For those that have suffered.

Contents

"[Psychopaths] exhibit a cluster of distinctive personality traits, the most significant of which is an utter lack of conscience. The number of psychopaths in society is about the same number as schizophrenics, but unlike schizophrenics, psychopaths aren't loners. That means that most of us have met many."

Dr. Robert Hare, 20th-21st century criminal psychologist

"The nature of some of their offenses can be so unbelievable that to normal people…we have to have an explanation. One of the most common explanations is, 'They have to be crazy.' But psychopaths are not crazy. They know right from wrong. If they were standing on a corner next to a police officer and wanted to commit a robbery, they would know not to do it as long as the officer is standing there."

Mary Ellen O'Toole, FBI Supervisory Special Agent

"One of the things that the medical students with whom I've worked have noted is that they're shocked at how *normal* psychopaths look, and how engaging they are. I do not know one clinician that has not at one time been fooled by a psychopath. [Psychopaths] can read an audience, or an individual, very well. While psychopaths appear to be speaking about themselves, they are constantly monitoring the facial expressions, responses from others, and other cues, and they will then 'tailor' what they say to see if they can get the response they want."

Dr. Greg Saathof, FBI Consultant Psychologist

"We know that in some people who have a very high IQ, there is a cost associated with this high mental functioning."

Dr. Paul Thompson, Neurologist

Psycho Save Us.

Chad Huskins

NOTE: All characters and events in this book are fictional. Any resemblance to real people and events is purely coincidental.

PSYCHO SAVE US

Edited by William Fruman

Cover art by Axel Torvenius

ISBN-13: 978-1482064735
ISBN-10: 1482064731

www.chadhuskins.com

www.forestofideas.com

Fans may contact: chadhuskinsauthor@gmail.com

Subscribe to YouTube channel: ChadHuskins

Follow the author on Twitter

1

It wouldn't have mattered which street they took home that night, it was going to end the same way. Later, when Kaley was huddled in a dark corner with her sister, a victim of violence, she would know this.

It wouldn't have mattered if the man behind the counter at Dodson's Store hadn't shorted them and required Kaley to return to the store, either. Somehow she knew that, too. But the lack of math skills from the man behind the counter *had* served one purpose. It had put them in sync with perhaps the only force in the universe that could have saved them. The Lunatic. She knew this, too.

Kaley knew these things in precisely the way most people thought they knew things, but really didn't. She had known them her whole life. Just as she somehow knew that her mother would not be alive for her wedding day. It was as self-evident to her as a scratch at the back of her throat meant the weather was about to change. Well, something else told her other things. She didn't pretend to know what it was, but it was there. She had become so accustomed to it that she often forgot it was there, and lived to regret it.

Tonight was such a night.

In years to come, she would kick herself and hate herself for not paying more attention to this thing, what some foolishly called female intuition. But Kaley knew it wasn't just listening to the tone in someone's voice that told women the intentions of a man or another conniving woman. No, her "charm," as her grandmother had called it before she died—God rest her soul— was a thing that had nothing at all to do with visual or auditory cues.

She did not listen to her charm that night, though it was there, all around her. She felt it even as she stepped out of the house with her little sister in tow. That would hurt the most. In the years ahead, between the times when she would be testing LSD and other mind-altering drugs to give her mind something to play with besides the guilt, she would never forget the soft, secure touch of Shannon's hand in hers. The touch would signify sisterly trust that would never be broken, no matter what had happened to them. But so simple a thing would linger with Kaley forever: the way a seven-year-old girl could hold her big sister's hand and just trust that no harm could come as long as she clung to that Anchor.

But all of those horrors were in their future. Presently, they were two sisters stepping out into the night. As they stepped out of the house, Kaley eased the door closed so that it didn't squeak and slam, waking up their neighbors. Beltway Street was quiet this time of night. It might've been eerily quiet to some, but the girls knew it too well. Beltway Street had been their home since their dad left them there. (Nobody knew where he'd gone. He went out for drinks with his buddies one night and never came back. Somebody said he was in Denver now, working at a Costco.) It was here that they had developed their own world of imagination, one that Kaley was just starting to grow out of at twelve, but one that she still visited with her sister. Again, to maintain that Anchor, which was all important at this stage in their life. Their mother was addicted to meth, what Shannon so innocently called "meff", and hadn't taken an interest in either one of them for a couple years now.

"We're gonna play ninja spies, okay?" she said presently. "That means we have to stay close together—"

"I'm the White Ninja!" Shan declared. For a reason that would remain forever obscure to Kaley, Shannon had developed a fascination with late-night kung fu theater on TV, and had learned to find lots of those kinds of movies on YouTube and was now obsessed with one called *White Ninja Meets Shaolin Crane*. She wanted to be the White Ninja all the time now.

"All right," Kaley whispered. "But keep your voice down. You'll—" It was at this point that Kaley first felt it. It started as a creep at the back of her neck, crawled up to the very top of her head, causing her hairs to stand on end. It was there for all of a second, and then retreated immediately. "You'll wake the neighbors," she finished. "Ninjas are *silent*. Remember? Jeez!"

"We have to get meff?"

Kaley paused at the end of their small yard and looked at her sister. She smiled, despite her displeasure with her sister's pronunciation. "It's *meth*. And no, we're not getting any meth for Mom. She gets that on her own, remember?" But Shan didn't remember. So far in life, things that were put to lips and made smoke were always meth. Their mother was inside smoking cigarettes, and had given Kaley money to go and get some things from Dodson's Store, the only thing opened this late at night in the Bluff.

Shannon had witnessed the exchange of money between Kaley and their mom, but hadn't yet developed the understanding that they were too young to fetch cigarettes for Mommy. Interestingly, though, Kaley had come to realize she *wasn't* too young to buy *meff*, though she never would—in years to come, she would buy a great many substances, but never that.

It was easy to buy anything in the Bluff. It was a relatively small area, only about 1 ½ square miles, but teeming with people leading the tail end of their disastrous lives. Though she was only partially aware of it at this stage in her life, Kaley had determined to leave these 1 ½ miles behind her someday. Tonight would cement that resolve.

"Watch out!" Shan shouted, pulling back on Kaley's hand.

"Ninjas don't shout—"

"You almost stepped on it," Shan whined.

Kaley looked at where she was pointing. A beetle was scuttling across the sidewalk. Shannon cared for all the creatures of the world, even the nasty ones. Kaley had too, once, but was starting to grow out of it.

They hustled across the street, Shannon putting one hand behind her and crouching as she had seen the White Ninja do. Kaley felt stupid playing along, but sometimes in order to get her little sister to go along quietly, she had to play ball. They moved past Stephanie's house, and Shannon briefly pulled Kaley into the shadow of the plastic garbage bin beside the decaying picket fence in the front yard. Here, Kaley indulged her little sister while she pretended to hug a wall and listened for bad ninjas to go past. Then, all at once, Shan stood up and yanked her big sister's arm nearly out of socket and took off in a crouch again.

"Slow down!" Kaley said. In that moment, she saw it. She saw it crystal clear. It happened in a flash, and was over before she could think on it. The low-ceilinged basement where they would be held was as real as the touch of her sister's hand. Indeed, in this charmed state, she could tell that Shannon was nearby, though not touching. She could smell…onions? And there was screaming…screaming from another room—

Another tug at her arm interrupted the vision, and Kaley did nothing more than shiver. Almost at once she had rewritten the future memory as nothing more than a combination of Big Sister's Paranoia and a cold wind, one born on a late-night stroll down an empty street that she walked with her litter sister, whom she had always tried to protect from everyone. Including Mom.

"I said, *slow down*!" Kaley said. This time, she yanked back on Shannon's arm, pulling the reins back on this little horsey. "Listen to me! Stop! Okay? Just stop it."

"I wanna run faster! It's not *fair*!" she pouted.

Shannon had entered the stage now where nothing was fair. It ended every sentence where she was arguing to get her way.

"We can play White Ninjas, but we have to be quiet—"

"There's only *one* White Ninja, and I'm it! You're Pan Lei! Remember?"

"I remember," she sighed. Pan Lei was the name of one of the White Ninja's few allies, a kung fu master who ran the White Lotus Clan. He was supposed to be a gifted kung fu man whose powers were undefeatable, or some such. "You're a *ninja*, though, remember? If you're too loud, you might alert the guards, and they'll tell Oni." Oni was the villain in two of the White Ninja films, a tattooed fat man who juggled several nefarious schemes at once. "Now, you gonna be quiet?"

"Yeah, yeah, yeah," said her little sister dismissively. But she obeyed now, and moved in low a crouch, creeping along with one hand out, staying brave as long as the other hand maintained the Anchor.

Kaley made sure each time they crossed a street, she made Shannon look right, then left, then right again. A single car drove past them, headed in the same direction they were going. It was a black Toyota Tacoma. Kaley knew because she was getting into cars, a hobby that so far hadn't extended any further than just reading about them and dreaming of her first car, but still made her a sharp eye for years, makes, and models. This one was a 2008 or 2009 TRD, and she marked it as strange immediately because she had never seen it around her neighborhood before, and there was never any reason for anyone new to visit her neighborhood at all.

Kaley held no illusions about where on Earth she lived. A decrepit neighborhood in the middle of Atlanta, one filled with apartments and townhouses for rent and nothing of real worth. She had seen enough reruns of shows like *Modern Family* and *Family Matters* to know that whatever was normal for the rest of America wasn't normal for her. She'd never seen a sitcom depicting even one motherly figure that enjoyed crystal meth. And everyone on TV had a car, no matter how broken down—Kaley, her sister and their mother all took the bus. In this neighborhood, cars were little more than lawn decorations, propped up by cinderblocks, or else missing some vital component that rendered them inoperable.

But the Tacoma, even in the dark it shined. No scratches or dents, no screeching of metal on metal as it rolled past. The truck was around the corner and out of sight within six seconds, and Kaley gave it no more thought. Although, some part of her *did* consider it. It was the charm, of course. She would come to know that many years from now. It revealed something to her. A cocksure smile, worn by a man she wouldn't want to rescue her in a million years, but one she would run to in time.

"Shhh," Shannon said. "I think I heard the guards."

Kaley sighed. Still playing the game, she crept in behind the White Ninja, slinking along and ducking from phantoms.

Dodson's was two blocks away from their house. Just two blocks. One day, when she went for her criminology degree, Kaley would learn that most crimes, including kidnappings, happened within a mile of the home.

The truck pulled to a sudden stop. The driver had just spotted the first lights on at an eatery of some kind, and an open sign. The first open sign for the last five miles or so. The hankering had come on him so abruptly his hands had started shaking on the wheel. *Or maybe that's just yer conscience, Spence ol' boy*, he mused, smiling. That was funny, because the docs at Leavenworth all said that he didn't have one.

He had parked the truck at the curb, just beside Dodson's Store. A few of the letters weren't lit up on the sign, so it looked like **D ds n's St e**. He pulled out a pack of Marlboros, one left by the owner of the truck. He lit it, inhaled gratefully, and exhaled just the same. He glanced into the rearview mirrors, gauging what sort of neighborhood he was in.

This was the Bluff, notorious throughout Atlanta for being the hub of heroin, meth, cocaine and prostitution. It was bounded by Donald L. Hollowell Parkway to the north, Martin Luther King Jr. Drive and the Atlanta University Center to the south, Downtown Atlanta to the east and Joseph E. Lowry Boulevard to the west. Splitting her in half was Joseph E. Boone Boulevard, creating the two distinct Neighborhoods of English Avenue to the north and Vine City to the south.

Up the street was a car title pawn shop called Strike Gold, and standing on the street outside of it were two young black boys, probably no older than fourteen. Spencer was sure they were holding.

On up the street a ways was a pair of cars, one a red El Camino and the other a black Expedition. Spencer reassessed the set-up. *Naw, the boys take the money, the men in the cars are the one's holdin'. They drive up, drop a bag, probably some fake shit made out of baby powder and mixed with Clorox to smell.*

Spencer smiled and took another toke. It was funny how the game never changed, no matter where one went in the wide world. Baton Rouge, Biloxi, Leavenworth, Atlanta, all the same. He wondered who it was that had first thought of recruiting kids to hang out on corners while the adults hung back, too afraid to reveal themselves to the cops who no doubt patrolled this area with the occasional undercover sting. Whoever thought up recruiting kids was a fucking genius.

He glanced up through the windshield when he spotted a helicopter swooping by, its searchlight flashing down. It was nowhere near him, but he stopped smoking for a moment, wondering, as he had for the last five hundred miles, *They lookin' for me?* He'd been very careful, using any back roads he could find on the GPS and changing cars every fifty miles or so.

When the helicopter moved on further west, Spencer leaned back and relaxed a bit. He took a few more tokes, glancing at the closed car wash across the street. Next to that was a closed tanning salon. Next to that was a gas station, closed at these hours, but a sign out front still declared in bold red neon letters **LOTTERY TIX SOLD HERE**.

Standing just outside Dodson's Store were four young men. Black men. *Niggers. A nigger neighborhood. What did I expect?* This was Atlanta, after all. Though his work had often taken him to places like this, Spencer typically proscribed such areas. He supposed even traveling salesmen had to get used to life on the road, and nurses had to get used to looking at blood and piss and shit. Every job had its drawback.

Spencer hopped out of the truck and locked it behind him, marking the look that the four black men were giving him and the truck as he stepped inside. "S'up, fellas?" he said. Conversation, hitherto clandestine but active, now ceased. Though they had been gazing at him in his truck with indolent eyes, there was a degree of intelligence in them—predatory intelligence, but intelligence just the same. They had made sure he saw them, so he made sure they knew he saw *them*.

He stepped inside, a jingling bell over his head had the musical accompaniment of Akon, saying he would "smack that." A waft of half-cooked meat met him, as well. Dodson's was part convenience store, part burger joint, it seemed. *Leave it to a nigger neighborhood to create such a nonsensical amalgam*, he thought. The word "amalgam" came to mind courtesy of the Leavenworth Rehabilitation Program. In the reading portion, Spencer had excelled at remembering the word of the day and its meaning. *You're a gifted reader, Spence*, Dr. McCulloch had told him. If Spencer recalled correctly, he had replied, *You're a good bullshitter, doc.*

Sad about McCulloch. Not a bad fellow, him.

The wall to his immediate left had a single stand full of books—romance and erotica novels with black people on the front, some *Penthouse* magazines with a dubious dash of Tom Clancy peeking out here and there. A spill on aisle three hadn't been cleaned up. Wires hung from the paneled ceiling.

"S'up, yo?" said a man behind the counter, satisfying his Pavlovian response to hearing the bell jingle over the door by tossing out the greeting. He was a tall, corpulent fellow, nearly as wide as the stolen Toyota truck parked outside. He had cornrows pulled back over his head, two of them sticking up like strays, though Spencer was pretty sure they were meant to be that way. *A nigger style if I ever saw one.* He wore a *faux*-classic #7 Michael Vick jersey, a black one from back when the man played for the Falcons.

I could pitch that shirt for a tent, Spencer thought. He fought the smile from his face and said, "Burger?"

"Fuh sho," said Fattie, and waddled away. He made it over to a table behind the counter, his ass bumping up against a few shelves holding an odd array of *TV Guides, Vibe* magazines, burger condiments and a copy of *Uncle Tom's Cabin,* opened and facedown. His feet stuck to the floor, an indication of many spills that were never quite cleaned. There were stains on the walls and around the sandwich area, all of which Spencer regarded with a degree of humor. *If I was in the joint, I would be eatin' better than this.* It was true. Leavenworth wasn't so bad. At least, not when it came to lunchtime.

Fattie had the good habit of pulling on plastic gloves, but that's where the professional etiquette ended. He reached over to the grill and lifted a meat patty with his hands, no tongs. He then opened up a plastic Sunbeam bag, and started pulling out sandwich bread.

"Regular sandwich bread?" Spencer asked.

"Yeah. Why? Problem?"

"What, ya don't have any hamburger buns?"

"Like what?"

"Whattaya mean, 'like what'? Like hamburger buns…never mind," he said, and lifted the cigarette to his lips.

"Yo, dude, you can't smoke in here."

Spencer smirked, looking around at the counter that wouldn't pass a health inspection by the Tasmanian Devil. "You serious, fat man?"

At this, Michael Vick's last fan in Atlanta tilted his head, half in sarcasm, and half in a challenge.

"A'right, a'right." Spencer crushed the cig in his hand and put it in his pocket.

"Ya better believe, 'a'right'. I may not look like it but I can jump across this counter an' whoop that ass."

"Before you do, would you mind telling me where I can find Pat's Auto?"

Here, the fat man looked up at him, halfway through placing the patty on the sandwich bread. Spencer thought, *I came to the right place. He knows.* Very quickly, the fat man went back to fixing the burger. "He up on Terrell Street. Closed right now, though. Most o' his folk got locked up, fuh real."

"That's what I heard," Spencer said.

"Whatchoo want on this muthafucka?"

"Oh, uh, cheese, mayo, mustard, ketchup, onions, pickles. Everything you got except lettuce and tomato."

"Er'thing but the healthy shit, huh?"

"You'd know all about healthy eating, I guess?"

"I dun tol' you to watch that shit," he said with a touch of asperity.

Spencer smiled. He liked this fat fuck. "Yeah, everything but the healthy shit. Does that come with fries an' a drink?"

"Does this look like a goddam McDonald's?"

Spencer laughed now. He nodded. "Then I guess that'll cost me more than a Big Mac meal, eh?" The fat man nodded wordlessly and went about finishing off the sandwich, slinging the pieces together without the affection he would have shown his own sandwich. Spencer glanced outside, noting the four black men hadn't moved. He looked back at the fat man. "What's your name?"

"We makin' friends now?" he asked, tossing Spencer's burger into a translucent plastic wrapper.

"Just curious what'cher name is, friend." Behind him, a door opened, and he heard someone enter and whisper. His natural instincts caused him to look, and saw two black girls walk in; one was no older than eight, the other not quite a teenager. The smallest was in blue jeans and a blue shirt with Jimmy Hendrix on the front, and the oldest (holding the little one's hand tightly) wore blue jeans with a green sweater. Both had cornrows with pigtails. The oldest girl paused in the doorway. No, froze. She froze there, looking at Spencer. He stared back at her, wondering if he knew her. She certainly looked astonished for a moment. *Probably never seen a white man around here before*, he thought, smiling back at her.

After a moment of tugging from her little sister ("C'mon, Kaley!"), the eldest nigglet stepped on inside and let the door close. They walked to the back of the store, hand-in-hand.

"Mac," said the fat man.

Spencer turned back to him. "What?"

"Name's Mac, playa."

"Mac?" he laughed, and saw the fat man tilt his head to one side. "As in Big Mac? As in big as a Mack truck?"

"As in MAC-10, muthafucka. Plop, plop." He made a gun with his fingers, and aimed it at Spencer's head.

"Go ahead an' charge me for a Dr. Pepper."

"Fuh sho."

"How much is that?" he said, fetching out his wallet. There was whispering behind him, and he glanced over his shoulder to check the status on the little girls. They had made their way over to the chips aisle. The oldest one had been handing her little sister a bag of pretzels. She was caught stealing a glimpse of Spencer, and darted her eyes away as soon as he looked. She finally dared to look again. He smiled at her, and again she quickly averted her gaze and pulled her sister down another aisle.

"Usually?" Mac said. "Two-fitty. Fuh you? *Three*-fitty."

"A rip-off, but I'll pay it. I earned it. I was very rude, wasn't I?"

"Tru dat, playa," he said, snatching the five-dollar bill out of Spencer's hand and tossing it into the register. He closed it without handing over change.

"Where's my change?"

"Asshole tax." This time, it was Mac's turn to smile. He revealed silver grill with his name carved in it: **MACTEN**.

"You know what?" Spencer said, taking his burger and soda off the countertop. "I like you Mac. I can honestly say that nobody could ever pay me enough to kill you." This must have unsettled Mac for a moment, because he looked taken aback. He pushed himself away from the counter. "Relax, it means I *wouldn't*, big guy. Ya know Patrick, huh? Of Pat's Auto, I mean?

Have you got a phone that I can—?" He paused and moved out of the way of the two girls who now approached the front counter. "Sorry, ladies," he said. "I'm very rude standing here and talkin' while you're waiting behind me. I prostrate myself before you and beg your forgiveness."

The littlest girl stuck her forefinger in mouth and started chewing on it, and looked up at him dumbly. The eldest girl gave him only a wary glance, and placed her bread, cheese, ham, mayonnaise, pretzels, orange juice and Pop-Tarts up on the counter.

"How's it goin', Kaley? How's yo momma?"

"Fine," said the eldest girl in a low mumble. "Here's what we've got." She handed over a few bills, none of it neatly folded. Mac rang up all the items, then took the money and handed back the girl's change.

While this happened, Spencer looked about the store, looking up at the camera in one corner. He looked beyond the shitty grill, and beyond it at a room with a large door that looked pretty solid, and next to it there was a window, undoubtedly Plexiglas. He imagined Mac had some kind of weapon just behind the counter. *Maybe a MAC-10*, Spencer thought. *Plop, plop.*

He glanced outside at the four thugs. Two of them were tossing surreptitious glances through the window into the store, obviously stealing glances at the lone white boy. If I stay here much longer, *I'm likely to go outside and find all my wheels missing.* He went to ask Mac another question, but when he did he caught sight of the eldest nigglet. She was looking at him again out the corner of her eye, and now looked away like a boy caught staring at his best friend's mother's tits. *The fuck's her problem?*

Paranoia crept in then. Paranoia like he hadn't felt since the joint. Strange, impossible scenarios occurred to him. Did the girl recognize him? Was she one of those weird, precocious nigglets who watched the news at a young age and kept up with shit going on in other states? Had she heard what he'd done? Did she know Spencer Adam Pelletier? Did she know about the shootout in Baton Rouge, or the convict that escaped from Leavenworth Federal Penitentiary two years ago? *Happens on* America's Most Wanted *all the time*, he thought. *Some random civilian up an' recognizes a killer that nobody else notices.*

Spencer looked at the girl for a moment, knowing she would look again. When she did, he shook his head at her, slowly but enough so that she noticed. It was a warning. *Whatever you think you know, don't say anything.* Then, he glanced down to the littlest girl, presumably her sister, and then looked up at the eldest again. *Remember, you've got a sister to look out for.*

The eldest accepted her change and her bagged groceries then turned quickly to get out of there. The door flew open, the jingling bells clanging against glass. The two girls jogged past the four black dudes outside, and were gone.

Spencer looked up at Mac and said, "You got a phone? I'm afraid I lost mine."

"Why the fuck would I let you use a phone when it means yo cracka ass be hangin' around here a minute longer?"

"Because," he said, pulling out a twenty, "there's something in it for you." Spencer really needed the phone. He needed to see if he had any friends left in this town.

But on top of being as big as one, Mac had obviously been *around* the block. He had knowledge of the kind of person Spencer was now. After all, he was asking for Patrick Mulley, owner of Pat's Auto, a chop shop with a great legacy in the A-T-L, so that right there said a lot. That's why "Big" Mac grew that smile, and why he knew he could get away with saying, "Make it a solid *fitty* an' you got a deal."

Spencer smiled. He had money, but not much. He reached into his wallet and pulled out five tens. "Ya drive a hard bargain, Mac, but I still love you."

"You a weird muthafucka," he said, snatching the bills out of Spencer's hand. "You know that." It wasn't a question.

"Phone. Now. Or I whip my dick out an' piss on this floor."

"You cleanin' it up, fool," he said, tossing Spencer his cell.

"Ow! You're hurting me!" Shannon was pulling her arm away from her big sister, but Kaley wouldn't let go. They had hustled down Kenton Street and were nearing Beltway. Almost home.

Kaley didn't know what had happened. She didn't know why she was even running now. It started when she opened the door to Dodson's. Her hand had frozen on the door handle, unable to let go. She'd looked at it, perplexed at first, then terrified when she felt a dropping sensation, like plunging from the top of a rollercoaster. As a small girl, she'd had vertigo. So bad that she often couldn't get out of bed because the world spun out of control. So bad that the doctor had prescribed pills that never worked, and Kaley had eventually just grown out of it. This was like vertigo, only not as sickening.

When she'd finally found the strength to let go of the door and gone to step inside, she had spotted the man with the kind eyes. Tall, thin, and white. Yes...white. *Very* white. Pale. Like the vampires in those *Twilight* movies. Only he didn't glitter like that...yet he did. No, he didn't, he just...he was paramount. Yes, that was the word. Somehow, he felt important. It wasn't just his otherworldly kind eyes, it was the Charm, she was sure of it. It was letting her know something about the man. Was he going to kill her? Was he going to kill Shan? Or someone else, maybe?

The feeling had passed as abruptly as it came, and she had stepped on inside to get their shopping done. Still, something had lingered inside of her, something that drew her to the man. A connection had been made. At least, that's what Nan would've said.

When she was as little as Shannon was now, Kaley had gone to Centennial Olympic Park with Ricky, one of her mother's boyfriends at the time. It was her birthday and all she liked doing back then was going to big, open spaces where lots and lots of people could be found. Kaley didn't know why. She wasn't especially social, she just liked being around all the excitement, and from Olympic Park, one could see loads of people walking amongst the fountains, with a backdrop of mirror-like skyscrapers surrounding you, lots of kids running around, and usually some kind of festival or concerts divvied up into smaller venues all around. She had gone there with Ricky and one of Ricky's friends—her mother hadn't made it, she was "sick", which really meant she was either on her meth or was too unmotivated without it to go—and had been leaning over one of the fountains and letting the water splash in her hands. Ricky and his friend had gone to get her a hot dog from a hot dog stand. She was alone. With her mind on the fountain and her back to the rest of the world, Kaley had felt something tiptoeing up to the forefront of her mind. It was an idea, a notion, one that filled her full of excitement and anticipation.

Someone's gonna propose to me, she thought. That didn't make any sense, because she wasn't nearly old enough to get married yet. But something had definitely made her feel as though that was going to happen. She couldn't say why. She turned around, following the general direction from whence the idea came. She saw a white man. He wasn't surrounded with an aura and he had no halo over his head, but somehow she knew it was him that was generating a feeling. It was her charm, and she was feeling the anticipation created by an intention directed at…someone.

Kaley had watched the man for a while. He paced about, checking his watch here and there until finally he was joined by a blonde woman. He spoke words that Kaley couldn't hear. Then, he sat the blonde woman down on the bench, knelt in front of her, and started talking. The man pulled out a small box, opened it, and the woman wept and laughed all at once. *What's that all about?* she had wondered at the time. It wouldn't be until days later that she would truly stew on the fact that she had somehow known it was about to happen. She had felt the man's anticipation over asking, and her young mind had believed the man's intentions were directed at her.

Kaley had played with this notion for a couple of years, until one day she had mentioned this to her mother and her Nan. Her mother had rolled her eyes and said, "Oh, whatchoo been tellin' this girl?" She had walked off, leaving the oldest and youngest of the family sitting at table together. Nan had leaned in and said, "Tell it to me again. Every last detail, chil'." And so she did. When Kaley finished, Nan looked troubled. "You dun went an' got the charm." She offered a smile, but it seemed sad, like she was offering her condolences. "Yo momma don' believe, girl. She won't never. She never listened to me when I would tell her. She won' listen to *nuthin'* I say," Nan had added.

"What do I do?" Kaley had asked.

"You *hide* it, girl. You hide it an' you don' tell nobody ever again." This was not the advice she had thought she would get from her Nan. Nan was always telling her to stand up for herself, stand up for what she believed in, and not to be "one o' these dumbass heathens lettin' our people backslide on what the good Dr. King dun went an' won for us." No, this wasn't like Nan at all. "You hide it an' only ever share what you see or hear or feel with *me*. Hear, now?"

"Yes, Nan."

And it had been that way, until the day Nan died from her thyroid problems. Kaley had gone to her bedside, holding her hand. Something had happened there, too. Something...that Kaley didn't like to think about. She was pretty sure these days that she was just making it all up, that she had invented the whole story in Olympic Park the way kids make stuff up and had just come to start believing in it. She also believed that she had made up every other feeling since then, that she was just blowing it out of proportion.

That still didn't help it any when she was frozen in stasis at times from what her Nan called the charm. The white man back in Dodson's Store had brought it on again, and fiercely. He was somehow emanating something concerning the future. He was on his way to do something, but he was also connected to her. At least, that's the way it felt. That's the lie she was telling herself.

"It skips a generation, ya know," Nan had told her. "That's why yo momma don' feel it. That's why she don' *believe* it. She can't never. It's like convincin' a blind man that there's color, only he can't see it. He either believes in it, or he keeps thinkin' it ain't there. His choice. Either way, he'll never really know. Only people that *see* will know. That's our burden, girl. We see." Nan had given her another warning. "Always listen to it. Listen to it, an' others will, too. Ya hear? Unnerstan?"

"Yes, Nan." Only she hadn't, and, near the end, hadn't wanted to.

Nan hadn't always known what she was talking about, anyway. It would take her a full year to start writing the dates on her checks correctly, and just when she got used to it another New Year's Day would arrive, kick-starting a whole new year of frustration for her. She thought Viagra was pronounced "Niagra".

She sometimes thought Bill Clinton was somehow still President of the United States, or could somehow tell "that dumbass in the White House now what he ought be doin'." Nan had been wrong about lots of things, even at the very end when she claimed nothing was wrong with her.

"This is stupid," Kaley said presently.

"What's stupid?" Shannon asked.

"Nuthin'. C'mon, we need to get back. Hurry. Did you pocket the money I gave you?"

"Yeah," Shannon said, and pulled it out to prove it was so. "See? Count it."

"We'll count it 1—" Kaley stopped herself short. She looked down at the money in her little sister's hand. Something didn't look right about it. There weren't enough bills. "Hold on." She set down the groceries in her hand, and took the money from Shannon. She counted it. She recounted it. They had had a twenty-dollar bill. The groceries had been $9.36. Kaley counted it again. "Check your pockets again," she told Shannon. "There's not even six dollars here." There were three dollar bills and the rest was in quarters, dimes and nickels. "I said *check your pockets*," she repeated.

"I am!" Shannon said. She turned them out, and there was nothing left.

"Did you drop some back in the store?"

"No!"

"Are you sure?"

"Yes!"

"We gotta go back." Then, a part of young Kaley's mind rebelled. *It's just four dollars and some change you're missing*, it said. *Let it go. Let this go, girl*. That sounded like Nan, strangely. And then she argued back. *It's not "just" anything. It's money that was owed me*. One thing Kaley shared with her mother, and not her Nan, was her anger over being cheated.

It was a mistake. You know Mac well enough. He's not gonna short you four dollars on purpose! Then, on the heels of that, *You don't know that for sure*.

And then, something else told her not to go back. It was a feeling, not any sort of argument with herself or with Nan. When she had been inside that store, Kaley had felt a looming threat from the white man. She didn't think it was aimed directly at her, but it was there. Of that, the charm had been perfectly clear. *I don't want Shannon in the middle of that.* And if she had listened to that last piece of advice from her charm, Kaley wouldn't have been plagued with nightmares for the rest of her life. She wouldn't have blamed herself to the point of winding up on a therapist's couch for years on end, trying to forgive herself for something everyone else had forgiven her for long, long ago.

He's got our money, she thought.

Then Kaley remembered the white man, him in his black hoodie and jeans, looking over at her at one point with his smile and feral face and…shaking his head? Yes, he had definitely shaken his head at her in a warning sign. *He even warned me away.* The more she'd been around him, the more she had known that he was no good. *He's not a nice man.* No, that wasn't right, he wasn't just not nice. He was sick. He was deranged. He was vicious. "You don' have to tell nobody why you decide the things you decide," Nan had told her. "Jes listen to yo charm an' let everybody think you're crazy. *You'll* know you made the right decision."

But it's not the right decision to let someone rip you off. It's just crazy. Charm may skip a generation, but when it comes to crazy, apples don't fall far from the tree. Kaley's mother was a crazed meth-head now, and Nan had been out of her gourd for the last few years of her life. Kaley was not going to be like them.

She thought about the warning shake of the head from the white man. *You imagined it. That's that.*

So that was that. With new resolve, she put the rest of the money in her pocket and said, "Here, pick up the orange juice. I'll carry the rest."

"We goin' home?"

"No. We're going back."

"But it's just—"

"It's another day's groceries! *That's* what that is!"

"I don't wanna—"

"We're going and that's final, Shannon!"

"That's not *fair*!"

"Hush now. Ninjas don't talk. C'mon. We're just gonna get what's ours."

They started back down Kenton. Up the street behind her, two cars were parked. An El Camino and Expedition. The El Camino flashed its lights twice, and the Expedition flashed once in response. The El Camino pulled down the street slowly, and the Expedition followed just behind.

Kaley felt a tickle at the back of her head. This one, too, she ignored.

The phone had rung and gone to voicemail eight times. Spencer looked over at Mac, who was sitting in a chair that completely disappeared beneath his wide ass. He had his arms folded, and had flipped on a small television that showed *SportsCenter*. Highlight reels of the day's games were rolling. The Bulls weren't doing so hot this year according to Charles Barkley, his host, Kevin Negandhi agreed.

Spencer dialed again. The phone rang four times, then came the message, "Yo, cut this, cuz. I ain't around. Leave a message. I'll holla atcha, a'ight? Peace!"

"Basil, it's me. Now answer your goddam phone, Yeti. You high or somethin'? I need what you have. Now. ASAP. I know you moved but I'll find out where you live. I'll be comin' around your place later tonight, you better believe that." He hung up, and then dialed two more times just to be sure. But Basil the "Yeti" never picked up. He sighed and stood there in the shop, the phone in one hand and Mac's special burger in the other. He took a bite and shook his head.

"Sounds like you a friendless muthafucka tonight," Mac said, calling that one over his shoulder.

Spencer looked at him. He tossed the phone back to the prick and said, "Catch." Mac caught it just in time, and put it in his pocket. "Know where I can get a good night's sleep around here? I got no ID, so I need that to be not an issue."

"I feel ya, playboy," he said. "Up the street three blocks. Take a right on Filmore. Second stoplight, make a right. You be Motel Quickin' like a muthafucka."

"Motel Quick? That's the place's name?"

"Ya heard me."

24

Spencer nodded and turned away. But before he walked out the door, he said, "Get a new jersey."

"Huh? Why?"

"You support illegal dog fighters?"

"You like eatin' dead cows?"

Spencer looked down at the burger in his hand. "Touché. You may not make a great burger, Mac, but you make one hell of an argument."

Mac tapped a finger to the side of his head. "I'm all wise an' shit."

"I see that now. Sayonara, Obi-Wan," he said, pulling his hood over his head. On his way out, Spencer lifted his Dr. Pepper from the counter and raised it in mock salute.

"Yo, I'm Yoda, playa," he said, popping open a can of Pabst Blue Ribbon. "Obi-Wan's a whiny-ass lil' bitch."

Spencer stepped out into the night and gave a quick nod to the four fellows hanging out outside Dodson's. He glanced up the street, saw that the two black boys outside of the car title pawn shop Strike Gold were still there. However, the El Camino and the Expedition were gone now. He checked his watch, and marked the time.

As he approached the driver's side of his stolen Toyota, a pair of stray cats darted out from underneath it. He watched them cross the lonely street, then opened the door. He paused again when he glanced down the street, and saw the two black girls returning. By now he'd come to realize his earlier paranoia had been unfounded. The girl was just curious, that's all. Her parents hadn't taught her that it was rude to stare.

Spencer heard some shouting behind him. He turned and saw a black man and a black woman walking on the sidewalk across the street. The woman was hollering inarticulate threats while she walked ahead of the man. A lover's quarrel, one the man seemed to hardly care about as he was busy texting someone on his phone.

Spencer hopped inside the truck and cranked it up. He looked out at the four black guys still leaning against the glass windows of Dodson's Store, and raised his Dr. Pepper to them. "A salute to your future schemes and depredations," Spencer Pelletier said. He took a sip.

And then several things seemed to happen at once. Tires screeched. Someone screamed. Then someone else screamed. The four black guys leaning against Dodson's Store bolted like their lives were on the line. There was some more shouting. "Get her! Get that one! Don't let her fuckin' get away!" Someone else screamed, "Run, Shannon! *Ruuuuuuuuuuuuuun!*"

Spencer threw his Dr. Pepper into the floorboard and put his truck into drive, then looked in his rearview mirror just long enough to see that it wasn't the cops, and the attack wasn't meant for him.

They were almost there. Dodson's blinking sign had just come within view, those few letters switching on and off indecisively. Kaley slowed down a bit when she saw the white man exit the front of the store. He had his burger in one hand and his soda in the other. He had pulled his hood up over his head, and was glancing right and left, combing the street like he was expecting someone. His eyes darted all around at all times, though Kaley somehow didn't believe he knew he was doing it. *He notices things with those kind eyes, things others don't. He marks things.*

She pulled lightly back on Shannon's hand, a sisterly communication that was immediately heeded, no matter how cross Shannon was with her. They both waited for the white man to hop inside his truck. "You think he bad?" Shannon asked, partially coming out of her sulking mood and looking at the white man with a mixture of curiosity and trepidation. Kaley didn't answer. Once he was inside and had cranked it up, they started moving again.

That's when she became aware of the dull hum from behind.

"It'll be quick," Kaley promised her sister, who turned away, remembering to sulk. "Just in an out."

The humming got louder.

Something happened then. Vertigo, or something close to it. She felt it deep in her guts. Her stomach leapt to her throat, and then it eased back down. She looked up and saw things in slow motion. She also saw her future. There was a black man holding her hand, kissing it. He was very handsome. Was he her husband? For a moment, Kaley was swimming in happiness, then darkness crept in, the way a bad feeling creeps in on a good dream and gives it ominous new undertones. Like the worst of nightmares, the bad feeling was *per*ceptual rather than *con*ceptual.

Then, she snapped out of it. Only a second or two had passed, and she and Shannon were walking again.

Then there was the humming. It was an engine. *Wonder what kind of car that is?* she thought, and turned to see. The El Camino was coming so fast she thought she was about to be hit. Without thinking, Kaley shoved Shannon out of the way. Her little sister screamed indignantly as she hit the pavement. Kaley put her arms in front of her and prepared to die...

And, oh God, if only she had.

The El Camino screeched to a halt. The Expedition came up right beside but didn't stop. Instead, the Expedition slowed down and pulled around to the curb. In an instant, Kaley knew what this was. Somehow she knew.

Someone shouted, "Get her! Get that one! Don't let her fuckin' get away!" That confirmed it.

Kaley flung her groceries at the El Camino's windshield. "Run, Shannon! *Ruuuuuuuuuuuuuun*!" The charm had told her, had fed her all the warning signs. She hadn't listened. She hadn't heeded Nan's advice.

Shannon, not understanding, got to her feet but didn't run anywhere. Lost without the Anchor, without the all-comforting touch of her big sister's hand, she stood there wide-eyed and confused. By now the tattooed white men had leapt out of the El Camino and were bolting for her. She turned and screamed at Shannon again, "Run!" This time, the Big Sister command jolted the little one out of her inactive state, and Shannon obeyed. But the Expedition had pulled in front of her, corralling both Big and Little Sister. Ahead of the Expedition, the four guys that had been hanging out outside Dodson's turned and ran, like they knew the score here and didn't want to be either an accessory or another victim. Shannon tried to run around to the back, but the Expedition stopped, went into reverse and cut her off. Just then, someone leapt out of the back driver's side door and reached out to snatch Shan.

"No!" Kaley screamed, and ran directly at the big man. This one was black and bald, and twice the size of Rick, Kaley's ex-stepdad. In those as-yet-unlived years of guilt, Kaley would hate herself for making another mistake. Instead of running for Shannon she should've run away. That would've allowed her to tell the police everything she'd seen and give a description. That would've been the *smart* thing to do.

But Big Sister Protocol performed an override of rationale, and it demanded she never leave Shannon alone, and so she hadn't. Kaley balled up her fist and smacked the big fucker across his face, just as he was bending over and snatching Shannon up by her right sleeve. This had *almost* bought Shannon time to escape. The man staggered back in surprise, and Shannon's Jimmy Hendrix shirt that Rick had bought for her before he left tore in the man's grip. Shannon got two steps before one of the tattooed white men got hold of her.

"No!" Kaley screamed, and leapt for her.

Then, a hand made of steel grabbed her around her mouth, jerked her head backwards and lifted her off the ground. There was something clamped between the hand and her mouth. It smelled sweet at first, then really awful, like the fumes of gasoline or Drano. Her head swam for a moment as she kicked backwards at the monster's shins. She heard him grunt, but otherwise she didn't seem to have any effect at all.

Someone muttered words she didn't comprehend. *"Bez problem."*

Someone else replied, *"Khorosho."*

Someone else said, "Hurry the fuck *up!*"

The world lurched, her limbs went numb and her eyelids became very, very heavy. She saw Shannon being lifted and handed off to someone in the back of the Expedition. *Rounded up...like cattle...*

It was the last coherent thing that passed through her head. The last thing she saw and felt was Nan's hand in hers. She was on her deathbed, shaking her head disapprovingly at her. On that day, Kaley had felt something. The charm, perhaps. She had also seen something in Nan's eyes, something akin to a great, inestimable pity. Kaley suddenly recalled the old woman's last words. "Oh, chil'…you got a lotta hurt comin' yo way…good luck…"

It had all happened so quickly that Spencer had barely had time to climb out of his truck. He hopped back inside when he saw the older girl getting tossed limply into the back of the El Camino, just before the two vehicles took off. The El Camino peeled out at first, then followed the Expedition up the street past Strike Gold. As the Expedition went past, Spencer spotted a white fellow in the passenger side seat, leaning an arm with huge biceps out the window. The bicep had a crimson bear on it, one claw lifted, preparing to swipe.

The two vehicles burned ondown the road, but they passed close enough, even the dark, that Spencer could make out the Georgia license plate. Bartow County, number AXC 327. The two cars made a hard turn at the corner of Cheshire Road, a maneuver that was at odds with the Expedition's size and tonnage. Its right-side tires momentarily left the pavement, then it stabilized, and then both vehicles were gone.

He jumped out again. The street was utterly silent, not even a honking horn in the distance. The four black men, who had seemed so eager to boast their confidence before, had vanished quick as a dream. Across the street, the black couple, who had been arguing just moments earlier, now stood looking dumbly up and down the street. Right, left, then right, then left again. They were probably wondering the same thing Spencer was. *Did I just fuckin' see what I think I did?*

"Huh," Spencer said to himself. "Ya don't see that every day." He reached into his pocket and pulled out another Marlboro, lit it, and opened the driver's side door to hop back in. He stopped, though, when he spotted Mac coming out of the store. The fat man barely fit through the front door, and he opened it more with his belly than he did his hand, the bell jingling hard against the glass. In his right hand he carried a weapon. Not a MAC-10, but a Glock, something that would do the job just as well. "They're gone, Yoda," Spencer said.

"What the fuck *was* that shit?!" he screamed, looking up and down the street. Mac's eyes found something on the sidewalk and locked on. He was panting, but his breathing slowed as he started to put something together. Spencer followed his gaze, and saw the groceries spilled on the ground, the artifacts of a perfectly normal life for two girls until seconds ago. Then Mac looked up at Spencer accusatorily. He raised his gun.

"Hey, hey, hey!" Spencer shouted, stepping so that he could get cover behind most of the Toyota. He reached behind him, touched his own weapon, a Glock Pocket 10, a concealable weapon barely bigger than his hand. "Chill out, homeboy."

"The fuck just happened here, white boy?" Mac demanded. "*Tell* me! Did ya see it? They take the girls?"

"Yeah."

"God *damn* it!" He pulled out his cell and started dialing.

"You knew 'em?"

Mac put the phone to his ear. "Yeah, I knew 'em! They momma live up on Beltway. Always high as a muthaf—*hey*! Where you goin'?"

"Good luck to you and them," Spencer said, stepping inside the truck.

"Hey, you can't just leave like this! I'm callin' the po-po, man! You gotta give a description an' shit! Give a statement! That's how this shit *works*, yo!"

"Ask the kind couple across the street," he said, pointing to the still dumbfounded woman and her man on the opposite sidewalk. "They probably saw more than I did."

"The fuck you runnin' from?"

Spencer said nothing, he just shut the door and got moving. *I can't be here when the cops show up. If anybody'll recognize me, it'll be a goddam pig.* He squealed out without a second's consideration, glanced in his rearview mirror once to see Dodson's Store and Mac's big ass diminishing behind him. Mac was holding his cell to his ear with one hand and waving desperately with his gun hand. *He could've shot me, or threatened to shoot me, but he didn't.* Spencer had gauged the fat man wrong. He wasn't like these other niggers around here, no, he was one of those that tried to defend himself from the rest of the garbage. The girls were part of his tribe, and he at least wanted to protect them.

30

Spencer made a turn on Cheshire Road, but in the opposite direction that the Expedition and El Camino had gone. He looked in his rearview mirror, didn't see them. *Wouldn't be able to follow them anyway*, he thought. *A crew like that, they probably have some safehouse nearby, a garage where they can dip in and hide.* Yes, they had moved quickly. A professional pull crew if Spencer ever saw one. *Just pullin' them off the streets. Snatch, snatch.*

He had already moved on. The past was past. The two girls had to fend for themselves. He couldn't be a part of it because it would undoubtedly bring a shitstorm down on him, as well. In fact, considering his record, the pigs were likely to think he had something to do with it. No, no statement. And no time to hang around talking to Mac about what he'd seen. It was time to move.

Something occurred to Spencer, though. He couldn't go to Motel Quick now, because Mac had recommended it and would know he was going there. Mac might tell the police. *And Basil didn't answer his fuckin' phone. Which means he may not even be in the state.* But Mac had told him Pat's Auto was on Terrell Street. He could go there, lay low, especially if Pat himself was there. After all, a favor was owed, and Pat, asshole that he was, had never balked on repaying one. And Mac probably wouldn't mention Pat's Auto to the police, since it wasn't the kind of place one wanted the cops to know one was associated with. *But then again, he might*, Spencer thought. *He seemed awfully concerned about those girls.*

But Pat's the only guy I really know in this town.

He took a quick right turn on Holcomb Bridge Road and said out loud, "Fuck it, I gotta take the chance." Spencer punched in the street name on the GPS. Terrell Street came up, whereas Pat's Auto never had. Patrick Mulley didn't advertise, and kept his little chop shop from coming up on most searches.

Spencer took a left turn onto McKinley-Parke Drive, toking on his cigarette and turning up the radio. Blue Öyster Cult was advising everyone not to fear the Reaper, and the voice of his stolen GPS said, in its usual fragmented way, "Go—two—*miles*—then—turn—*left*—on—Winston—Street." The smoke felt good in his lungs. He exhaled, singing along to the music, remembering the hilarious "more cowbell" sketch Will Ferrell had done on

Saturday Night Live with Christopher Walken, like, what, back in 2000, or 2001? *Back before the towers had even fallen*, he thought. That led him to think about what Will Ferrell had done since then. Associative thinking like this took him down more roads than he drove that night, and the only time he thought of the black girl in the green sweater again was when he considered how she had stolen glimpses of him while paying for her food.

Spencer thought back to those piquant eyes. Why had she kept looking at him? Not just at him, but looking him in the eye. She hadn't looked him over out of curiosity, she had watched him. Like she knew him. *Crazy fuckin' nigglet*, he thought, and turned the music up some more. The universe was full of random encounters. So much going on in what that Carl Sagan guy had called the cosmic fugue (inside Leavenworth, Spencer had read Sagan profusely, particularly *Cosmos*). Things happened randomly. Indeed, the very event that kick-started life on this planet was random in itself—random interactions causing haphazard chemical reactions just so happened to synthesize some amino acids and other organic compounds from inorganic precursors.

Tonight's encounter had been no different.

"Come on, baby," he sang. "Don't fear the Reaper, baby take my hand, don't fear the Reaper, we'll be able to fly…"

Echoes…

The dreams were spotted and menacing. She came and went. Sometimes, she was in the back of the car, and other times she was treading water. No, not water. A viscous liquid; dark shapes swimming just beneath its surface. She swam in a dark room with tenebrous shadows that fell over her, no, *reached* for her.

Echoes…

People were calling to her. She looked around to see who it might be. There was her mother, despondent and alone on her couch, crying for Kaley's father, Maury, wishing he would come back home. The pipes she smoked from were made out of glassblown Pyrex tubes or light bulbs. In this vision, one was now in her hand, burning the powder and transforming it into a substance of magical fumes that made Mom feel so good…but the dream also revealed to her those desperate times when Mom had to heat it in aluminum foil over a flame. Like the time she had gotten so angry with little Shannon for running around and playing with their cat Mr. Peps and stomping on her pipe. "Shan! I told you, stupid girl, *watch yo step*!" Mr. Peps mysteriously vanished the next day.

On some level, Kaley knew. *Nobody's gonna come for us. My mother's a meth addict and she'll probably wake up not even knowing she sent us to the store*. The thought echoed, and with it, pain. This was common. Mom gave them a chore, or sent them to their Aunt Tabitha's, or saw them walk out the door to catch the bus, and woke up not knowing where they'd gone. It was Kaley who prepared their school lunches now. It was Kaley who collected Shan's laundry and washed it all. Mom had become a word sometimes uttered around the house to refer to the husk that roamed about their home, occasionally burning something and occasionally issuing an "I love you" in their general direction. *Nobody's going to save us.*

Echoes…

"Romeo and Juliet…are together in eternity…we can be like they are…"

Who's singing?

None of her thoughts had much substance, because Kaley didn't even know where she was, or why she was so worried. Part of her knew that she was now in the clutches of bad people. The worst people. She knew it, and not because it felt so real, but because it felt so *surreal*. Her black, liquidy, nonspecific dream of echoes was loaded with the knowledge, and the intense feeling. The feeling a person got when they felt like they had stepped into someone else's life. *This doesn't happen to me*, one thinks to oneself. *This is supposed to happen to someone else, but not me.*

That had happened at Nan's bedside. The feeling of disbelief that her Nan had felt had washed over Kaley, causing her to feel death. The actual coldness of it, and the utterly despairing part of her grandmother reaching out to someone, anyone, finding only the granddaughter who shared the charm with her. Kaley had shared in death, had felt pulmonary functions ceasing, had felt the lungs shutting down. She hadn't been able to feel her feet. *This can't be happening*, her Nan had thought. And Kaley had shared the same thoughts on the matter. *I can't be connecting to death*, she had reasoned. *No one can do that.*

But she had. Just as she had connected to the feeling that emanated from the white man in Olympic Park who had been bursting with excitement over proposing to his girlfriend, so much so that Kaley had caught it like she were a sail and his enthusiasm the wind. It carried her, and filled her.

Echoes…

Her thoughts were carried by those dark currents. Directionless and without origin, but everywhere and altogether paramount. Sometimes they were like voices, but with tangible weight. The sounds were heavy and weighed her down. Other times, they were light whispers carrying in a cavern.

Somewhere in the cave, Shan was crying. Kayle struggled weakly, but the current was too strong, holding her fast and carrying her deeper. She wanted to fight the current, to try and swim against it, but she could not summon the strength to do so. Somewhere in her unconscious mind she could feel the bonds holding fast against her wrists and legs. Still, Shan was crying, but her voice didn't echo like all the other sounds. Her voice was very, very close, and didn't carry. But still there were others.

Echoes…

"Seasons don't fear the Reaper…nor do the wind, the sun or the rain…we can be like they are…"

That singing again. Who was doing it?

More uncertainties crept in. Those were the most terrifying things of all. Was she awake or was she asleep? Was this real or was this imaginary? *Parts of it are real*, she decided. *The parts that are the worst.*

There was the sound of a baby crying. Crying loudly. It sounded like it was pain.

Kaley's eyes opened. She was pretty sure the world she was seeing was real this time. But she could still feel that dark current moving around her, threatening to carry her with it. She could still feel the movements of the shadowy bodies that swam beneath its surface.

She was on a floorboard, seated between two heavyset men, one white and one black. She looked up, saw the white man looking down at her. He smiled and then looked away. Her kidnapper actually *smiled*. "Where's...?" She wanted to ask where Shan was, but her words wouldn't work. The current surged with that smile, and took her voice away. That smile washed over her like a thick sludge. She could taste it in her mouth, its rotten smell invading her senses. She could feel it in her mind. In that smile, she could feel the pride of earning something and yet being humored by the notion that someone else had to suffer for it. It was the smile of thinking about tasting the goods before they were sold. It was the murky, messy smile of a mind that had never learned to pick up after itself, and had left litter out in the streets, cluttering avenues of thought and morality.

It was the smile of the big, bald white man. Him with the red bear tattooed on his right arm. It was the smile of his lust. His lust in all things.

The smile echoed...

And it carried her away, dislodging her from whatever fragment of reality she clung to. Deeper, again the current carried her deeper.

Kaley had learned all about lust. She had known about it long before she got her first period. Her cousin Tyrese had taught her all about it, though he never knew it. It was Christmas, they had traveled to Memaw's house—her Nan's nan, in the last year of her life. Ricky, Kaley's ex-stepdad-to-be, wasn't even her mom's boyfriend back then. Shannon was inside her mother, but nobody knew it yet. Kaley was very small. She drank a lot of Coca-Colas that night. Her bladder had warned her that if she didn't get to a bathroom very quick, she would need a mop. Kaley hustled to the bathroom at the end of the hall, but it was occupied, locked. She found a paper towel roll in the kitchen and went outside, in the dark, all alone. Out there was Tyrese and his two older brothers. He followed her, though she hadn't known it at the time. She hadn't known it until she got out in the woods and dropped her pants and squatted. She had been cleaning herself up when something hit her. It was the charm. She felt...curious. Curious about someone else. She felt wanted, too. Emotions that she wouldn't understand until she was in her twenties had swirled and coalesced. She pulled her pants up quickly, because something else made her shiver, and it wasn't the cold December wind. Kaley remembered turning around, looking back towards the house with the lights on, and seeing Tyrese's silhouette there. He was twelve years old at the time, and he was coming for her. He didn't even know it yet, but he was. He thought he was just curious. He thought he was only going to see how little girls peed, maybe see what their plumbing looked like. "Hey, Kaley," he said. He might as well have screamed, "I'm here to kill you!", because she gasped, stood, and ran. She couldn't go back to the party because he was in her way, and he would stop her, talk to her cousin to cousin. Tyrese would laugh and convince her there was nothing to be afraid of. And Kaley would believe him. She would doubt her charm, just as she usually did. In that moment, she knew she couldn't let that happen.

That night, Kaley ran from him. She ran deeper into the woods. She came out onto another street and got lost quickly. Later that night she would get a mean spanking after the cops were finally called and found her wandering blocks away. Mom demanded to know why she'd done it, but Kaley hadn't told her. In truth, she hadn't known, either. How does one explain a premonition that they doubted had really happened themselves? Kaley felt stupid, and part of her had determined to never make herself look that stupid again. She now realized that that night had been the beginning of her new, sanity-saving programming, the programming that told her not to listen to such stupid "feelings" again or else she would suffer more humiliation. For proud girls like Kaley, saving dignity was everything, and that placed her at constant odds with her charm.

She had listened to her charm back then. It had probably saved her. *I should've listened to it tonight.*

Echoes…

There was that crying baby again. Someone really needed to *do* something about that baby.

Now, her dream became displacing, and she had no idea of where she was or what she had been doing. She wasn't even sure this was a dream. Kaley suddenly realized she needed to be some place, she knew that inherently. But where? She had forgotten. It was important. It was *vital* that she get there. Yet, what good was being there if she couldn't even recall what she needed to be there *for*? So she remained. She remained where she was, with neither the ability to choose nor the will to choose. She remained. Deep, deep within herself, there was the ghost of panic haunting her. She felt constricted, and she always would. She knew it. On some fundamental level, she knew that she would always be *confined* somehow.

And then, all at once, she saw him. The smiling man. Pale. Pale as bone. Pale and black-hooded, and with kind eyes. He smiled across at someone else. He was torturing somebody, and he was delighted. It wasn't the torture he was enjoying, though. Her charm told her this much. Her charm, or the fancifulness of her dream. No, he was enjoying...freedom? Yes...yes, that was it. He was free and he hadn't been for a while. But he was free now and loving every minute of it.

Then, she saw *it*.

Oh God, she thought. *He's going to kill everyone.*

She parted her lips and groaned, "Please...please, we have...we have to go...we have to run...far away...from him..."

The big bald white man glanced down at her. He smiled again, and she felt the wash of lust. "Shhhh. Just relax. It'll all be over soon."

"We   have...to   go...please...you   don't understand...he's..." Her eyelids felt so heavy. So very, very heavy. "He's...he's going to kill...and the imps...he'll bring the imps...and the chains and the...the...briars..."

Somewhere in the car, someone's phone rang.

And someone was...singing.

"Come on, baby...don't fear the Reaper...baby take my hand...don't fear the Reaper...we'll be able to fly...don't fear the Reaper...baby I'm your mannnnnnnn..."

2

People found out about Spencer Adam Pelletier when he was thirteen years old. He was still in the fifth grade, having failed two years in a row despite having breezed through all previous four grades with straight A's. During that time, he had been the kind of kid who was prone to acts of kindness, sharing his lunch with poorer kids and sometimes just giving his lunch money away to the kind of kids that didn't eat at all and had to keep pretending that they'd lost their lunch money every day, or that they just weren't hungry.

Teachers had commented on just how terribly good Spencer was in all things, and found it refreshing to talk about a child who was so giving. He never mocked other kids, and stood up for those that were getting made fun of. If he couldn't do anything about it himself, Spencer made sure to tell a teacher. He actually did this three times in a row in his third-grade year, enough to be put on a school poster. Beneath his face had read the words **BULLYING IS NOT ACCEPTABLE: BE LIKE SPENCER, IF YOU SEE SOMEONE TREATED UNFAIRLY, BE SURE TO REPORT IT.**

Before he was ten years old, many kids were already calling him a narc. But that was fine, because Spencer enjoyed it. You see, long before anyone else in the world or in his family found out the truth about Spencer Adam Pelletier, he'd found out about himself. He hadn't been doing the right thing because he found it moral. No. Not at all. He'd been doing the right thing because he liked the look on the faces of those who thought they could get away with something when they suddenly realized they were *not* going get away with it.

That's a slight distortion. Spencer didn't just like seeing this look on people's faces. He relished it. He relished it the way a person well-versed in tantric sex will relish the build up to the finish, with almost no attention at all paid to the final squirt at the end. And, like a person versed in tantric sex, it took practice to become good at it.

Spencer understood that there were all kinds of people in the world. That there were those who were born with a certain powerful or beautiful body type, which allowed them to look down on others and society gave them the okay to do so, no matter how many anti-bullying campaigns were launched. Other folk were prone to kind acts because, being bullied themselves, they could empathize with those who were pushed around. It was a survival mechanism: *We should band together. United we stand, divided we fall.*

But no matter which of these personalities a person happened to be, no matter what their body or personality type, they will almost always do what they do because of a perceived consequences and rewards system. And Spencer understood that system to be based off of what a person believed they could reasonably get away with.

And *that's* why few people understood Spencer Adam Pelletier. Turning in a bully was never about getting a pat on the head or his face on a poster. Quite the contrary, Spencer had perceived those "rewards" as *drawbacks* to what he liked best— chopping people down. Chopping down a teacher off her moral high horse, or chopping down a mob boss in B cellhouse of the prison rotunda's east wing. There was never any reward for that. In fact, there was almost always punishment for it.

But another facet of Spencer's personality that his mother and father would come to find disgusting was his blatant masochism. He thought pain was funny, interesting, and, quite frankly, a turn-on.

An understanding of this concoction was what was essentially missing when folks tried to suss out why Spencer did what he did to Miles Hoover, Jr. in the school library during his second repeat of the fifth grade. And why things had only escalated thereafter.

Presently, Spencer sat in a new stolen Ford Aerostar minivan outside of Pat's Auto—he'd ditched the Tacoma thirty minutes and six miles ago because he figured Mac would give the po-pos his description as well as the truck's—inhaling deeply of his last Marlboro and exhaling ostentatiously, thinking back fondly on Miles Hoover, Jr.

In those days, he'd been quite the angel, and undoubtedly his parents' favorite amongst their three sons. Fast-forward fifteen years, he was a murderer on the loose and his brothers, Brian and Collin, had become a lawyer and a nightclub owner, respectively. Brian Pelletier was working on cases for old people who had undergone hip replacement surgery and now needed to sue their medical providers for giving them artificial hips that had been recalled, Collin was battling cancer while facing low customer turnout in a bad economy, and Spencer was waiting on lights to flick on in the windows of a chop shop. O, the paths we take.

When a light finally did switch on inside Pat's Auto, it was at the back of the shop. A single light in a single window. *Bingo*, he thought. *Just in time, too. Down to my last smoke.*

Spencer checked his watch—it wasn't quite midnight—so he waited another ten minutes or so. Just about time for the third shift boys to start showing up and performing tasks that the first and second shift guys would never dream of. Pat's Auto, while having no clearly defined off-limits areas, was no less able to somehow convey a sense of restricted ingress—a curb with no incline and a few junkers parked at irregular intervals around the premises made the place *feel* off-limits.

"Here they come," Spencer said to no one at all. First it was a navy-blue Nissan Altima, which killed its lights a block up and pulled around to the back. Next was a red, four-door Pontiac Grand Am, an old one, possibly late 90's. Following quickly on the Grand Am's heels was an old, beat-up Buick that had probably once been red, but was now every color conceivable. The two cars pulled around back and parked beside the Altima.

Spencer waited to watch the figures step inside. They were barely more than silhouettes under a not-quite-full moon. From where he was parked, he could only just make out the back parking lot and its numerous junkers and other cars left overnight; the latter being there to keep up appearances of honest business. The three drivers stepped inside a side door that Spencer couldn't quite see, and a few seconds after they were inside, more windows were filled with light.

Atlanta's premier chop shop is now open for business, ladies an' gents.

Spencer hopped out of the car and crossed the quiet street. Terrell Street was as vacant as it would be after the Apocalypse. One survivor of that event, possibly a radioactive mutant, crossed the street in a slow limp, holding a bag no doubt filled with his liquor for the night and illuminated only by a single dim orange streetlight. The desperate mutant paused only an at overturned trash can to rummage through it, then soldiered on down the street and disappeared, presumably off to scavenge the rest of the wastelands.

Yes, quite a dead avenue. Still, one never knew when the law would finally catch on to Patrick Mulley's secret, so it behooved Spencer to check up on the various parked cars along the sidewalks. There were three of them—a van, a station wagon, and a truck—and he checked all of them for possible surveillance teams before he finally walked right up to Pat's front door and knocked.

The door was made of glass and had faded stenciling on it. The lobby through the glass was pitch-black, not a single photon of light bounced its way from the work area in the back. He knocked again.

This time, he heard something drop. A wrench or a crowbar clattered to the ground, and someone hollered something like, "Hear that?" or "What was that?"

Spencer waited a few more seconds, still humming the Blue Öyster Cult song to himself and thinking about the first time he had heard their music. His older brother Brian had introduced him to music of the 60's and 70's, back when they were still talking, back before things changed and the family looked at the youngest and favorite with new, terrified eyes. Back then, Spencer wore turtleneck sweaters, pants with suspenders, and even pocket protectors. Brian had been the hellraiser and chick-banger, and Collin his faithful sidekick and confidant. The two of them had given Spencer his first beer when he was twelve, in secret and for his birthday, but had forbade him to ever act out as they had. Mom, the Christian fundamentalist, still swore that the music and that first taste of beer had planted a seed. She didn't comprehend or believe in contemporary psychology, and so couldn't understand that what happened to Miles Hoover, Jr. in the Brownfields Elementary School library had nothing to do with taking a single sip of beer or Blue Öyster Cult. *They're called a cult for a reason!* she had screamed while Dad sat in his rocker, backing her up by saying nothing at all. *These rock an' roll creatures aren't even tryin' to hide it! They're proud of it! Don't you see! Same with these Nirvana idiots! Tryin' to seduce you away from God!* That had come about because Spencer was way into Kurt Cobain way after his suicide.

Spencer smiled. *Funny how music sends one back in time.*

A light flicked in a room at the back of a hallway, and another dark silhouette appeared at the end of it. Spencer looked at the unknown person, and the unknown person looked at him. The staring contest lasted a few seconds, and then the dark silhouette approached the glass door slowly. He couldn't see much, just the teeth of the man in the moonlight. "Yo, dude, what'choo want?" the man hollered from the other side of the door.

The voice was a little different than Spencer recalled, but it was him. He reached up and pulled the hood back from his head and smiled.

It took a second for the black man on the other side to imbibe his image—or perhaps he was just trying to conceal his shock—but finally he said, "Sheeeeeeeeeyyyyyyiiiiiit!" It was said with equal parts derision, surprise, humor, and trepidation. He called back to his cohorts. "Hey, yo! I'm gonna open this doe! Naw…naw, it's cool, money! I know this bitch!" He fiddled with the lock a moment and opened up, glancing left and right. "What. The. Fuck?" Patrick Mulley was shaking his head ruefully. "We got some lazy-ass fuckin' cops in this town when yo crazy ass walkin' the streets an' ain't none o' them snatched you up yet."

"I'm like a sunburned penis," Spencer said. "You just can't beat me."

That made Pat laugh. Humor was the best path to Patrick Mulley's heart. Anyone that could tell a good joke could easily slip into his life and start manipulating him, if only they understood how to approach it. And Spencer did. He understood how to approach anybody.

Patrick shook his head again ruefully, as if he was already regretting the mistake he was surely going to make by permitting

Spencer into his domain again. *He already knows he's gonna let me in. He just doesn't want to admit to himself he's that easy.* It was funny this dance he had to do with "normal" people.

"S'up, Pat?" he said. Each man's right hand went wide, then slapped hard as they connected, squeezing one another's fingers and snapping as they came loose. The time-honored "street greet" might not ever go out of style.

"Not much, cuz. Work." He said this the way a family man of twenty years would describe his days spent laboring in the factory. *Same shit, different day.* "S'up wi'choo?"

"Not much. Work," he replied.

"Uh-huh." Pat didn't quite smile. He looked Spencer up and down, studying him for a beat, then took another look up and down the streets. "Izzat what brings yo white ass to my humble establishment?"

"Man's gotta earn a living."

"Uh-huh," he repeated, even more skeptical this time. Another glance up and down the street. Spencer had noticed that so far Pat hadn't moved out of the doorway. He hadn't yet decided if he wanted to allow the wolf in. Pat knew many of the same people in Spencer's world. He'd done ample business with the guys up in Kansas, and plenty with the boys in St. Louis, so he knew the rumors. He knew what had happened at Leavenworth, too. Anybody who watched *America's Most Wanted* with even passing interest, or who visited www.fbi.gov just to check out the Most Wanted List from time to time, would know what happened at Leavenworth.

But does he know about Baton Rouge? That's relatively recent.

"You gonna let me in, or leave me out here to freeze my nuts off the rest o' the night?"

"It ain't that cold." He was right. Spring was edging into summer, and one could feel it now even at night.

"It is when you don't have a friend," Spencer said, giving a frowny face and wiping away an imaginary tear. This earned him another rueful smile and Pat backed away from the door just a smidgen, still not letting him in, but wanting to. Apart from being able to do what others felt was unconscionable, there was really only one other benefit to being a certifiable psychopath, and that was the ability to emotionally detach oneself so utterly from the outcome of any situation that one didn't panic the way others did when things weren't going their way. Thus, total attention could be paid not to the "what ifs" (as in, *What if he doesn't let me in? Where will I go?*), but to watching the subject carefully to see what needed to be done, what action needed to be performed in order to allow one to slip right on inside another person's confidence. This sometimes took careful navigation, playing with a human being's emotions, toying with their tendency to believe in the inherit good in others, and trusting their fear of offending another human being so that it would override their good sense that would usually told them to turn and run.

Like the two little girls earlier, he reflected. He thought on how people got themselves into such trouble by not knowing themselves. Those kind of people condemned creatures such as Spencer, claiming there was something wrong with *him*. *I'm not the one getting raped right now, though*, he thought with a smile. A line out of *A Midsummer Night's Dream* suddenly came to mind: *Shall we their fond pageant see? Lord, what fools these mortals be*. Billy Shakespeare knew what he was talking about.

The smile was right on time. He'd aimed it right at his old acquaintance—not a *friend*, psychopaths didn't have or understand friendships, but knew how to mimic them—and it had done the trick. Pat backed away from the door and said, "Get the fuck in here 'fo the five-oh sees yo stupid ass on my doorstep."

"You're the boss."

"God damn right, son."

Officer David Emerson and his partner, Officer Beatrice Fanney, were the first on the scene, and the first to start taking statements. David stood in front of the titan that had called in the 207: possible kidnapping. The only man to call it in, and so far the only person in the area who had reported anything at all tonight. He might've thought the big fucker Terry "Mac" Abernathy had made at least some of it up, but then there were some telltale signs in the area. Skid marks aside, there were the spilled groceries, and the footage taken from the outdoor camera, which unfortunately took everything in one-second stills and not smooth continuous video. Still, it showed a couple of automobiles come halfway onscreen, a brief struggle between two or three blurry assailants and a pair of equally blurry small children, and then a speedy getaway. Not enough exposure in the camera to catch the license plates.

David glanced over at Beatrice, who was taking out the small orange cones from the patrol car's trunk and placing them at intervals around the sidewalk, around where the best of the skid marks were. A detective would have to haul his ass down here in the next hour or so to start taking pictures, but David doubted it would happen even that quickly. No investigation he'd ever heard of happened quickly in the Bluff, no matter which side of Joseph E. Boone Boulevard you were standing on.

"So, you didn't actually see the abductions yourself," David verified, scratching the back of his ear with his pen.

"Naw, man. Like I said, I was inside watchin' *SportsCenter*," said Abernathy, who had first introduced himself as Mac. David had to wonder if the nickname came from the famous McDonald's sandwich. "I heard this commotion, knew somethin' was up, ya feel me?" David nodded that, yes, he felt him. "I heard screamin'. I heard some kid sayin' 'Run, run, run,' an' I heard some men yellin'. Got up, got my Glock, headed out the front doe. By the time I got outside they was squealin' off. I barely got a look at 'em."

"El Camino and an SUV of some kind, right?"

"Yeah. Full-size, fuh sho."

David updated dispatch with the information. When he was done, he licked his lips and looked back at Mac. "And you're pretty sure it was these girls you know? What were their names?"

"Kaley an' Shannon Dupré," Mac supplied. "Yeah, it was them. Had to be. That's they groceries right there, Officer."

David glanced at the smashed orange juice container and the paper bags that spilled ham, pretzels and Pop-Tarts. "Home address for the girls?" he said.

"I don't know they address, but I know they be livin' with they mom, Jovita. Fuckin' meth-head bitch. 'Scuse me, Officer," Mac put in, proving that he was a rough but congenial giant, which David found both unusual and refreshing for the Bluff.

"Jovita Dupré. Got it."

"She always cooked outta her damn head, don't pay them kids no mind like she should. She need her ass whooped lettin' them kids walk out here alone like that!" He fumed for a moment.

David figured Mac was one of "those" kinds of people in places like the Bluff. A lone spirit who despised his surroundings, wished people would act right, and would never up and leave it. "So, you *don't* have an address. Have a street, or a description of her house?"

Mac nodded enthusiastically, like he'd just been invited to go up there himself with the two officers and smash Ms. Dupré's head in. He looked like he would enjoy that very much, and David believed he would. "She up on Beltway. I forget which house, but it's one o' them where ya pay based on how much ya earn a month."

"Public housing," David said, nodding as he jotted that down. There weren't many other kinds of houses or apartments around here. The Bluff was the pinnacle of poverty in all of Georgia. "Got it. Descriptions of the girls?" Mac gave approximations of their age and height, as well as what they were wearing. "Did you see anything else? License plates on the vehicles? Special rims on the tires maybe? Distinguishing marks on the men who did this?"

"I didn't see shit, Officer. 'Scuse me. By the time I got out here, they gone." David went to jot that down, and then Mac added, "They was this one muthafucka, though. White boy. Drivin' a pretty new black Tacoma." David glanced up at this, interested. White was unusual for the Bluff, especially this late at night, and especially driving a new-looking truck. "He came in an' bought a burger an' a Dr. Pepper from me, walked out about the same time all o' this happened, an' then dipped when he found out I was callin' the police."

Mac had pronounced it *poh-leece*. Internally, David was just grateful Mac didn't refer to the police as "po-pos," at least not in his presence. "Description?" he said.

"White," he said. "An' I mean like *white* white, Officer. As in as pale as that moon over yo head. I mean, not albino, but fuckin' white, ya feel me?"

David nodded. "What else?"

"Tall, thin."

"How tall? How thin?"

" 'Bout six-one, six-two, an' maybe one seventy-five. Nazi poster boy, 'cept fo his black hair. Blue eyes an' tall an' German-lookin'. Ya feel me?"

Again, David nodded. "Clothing?"

"Blue jeans. Brown shoes. Converse, I think. He wearin' a black hoodie. Pulled it up over his head befo he left."

"He say anything to you before he left?"

"Yeah, a whole lotta shit. Talkin' this an' that. He ran his mouth a lot. Talkin' about my name, how big I am, an' tol' me I oughtta buy a new jersey because Michael Vick's a dog-fightin' fool. I pretty much tol' him to kiss my ass an' he left. When I came out, I started to call 911, an' he got the fuck outta here like his head was on fire an' his ass was catchin'. Ya feel me?"

Once more, David nodded. "And you said that the only other witnesses were some guys who bolted, and a couple across the street that walked away a few minutes after all this happened?"

"Yeah, word. I don't know who the fuck they was, but the four bitches who cut an' ran were some fools I know from Vine, near MARTA."

He meant Vine City's MARTA station, which meant David wasn't likely to find or get much out of those four black youths tonight. That area held nothing but people who were supremely mistrustful of the police, slamming doors anytime the word "warrant" wasn't specifically uttered. A land of people who'd gotten to know the Atlanta Police Department so well that, despite sky high on meth and H all the time, most of them could quote civil rights laws back to the officers who appeared warrantless at their doorstep. It was ranked as the number one most dangerous neighborhood in Atlanta, and number five in the entire United States. David had only been working Atlanta for a year, had never gone to that area once, and didn't know many cops who did. That's how he knew it was a lost cause looking for those witnesses.

Which means probably a lost cause for those girls. He didn't like to admit it, but history was history, and facts were facts.

David sighed, and closed his book. "All right, I think we've got your full statement. A detective will probably be around in a short while, so—"

"Ho, wait, you leavin'?" Mac said, taking a step forward and forcing David to take a step back. He didn't like being made to take a step back. "You can't just let this up an' slip right now, Officer. We can't wait on no detectives to show up four hours from now—"

"Mr. Abernathy, I understand your concern," David said mildly. "Believe me, I do. But right now the quickest way to get some results is for us to put this on the AMBER Alert system, get the description of the girls and their names out in public, as well as the two vehicles associated in their abduction."

Mac's eyes went wide in supreme disbelief. "You gonna wait for a snitch around *here*?"

"We'll keep looking. My partner and I will patrol this area, and for the rest of the night we'll be looking for the vehicles you described. In the meantime we'll put the descriptions out so that maybe an aware citizen—" He paused when dispatch called something out over the radio attached to his chest.

"All units in the vicinity of Madison and Dawnview, please be advised of a 211S in progress—" David turned the volume down. A 211S was a silent robbery alarm going off. Madison and Dawnview weren't anywhere near him. He turned back to Mac and started to finish his sentence.

"An aware citizen," Mac said skeptically. He took a step back, and started stroking his chin. "Man, I'm tellin' you, you can't come at it like that, Officer Emerson. I mean, no disrespect or nuthin', sir, but these muthafuckahs was organized an' shit. They came up on those little girls an' moved with a purpose. They had dat shit *planned*, yo. Ya feel me? An' that white boy, he probably a scout or some shit for 'em. You know, scoutin' out easy victims an' all that?"

"We'll put a description out on him and the truck he was driving," David tried to assure him. Mac was breathing heavily now, though, forcing David to touch at his pepper spray and glance for his partner by reflex. Officer Beatrice Fanney, her of the round ass and unfortunate last name, had noticed the exchange. She'd finished placing the cones and called in an update to dispatch, and was now moving around the other side of the patrol car to back her partner up. "Call us if you think of anything else that might help us."

"A fuckin' *AMBER* Alert?" Mac went on. "That's it? Yo, Officers, I read *Time* magazine an' shit, an' those AMBER Alerts are bullshit! They only ever work in, like, *minor* abductions, like when kids are taken by a noncustodial parent or another family member. Kids that get abducted by total fuckin' strangers *never* get found by AMBER."

David said nothing to that, because, of course, Mac was absolutely right. While the alerts were a good idea, and certainly couldn't hurt, there was very little evidence to show that they helped. "Mr. Abernathy—"

"Just go, man." No more "Officer" now, just "man". Mac turned back towards his store. "You nuthin' but a fake-ass nigga anyway," he derided. "I guess I'll wait on the fuckin' detectives. If they even fuckin' show," he added.

David turned back to his partner and nodded towards the patrol car. Beatrice got in the driver's side and David sat in the passenger's, removing his hat and running a hand over his balding scalp. He looked at Dodson's Store, saw Mac squeezing his way through the front door with shoulders slumped, defeated. *So I'm a fake-ass nigga, huh?* he thought. *I guess that's because blacks shouldn't become cops. Who'd keep you, then, Mac? Huh? Who'd even give a fuck about—ah, fuck it.*

After David finished calling in the descriptions for the AMBER, he and his partner both sat there for a moment finishing out their notes.

"Gotta hand it to him," Beatrice said, cranking up the car and pointing at Mac, who was just visible through the window. He had already gotten to work stocking shelves full of cookies. "Two girls get kidnapped and six or seven people just dash. 'Fuck the girls,' they said. 'I'm getting outta here. Not my problem.' But he comes out with a Glock in hand, makes the call, and obviously has a lot of passion about finding them."

"Guy like that shouldn't be living in the Bluff."

"If guys like that didn't live here," Beatrice said wisely, "who would've called it in?"

David smirked. "Good point." Then a cloud came over him. "Fat lotta good it'll do, though. If the kidnappers belong to who I *think* they belong to, those girls aren't gonna pop up for another five or six years. They'll be coked outta their minds, giving blowjobs to johns in skuzzy crack houses and so fried that they won't be able to recall that it wasn't *their* idea to become prostitutes." He added, "If they're lucky, that is."

Beatrice nodded. "The Russians? The *vory v zakone*?"

David rubbed his eyes and pointed at her like, *Bingo!*

"If that's the case, the girls might not even be in this country by sunup."

Before they drove off, he glanced at the flickering sign of Dodson's Store. He thought about Mac's last words. *If they even fuckin' show.* Unfortunately, the detectives never showing up was a real possibility, and something that never got reported on shows like *Dateline*. Those were the breaks for those who opted to eke out an existence in the Bluff. You can get your H fine and dandy, but you became what David called an Outlander. *You don't really exist out here.* Everything from the plumbing to the policing worked differently down here in the Bluff; no one liked to admit it, but there it was.

The timestamp on Dodson's security footage showed 10:58 PM as the time when the two vehicles pulled up to abduct the two girls. If it was the *vory v zakone* that had done it, then Officer David Emerson and his cohorts at the APD probably had less than twenty-four hours to find them. Maybe a bit more if it was the Juarez cartel boys or the guys from the Crips.

"Car one-Adam-four, this is dispatch," said a friendly woman's voice over his radio.

David touched the button. "This is one-Adam-four, go ahead, dispatch."

"We've sent a patrol car up to Beltway to give a knock on the door of the home where your abducted girls live," she said. Beatrice had been updating them while she listened in on David's interview with Mac. "They'll notify the mother. All cars in your area have been notified to be on the lookout for your abductees and the vehicles—a red El Camino and a black Expedition."

"Copy that, dispatch. I've got another one for you. Caucasian male driving a Toyota Tacoma. May be nothing, but then maybe something." He gave the description Mac had given him: 6' 1" or a bit more, 175 lbs, short black hair, blue eyes, *pale white*, wearing a black hoodie with blue jeans and brown Converses. David had no way of knowing if the white fellow had anything to do with what had gone down here almost an hour ago, but he was willing to bet someone would spot a white man driving that truck before they'd spot a pair of black girls in the Bluff.

"We'll get that description out to cars in the area," said the dispatch lady.

"Ten-four. We've just finished taking the only statement of anybody willing to give one, and we're about to start canvassing the neighbors." *For what it's worth*, he thought but didn't dare say.

"Ten-four. Will advise detectives."

Will advise detectives, he thought. *Advise them of what?*

There wasn't much to go on. The clock was ticking. But the AMBER Alert had been sent out, and a cop's gotta eat sometime. The detectives would handle most of it from here. "Let's cruise the area a bit, knock on some doors, see what's up. If nothing turns up by the time the dicks get on it, let's hit the Waffle House. What do you say?"

Officer Beatrice Fanney pursed her lips and nodded in a way that suggested it sounded like a plan to her.

3

When she woke, Kaley discovered that her pants were gone. They were on the floor next to her. She tried to sit up, and found that she had to use her elbows because she was handcuffed at the wrists and ankles. She kicked out against a phantom attacker. There was no one else in the room. Except…she heard a whimper, and turned to see a truly terrifying thing.

Shan was bound and gagged on the floor with her, and looking up at her big sister with huge, tear-dripping eyes. Kaley tried to say something, tried to yell, but found that she was gagged, too. Something soft and large had been shoved into her mouth, and something else held it there. Upon her first scream, she almost swallowed it, and would surely have choked on it.

Panicking, Kaley tried to wrench her hands apart. That didn't work. The handcuffs were closed tight, cutting off circulation it felt like. It was dark inside the room. Bars of moonlight came through the shades of a window above her, casting her and her sister in zebra stripes. On the floor of whatever room she was in, toys lay strewn like so much detritus. There was a space heater, but it wasn't currently running. A ceiling fan overhead blew on its lowest setting, giving off a light gust that in her latest dream had manifested itself as the wind blowing in her face as she stuck her head out the bus window on the way to school.

There were voices. Perhaps the echoes from before? No, new ones. These came from someplace. They came from somewhere inside the house. Sounded not too far away. An adjacent room. There were three or four different men, all jockeying for position in the conversation. She caught snippets of English words, but there was also plenty of some other language to conflate the topic being discussed. At times the voices raised, then lowered, and even whispered before rising again.

An argument?

Kaley kicked out with her feet again, trying to break free of the cuffs by sheer power. She had heard of people becoming uncommonly strong when they were under pressure, but she was issued no such magical powers now. She screamed through her gag and writhed in emotional anguish, and in frustration at herself for not listening to the charm.

Beside her, Shannon sniffled. Fresh snot was moving from her nose and collecting around her gag. Her eyes were like saucers. She was missing her pants, too, but still had on her Powerpuff Girls underwear. Kaley crawled over to her and threw her cuffed hands around her neck, hugging her closely, briefly, hoping that this would assuage her long enough so that Big Sister could do what had to be done. "I have to leave you," she tried to say. But what came out was, "Ah hah tuh luh yuh."

Shannon—poor, poor Shan—she got the gist of this and shook her head violently. She clung to her sister, who was trying to separate from her. Then, Kaley touched her forehead to her sister's. She closed her eyes. She couldn't speak, but had to make her sister see. She had to make Shan feel what Big Sister had to do. What happened next was closely akin to prayer, only not directed towards the heavens. For a moment, Kaley felt something. It was Little Sister Terror. Then, Shan's body jerked, and she peed herself. But peeing herself was good, because after it was over it calmed her. When Kaley opened her eyes, Shannon was looking at her. Her little sister nodded reluctantly. She didn't like it, but she understood. *Big Sister must leave to go get help for Little Sister.*

Kaley then pushed herself away from Shan and found the nearest wall. She couldn't stand right up, of course, because her feet were bound. She inch-wormed until she got her back pressed against the wall, which was made of cheap paneling and had a ghoulish poster of Marilyn Manson half torn and hanging from it. Other than that, there was no other decoration to this room.

Kaley pushed herself up to her feet, and then hopped twice before the door swung open. *"Dorogaya moya,"* said the burly white man, half ensconced in shadow. *"Kak vashi dela?"*

Kaley screamed through her gag and dived for the window. It was closed, of course. On the other side of the shades were steel burglar bars. She had just enough time to ram them once with her left shoulder, hearing a pop from within the socket, and then the burly white man was on her. He snatched her by her hair, tearing some out and flinging her to the ground, landing atop her sister who wriggled to get out of the way but only made it halfway. Kaley landed in Shan's urine, and quickly spun her feet around to face her kidnapper. She kept her knees bent, both her cuffed feet cocked and ready to kick at his knees or shins if he approached.

The big white man stood over her for a moment. And then he laughed. He laughed long and hard, even slapping his knee like he'd just heard the greatest yarn. He wore a black wife beater, gray khakis, and a chain for his wallet. His face had multiple piercings, and a tattoo of barbed wire or a twisted tree branch that went down the right side of his face. Another tattoo, this one of the crimson bear, was on his right arm. Kaley recalled that tattoo from her time in the floorboard of the Expedition.

A mountain of muscle, he towered over her like Oni from *White Ninja Meets Shaolin Crane*. For a moment, she thought insanely, *We're in his clutches. Oni has us.* It was the kind of thought born of delirium. Her head still spun from whatever they had used to knock her out. *Probably that stuff—what's it called?— chloroform!* She's seen an *NCIS* episode where a woman got kidnapped by her ex-husband using that stuff.

"*Ti takaya prelesnaya,*" said Oni. He leaned forward, the moonlight revealing two tusklike protuberances at the edges of his mouth—large steel studs pierced there. Kaley saw that face grin at her ravenously, and she kicked up at his face.

Quick as a snake, he snatched up her feet, held both ankles in one big hand, and ran his fingers down the length of them. "*Ya ischu devushku, kotoraya khochet lyubit i bit luybimoy,*" he tittered. His voice was much higher than his size hinted at.

Kaley struggled to kick again, but couldn't get her feet free of him. She felt…sick. It was on her again. The lust. The terrible lust. A thing so hideous it would make it difficult to trust another man for years to come. She shouted something obscene at him, but he only laughed and tickled her legs.

"Hey, yo!" someone called from down the hall.

The smile on Oni's face died. He dropped her legs immediately and looked over his shoulder. He looked down at Kaley, tilted his head to one side, considering something. And she felt wanted. She felt *his* want of her. And the terror that rolled right off her little sister next to her swirled and mixed with this lust, causing an automatic cringe of revulsion from both. For a moment, she was the bearer of two great burdens.

Then, someone shouted something down the hallway, out of sight where Kaley couldn't see. This robbed the white man of almost all his lust as he made for the door. He paused in the door, though, and through the pale moonlight, she could just make out his wink. He did something with his lip that caused the steel studs to click against his teeth. "*Do vstrechi,*" he said, and shut the door. From the other side, she heard it lock.

To her, his last words had seemed (felt) like a promise.

As soon as the door closed, Kaley reached up to her gag. She tried pulling at it, but it was tough. A sock or something like it had been shoved into her mouth, several loops of duct tape had sealed it tightly against her head and something like a zip tie had been added for good measure. Her sister appeared done in the same way. No matter how they both struggled, nothing loosened these gags.

They wound up clutching one another again.

Emotions swirled about Kaley. Her sister's terror was the most powerful. She was redolent with it. But other emotions ebbed and flowed throughout the house, permeating the walls and permeating *her*. Like wading through water at first, but then someone had added cement to the mixture. It was thick and oppressive on her. Distrust, lust, and anger welled in her. She felt the abductors falling apart already.

Minutes later, Kaley and her sister heard more raised voices. Then the door flung open again and in walked three men. One of them was the burly white man from before, but the others were black men. This gave her hope. She hoped they were men from her neighborhood who would recognize her, realize they'd made a mistake and grabbed the wrong kids (who were the *right* kids?) and would set them free with the promise not to tell anybody.

But this didn't happen at all. Instead, the men said nothing as they dragged both Big and Little Sister over to the space heater. More handcuffs were produced, and though Kaley struggled the whole time it didn't stop them from cuffing her and her sister to the space heater.

One of the black men, a tall one built like a basketball player and wearing gold chains with a cross about his neck, turned and said, in the most rational voice one could imagine, "Let's see her kick you now."

The white man, who before had spoken in the foreign language, now spoke in strained English, "She not a problem. Not problem for me. I not worried. Room secure. My people—"

"Yo people call you a regular fuck-up," the black man said, wearing a half smile of satisfaction. "That's why yo ass got some help tonight. Now get the fuck in the livin' room an' let's talk the rest o' this out like men do." But the burly foreigner with steel studs in his mouth didn't go anywhere.

Another black man, this one short and skinny and wearing pants pulled so low his underwear was showing, waited by the door, shifting his weight back and forth, fidgeting. He touched the pistol tucked in his waistband impatiently, glancing up the hallway like he was expecting someone to show at any time.

The bigger black man knelt so that he was eye level with Kaley. "This yo sista?" Kaley didn't move. "This yo sista." It wasn't a question this time. "Imma kill her if you try anything again. White boy over there says you tried to dip. Don't." He pulled out a pistol. Kaley didn't know what kind it was. Cars were the limit of her boy stuff knowledge. He touched the gun to Shannon's head. Oh, God, it was *touching her sister's head*! "I won't kill you, I'll kill *her*. Got that, lil' girl. Now, I'm very sorry this had to be you tonight," he said, and Kaley sensed immediately that he wasn't sorry for anything, "but that's how this cookie right here crumbles tonight. A'ight?"

Kaley nodded vehemently.

He gave her a second, judicious look. "Stay cool, an' this'll all be over soon," he said. She didn't think so, but she certainly felt that he believed that.

The two black men filed out quickly, and Kaley watched with mounting terror as they all left. She was terrified because she knew what was going to happen. She knew the same way she'd known this was all going to go down like this tonight, only now she was listening to that charm her grandmother had passed down to her instead of ignoring it like she always did.

The burly foreigner with the avid eyes and the red bear tattooed on his arm and the steel studs in his lips was going to kill them. He was already thinking it. She shouted through her gag, trying to warn the two black men. *He's already thinking it! You can't let your guard down around him! He's waiting for you to let your guard down and then he's going to kill you and then…he's…*

The look the white man gave her before he shut the door told the gruesome story. He knew exactly what he intended to do with the two girls. He knew it. Kaley knew it. And even Shan probably knew it. Everybody knew it except the two black men. They thought they had a deal. They thought they were going to get something out of this. They didn't know how this was going to end, but Kaley's charm told her that if she could help them survive then this would all go differently.

She tried to reach out to them before the door closed, but the farther they got away the harder it was to feel what they were feeling, thus it became impossible to influence them at all. The charm was too dim for that kind of connection. If, that is, Kaley wasn't totally insane and only wishing the charm was all that her Nan had made it out to be. *It has to be! It needs to be! If we're going to survive this, we have to reach someone—*

When the door shut, it came to her. *Reach someone.* All at once, she recalled her cell phone. It was still in the back pocket of her pants. She looked across the room, to where her pants lay on the floor. *Stupid girl! Stupid, stupid, stupid! You should've made a phone call when you had the chance! You couldn't have made a sound but someone could've traced the call, maybe! Now your hands are chained up! Good job, Big Sis!*

A whimper.

Kaley looked over at Shannon. Her sister was sniffling and looking down at her lap dejectedly. A wave hit Big Sister. Ultimate fear of the unknown. Also…yes, yes…Shan had a sense of something shifting unfairly. Yes, hope had been unfairly dashed. *It's not* fair, *she's thinking.*

And there was something else. Deflation? Yes, deflation. *She's thinking we're not such awesome ninjas anymore. She's thinking about what a stupid little game it was. She's yearning…yearning…for* Mom*? Mom, the meth-head? Mom, the woman who never remembers to pack her a lunch or give her lunch money?* Yes, it seemed that no matter how dedicated a mother was to earning the Worst Mother of the Year award for the tenth year in a row, a little girl would always crave her mommy.

She's feeling like we're gonna die without her.

"Mmmm," Kaley said, because it was about all she could manage. Shan looked over at her. Big Sister leaned over as far as she could, and looked Little Sister dead in the eye. *We will make it through this*, she thought. Kaley didn't blink, and kept sending the thoughts. Or rather, the feelings. But she couldn't send a feeling of confidence when she didn't feel confident herself. Still, Shan seemed to get the idea, and nodded. She hadn't picked up on any confidence, but she'd gotten the intent, the love, the caring of Big Sister, which would have to do.

Another wave hit her. Something from down the hall. Tension. Anger. Men were getting heated.

Yes, it would just have to do.

"Dig, son: welcome to the new an' improved Pat's Auto," said the proud owner. Pat took him to the back work area and opened the door, which swung on new hinges. On the other side of it was a new peg board that held pneumatic drills, socket wrench sets, tubing, funnels, pliers and spare nuts and bolts.

"Nice," Spencer said, unimpressed but pretending to be. The chop shop was almost exactly how he remembered it. His ears were assaulted by the sound of car work being done. A Lincoln Town Car was jacked up, half of it gutted. Beside it was a Mazda3, up on the hydraulic lift, two grease monkeys working underneath it with a VIN scraper. There was the same parts room off to one side, the same three bays with the hydraulic lifts. There were *some* improvements, but they all had to do with a certain cleanliness and order being kept—shelves filled with engine blocks, boxes of carburetor pieces, drive shafts, wheels, tires, screws, bolts, spark plugs, and the engine hoists all appeared more organized. The floor was cleaner. The lights weren't so dim as Spencer recalled. Things were more efficient now. The pneumatic hoses drooped down from overhead, no longer creating a troublesome web the floor. The three grease monkeys Pat had working for him were either white or black. No more Mexicans, which was smart. Pat was figuring this shit out.

Pat hollered out, introducing Spencer to some of his employees. Their greeting was a lot less effusive than Pat's had been. They were busy with their work, and none of them deigned to give him more than a cursory, and slightly suspicious, glance.

Many of the improvements Pat spoke of were invisible to the naked eye, though. Before he came up from Baton Rouge, Spencer had learned from a cat named Uncle Ben what sort of operation Patrick Mulley was now running. Since Spencer's last visit this way, Pat's Auto had become a multifaceted criminal venture, dealing a lot with the local gangs and cartels, providing reconfigured vehicles with sly compartments for hiding contraband. No more selling stolen parts for scrap or to unknown buyers online. Pat had moved up in the world.

Moving up meant newer, bigger connections. And with these new connections, he'd begun establishing himself as a key provider of perhaps the most important service in any big money scheme—Pat's Auto was a haven for the placement of ill-gotten money, then the layering of it, and then the integration of it: the three main steps to money laundering.

Spencer walked slowly with his old acquaintance, taking it all in with the studied look of a man appreciating a young artist's growth, but also seeing where the artist had yet to truly see his own potential, seeing that he was just on the cusp of his greatest breakthrough. *This is the stage where most artists flounder*, he thought. The first change that needed to be made would be taking such an operation out of the Bluff—Pat had enough friends now to help him do that, so why was he hanging out down here in Vine City with all these losers instead of going for the big-time?

One word answer: *nostalgia*.

Pat wouldn't leave this town until it left him. He no longer needed its seclusion and safety from the police, yet he would remain. He would remain here until the day he got caught, probably sold out by one of these grease monkeys in overalls.

"What'choo think, money?"

Spencer sighed. "You've come a long way." *An' still got a long way to go. But what do I know about these things? I've never been in charge of a chop shop.*

"Yo, Eddie, m'man!" Pat shouted to one of the grease monkeys. "Me an' my boy here gonna step inside my office fo' a piece. I want them VINs scraped off."

"You got the VIN books on the new Lincolns?" asked the skinny dude in blue overalls. "Because if you ain't, we ain't gettin' all these VINs off tonight."

"I gave those books to G-lo over there," Pat replied, a bit testily. "G-lo, man, don't tell me you lost them books, boy."

"I got 'em right here, Pat," said a big, solid-looking black fellow in a tone that said Pat should get off his ass about it.

"You boys better communicate better. Ya daddy here ain't gonna be around forever." He was referring to himself, of course.

Spencer watched them pull out their VIN scrapers and get to work.

Vehicle Identification Numbers were hidden all over cars and car parts, and some of their locations were kept very secret, known only to those in the know throughout the industry. If a fellow had connections like those that Pat had culled throughout the years, he could get a hold of the books that documented how many VINs had been etched onto the vehicle and where they were hidden. A VIN was a car's fingerprint. If all the VINs couldn't be scraped off and changed, then there was as problem if a driver got taken in, because it would be very easy to find out he was driving a stolen vehicle by checking the VIN.

Spencer knew this because he was a booster. Not from the sexy *Gone in 60 Seconds* type of bullshit, but the real, more mundane variety. It wasn't actually all that exciting. Just scope out a Mustang GT you wanted and follow it to the owner's house. Come back a week or a month later and smash the window. Toss down a towel so you don't sit on glass, then use a screwdriver to pry out the ignition cylinder. Jam the screwdriver into the slot that fit a flathead so well you had to wonder if the idiots who made the car had purposely *made* it easy to steal, and then you're off with your brand new Mustang, all without having to play that *Price is Right* game show like a sucker.

Spencer took in the entirety of the chop shop and wondered, *Why would anyone wanna live the life of a simple sucker? How could anyone feel the energy of this kind of operation an' not want in for the rest o' their lives?*

Pat clapped him on the back and opened his office door. " 'Step into my parlor,' said the spider to the fly. Remember you said that shit to me, what, twelve years ago it's been since we met in New Orleans?"

"Thirteen," Spencer said, stepping inside and taking a seat in a squeaking rolling chair. "But who's counting?" He looked about the office, which hadn't seen as much orderly improvement as the shop itself had since the last time he'd been here. There were two empty Dorito bags that sat on top of a desk piled high with folders that were in desperate need of a cabinet and filing system. A *Hustler* magazine peeked out from this pile, as did a number of used yellow legal pads and a copy of *Fortune 500*. Spencer pointed to the Steelers flag on the wall, unchanged since last he was here. "Still bettin' on those guys?"

"Yeah. Dig: lost three g's on 'em last week. Fuck me," he laughed.

"Need to start betting with yer head and not yer heart, Pat."

"Ya don't turn ya back on where ya came from, money. Thought you woulda figured that out by now."

Spencer smiled and leaned back, interlacing his hands across his belly.

"So?"

Spencer shrugged. "So?"

"So *talk*, nigga. What'choo showin' up here fo' like a lonely muthafucka in need of a friend?"

"I told you. Work."

"Bullshit. They's somethin' else."

"No. Honest to God. I need work." And he really did. Money wasn't just scarce these days, it was nonexistent.

Coming up from Baton Rouge he'd managed to work out a few ways of wrangling what he needed to get gas and food, but most of that had been ill-gotten. The Baton Rouge PD was still looking for him when he came across the Chevy Tahoe, one of the easier vehicles to boost because of its limp ignition cylinder setting. The damn thing had been sitting nearly on empty, though, so he'd only managed five miles before he had to pull over and snatch up an F-150 from a Wal-Mart parking lot. He'd gone straight for the Ford because there was a gun rack on the inside of the back window, but, alas, once inside he found no guns at all. Fifty miles later, though, he got his weapon. A Glock sitting in the glove compartment of an old Camry. He'd selected this one because of the NRA bumper sticker, right next to the sticker that said **WORST PRESIDENT EVER** with the O replaced with the Obama logo with the half blue circle at the top and the three red stripes at the bottom. One could always count on a card-carrying NRA redneck who despised the first nigger president to have a weapon nearby.

Never know when the End Times will come an' the Anti-Christ will emerge, Spencer had thought at the time.

The Camry had gotten him forty miles into Mississippi. Spencer had gone far, far south, into a town called Spenceville (which he thought was providence) and knew that he was probably plenty safe when he started seeing billboards that relayed messages from God Himself. The first one was black with only large, white bold letters saying, **God, why don't you answer our prayers and send us a person who can cure AIDS, cancer, and all disease?** Two miles down the road, God gave his answer on another billboard, **I sent you that person and you ABORTED him!**

Yes, Spencer had entered the realm of Hallelujah and Amen! Churches were placed literally every three miles, sometimes four, but that was a rarity. The Camry ran out of gas and he felt safe enough to stop at a station to fill up, but only went another fifteen miles down the road to a parking lot behind a Ryder truck factory in Buford County. Here, where third-shifters had been toiling away their nights, he obtained a Civic. He quickly switched the plates with another similar car nearby, then hotwired that sucker and got to movin'.

The Civic was a piece of shit. It kept listing off to the left and its engine made enough noise to raise the dead. *You don't wanna raise the dead in the South.* Spencer's mother used to say that. He never knew what it meant, only that she said it whenever talking about how difficult it was to debate anyone with a Southern accent.

Spencer stayed off major highways, feeling far safer in the back roads that took him through towns of simple country folk. These people would be more likely to shoot him if they knew who he was and what he'd done, true, but they were also less likely to pay attention to anything besides Fox News, and anyone with an IQ above 110 knew that channel ran almost nothing but political rhetoric that soothed these humble, smalltown folk and eased them to bed at night, confident that they were right about the liberals and how the country was going to hell.

He hadn't even sweated seeing patrol cars while pushing through these territories. Once in Alabama, he switched cars twice; first into a Mazda Miata that had an awesome CD collection for him to listen to while he blazed a cigarette from a pack of Marlboros he'd found in the Civic, and then into a Dodge Grand Caravan at Tallapoosa County.

All during this long game of musical cars, Spencer had checked in with news radio stations. So far, there wasn't any mention of what had happened in Baton Rouge. Amazing to think that as violent as it had been, there was still other shit in the world that people cared about more. He *did* learn, however, that Kim Kardashian was rumored to be engaged again.

Now there's *knowledge I can really use*, he thought, chuckling and burning another Marlboro. It was little wonder Spencer got away with all that he'd gotten away with in life.

He chanced Interstate 20 for a few miles before he hopped off again. The Caravan he was in came with a detachable GPS, which was pretty sweet to have.

The next car he stole was in Muscogee County, right near the Chattahoochee River. That officially brought him to Georgia, the land where local legend had it a young man named Johnny had an epic duel of fiddles with the Devil. It was a Chevy Blazer that carried him thirty miles to Troup County, where he came across the Tacoma in the parking lot of a hair salon. He'd moved through Heard, Carroll, and finally into Fulton County, all the while using the same screwdriver to tear off ignition covers. By this time, the game had changed, gotten tenser. The closer he came to the cities, the more wary he had to be of police vehicles.

Once there, he hadn't stopped until he was in a city called Roswell. There, he'd approached an unsuspecting well-to-do-looking man in an empty parking lot and clubbed him over the head with a tire iron he found in the back of the Tacoma, taking his wallet. Spencer had tailed the man into a gas station, watched him count out some cash, and knew this was the guy. He'd taken off in the Tacoma, leaving no witnesses (as far as he knew) and perhaps leaving the man for dead (also as far as he knew).

It had been a long journey, and it had been fun so far. In fact, reflecting on it now, the mad dash to get away from Baton Rouge had been one of the most liberating experiences of his life. Second, perhaps, only to his escape from Leavenworth. And speaking of Leavenworth, it appeared Patrick Mulley had read his mind.

"Yo, Spence dawg," Pat was saying. "Befo' we get into any kind o' business arrangement, I just gotta know what up. Ya feel me?"

"What's up with what?"

"Leavenworth, playa."

"You really wanna know?"

"I asked, didn't I?" He leaned forward, elbows propped up on his knees. He reached into a mini fridge beside his desk and plucked out an ice cold Bud, tossed it to Spencer without asking if he wanted it. Spencer caught almost without looking.

Spencer popped the top of the bottle—and was glad it was a bottle, because it didn't taste as good in a can—but winced when he heard the *snap-hiss-pop* of the cap coming off. He'd never liked that sound. It got under his skin. Like Miles Hoover, Jr.'s voice had done. He took a sip, savored it. "It's been two years," he said. "I'm sure ya heard it all by now. It was on the TV for a minute."

"Yeah, I heard," Pat conceded with a knowing smile. "But I wanna hear *you* tell it, playa-playa. I wanna know what *really* went down. 'Cause it went down a bit differently than they reported it, didn't it?" Spencer smiled at him, and Pat smiled wider. "Didn't it?"

Spencer leaned back in his seat and put his feet up on a desk, knocking over a Burger King bag and a paperback novel that looked like the binding had never been cracked. "What do you wanna know?"

"E'rythang."

So Spencer obliged him.

At 12:13 AM, the Fulton County Police car pulled up to 157 Beltway Street. It was the left half of a boarded-up duplex that had been built in 1965, with repairs performed repeatedly down through the decades, but always to the plumbing and electrical work, never to anything that reinforced the integrity of the structure. Many times over Atlanta City Hall had debated condemning the entire area around it and tearing down the apartments, townhouses and duplexes that made up this section. As one city councilwoman once famously said of the homes there: "Those aren't houses. It's a bunch of cockroaches doing handstands on each other's backs."

Jovita Dupré didn't see the patrol car pull up. She had been near the window, curtains drawn, but the light that splashed across them looked like a white fire blooming against her shut eyelids. When she opened her eyes, Jovita blinked. Her mouth had been open while she was sleeping. Her collar was soaking wet with drool and her tongue was as dry as sandpaper.

The light from the headlights pried her eyes open, slowly and painfully, until finally she realized she was back in the waking world. Back in the slowed down version of reality. Back in the uninteresting part.

Jovita's bones hurt. She wondered how long it had been since she had moved. She wondered what time it was. She wondered a lot of things.

As she stood up, Jovita became faintly aware of the knock at her door. Paranoia, distant but familiar like an old friend that hadn't called in a while, settled in for a visit. She blinked. Her eyes felt dry, and her vision was blurry. A stark contrast to the sharpness she had experienced earlier, a distinction to the vibrant colors that had defined her life. There was also a cluttered mess in the place where her former clarity had been. Jovita's thoughts moved sluggishly, trapped on a freeway during a rainstorm where an accident had happened way, way up ahead, too far to actually see. The great importance that she had felt for both herself and the world around her had now evaporated. The world was topsy tur—

Shan! Kaley!

Paranoia called up his cousin, Fear, and they had a little get-together in Jovita's brain just then. The last thing she recalled was that she had handed something to her daughters. Maybe some money? Told them to go get something? Groceries? But now they were gone. Jovita searched the room for another kind of light, those being the red numerals of the alarm clock on the living room table (the living room had been her bedroom a lot lately). But those reassuring red numbers were nowhere to be found.

There was more knocking, and for a moment she just put her head in her hands. Nothing seemed very important. Then, she recalled her children again, and that became imperative.

She fumbled in the dark for the clock, even as the knocking grew louder and a part of her somehow sensed that the knocking was more important than the time, but then again it wasn't. The meth-addled mind knew so very little about itself when it was coming down.

Jovita's hands found the familiar contours of the table in the dark, and her fingers did a little nervous dance across magazines, food wrappers, a spilled milkshake, and the remote to the TV before finally coming across the infernal clock. When she flipped it, she discovered it was 12:16. But that didn't make sense because there was no light outside. It took her a moment to recall that the light on the clock that indicated AM or PM had gone out long ago. *Past midnight, then*, she thought. *Where are my girls?*

She sat there for a moment, trying to concentrate. Were they with Ricky? No…no, that wasn't right. Her brain had just brought up the old, corrupted file that reminded her Ricky was ancient history.

The knock on the door got louder. "Ms. Dupré?" came an insistent voice.

Jovita started primping herself. It was then that she discovered she had no clothes on. *Oh, God, did I…?* Her hand went down to her crotch to check herself. Once she felt around and made sure she hadn't seen any of her customers tonight, she relaxed a little and stood up. Her balance was a little off. She pitched sideways on her way to the light switch and slammed against the wall. Jovita flipped the light switch up and down, her brain refusing to recall why the lights wouldn't work. *Power bill?*

No. We paid that. Her sister Tabitha had sent the money and she had paid for it this time, Jovita was sure of it. *Light bulb. Yeah…light bulb's blown.*

"Ms. Dupré?" More knocking. No, it was hammering this time. Someone was hammering on the door.

Jovita stumbled over to one of the lamps by the front door and managed to switch it on. She was proud of herself for this momentary coordination. She almost opened the door before remembering to check the peephole. When she did, her old friend Paranoia came back to reside.

Police. What'd I do? Or was it somethin' the girls did? Maybe they got my girls! Damn pigs! Again, she almost opened the door, but stopped herself long enough to search for some clothes. "Jes a minute!" she hollered. Jovita looked around in the dim light, searching the cluttered floor of overlapping clothes, Ricky's old toolbox, a recliner with more duct tape holding it together than thread, and an upside-down table that was missing one of its legs. Ricky was supposed to fix that before he left, but never did. *Till death do us part, my ass!* she thought, snatching up a shirt hanging from one of the table legs.

More hammering. "Ms. Dupré?"

"I said, *jes a minute!*" She found a pair of pants, but those were Kaley's. "Fool girl needs to do laundry!" she cursed, still on the prowl for something to cover her lower body. She eventually found one of her robes, threw it on, and was still tying it when she opened the door. She didn't remove the chain from the door, though. Jovita wasn't stupid. She remembered what happened to 92-year-old Kathryn Johnson up on English Avenue, who got shot in her own home by Atlanta PD officers who raided the wrong home. The story made national headlines back in 2006 was still fresh on the locals' minds, and would always be. "*What?*" she snapped.

The two officers standing on her doorstep were black. It was mostly black officers that came down to the Bluff these days. *White man don't wanna see what he's done to us*, she thought, looking the traitor niggas up and down. "Are you Jovita Dupré?" the lead nigga asked.

"I—" Her voice caught. Her mouth and throat were very dry. How long had she been coming down? It seemed so much easier these days to sleep through the periods of her life where meth was scarce. These periods of rest became longer and longer, though. She was getting exhausted in her late thirties. Soon, she'd have to start sending Kaley out to fetch her stuff for her. Jovita was not proud of that fact, she was just a practical woman. She cleared her throat, swallowed, and said, "I...I am. What's this about, Officer...?"

"Jameson," he said. He was a big, barrel-chested nigga who looked like he made time for the gym every day. He glanced over his shoulder at his partner, a slightly smaller version of himself. "This is Officer Manning. Can we speak with you, ma'am?"

"What about?"

"Your children, ma'am. They—"

He stopped speaking when she slammed the door in his face, undid the chain, and flung it open wide. "Where they at? You got 'em? I'll tan they little hides, an' yours too, if you got 'em handcuffed in that squad car!"

Officer Jameson raised his hands in a gesture that told her to ease up, a gesture that she had seen directed at her many times in her life from men of all sorts, and always thought insulting. *They all think I'm crazy*, Jovita thought bitterly. "Ma'am, are you telling me that your daughters are *not* at home with you at this time?"

Jovita scoffed at him. "I think I *know* where my damn kids are and are *not*, Officer Jameson—"

"So where are they?"

"I sent them off to the sto'," she said. As quick as she'd needed it, the memory suddenly surfaced. Yes. Yes, indeed, that *was* where she had sent them, wasn't it? Yes, Jovita felt certain of that. It was so. Just before the haze had taken her, just before things had started to be less interesting, she had given Kaley some money and sent her with her sister to get a few things. She was hungry and Shannon would need something for lunch tomorrow. Sandwich stuff. Yes, that was it. That was it.

"You sent them to Dodson's Store up a couple blocks?" the officer inquired. A notepad and pen had magically appeared in the hands of the officer behind him.

"I did. Where they at?"

"Ms. Dupré, there was an incident at Dodson's S—"

"What kind o' incident?" she demanded. Then, Jovita sighed. She realized what it must be. "Shit, did Shan try to put somethin' in her pocket? I thought that girl done grew outta that already! Bring her out here! I'll tan her black ass—"

"They didn't steal anything, Ms. Dupré. They made a few purchases and got on their way. They turned back around for some reason and went back. Possibly they forgot something at the store. It was at that time that two vehicles approached them. A few men got out, grabbed them—at least, we are fairly *certain* it was your daughters now—and put them in a car. The two vehicles took off. We got their descriptions, but—Ms. Dupré? Are you listening?"

"Yeah..." But she wasn't. Once things became a dream, why pay attention anymore? It's all just bullshit anyway. Officer Jameson had started talking so quickly and casually about "the incident" that Jovita was now confident that it couldn't be happening at all. Nobody could talk about such a horrible thing with such nonchalance. It just wasn't possible.

"Ma'am, could we step inside to finish this conversation?"

"I...I d-don't think you..." Jovita swallowed sandpaper. She tried licking her lips, but her tongue felt as dry as her skin. Only now her skin wasn't so dry. She was sweating. Sweating profusely. She felt nauseous. "What...what're you *sayin'*, Officer? I don't...I don't think you're makin' yourself very clear. You're not very good at your job..."

Officer Jameson swallowed this pill and said, "We believe your daughters have been abducted. We need to know if you know of anyone who might have reason to—Ms. Dupré!" He rushed to catch her as she was falling.

Jovita felt her knees buckle. It was time to wake up. Yes, that was a good plan. Once she woke up, she could score another jab perhaps, maybe find some H, who knows? That would do away with these dirty, icky dreams for good.

4

Two years, three months, six days and seventeen hours before he entered Pat's Auto, Spencer Pelletier entered the American prison system for the first time. A series of robberies had been what did him in. Not the murders. No one knew about those yet, and, unless someone found a cure for death by hydrofluoric acid, no one ever would.

The robberies he committed were fairly nonviolent, and they were the kind of stuff that would have him called "Brainiac" for a time by some FBI fellows who needed to give everyone they were after a nickname, the "Master Mimic" by those in the press with the same inclination, and "a master of deception" by the host of *America's Most Wanted*. But those names would only come *after* he'd escaped Leavenworth Federal Penitentiary.

The crimes were fairly simple, and Spencer would always feel that it had nothing at all to do with his intelligence, but rather everything to do with the fact that most people were stupid. Just stupid. They just didn't think. And they were eager to go along with the rest of the herd.

This would be a common argument of his: his sincere belief that he wasn't anything special. In Leavenworth, Spencer had been tested for his IQ, and when Dr. McCulloch told him that it was superior to most others, that Spencer was quite the perceptive intellectual, and had asked him what he thought about that, Spencer had merely replied, "Then you need to raise the standards for IQ testing, because I'm no Al Einstein, doc."

The first bank he hit was a Bank of America in a small town called Marble Falls, in Burnet County, Texas. It had been a sunny October afternoon during an autumnal cavalcade like no other. High winds were blowing dead leaves off of trees, creating miniature, swirling funnels of multicolored leaves dancing up and down the streets, a few of which danced across the parking lot as Spencer had approached the Bank of America wearing overalls, large rubber gloves, a reflective orange vest like a road worker might wear, and carrying a bullhorn. The radio clipped to his side was for effect, as was the hardhat, gas mask and the Geiger counter.

Spencer had opened the door and hustled with purpose right over to the manager's office. Two female employees were within earshot, which was good. There were four customers in line waiting, one of which had spotted him, which was also good. They all saw his urgency. The unease was already palpable, and soon would spread. "I need to speak to the manager," he told one employee. "What's his name? Mr. Ottey?"

"Yes, he's—"

Mr. Ottey had heard and seen Spencer's hasty entrance, and had hopped up from his desk to run to the doorway. "Yes? What is it? What's going on?"

"Gas main leak, sir," Spencer said in an officious tone. He pointed out the nearest window, where the van had been parked. One week prior, Spencer had rented it and had a friend of a friend of Pat's over in Alabama put on letters and stenciling that made it appear legit. It read **MARBLE FALLS GAS & LIGHT** on the side. Like the hardhat and the radio clipped at his side, it was only for effect.

"Gas main—?"

"We need to move everyone into a secure location. *Not* outside! A chemical truck wrecked outside and may have caused the rupture while the road work was going on, hitting the exposed main line." Spencer said it all so quickly that Mr. Joseph Ottey never had any time to register it, or to recall that there was no road work going on outside, and no one digging up a gas main. "The chemicals spilled may mix with the gas leaking and become *highly* combustible! We need to move everyone to a secure location inside the bank."

"B-but…well, okay, but where?"

"I don't care, um…" Spencer touched the button on his radio, pretending to be in a hurry to ask the question of someone else. "I…just…just put them in the vault. Do you have a vault or a back room or *someplace* you can put them?"

Mr. Ottey nodded and said that he did. He pulled out a set of keys and described a back room where counting was done. By now, others had started looking. Customers were unnerved at the frenetic exchange. Spencer made sure to speak in tones just barely audible, increasing the trepidation and fear of those around him.

Then, once he had the full support of the bank manager, the alpha male, it had been easy to get them all to fall into line. "Folks!" he'd hollered. "This is an emergency! Listen up! Listen *up*! We've got a leak outside that's emitting highly volatile chemicals! There's a chance that it may rupture and explode! I'm going to have to ask all of you to move to safety immediately! Do *not* go outside to your cars! The risk of combustion is too great! The fumes are also highly noxious! The bank manager here, Mr. Ottey, is going to escort you all to the back counting room! Now—" Here, he paused suddenly to pretend he was getting something in from his radio, when all he'd really done was touch the button which made the staticky sound. To others, it would sound like a transmission coming in. Spencer touched his ear, which had no earpiece, and checked the Geiger counter before saying, "Yeah. Yeah, that's what I'm reading, too. Some of it's seeped in through the front door. I'm getting everyone to safety now."

Most people were too stupid to know that a Geiger counter didn't detect gaseous emissions leaks. Most people wouldn't even know a Geiger counter if they saw one. But Mr. Joseph Ottey was already standing behind Spencer, lending him his support. With the bank manager at his side, his story now had verisimilitude. He was valid. He was in control of them.

They had gathered in the back room, and were left there for God knows how long after he left. Spencer had locked the front door at once. He then took the crowbar out from inside his overalls and pried open all of the tellers, robbing all six of them. He'd also come across a bagful of deposits not yet entered into the system. He went outside, got inside the van, and drove two miles before he came to his other rental car, hopped in, and drove off with his money. He'd come away with a mere $37,893.

It wasn't genius. His schemes never were. It was the fear and gullibility of people that allowed him to get away with it all.

Two months later and three days after Christmas, Agent Gary S. Chalke of the Secret Service walked into a SunTrust bank in Brandon, Mississippi. He stepped right inside, dressed all nice in a black suit and red tie with a tie clasp in the shape of handcuffs, his expensive shoes clicking on the marble floor as he approached the manager's desk and pulled out a badge identifying himself as a member of the Secret Service. He'd pulled out a series of hundred-dollar bills he claimed were all counterfeit and said that every single one of them had come from this bank.

"Oh, dear," said the Mississippi bank manager, a man named Mr. Tanner, who bristled a bit at the insinuation his bank was somehow involved in a nefarious scheme.

Agent Chalke talked fast, making it clear that he meant no such implication. In the next few months, Mr. Tanner would try and convey to law enforcement officials just how fast Agent Chalke talked, and how utterly confusing some of the things he'd said were, yet how he had spoken with such confidence and authority that it was difficult not to believe every word he said.

At one point, Mr. Tanner asked, "Is this all, you know, for *real*?"

"We're a part of the Department of Homeland Security, sir. And our role with the Treasury mandates we monitor laundered or counterfeited money like this if we're to stay a step ahead. We take this very seriously." Mr. Tanner had protested very little after that.

Over the next thirty minutes, Agent Chalke convinced Mr. Tanner to bring him samplings of other hundred-dollar bills. He produced a kit that could chemically test the bills. Chalke had dipped a small brush in liquid and fanned it delicately across the paper, turning all of the bills yellow. "We've got a serious problem here," Chalke had said. Mr. Tanner almost phoned someone, probably the regional manager, but each time Agent Chalke had assured him that it wasn't necessary. "All the essential people are being informed as we speak," he told Mr. Tanner.

Agent Chalke convinced Mr. Tanner to bring him more and more samplings of bills, tested only a few and they all turned yellow when tested with the liquid. Chalke had nodded knowingly, broodingly, and asked for more. Eventually, he had Mr. Tanner bring him a few dozen stacks of hundred-dollar bills. It was around this time that Mr. Tanner had started getting suspicious, and just as he'd asked to see Agent Chalke's badge and identification again, he'd been hit over the head with a hammer.

Agent Chalke had made sure the manager's door was suitably closed just before that happened.

Of course, there was no such person as Agent Gary S. Chalke, and the liquid he'd used to test the money had been an ammonia mixture that turned all money yellow. Spencer had made off with $54,300, and Mr. Tanner had been hospitalized with brain injuries for six months.

The story made a few headlines, but was mostly just told as a side story to other more important things in the world—the withdrawal of U.S. troops from the Middle East, the latest development in the scandal involving that senator from Idaho, and a sexting story involving a bunch of high school cheerleaders that had the media ostensibly in an uproar while at the same time daring to give away the most titillating details.

"The last time I saw ya was around that time," Pat said presently. "That's when you came around an' needed that spruced up black sedan, right?"

Spencer took a sip of his Bud, and nodded. "Yeah, but I ended up not needing it. But if anybody saw me driving up in a van an' then hopping out an' saying I'm a Secret Service agent, it wouldn't have been convincing. But nobody saw me hop in the sedan when I arrived or when I left. Still, it was a precaution. It was clean, so I brought it back to you, if you recall."

"I do. So, what happened next? If ya got away clean, how'd they bring ya in?"

"Random fucking traffic stop. Can you believe it?" Spencer laughed mirthlessly and rapped his knuckles on the desk beside him. He downed the last of the Bud, belched, and tossed the bottle into an overflowing trash bin beside Pat's desk. Outside, some pneumatic drills were getting to work on the jacked up Lincoln. "Cop pulled me over for a roll-and-go at a stop sign in, uh, let's see…I think it was some fuckin' town called Foley?" He scratched at the back of his head. "Yeah, yeah, Foley, Alabama. Goddam tenacious motherfucker, this cop was."

"S'what happened?"

"I gave him my ID. Fake, o' course. I got it from Basil—which, by the way, I need the Yeti's new address from you later, get some more fakes he's supposed to have waiting on me—but anyway, the cop knew my face. By that time an enhanced image

74

of the banks' security cameras started circulating, courtesy of the FBI."

"Yeah, I remember that shit. I was tellin' e'rybody around here, like, 'Spence done fucked up now.' I was still pullin' fuh ya, yo," he said, toasting the memory of the Spencer That Was and downing the last of his beer before grabbing another one from the fridge. "I heard ya beat a fuckin' cop nearly to death before they pulled ya in. Didn't go out like no punk, eh? Was it the cop that pulled you over?"

Spencer nodded. "Yep. He asked me to step outta the car. Now, I knew what the score was. He was gonna check me out, pat me down, but his back-up was probably already on the way. He didn't wanna just ask me to stay inside my vehicle because he was actually pretty smart. He figured if I lingered much longer, I'd know that he recognized me and I'd speed away. So he asked me to get outta the car. I got maybe two steps out before I head-butted him an' then he an' I went at it. He went right to the ground but snatched the collar of my jacket and pulled me down with him. They're not supposed to do that, they're supposed to roll so that they can get to their gun or Taser and make space to shoot, but I guess it's the animal in fighters like us. An' *fuck*, was he a fighter."

"His back-up show up an' fuck you up?"

"Yep. But not before I fucked him up good."

"How so?"

Spencer looked up at him. "You sure you wanna know?"

"Uncle Spence, please tell me the story o' the little piggy ya fucked up." Pat had on a childish grin. The folks in the Bluff had ever despised the police, and it would surely always be so.

"I bit off his nose," Spencer started. "I swallowed it. They tried to give me syrup of ipecac—you know, the automatic vomit stuff?—and tried to see if I could puke it up so that they could reattach it to his face. I held it down as long as I could, but it finally came up. I hear they reattached it, but it doesn't look too good. Had to take some flesh off his ass and grow it on his forehead to make it look better, but still..." He shrugged. "I bit off a finger when he pushed at my face, but I didn't get a chance to swallow that one. He pulled out his Taser with his free hand, screamin' the whole time, but he couldn't make it work and I just kept head-butting him. He was goin' unconscious by the time the other two patrol cars pulled up."

Now, Pat's smile had died. He'd wanted to hear about a pig getting fucked up, and he'd gotten it. *Only it's not exactly what he thought he'd hear*, Spencer thought. *A couple of punches, maybe. A knee to the groin. Maybe a broken limb or somethin'. But not a face bitten off. Not a finger that I meant to swallow an' a nose that I did.*

But what Spencer had left out was a thing he felt not even Pat could endure, because most people couldn't. After all, how does one explain that the more he bit and tore at the police officer's face, the more aroused he'd become? And how would Spencer be able to explain—and make Pat understand—how he'd come in his pants during the beating the cops gave him. He'd relished it, every knuckle and boot heel that smashed against his body.

Pat took a sip of his beer, and said, "I bet they—fucked—you—*up*, didn't they?"

"A tweaked elbow and a dislocated shoulder that got fixed up courtesy o' the taxpayers," he said, chuckling. "Otherwise, just some cuts an' bruises. Some bleeding, of course. Nothing that didn't heal up completely in two months."

"An' then?"

Spencer looked up at him. "Then, what?"

Pat reached out and smacked Spencer's knee. "Don't leave me in suspense, nigga! I axed you about Leavenworth? What happened when ya got in the *joint*, playa? How the *fuck* did you get outta there?"

"That'll require another cold one," Spencer said, holding out his hand.

Pat sighed, and gave a knowing smile. He reached into the miniature fridge and plucked another Bud out, tossed it at him, and fixed him with a look that said *No more bullshit*.

"They said I found a weakness in the fence, a minor hole that's since been covered up, and that I snuck away in the night, got picked up by some friends waiting for me nearby, and we drove off."

Pat nodded. "But that ain't the whole troof, is it?"

"No. You want the *whole* truth?"

"Fuh sho, money. That's what I been askin' this whole fuckin' time!"

Spencer popped the lid off his beer, wincing again at the *snap-pop-hiss*, and took a sip. He enjoyed the buzz he was getting for a moment, then lowered the bottle and said, "I walked out." He took another sip, and savored the look of disbelief on Pat's face as he stared at him over the bottle. He lowered it, smacked his lips, and sighed. *This is the life.*

"You walked out," Pat said skeptically.

"That's right," Spencer said. "Right out the front fuckin' door."

"Bullshit."

"It gets even better."

"Yeah? How?"

Spencer smiled. "They opened it for me." He couldn't help it anymore. He laughed so hard he nearly pissed himself. For a moment, for just one instant, he thought he heard children screaming. And he thought he heard them close by, although their screams were muffled, like they had something in their mouths. It interrupted him for maybe only a second, and the sounds were gone. Probably just the drills in the shop going to work.

When the first gunshot went off, it jolted Kaley, who had gasped an instant before it happened because she felt it coming. She *had* felt it coming. That sickening anticipation, like having to go number two but having to hold it. It hurt. The anticipation hurt everything inside her. The others hadn't known it was coming, but the burly, lusty white man with the crimson bear tattoo had known. It had been his plan all along.

First, there was loud, rancorous bickering just down the hall. Lots of raised voices. Adrenaline surged through her. It was the adrenaline of the dying. Each gunshot hammered in her head and in her heart. She felt the fear of the others who were taking the bullets. She also felt their pain, and the sinking knowledge that they were going to die.

BANG! BANG! BANG! BANG! BANG!

Glass and furniture crashed. There was the sound of heavy objects hitting the floor.

Bodies, she knew.

Kaley started yanking and pulling at her cuffs throughout this madness. She jerked and pulled and wrenched against her bonds until they bit into her wrists and brought blood.

A few minutes ago Shannon had lowered her head, closed her eyes, and looked ready for sleep. *That's good. Let her sleep*, Kaley had thought. She needed it.

The gunshots jolted Shannon awake. The Little Sister Terror that Kaley now felt was at a crescendo. She was taking it all in again—the dark room, the cluttered floor, the ceiling fan on its most sluggish setting and the Marilyn Manson poster on the far wall—and was recalling with startling clarity where she was and what sort of predicament they were in.

The Little Sister Terror made Kaley dizzy, nauseous, and she almost blinked out.

Four more gunshots followed, along with screaming. *BANG! BANG! BANG! BANG! BANG-BANG-BANG!* "Fuck you! Fuck you! Fuck y—!" Another shot fired and silenced that screamer forever. Somebody else started begging. "No, man…no, no, no, please, dawg, no, man, *NO!*"

BANG!

Somehow, that last bang had finality. The period at the end of a long, angry sentence.

Kaley sat there, panting. She smelled something. Faintly, she was aware that Shan had peed herself again. She looked over at her little sister, saw that she was looking up at the ceiling with tearful eyes. *She's asking God for help.* Kaley didn't feel that, she just knew. They didn't go to church very often, just whenever Mom sent them to Aunt Tabitha's. Aunt Tabitha always made sure the girls had nice clothes to go see the Reverend, and though Shannon was very small (or, perhaps, *because* she was so very small), she understood that some powerful being was "up there" somewhere, and was supposed to be a just and considerate Lord that protected the weak and punished the wicked.

We need that kind of help. Oh God, help us! Help us, please! Send your best angel! Then, she felt something twist inside her guts, she felt the violent yet joyful emotions of the white man down the hall, triumphant now with the final shot fired. *No, send your worst! Send the ugliest fucking one! Help us!*

A minute went by. She heard nothing else from anywhere in the house. Not a footstep. Not a television. Nothing.

They're dead, she thought. *They're all dead except the tattooed white man.* Kaley knew it was true. *The black man who put the gun to my sister's head and threatened to kill her is dead.* There ought to have been satisfaction in that thought but there wasn't. There should have been because, strange as it was, they were now trapped with the creature so abnormal the others had repudiated him.

Like two dogs fighting over a bone. And we're the bone.

She heard talking. It was the burly white man, talking to himself. Or, no, probably not to himself. Probably on the phone with someone. His voice approached, and when the door flung open and Oni came inside with that wife beater of his bloodied and his brow glistening with sweat in the moonlight, both Kaley and Shannon froze. It was probably something ingrained in every animal. *Don't move, and the monster won't see you.*

Oni flipped on the light switch with his gun barrel—it was some kind of silver pistol that Kaley didn't recognize—and he held a cell phone to his ear with his other hand.

"*Harosho. Da, harosho,*" Oni was saying, glancing at the two girls and checking on them the way he might a pair of dogs, worried that the fracas between humans would've caused them to thrash against their bonds and kill themselves. "*Ya tebya penimayu. Da. Da.*" He walked right over to the girls and leaned over them. Both Kaley and Shannon now tried to roll out of his way, but their hands were firmly secured to the space heater. He parted the curtains above Kaley's head with his gun and said, "*Shto? Net, net. Ya pozvonyu tebe pozdnee.*"

What language was that? Russian? German? It certainly didn't sound like French or Spanish, at least no kind that Mrs. Moore at English Avenue Middle School had ever taught.

Kaley felt something swell inside her. It wasn't the lust from the white man. No, that had been replaced by his need for survival. And that was what she felt. He looked panicked. His eyes were wide and wild, darting here and there, talking rapidly to someone over the phone and mostly ignoring the girls at his feet.

Why be concerned with us? We're nothing. Less than human. We're a...a...

She searched for the word Mrs. Holloway used in advanced economics. *A commodity. We're something to hold onto, an investment.* Yes, they were something that accrued worth over time, something to barter with, but something that would depreciate over time if not handed off quickly. *A hot commodity.*

"*Da, neplokho,*" Oni was saying. He checked his watch. "*Chas? Da. Do vstrechi.*" He hung up, and looked down at her. "You stay calm now. We leave soon." He put his cell phone in his side pocket. "I be back with keys." He left the room and was gone for over a minute. During that time Kaley tried to send some feedback to Shan via her charm, since she could not reach her to hug her or just be close to her. Kaley tried to send reassurances, but nothing was getting through. Shan was alternately whimpering and sobbing, and wouldn't (or couldn't?) look at her sister.

When Oni returned, he did indeed have the keys to the handcuffs. He knelt in front of Kaley and said, "You try to run, I kill her." The same basic threat that the black guy had given her. "Nod." Her head felt like it was filled with cement. She nodded so sluggishly, still hating herself for not listening to the charm like Nan had told her to do so many times before. *I called her crazy once to her face*, she recalled. And she remembered the hurt expression on Nan's face. It hurt to recall that expression. Then she recalled Nan's last words to her: "Oh, chil'...you got a lotta *hurt* comin' yo way...good luck..."

Satisfied that his threat had been respected, Oni undid Kaley's handcuffs, and then immediately snatched her up by her twisted hair and flung her to the floor. Her head still hurt from where he'd torn hair out when she tried to escape. Kaley had forgotten about that until now.

Shan was even easier to deal with. Oni made the same threat to her ("If you fucking fight me, or try run, I kill sister, *da?*"), and got a weak nod. Kaley watched as her sister's bonds were undone and she was lifted off the floor. She was so limp she looked like she was a cripple. *I know how she feels.* Their shared experience—shared both in reality and via the charm—had made Kaley's legs weak as water.

"Outside," said Oni, a villain unlike any the White Ninja had ever had to face in his long and storied career.

The two sisters both struggled to their feet, helping each other up—Kaley helping Shannon mostly—swaying uneasily on their way to the door. She thought her little sister would have to wait to see a dead body—Kaley had only been to one funeral herself, and she had been so young she almost didn't understand it at all—but it seemed that tonight might have more terrors in store for her. Spur of the moment, she reached out to hug her sister and cover her eyes, confident that Oni would stop her from doing it but trying it anyway. Lo and behold, Oni didn't try to stop her. As they walked down the quiet hall, Kaley kept her hands cupped over Shannon's eyes, both of them sniffling as they shuffled slowly, like how they had done years ago when trying not to get caught searching for presents on Christmas Eve. Even though the cuffs had been removed from their feet they both took such baby steps.

The first body was laying arms akimbo beside a kitchen table. Kaley hadn't been ready for it at all. They simply rounded a corner, and there it was. It was one of the black men, the shorter one. He was on his back, two red holes at the center of his chest that were still spilling out his life's blood. Kaley *felt* him. She felt him still dying. His chest wasn't moving up and down anymore, and his eyes stared vacantly off to one side, trying to remember something. He wasn't moving, and wasn't breathing, but he wasn't entirely dead yet. Somewhere deep within him, there was still his essence. She felt it.

A comb that had been placed decoratively in the dead man's hair was now lying in the pool of blood spilling out the back of him. Kaley stared at the comb, fixated for a reason she couldn't explain. She would remember that comb for a long, long time.

Shannon trembled in her arms beside her. Kaley tried to say, "Don't look," but all that came out was "Nuh huk."

"Fucking move," said Oni.

They shuffled through the kitchen, passing into another hallway where a bedroom door stood wide open. They moved past it. Kaley chanced a glance, saw a pair of legs on the bed, the torso hanging off the other side, and a blood spatter against the wall in a pattern that reminded Kaley of fireworks, the trails they left behind when their various arms fell back to earth just before they winked out.

"Fucking *move*," Oni insisted.

Shannon sniffled.

They moved into the living room, where the real havoc had happened. Four men lay dead in various positions—one sitting in a chair, one on the floor with his arms up across a coffee table, one near the door (almost made it), and one crumpled in an odd, upside-down fetal position between a recliner and a TV stand. The closest one to Kaley was the one sitting in his chair—probably had been standing until blasted backwards. He rested comfortably now, looking ready to watch tonight's football game. His right hand was hanging off the armrest. He had a gun on the floor beside that hand (almost made it). Two bullets had ended him, one to the chest and one that tore through his face, ripped off half his nose and exploded one eye socket. Blood and mucous leaked out of the socket like fake movie blood. Strangely, Kaley thought, *Looks like* White Ninja Meets Shaolin Crane *got it right.*

It was shock. Shock that was somewhat tempered by the strange sense that most of these men weren't entirely dead yet. There was still something inside them, something that lingered. It would someday terrify Kaley to consider that, once *she* died, she might linger inside her own body as well, and she might potentially feel everything the coroners and the morticians were doing to her—removing her intestines and replacing them with newspapers, the whole embalming process, et cetera—perhaps right through the burial and everything. Every piece of these people was alive. The smallest biological pieces were living, all the cells, all the bacteria inside the stomach, it still had a purpose. And, on some level, the brain was still working.

I don't want to die like this, she thought, looking over at the man crumpled between the TV stand and the recliner. He was still inside there, his spirit or his soul or his thoughts or whatever still lingering. *Not like this. When I die, I want to* die!

A part of her worried that Shan felt it, too, that tenuous place between life and death. Her Nan had once told her something that was supposed to be helpful, although Kaley wasn't sure what it meant: "To be living is to be dying, and to be dying is to be living." It had made sense, yet was senseless, and it was all she could think of as she looked at the blood leaking out of the crumpled man's ears and nostrils. The hole at the center of his head, surprisingly, wasn't leaking at all. *He's dying...so he's still living.*

"Move," Oni reminded her.

And so they did. They moved a bit more quickly now at his urging. The gun touched Kaley once at the back of the head, and twice at the back of Shannon's. They moved around an easel that had fallen over and hustled out the front door into a dark, secluded neighborhood that she wasn't sure she recognized. Two orange streetlights were all that lit the street, which was surrounded by briars, bushes and brambles. *Where are we? Where did they take us?*

"Move," Oni said. "Over there." He used his gun to gesture to a narrow patch of woods she didn't recognize.

Kaley obeyed, and kept her hands cupped over Shannon's eyes because there was still one more body in the yard, just beyond the doorstep. He was facedown, two bullet holes in his back and one in his head. He didn't have a gun anywhere near him, just a pocketknife in his hand but unopened. He looked like he had crawled a bit because the blood trail was smeared behind him, all the way up to the doorstep. *Almost made it*, Kaley thought. *All of them. Almost made it out. But Oni drew down first.*

The El Camino and the Expedition that had brought them here were both parked side by side in the yard. She thought, *Which one will we take?* The answer was neither. They kept moving towards the woods, away from the vehicles and the street. *Where is he taking us? We can't get far on foot. Somebody will call the police about the gunshots.*

But on consideration, Kaley figured that wasn't likely, either. This street was desolate, like the world in that movie *Book of Eli*, and while the center of the Bluff could be a ghost town this late at night, especially with it this cold, she knew that this wasn't anywhere near the center of the Bluff. *Where are we? How far outside Vine an' English did they take us?*

Barefoot and trembling in the cold, the two girls walked ahead of their last surviving captor. They stumbled when Shannon stepped on one of many discarded bottles and it rolled beneath her foot. Kaley's feet were fine stepping on twigs and sharp fallen branches, because she went barefoot everywhere around their neighborhood, unless she was traveling far, and so her feet were hard and callused. But she worried about Shannon, who never went around the *house* without both socks and shoes on, much less anywhere else in the world.

"Move," came the same command as ever. "Move."

They stepped around a piece of corrugated steel that lay half buried in the soil. Kaley glanced across the street to the only other house around. It was a boarded-up structure on the verge of collapse, as many were in the Bluff (but she still didn't think this was the Bluff), and had various designs and phrases spray-painted, including one that said **FUCK KASIM REED**, and another that just said **CRIPS**. A crack house, probably, one condemned and belonging to everyone and no one. There were no lights on in the house. Nobody to pay the light bill. *No help's comin' from there*, she thought.

There were a few clouds out now, though the moon still shone true. There was a dampness in the air. Kaley predicted rain within the next hour or so, but that wasn't her charm at work. Or was it? She'd often predicted when it was going to rain, grabbing a raincoat and tossing Shannon hers on mornings when there had been nothing but skies as clear as the water in heaven. *But it won't rain for long. Just a drizzle. For half an hour, no more.*

They walked about forty steps into the woods before Oni hissed, "Stop! Wait here."

They did. Kaley turned to look at him. After a few minutes, Shannon reached up with quivering hands and slowly pushed her big sister's hands away from her eyes so that she could have a look around. Kaley almost resisted, but figured, *What's the hurt now?*

They were in deep darkness, barely able to see each other's face in the pale moonlight and what faded orange glow made it through the trees from the streetlights. Nearby, there was a large rock covered in lichen. Except for their breathing and a dog barking a mile or more away, there was no sound. Not even twigs fell out here. The silence was inutterably complete.

Kaley chanced a looked up at Oni, who seemed to sense her look even though he never glanced at her. "We wait," he said. His tone made it a warning.

84

Part of Kaley wondered if Oni had the charm, too. Then she decided that, no, that wasn't possible. Anyone blessed with the extreme empathy that the charm granted could never be doing what he was doing.

Kaley reached out and hugged Shannon, who had started whimpering loudly. She wanted to say, "Shhhhh." Such a simple appeasement, requiring no articulation at all, but with the gag still in her mouth she couldn't even give her sister that much. Part of her reached out for her mother, trying to pray or wish some kind of heroic action on her part. But another part of her knew that was eternally hopeless. *We're all alone. We're going to be sold or killed or something.*

A little over an hour ago she had been buying groceries and playing White Ninja with her little sister. Back then, ten thousand years ago, it seemed like that was all there was, all there would ever be. Kaley had grown up hearing gunshots late at night, had gotten used to them, but none of it had ever been directed at her or hers. She had survived just fine, not getting mixed up in the gang nonsense, and, for all her mother's faults, neither had she. *We were fine an' clear.*

True. They were fine and happy until tonight. *I should've known when I saw that white man. I should've known that something wasn't right about tonight.* Then, she corrected herself. *I did know. I knew and I did nothin' about it. Now Shannon and I are—*

Are what? What was going to happen to them? Kaley knew, just like she had known about the pale white man. And, just like inside Dodson's Store, she didn't want to admit it to herself that she knew where all of this was going. She was ignoring something else her charm was telling her. It was there, just in her periphery, a monster in a dream that somehow the dream told you wouldn't hurt you as long as you didn't look at it, if you didn't even think about it.

Instead, Kaley retreated to meditating on what *might* help them. Mom was out of the question. *The cops?* She wanted to believe that. Officer LeBlanc at English Avenue Middle School was certainly the kind of police officer one could trust to care, but the cops at EAMS knew the kids personally, and that's why they had always seemed so caring, especially LeBlanc. Other cops wouldn't care as much. Kaley knew enough about how the world worked to know that Officer LeBlanc and others from EAMS wouldn't be the ones assigned to track her and her sister down. *Some detectives or somethin'. People who don't even know us. Will they care? They're supposed to.*

That wasn't reassuring. Kaley had lived in the Bluff all her life. She had seen how the police treated everyone who lived in Vine City and on English Avenue, had seen how they viewed her and her kind with skepticism. She had seen the dull, listless faces of the officers who took Ricky's statement when he'd reported that their house had been broken into and two men he knew had made off with their TV and a CD player before he could catch them. It was the same look the two policemen had given Jamal Rhinehardt on Beltway when he'd described the three Crips that beat the tar out of him. Disinterested, mandatory, and dutiful; all these words she'd learned from EAMS, and all these words described the police in an around the Bluff. No one would never accuse them of being passionate about their jobs.

Who, then? she thought. *Who's gonna come for us?* The immediate and obvious answer was no one. Mac, the clerk at Dodson's, would almost assuredly report it, but he wouldn't and *couldn't* be expected to pound the pavement. *Especially now that we're not in the Bluff.*

So now, Kaley was down to the ultimate conclusion. I *have to get us out of this.*

She glanced at Oni's gun, but he kept it in his left hand, away from her. *By choice?* she wondered. *Is the gun in his far hand because he senses an ulterior motive in me?* Oni seemed like a thug, but Kaley sensed he had a mind of meddle. He was one who liked to interfere with others' schemes, thus developed counter-schemes of his own. Not brilliant, but sharp. After all, he'd gotten the trust of the other kidnappers, hadn't he? They'd trusted him so much they hadn't had time to draw down and return much fire.

So she wouldn't be able to reach the gun. So what to do, then? Kaley thought about a distraction, or of just rushing him. Yes, rushing him. Her mind was alternating between sluggish and harried. In that moment, rushing Oni seemed like a plan. It was no great plan, but at least it was a plan. If she got lucky, she might

86

even be able to scramble for the gun. *If I take him by complete surprise, he might even drop it or something.*

Kaley made her decision. They were alone out here and if she could tackle him at his legs, it might give Shan the chance to run. *That's all I need to give her. A chance to run. Out here in the dark, Oni will never find her. A Black Ninja vanishing in the night.*

She raised her hands away from her sister, having to pry Shannon away with both her arms and her heart. Kaley sent waves of assurances, and when their eyes met in the moonlight, Big Sister made Little Sister understand what she must do. They nodded. There was an understanding, a shared plan. Kaley would tackle him, potentially sacrificing herself, and Shan would run. It was a horrible yet persuasive idea. Persuasive, because Shan would survive. That was what Big Sister was for. That was what she functioned for.

The sisters touched one last time. Then, Big Sister severed the Anchor, and turned to face their tormentor.

Kaley turned slowly away from Shannon, who was still sniffling, still keeping up her part in this game. Then, all at once, she felt worry wash over her, and Shannon reached out to touch her elbow. When Kaley looked back, Shannon was shaking her head. Kaley gave a sharp but almost imperceptible nod. Shannon was terrified that Big Sister would be killed if she tried. Kaley tried to send her a wave that told her this was their best shot, their *only* shot to be free of Oni. She would dive at his legs—his knees, because those were the weakest and would buckle, causing Oni to topple—and Shan would have a few seconds' head start.

Shannon shook her head again vehemently.

Kaley turned away from Little Sister, and huffed up the courage. Then, there was the sound of a rumbling engine and squeaky brakes. Headlights splashed across the street, blinked twice, and Oni reached down to snatch her up by the collar. "Come on. We go."

There was a terrible instant when Kaley felt conflicted. She felt the moment slipping away. Her focus dwindled, and her courage with it. Because she was now susceptible to Little Sister's fear, which washed over her and utterly drowned the part of her that had devised the plan and built up to it, she was diminished.

They stepped out of the cover of woods and onto the street. The girls were shoved ahead of Oni. The car pulled up to them and slowed down. It was a dark-red Dodge Durango with tinted windows. The back door opened for them, and in the back seats were two white men, both of them blonde and wearing black jackets, both of their faces and hands adorned with various tattoos.

"Get in," said Oni from behind.

Kaley had one last moment where she thought she would proceed with her plan, but the barrel touched the back of her head, convincing her not to. *He doesn't have the charm, but he does have something. He knows what I'm thinking.*

Kaley climbed meekly into the back seat, Oni behind them. The door was shut behind her and for a horrifying moment she thought Shannon was being taken someplace else. She started to struggle but stopped when Shan was brought around to the back hatch and shoved inside, landing beside someone else. There was another girl there, a black girl a few years older than Shan who was similarly bound and gagged. She wore a red coat and tattered blue jeans. A silver locket hung from around her neck, one that she clutched as she stared up at Kaley hopefully.

The girl looked passing familiar, but Kaley couldn't place the face.

Kaley felt the young girl's heart leap, then deflate when she saw that Kaley and her sister were in the same boat she was. She felt the young girl's hope diminish just like hers had in the woods only seconds ago.

Oni hopped into the front passenger seat. To the driver, he said, "*Zdravstvujte, dorogaya moya.*" He blew kisses at the driver, a man even larger than Oni and who reached out and smacked him across the face, laughing.

On either side of Kaley, there was a pair of men who might've been twin brothers—buzzed blonde hair and cold hazel eyes. The only thing that separated them was the one on the left had yellowish skin, what Kaley had learned in school was called jaundiced skin. They all chuckled, and the jaundiced man pulled out a cell phone and started chatting leisurely with someone. Kaley wanted to scream for help, that maybe the person on the other end would hear and come to save them, but her charm told her that that wouldn't help at all. She could feel the comfort the jaundiced man had with his conversation partner. *He's talking to someone who's just like him. Someone who wouldn't care if they heard a screaming girl.*

As they started to drive off, Kaley looked back at Shannon, who was staring across at the other bound girl. For a moment, they shared a connection. They were both too frightened to know what was really happening to them, and far too petrified to move or do anything besides wonder what horrors waited for them.

"Don't worry, little girls," said Oni from the front seat. Kaley turned to look at him. He had twisted in his seat and was smiling back at her. "Don't worry. We fuck you soon."

The SUV erupted in laughter. The aggregate of her sister and the other girl in the back seat was almost impossible to take without passing out. Kaley cast her eyes down at her knees, wishing she could turn back time and tackled Oni in the woods while the son of a bitch wasn't expecting it. *That's the second time I've not listened to my gut tonight*, she thought. Kaley made a solemn vow to herself. *There will not be a third! God as my witness, there will* not *be a third!*

The truck was found at 12:42 AM on the south end of Joseph E. Boone Boulevard. It certainly matched the description that the clerk at Dodson's Store had described. The Tacoma's license plate had it from Troup County.

The plate's almost certainly been switched with another vehicle's, David Emerson thought. If so, then trying to track it down would do little good, because the owner of the *other* vehicle, whose license plate this really was, probably wouldn't know his license plate had been swapped for someone else's for quite some time. Few people knew their own license plate number, or knew when it had been swapped. They'd have to find this license plate's true owner, wherever he was (hopefully close-ish), take a look at *his* license plate, and then figure out who this Tacoma truly belonged to.

David had pulled on his raincoat since a drizzle had started. He handed Beatrice a Slim Jim to open the driver's side door. She popped the door, and began checking inside with her Mag-Lite while David bent to one knee and checked beneath the carriage. So far, they hadn't found anything suspicious or illicit—no weed, no coke, no meth, and no weapons of any kind.

Headlights poured over the car. He looked up. A black sedan had come up. It was one of the dicks, but he didn't know which one until the mountain stepped out of the car.

Leon Hulsey looked as impermeable as a brick wall. He was a regular down at the gym, and David knew him well. The guy had been a beat cop with the APD for almost a decade, working Zone One (the area containing the Bluff) that whole time before finally taking the exam that put him in the League of Detectives, as Hulsey was known to refer to it. He was a comic book fan, and his favorite team was the Justice League. David happened to know that Hulsey had a Superman symbol tattooed on his left pectoral, and that it was large enough that it had excluded him from undercover work years ago. A much too obvious and defining mark that wouldn't be forgotten by Atlanta's underworld.

Hulsey was an old hard ass with very little sense of humor. Gerard Laurent in Robbery/Homicide said that Hulsey had it amputated the first week he started working the Adult Missing Persons Squad.

And that was the thing. David knew Hulsey worked the *Adult* Missing Persons Squad, not Missing and Exploited Children. "Hey, Hulsey. What're you doing here?"

"I was closer than anybody else, I suppose," he said, extending his hand. They shook hands briefly, and then Hulsey put on a pair of rubber gloves and looked ready to give a rectal exam. "You guys find anything yet?"

"No."

"Called the tow company?" His breath smelled like Tic Tacs.

"Yep. They're on their way. Hopefully forensics can find a print or a hidden compartment that'll give us something."

Detective Hulsey pursed his lips. "I doubt there's a compartment large enough to hide two little girls in here."

David stiffened. "That's not exactly what I meant, but..." But he didn't finish his statement. It wasn't necessary. Hulsey was moving on around the car and ignoring him now.

"Beatrice," Hulsey said. "How's things?"

"Good," she sighed, and pulled the hood of her raincoat up over her head.

Hulsey had no raincoat or umbrella. He just turned up the collar of his long coat and walked, for all intents and purposes oblivious to the rain. "Howard and the kids all right?"

"Yep. Right as rain."

"Keepin' 'em all straight, huh?" he said without a smile. Asking generic questions about home life was the closest Hulsey ever got to being amiable.

"You know it," Beatrice said.

David walked over to join them. Hulsey had already reached beside the steering wheel to pop the trunk. He walked around and opened it wide, glanced at a few things, and nodded to himself. "Something?" David said.

"I got an update from dispatch just before I got here," Hulsey said. "A Tacoma was reported stolen outside of a Great Clips hair salon in Troup County about this time yesterday. The owner said he had just replaced the alternator and the battery. I can see here that both are new. Looks like we got our stolen Tacoma."

"Fella did this knows how to hotwire," David said. He waved Hulsey over and showed him, aiming his flashlight at where the ignition cover had been removed at the steering column and the power and starter wires had been connected. Other wires were still hanging out like the entrails of a gutted chipmunk.

"Hm," said the detective.

David saw that look on Hulsey's face, and said, "What's up?"

Large, callused hands touched the space just beneath his iron chin, and tapped it a couple of times, like he expected a fresh thought to pop up. "The guys in Troup County said that another stolen vehicle was found about a quarter-mile hike from where the Tacoma was stolen. The vehicle was a Chevy Blazer, reported stolen in Muscogee County off a turnpike. Not too far from where the Blazer was reported stolen, Muscogee police found a Dodge Grand Caravan that was taken from Tallapoosa County." He reached in to touch the dangling wires. "That's in Alabama," he said over his shoulder.

I know where Tallapoosa is. David considered what he had said. "We got a guy playing leap frog across the South?"

"Looks like maybe that's the case," he said, hopping inside the Tacoma and opening up the glove compartment and checking things that Beatrice and David had already checked.

"So that'll kick this case over to ATTF."

"*Also,*" Hulsey said.

"What?"

"That'll kick this case over to ATTF *also,*" said the large man. He hopped out of the Tacoma, and the thing lifted a few thankful inches as he did. David even fancied he heard a sigh of relief from the truck. "I'll be coordinating with them for tonight, and give the Missing Children guys a bit of a hand. ATTF won't like it, especially since the car got dropped off down here in the Bluff."

"They still lookin' for the right chop shop?"

Hulsey nodded and looked up and down the street. A few late-nighters had paused to see what the cops were doing. A trio of young toughs had gathered around a spray-painted mailbox, and up the street from them a bearded fellow in a blue flannel shirt stood as still as a statue, just staring at them like a deer in headlights. "Almost two dozen auto shops in a ten-block radius, but none of the ATTF boys are sure which one's their big flipper."

David turned and looked up the street, where a few cars had stalled at a stoplight, even though it had turned green. Everyone was so curious tonight, even more so than usual. It's like something was in the air. *Something's changed*, he thought, and knew he was being silly.

Or was he?

The Bluff had always had a weirdness to it, especially at night. No one denied that. A lot of local church leaders had started campaigning for the revitalizations of areas in and around the Bluff, and had started programs to coordinate with police, even going so far as providing safe havens for informants that needed to disappear for a while. But Atlanta's Major Crimes Division had its work cut out for them when it came to this end of town. Abductions were on the rise. It wasn't anything quite so alarming as what you'd see in Phoenix, but the same drug cartels that had moved in there had now taken up residence in the A-T-L, plus a few extra, such as the *vory v zakone*, who conducted organized kidnappings like the Mexicans but for different reasons. At least, that was the new report that was moving fast out of the rumor mill and headed directly for the land of certified fact.

The *vory v zakone*, the influx of Mexican cartels, the new human traffickers and the Auto Theft Task Force's frustration at not finding this major chop shop, which they were all positive was helping these other groups and was *some*-God-damn-where in this area, were just other symptoms of the changes here. Once, the Crips and the Bloods had been the big problem. Then had come the brief occupation of heavy hitters from the Five Families. Now, people from other countries were calling the shots here. They had proxy groups and proxy gangs doing their deeds for them, and they never even had to leave their home soil.

A sign of the times, David thought. *Crime isn't for the locals anymore. It's gone international. We're outsourcing the criminal work.* He smiled whenever he thought about how criminals were finding it difficult to find work with other criminals, just like the law-abiding citizens in the standard economy were finding it hard to find a job not taken by foreigners. Hard to believe, but criminal jobs were disappearing overseas, and many of the important ones that remained here were going to the cousins of those lieutenants in other countries. These made up the proxy gangs.

The rain got a bit heavier. Small puddles had started collecting just since Hulsey arrived. The big detective removed his rubber gloves and tucked them in his back pocket. "That's weird," he said.

"What is?" David asked.

"Well, a Caucasian car thief hauls ass across the South for more than forty-eight hours, maybe longer, just to come here to Atlanta—the fucking Bluff of all places—and then helps with the kidnapping of two black girls?" Hulsey shook his head. "Just weird."

"You think they're unconnected?"

"Yeah, I think they're unconnected. But he still saw something at Dodson's Store, and I wanna know what, and why he ran off like that. Maybe if I help ATTF find their man, their man will help me find Kaley and Shannon Dupré."

Beatrice, who had been quiet throughout the conversation, spoke up. "David here thinks it was the *vory v zakone*. Ain't that what you said earlier?"

David stiffened again. He knew that Hulsey was one of those guys who didn't like needless speculation, especially from people who weren't detectives. Hulsey himself had obeyed that rule when he was a beat cop; never second guessed a detective or voiced his opinion in the presence of another detective, nor in front of David himself when they worked out together.

Hulsey grimaced. He lifted a finger and pointed up the street. "Here comes the tow truck."

The big man walked back to his car, folded the collar down from his long coat, and hopped inside. His sedan rocked hard and tilted to one side as he settled in. He started it up, and drove off with a lifted index finger as his only farewell.

David turned to Beatrice, and said, "Please, *please*, if you were ever my friend and wanted to help me make detective, don't ever tell Leon Hulsey that you or I have an opinion."

Beatrice thought about that for a second, and made a hissing sound. "Oops. Sorry, Dave."

"Don't worry about it." David said it a little more sharply than he'd intended. He wasn't really cognizant of it, but he was still upset over what the guy at Dodson's ("Mac" Abernathy) had called him earlier. *Fake-ass nigga.* He had thought he could drop it, leave it behind like he had so many other times before. But he couldn't. Not tonight.

And now Hulsey, and Beatrice's indiscretion...

David looked at who was hopping out of the tow truck. "C'mon," he said. "Looks like they sent Saul. He's got that bad knee and moves slower than a snail in Jell-O. We're gonna have to help him if we wanna get outta this weather."

The clouds had moved in from nowhere. They were thin, spread out. They didn't look like rainclouds at all. David looked about the street, and saw that they still had an audience. In fact, it had grown. Three woman in the skankiest clothes now stood at the corner of the block, just staring at them. They were staring at the truck. *They're drawn to it*, he thought for half a second, then walked over to greet Saul.

Yes. A strange night.

Leon Hulsey drove a couple blocks away to Brandi's Grill, where he sat for a moment, thinking. There were only two other cars parked near him, waiting for the curbside service Brandi's was known for. When Theresa, one of the waitresses, had approached his door, he'd waved her away.

The Tacoma and its thief had him vexed. "It's not easy to know how to hotwire that many cars," he said out loud. To think better, Leon liked to get away from people and have a conversation with himself. He knew that they would think him weird, so he always sought seclusion and hammered it out. "There's no universal color-code system for the wires underneath ignition covers." He thought for a moment. "Only an owner's manual would have that much information, let you know which wires are which, but a car thief in a hurry like this guy couldn't stop to consult every single owner's manual in every single car he targeted. It would take too long." He nodded to himself. "Yep. Besides, not all of the cars would have the owner's manuals inside."

He glanced outside. Theresa had walked up to him again to check on him. Leon waved her away again, watching her sashay her ass in those tight blue jeans. Half the reason he came to Brandi's Grill right there, because the hot dogs and burgers were shit for sure.

The rain had slackened to a light drizzle again. Rivulets ran down his windshield, and Leon watched them merge and form temporary rivers before separating again.

"But a pro would know that the red pair is *usually* the set that provides power to the car," Leon went on, sussing it out. "And the brown, which can be a single wire or a pair of wires depending on the car, handles the starter. A pro would know that, too. Sure. Someone who had done this a lot. No standard booster or avid *Grand Theft Auto* video gamer." He shook his head and waved a dismissive hand. "No, not like that. A lifer. Done this since he was old enough to look over the dashboard. For sure."

Leon considered the kinds of cars that had been selected. The thief, whoever he was, had selected all models of cars that *didn't* have the locking mechanism that would require a key before unlocking the steering column. Had the thief tried it on, say, a Mercury, he would've been able to start it but wouldn't have been able to turn the steering wheel. "A lifer. For sure. Knew which models to look for. Yeah. For sure."

Leon tapped his teeth for a moment, ruminating, then reached over to the passenger's seat and lifted an issue of *The Dark Knight Returns*. He hadn't removed it from its flimsy plastic wrapper yet, and savored removing it now, just as much as he then savored flipping through the pages and sniffing the age. This was an old Frank Miller special, one of the greatest runs an artist or a writer ever had on a comic series. Leon hardly read comics anymore, but he enjoyed the artistry, the pageantry and the mythology. Miller's gritty, film noir-style of art particularly appealed to him. The streets weren't clean in Miller's universe like most cities appeared in comics or film. The streets were filthy, grimy, all the people had rough lines on their faces that showed how hard the world had been on them, how it had abused them before moving on without them.

Like Atlanta, Leon thought, glancing up at the rough streets of the Bluff all around, and the juxtaposed skyscrapers looming miles away. He looked back down. The comic provided a temporary distraction, one that settled the growing black tumor of knowledge that he'd been trying to avoid ever since he peeked inside the Tacoma. There was no denying it. *It's one of Pat's guys. For sure.*

Yes. For sure. His grandpop had passed down this piece of advice: "If it looks like a duck, walks like a duck, an' quacks like a duck, then it's a safe bet you don't got an orangutan's smelly turd on yer hands." If it wasn't one of Pat's guys, then Pat would know him. Leon was willing to bet on that.

For a moment he continued flipping through the pages of his comic. He took in the rough textures, ran his finger across the faces of the characters like he did as a kid, almost expecting to feel them. He considered where he'd be now if he had opted for the art scholarship instead of following his father's footsteps.

"Why are you stalling, Leon?" he asked himself sternly. "What else can it be? Remember what Grandpop said." He gave it another moment's thought, then nodded his certainty. "So that's it, then," Leon said, closing the comic book and putting it back in its plastic wrapper. "Pat's Auto." He still doubted it had anything to do with the kidnapping—nothing else about it lined up—but it was worth a shot to see what Pat, or one of Pat's drivers, might know.

Leon cranked up his sedan, backed out of Brandi's with a final wave to Theresa, and then headed for Terrell Street. It had been a peculiar thing, trying to find reasons *not* to go to his brother-in-law's chop shop, but no one ever said being a cop was easy.

5

Pat pulled out a Caran D'Ache lighter, and lit the cigarette pressed between his lips. He obviously did it without thought to show off, but to Spencer the black Chinese lacquer finish on the lighter was a sign of just how high Pat had risen. He offered a cig to Spencer, who declined. Some people thought beer and cigarettes went hand in hand, but Spencer had a different philosophy. He'd smoked Marlboros earlier in lieu of a beer, but he had a good buzz going on now so to hell with the nicotine.

There was a loud clanging outside, and someone shouted. Pat huffed and went to do the door. He stepped outside and started hollering at Eddie and the other grease monkeys. Spencer remained in his seat, leaning back and staring up at the spackled ceiling and listening to the light tinkling of rain on the roof, thinking about all the nights spent in the joint with little else to do but listen to the rain, or talk to Martin Horowitz.

When Pat plopped back down his squeaky chair, he did so with a sigh and a rueful shake of the head. It was interesting to see him behave in such a way, like a man with actual responsibilities. "And so," he said, taking a toke of his cigarette (it was a brand with a name Spencer couldn't pronounce). "When last we left our hero, his stupid ass was locked up inside Leavenworth Federal Penitentiary. An' now fo' our excitin' conclusion, folks. How *will* Spencer Adam Pelletier escape the evil clutches of the Man an' keep his asshole virginity intact? Stay tuned."

Spencer took a sip of his Bud. There was only a quarter of the bottle left, and he held it up to the light and sloshed it around for a moment. "I already told you," he said. "They opened the door for me and I walked out."

"Uh huh. The full story, if ya please, sir? Pray tell."

He sloshed a bit of the beer around again, considering how much he ought to tell. He shrugged, and figured, *Why not everything.* "I was transferred from CRC, Coyote Ridge Corrections, which is a state prison in Washington."

Pat nodded. "I know the place. Remember Enrique Lopez? Gay-ass Puerto Rican with a lisp? His brother locked up in that joint."

Spencer continued. "They were initially going to send me to a level-three maximum-security prison, one down in Tennessee, but then a few inmates at CRC lied on me, said that I'd been givin' them all these threats of violence. I *did* get in a fight with one o' them—this one fella who stepped to me, he was a member of the Aryan Brotherhood, an' the AB don't forget. Since I was about to be moved out soon, and would be away from the reach o' their vengeance, they concocted a story that had me attacking a whole bunch of 'em during the six short weeks I was there. They claimed to all be scared of me. They did this and presented the one AB guy whose ass I'd beaten in the shower room as evidence. It was a last ditch and pathetic effort. One that worked.

"They sent me to Leavenworth after a reevaluation of my conduct and misbehaviors. A prison shrink named Armand suggested at one point that I might be a psychopath. I never paid that label much mind, but as it would turn out, I guess he was right. I'd done a good job blending in at CRC. I carried myself like a lifer, an' everyone seemed to regard me as someone who'd been around prison for a long time, even if it wasn't *that* prison. But the AB's lie ended up helping to expose me for what I really am."

"What'choo really are?" Pat said, blowing out his smoke with a quizzical face.

"A psychopath," Spencer said, shrugging. "At least, that's what they tell me."

"They actually *diagnose* muthafuckas with that? I thought that was just a word."

"They gave me the PCL-R. The Psychopath Checklist-Revised. It's a forty-point personality test. The test isn't given to everyone, only some people. Doctors actually have to pay *royalties* to this guy named Dr. Hare, the guy who invented it, like the way radio stations have to pay Prince a little bit o' money every time they play one o' his songs." He took a sip and shrugged again. "So, they don't use it very often, and Dr. Hare even suggested that it not be used too liberally, only when a clinician is highly confident that a subject warrants testing."

"Warrants testin'?"

"*Needs* it," he clarified. "The head doc up at Leavenworth was a guy named McCulloch, an' he agreed with Armand back at CRC that I needed the PCL-R. It tests a person in two main categories or *factors*, Personality and Case History, which are divvied up into twenty subcategories. The Personality Test has to do with things like pathological lying, cunning and manipulation, lack of remorse, lack of empathy, aggressive narcissism, shit like that, ya know?" Pat nodded, but he did so slowly. To Spencer, his old acquaintance had the look of a man who had just realized he was in quicksand, and didn't want to move too much or else he might sink faster. *Is he wondering how long I've been a psycho? Is he wondering if it's somethin' he can catch?* Spencer had to fight the smile. "The Case History Test looks for things in the past that back up what's being seen in the subject in the present— childhood shit like early behavior problems, juvenile delinquency, a need for stimulation, impulsiveness, and a proneness to boredom. The highest score a person can get is a forty, but that's incredibly rare. I scored a thirty-six." Pat nodded. Spencer added, "That's pretty high."

"No, I got it," Pat said. "I feel ya. What parts didn't you score high in?"

Spencer took another sip, belched. "Apparently, I show no signs of a parasitic lifestyle—I don't tend to cling onto others and feed off of 'em—and I don't necessarily have a grandiose sense of self-worth as most psychos do. Dr. McCulloch actually commented that I'm, quote, 'Quite humble.' "

"*Pshhh*. Humble? You? My fuckin' ass."

Again, Spencer shrugged. "I'm just tellin' you what they told me. McCulloch said my superficial charm conceals it. He said he thinks that I like to *pretend* I have a grandiose sense of self-worth, but only because he suspects that I have discovered how many people find large egos attractive—men respect those kind o' men, even if they don't like them, and women find them attractive and controlling. In short, I apparently pretend to view myself as High an' Mighty because it helps me control weak-minded people. It's actually what gave me the highest score in the manipulation section of the test." Spencer downed the last of his Bud, tossed the bottle into the garbage bin, and snorted derisively. "Thus spoke the Great and Powerful Oz!"

Pat managed a smile. Spencer watched him closely. Was he just now smiling because he sensed it was time to smile? Did he think he needed to smile because the psychopath required him to? Spencer thought he detected a glimmer of uncertainty in Pat's eyes. *He's recollecting all of our past encounters, all the times we worked together, an' reevaluating each moment.* Spencer figured that was fine, because ever since he'd received Dr. McCulloch's diagnosis, he'd done the same thing, too. How else does one react when their told they don't have emotions? At least, none that are quite like those the rest of the human race experiences.

He learned later that it was estimated that there was one psychopath for every one hundred or two hundred people. People just like him were all over the globe, floating throughout society, not experiencing any *real* emotion. Psychopaths assumed that emotions were all part of a societal game, and that they had to be better at the game than anybody else if they wished to get the upper hand. That's why psychopaths didn't *know* they were psychopaths, because they assumed everyone else felt the same way.

Dr. McCulloch had put it like this: "Try to convince a blind man that there's color. You can't. He has to take it on faith. Faith, and the testimony of others. But he'll never see. He can use the same words as others to represent them—white, black, red, blue—but he'll never have any *command* over those words, he'd never share a connection with them the same way you or I do, Spencer. When it comes to emotions, you're color blind."

Upon further research in the prison library, and on Dr. McCulloch's recommendation, Spencer had read up on psychopathy and those that had studied it the most. According to what he'd found on the subject, most psychopaths actually never killed anybody—but if they did they didn't give a hoot. Indeed, it was mostly normal, emotional people who got caught up in their emotions and killed others. Most people in prison were *not* psychopaths. Most psychopaths lived (ostensibly) normal lives. They mimicked the most socially acceptable behavior, sometimes too well, and knew how to predict the outcome of a conversation. Thus, they were great liars and manipulators.

The most shocking discovery Spencer had made had been when he'd read just how many world leaders were suspected of being psychopaths. Apparently, many modern psychologists agreed that psychopaths were everywhere, completely undiagnosed, the secret leaders of society, and said that one must *be* a psychopath (at least to some degree) in order to have the mental fortitude run for public office. Emotional people couldn't handle the rigors of campaigning, of being caught in contradictions and having your family's name dragged through the mud. It took a great and mighty ego to be the leader of the free world, to see yourself as the Prime Minister of England, or to view yourself as a great civil rights leader that others must follow. To Spencer, this suddenly explained a great deal of life, because this meant even the good guys in history were mostly psychopaths.

"Can I ask a question?" Pat said presently.

"Sure." *Here it comes. He's gonna ask me if I've always known what I was.*

But to his surprise, Pat asked a very simple question. "What part did ya score highest on?"

Spencer cocked his head and *tsk*ed. "There's only one way to score on the PCL-R. You get a *zero* if the trait doesn't apply at all, a *one* if it applies somewhat, and a *two* if it fully applies. I got a two on everything besides parasitic lifestyle an' grandiose self-worth, for which I scored zero. However," he said, having something spring to mind, "my old friend Dr. McCulloch said that I scored a *two* on something that most psychopaths show no aptitude for whatsoever, an' that was in the section of criminal versatility."

Pat smirked. "You a versatile muthafucka, eh?" He pronounced it *versa-TYLE*.

"That's what they tell me. An' that's why I was put away from the rest o' the inmates within the first month that I got to Leavenworth. Dr. McCulloch was very honest with me. He said that he was gonna recommend to the warden that I stay away from the common rabble 'cause he thought I might, uh, how did he put it?" Spencer spoke in the thick Jersey accent McCulloch had tried to cover up, but never to any avail. " 'Inspire loyalty in convicts less intelligent, and who might follow you once they figured out you are a superior thinker.' In other words, they were worried I might get a bunch o' guys together and we'd escape."

"Did ya?"

"Nope. I did it all alone. Well, *mostly*."

"Alright, alright, enough o' this shit, muthafucka. How *did* ya do it?"

Spencer tried to paint the picture for him. He started by describing the flight from Washington down to Kansas. He got to ride "Con Air" for the first time, feeling notorious amongst some crazy serial killer who was missing an eye, a small Italian shrimp who claimed to be a member of the Gambino family, and a couple of contract killers from the Latin Kings who were all chained up in their own separate cages, same as him.

Then, Spencer described the long, lonesome drive up to Leavenworth Federal Penitentiary, how he'd sat there looking neither right nor left. Most of the men around him had stared out their windows at the green fields, taking in the last view of the outside world they would see in a long time. For some of them, this would be the last view they ever got of that world.

Spencer described the front gate opening, and the large sign off to one side of the gate that read:

LEAVENWORTH
Proud of where we have been
Proud of where we are
Proud of where we are going
Pride in a job well done

He had shuffled off the bus same as all the others. The young man chained up behind him, a red-headed boy no older than nineteen, had already started crying. "I remember thinking, this kid's gonna be fucked in his ass before the week's out. An' ya know what? I was wrong. It cost him two months of doing chores for other inmates to buy him safety from the blacks on D cellhouse who wanted him so bad you could smell it. His name was Tommy Svenson, and eventually he was sold for two packs o' cigarettes. He was lured by one o' these guys into a certain part o' the shower room, which he was supposed to help clean. It was his cellmate who did him the first time, pretending he wanted to protect him outta the kindness of his heart. But it wasn't the kindness of his heart, but the piece lower down on his torso that *really* wanted to help the red-head. I was in the shower the day it happened. He screamed. The guards had to hear it, but nobody did anything.

"After that, Tommy was just a prison punk, passed around like a joint, shacking up in a different cell every few months because some low-risk prisoners they let do that. After that, they used him for his girlfriend on the outside, who became a mule— someone to sneak H an' other shit in an' outta the joint during conjugal visits and whatnot, you understand. She would come in with the stuff in her vagina, then slip off to the women's bathroom to remove it and put it in her mouth. Prisoners were allowed to kiss their visitors once at the beginning of the visit and once at the end. She'd kiss her red-headed boyfriend, an' Tommy swallowed the H an' either vomited it up later or shat it out. He did all this to stop the rapes from the black guys, see?"

For a moment, Spencer went silent. None of this had much to do with his escape, but he found himself thinking about it the more Pat pushed him about Leavenworth. He didn't know why. Perhaps it was the thought of predators and their prey, and how it was the same all over the world. It was sometimes easy for Spencer to become lost in these sorts of thoughts. Dr. McCulloch told him that was normal for many psychopaths. It's how they whiled away their alone time, thinking of how so many people were easily manipulated.

"You ever been to the pen, Pat?"

Pat shook his head. "Naw, dawg." He said it with wonder, like a young boy hearing the story of the ancient haunted cave that only his grandfather had returned from.

"It's a fascinating place." Pat laughed at that, but stopped when he realized Spencer wasn't being facetious.

He went on describing the basic processing procedures. He didn't go into detail about having his asshole fingered. What Spencer *did* mention was that, while the inspections were going on and the red-headed boy was trying to stifle his sobs, he noticed that the guards had such dull looks on their faces. "There was only one hack who screamed like he meant it. His name was Brummel, and he hollered shit like, 'This is my house! You understand me? You disrespect this house, you disrespect me! I will *not* tolerate disrespect!' Besides him, the rest o' the hacks at Leavenworth were dull-eyed an' really just bored-looking. At least, that was how it appeared to me."

Spencer described the changes the American prison system had been going through at the time. Leavenworth was on its way to being downgraded from a level-four maximum-security prison; almost the highest rating in the nation. Luckily for him, the transition was happening around that time. The BOP, or Bureau of Prisons, had people in and out of there at all hours, checking this and inspecting that. The rotundas were going to be renovated to allow for better prison management, and there were going to be different areas for different groups—high-level gangsters would have their own section (the prisoners called it "turf" or "territory"), and thugs from groups like the AB or the Crips or the Bloods would have their own allotted section. Like many prisons at the time, Leavenworth was transitioning to smaller buildings spread out over a compound and relying on more electronic surveillance, rather than the large domed structures it had been known for where a mixing of all prisoners of all races had been the norm. This meant that the hacks (the guards) wouldn't be as familiar with all the prisoner's faces as they once had been.

"At CRC, my goal had been to match the profile of a lifer. But in Leavenworth, I felt it was best *not* to blend in. Instead, I went for a different approach. I disappeared," he said, reaching out to the pack of cigarettes. With his Bud gone, he'd had second thoughts about Pat's previous offer. He plucked a stick out and put it between his lips. "There are more than 2,000 inmates at Leavenworth, and though they weren't being allowed to mix as much as before, they still mixed more than at most other joints."

"How could ya disappear, money? I mean, the hacks *had* to know yo face after ya beat that cop's ass an'…ya know…*bit his fuckin' nose off*," he finished with a nervous laugh.

Pat handed over his fancy lighter, and Spencer lit up. He inhaled with relish, blew it out, shook his head. "Naw, man. Only the feds workin' the case of my robberies knew me. I had a bit o' local fame when I attacked that cop, sure, but a few months had passed and I'd been at CRC for a while. By the time I got to Leavenworth only Brummel and Warden Plink made time to talk with me. I got the same twenty-two-page book with the prison's rules an' regulations that everybody else got, had a short talk with 'em about how things would go—I say 'Yeah, yeah, yeah, yeah, yeah, you the boss, man, nobody but you,' and then I'm on my way.

"I was shown to my cell. Ended up in A cellhouse with a pedophile named Martin Horowitz for a cellmate. That was a bit o' good fortune, because all he wanted to do was stay low-key, just like I had planned to do myself. Ol' Marty actually glommed onto me pretty fast because I was the only person who would pay him any mind and who didn't judge him. I didn't *like* the guy, mind you, but I knew a Santa's Little Helper when I saw one. I struck up conversations with him at night—never in plain sight of anyone else, never while jogging the blacktop track in the prison yard or anything like that, because I didn't wanna be openly associated with him, because ya know what targets pedophiles make in the joint—an' was glad that I did. Turns out, Marty had been in for nine years, an' had survived with his own asshole intact by kissin' the hacks' asses, as well as providing Warden Plink on the goings-on of other inmates. He was a snitch. And sometimes, he helped out with filing work for the prison. He had earned that privilege and liked it very much. He lacked one thing: a friend. I was his answer to that.

"So I listened to what he had to say. We would talk for long hours at night. At first it was just this an' that—do you have any family, where are you from, how much longer you got on your stint—but eventually I got some o' details about Leavenworth from this fat prick. There were exactly five hundred and three employees at Leavenworth, all of 'em broken up into groups," Spencer explained. "Three hundred and fifty of 'em were hacks, but the rest were cooks, hospital workers, maintenance men, psychologists, counselors, teachers, an' administrators. I learned a lot from him. I learned that the hacks earn less than anybody else in the prison, but the hacks have more clout—their word is Law.

"However, I also learned that the hacks were also complaining about how much they're left outta the loop. Marty told me that they despised oversight committees from the BOP who sent inspectors to check everything from the fire extinguishers to the inmates' well-being. I heard about a hack named Pembry, who was getting a divorce. I heard the hacks were gettin' pretty tired of unannounced inspections from the BOP. I heard about a secretary named Connie Ayers who got a transfer over to ADX prison in Florence and wasn't happy about it. I heard about a hack named Middleton who the other hacks secretly hated because he was always kissin' BOP ass, lookin' for a promotion. But that's all mostly tangential." He added, "That means only slightly connected."

"I know what tangential *mean*, muthafucka. You ain't the only one reads books."

"The important part is that Marty an' me became close at nights," he went on, blowing out another cloud of smoke. "Close enough that he tried to get freaky one night. I pushed him away, told him that I wasn't ready for that kinda relationship yet, but that I was open-minded to it. This kept his interest in me, and in our talks, for a good while longer. Long enough to get all that I felt I needed.

"I had been assigned to laundry duty and cleaning work inside the prison, but I cordially volunteered for the crafts shop of the prison, which Marty had told me had a shortage of volunteers since no man liked to sew all that much. I was willing to learn and I picked it up fast. Did ya know that the furniture an' clothing manufacturers inside Leavenworth have built chairs and clothes that presidents an' politicians have worn? As gifts from the wardens, of course. Some o' the prisoners there become quite the craftsmen and seamstresses. John F. Kennedy's rocking chair was made there."

"Naw, I didn't know that."

Spencer went on, looking at his solo audience through the billowing cigarette smoke. "I was worried that Dr. McCulloch might suspect something an' deny me the job, but I suppose he never considered it, or if he did maybe he allowed me to do it out of clinical curiosity. Guess I'll never know. What I do know is that I was able to gather the necessary textiles and materials over time to create what I needed.

"I eventually volunteered for the kitchen and the metal shop, because there were things in those areas that I needed, but I didn't always get those assignments. Maybe someone somewhere got suspicious. If they did, they weren't in time to stop me.

Besides Marty, I'd gotten to know a couple o' guys from the TV room in A cellhouse who worked in the metal shop. They got me what I needed, an' I got them what they *wanted*."

Spencer left it with that for a moment, enjoying another toke while Pat leaned in. Outside the office, the grease monkeys were still drilling away. "So I got what I needed. It only had to look passable, I knew. People aren't very smart, even police officers—the cop that pulled me over was the exception to the rule—and especially not these hacks. They're constantly on the lookout for an attack. Tension between inmates an' hacks is so high you can almost feel it inside that place. But the hacks're lookin' for a surprise shiv in their back, *not* an Uzi. So, I reasoned, they're lookin' for escapees to dig holes under the fences, *not* a member of the BOP."

Again, Spencer went silent, just toking on his cig. He allowed Pat to sit there with a look of perplexity for a few seconds. *Let him figure that one out.* Finally, Pat did. His eyes widened just a tad, and his posture went straighter. "No way."

Spencer nodded. "I put on my passable suit with its red tie an' all. I'd made it myself from bits an' pieces in the crafts shop. I wore what I'm sure looked like a pair o' pressed khakis, but was actually made outta the cloth they used for laundry bags in the prison. They didn't look *great*, but they didn't look like prison fatigues, either. I made 'em baggy enough so that my prison-issue shoes wouldn't be too noticeable, just the tips. Hopefully, as long as the first stage worked out okay, nobody would be lookin' at my feet.

"So, I walked right up to Middleton—the hack that Marty assured me was always kissin' ass an' lookin' for a promotion— and I started up a conversation. Almost none o' the guards in that whole place could've picked me out of a line-up. I'd been so quiet, kept just to myself an' Marty for the most part. I'd taken extra special caution against doing anything unusual in front of Middleton, anything at all, just so he wouldn't know my face when it came time for me to walk out. So, when I saw him glance at my tie and then at my face, I knew I had him. See, the guys from the metal shop had gotten me what I needed—they didn't know *why* I needed it, but they'd given it to me just the same. A metal tie clip and a matchin' pin that were both shaped like handcuffs."

Pat slapped his desk, chuckling. "Just like when ya walked in as Agent Chalke at the SunTrust in Ole Miss."

"You got it, my brotha. And I had a clipboard with me, which I actually got from the red-head, Tommy, who by then was already getting his girlfriend to sneak in all kinds o' shit and brought him gifts, some of which he was allowed to keep because of his good behavior."

"What did ya say to Middleton?"

"I said, 'How's it goin?' He looked back at me an' said, 'Not bad, sir. You?' I had him an' I knew it. He called me *sir*, after all. I told him I was just finishing up my inspection of A cellhouse, and then we both bullshitted about how things were going around the prison. I let *him* ask the question, 'You from BOP?' To which I replied that, yes, of course I was. I quipped that I wasn't a nature hiker who'd gotten lost, and we both had a good laugh over that. A few more minutes of bullshittin', then I asked him to please unlock the door to the prison visiting room."

"Don't tell me that muthafucka obliged!"

"Oh, he obliged, all right," Spencer said with a self-congratulatory smile. "And I was pretty sure he would tell the guards inside the visiting center that they had a BOP inspector on the way—Marty had told me how the hacks always gave each other the heads up, but he didn't really need to tell me that, because it's human nature for employees to warn other employees when a boss-type is comin' around, right? One by one, all of 'em vouched for me to the guards in the next section, opening doors and waving me right through, and I never had to show any ID."

Here, Spencer stopped. It was a pregnant pause, one where he pretended to be considering how to tell the next part of his story, but actually he was shaking away a distracting thought. It was unusual for him to be thinking about something he thought he'd completely discounted, but there was the big-armed man in the Expedition, staring at him almost challengingly, his arm with the crimson bear half hanging out. *Was that a warning? Did that motherfucker think I was afraid of his biceps or somethin'?*

He also felt…cold? Yes, cold. An image came to him of a forest someplace. He was barefoot and walking in the woods in the dark. Was this a memory? It certainly felt familiar, like it had happened when he was a child. Or, rather, he felt like he was *seeing* it through the eyes of a child.

All at once, it was gone. As quickly as the spell had come, it was over with and all that was left in its place was Middleton the hack and his overzealous ass-kissing. Spencer cleared his throat and got back to his tale.

"So, of course, I got outside of the visiting center thanks to Middleton's warning. The hacks here didn't ask to check my badge or ID either, because of course Middleton had already told them who I was an' I just moved right on through, lookin' harried an' whatnot. I would stop here and there to make notes on my clipboard about a fluorescent light that was blinking out overhead and an empty Coke can that someone had left on the floor, an' everyone was anxious to open doors for me.

"I walked all the way out, not really knowing where I was going because I hadn't ever been through this administrative portion of the prison before. So whenever I got lost I just paused and pretended to jot down some notes, made some conversation around a water cooler with a chunky woman who'd probably do a fella just fine in the sack, then continued on my way. I had to look in a hurry, but not *too* much in a hurry. The whole time I was just worried about running into Brummel or Dr. McCulloch, because they were the only two guys who I was sure would recognize me.

"I made it to the front desk of the Administrations Annex and said my cell phone had died and wondered if I could use one o' theirs. They were only too happy. They'd probably been called and warned that they were getting another damned unannounced visit from the BOP inspectors, an' so all I got from the secretaries were smiles so big you'd think I was the warden himself. I dialed 411 to get the number to a local taxi service and they sent a cab and had it waitin' on me outside within fifteen minutes.

"I walked outside, waving and smiling and nodding to people as I went. I made small-talk with one o' the hacks by the gate for a few minutes, talking about the Royals and how they couldn't catch a break while I waited on the cab. When it arrived, I walked out the front gate, hopped inside and told the cabbie to take me to the nearest town. I didn't know what else to tell him because I didn't know Kansas at all, and he didn't care to ask me for clarification, just took me into town."

110

Spencer put the cig back in his lips, and took a good, long drag, like it might be his last on Earth. Telling the story had invigorated him. He had never told anyone what actually happened because he hadn't known anyone well enough in the intervening two years to trust them to keep his secret. Most people didn't even know who he was. That was two years ago, the episode of *America's Most Wanted* with his story (most of his escape altered so spare law enforcement humiliation) had come and gone, and Spencer was mostly a nobody again.

"I was only in for a few months. But being inside there…I guess I kind of skipped over what it was like bein' in the joint, really. All I can say is that not seeing a horizon except in a magazine, not seeing any forests for all the God damn walls, not seeing any women in bikinis on the beach, an' not being able to step outside to go to a KFC whenever I wanted some chicken, even though I fuckin' hate KFC…well, it felt good to see the wind in the trees again. To *touch* a tree. To drive. To walk in the streets. To smoke this cigarette here without havin' to smuggle it and hope somebody didn't cheat you. I saw the looks on the faces of the guys who'd been in there ten years or more. An' I made a promise to myself that I'm not going back to that place. Not ever. No matter what." He took another toke as a reward for finishing his tale.

"They didn't give that side o' the story," Pat said. There was something else in his eyes now. Admiration, perhaps? Spencer thought so.

"You're damn right they didn't. It's gotta be pretty embarrassing when you opened the door an' let the bad guy walk right out."

"I'm sittin' here listenin' to ya say it, but I ain't hardly believe it m'self, man." He pronounced that last word *main*.

"Believe it or not, that's my story and I'm stickin' to it."

Pat nodded. "Okay. Just one question. You said ya got the metal necessary for the tie clasp in the shape of handcuffs from two guys from A cellhouse. You said they gave ya want ya needed an' you gave them what they *wanted*. What did ya mean by that?"

Spencer smiled. "That's enough story time for tonight, Patty. I came here tonight for a job. And for any other contact information you might have on Basil. Now, I paid for my part here with my tale. Time to pony up."

Pat sighed. "I s'ppose you want some green fuh that piece o' shit Ford minivan you got parked outside."

"It'd be a start."

The chop shop owner took on a bargaining face that only a long-time businessman could summon. "I can't take somethin' like that so soon after it's been taken, an' I presume you *did* take it pretty recently. We're old friends, podna, but how do I know that car ain't too hot to handle?"

Spencer had seen this coming, and admitted it made good business sense. "All right then. I'll get you another vehicle tonight. Any kind, your choice. I'll have it to you before sunup."

"Befo' sunup?"

Spencer nodded.

Pat considered him for a moment. He leaned back in his squeaky chair, rocking back and forth, unknowingly in time with a few short bursts of drills out in the garage. "A Dodge Dart," he said.

"We talkin' 60's or 70's?"

"The 2013 model."

Here, Spencer had to laugh. "Bullshit. They're barely even out yet." Pat just looked at him. "You got a peg on one?"

"Sho do. Rich muthafucka up on West End, in one o' those gentrified neighborhoods. He got exactly what I need." Pat tilted his head back, and scratched briefly with one finger underneath his chin. His eyes wandered for a moment before looking back at Spencer.

"But?"

Pat shook his head and *tsk*ed. "Electronically locked."

Spencer nodded. "I see. Can't be hotwired the standard way. Gotta have an RFID key to unlock the steering column, right?"

"Word. But I know where to find an RFID chip from the manufacturer that'll work. It doesn't come attached to any key, but…"

"Then what's the problem? I'll go get it, hotwire the Dart an' tape the RFID chip to the side of the steering column. That's worked before. So what's the—?" Spencer caught himself. "The chip isn't anywhere that's easily accessible." To this, Pat nodded silently. "Then why even go for it? It's just another shiny four-door compact sedan. Gotta be easier targets worth the time."

"I got people with specific, uh, *needs*. Ya feel me?"

Spencer believed he did. Pat's clientele no longer included shitty street punks. Now, he catered to the kind of people who had acquired tastes. Such newer cars relayed a certain validity that made them the least likely to be searched under various circumstances. As well, there was probably something to the Dodge Dart that Pat wasn't telling him just yet, some specific feature that made it ideal for creating hidden compartments (perhaps convenient hollow areas near the rear) in which one could conceal various types of contraband.

"Alright," Spencer said.

"Alright, what?"

"Alright, I'll do it. Tell me where the RFID chip is an' I'll go get it. Then I'll go an' get the goddam Dart. But since this is a two-parter my fee is double for the doubled risk."

Pat spun back and forth in his squeaky chair, cogitating. Finally, he consented. "A'ight."

Spencer leaned forward, elbows propped up on his knees. "Where's it at?"

"You gonna tell me what'choo did to get the tie clasp an' the clipboard?"

For a few seconds, Spencer considered telling him. Then shrugged. "I can't be expected to spill *all* my secrets. Must leave some ambiguity." He added, "That means vagueness, uncertainty—"

"Fuck you, then." He shook his head laughing, but had the look of a man who wanted to capitulate but needed a good reason.

Spencer leaned in closer. "Pat. This is me askin'. You know I can get this ride. Now—where—the—fuck—am—I—going?"

Pat hesitated a moment longer, then took a deep, deep breath, and let it out slowly. He told Spencer where he had to go and what he had to do. After that, Spencer stood up and went to the door. "Guess I got my night cut out for me. Oh, hey, contact info for Basil?"

"That muthafucka three blocks up on Maple. Hillside Apartments. Number fo-fo-eight."

"Thanks, Pat. You're the best nigger a cracker ever had." Spencer turned to leave. Then, something struck him. He couldn't say what it was that brought it suddenly to mind, but he just had to ask. "Hey, I saw these guys earlier drive up fast in an El Camino and an Expedition. They snatched up some people an' drove off. One guy was white, had a tattoo of a red bear on his right arm. You know him?"

Now, Pat took on an entirely different look. All humor evaporated from his face and he teetered somewhere between pissed and frightened. "You seen the *vory* snatchin' up somebody an' they didn't shoot yo ass?"

"Who're the *vory*?"

"The *vory*? The *vory v zakone*?" It sounded like *voreev zakonya*. "They the only ones I know wear them tattoos. They're Russians. It's a Russian bear, done in red because o' they flag. The top captains have a sickle tattooed below the bear's head. You never heard of 'em?"

"I can't even pronounce them," Spencer laughed. "Who are they?"

"Some muthafuckas you don't wanna mess with." He pointed to Spencer. "You ain't mixed up with 'em, are ya, money? 'Cause if you are just tell me now an' we'll dissolve this fuckin' partnership right here."

"Pat, I was just asking. No harm in asking, right?"

"Depends on who you ask," he said, perhaps unaware of that sentence's double entendre. Pat looked him up and down, maybe reconsidering for a moment, then said, "Now gawn. Get my fuckin' Dart."

Spencer left out with only a nod to the three grease monkeys, who were just now putting some new hubcaps on the Lincoln.

Out the front door and into fresh air. The city was dead. *Not a creature was stirring, not even a mouse*, Spencer thought as he glanced up and down the street. The rain he'd heard pounding against the roof earlier had since tapered off. The air was still damp, though, as was the street. He stepped around a pothole that had gathered most of the water and hopped inside the minivan. He sat there for a moment, thinking about everything he'd told Pat. He started the van up using the wires again, then turned on the radio and found a news station. There wasn't anything on Baton Rouge, at least not at the moment. Just some B.S. about an anthrax scare at a post office somewhere in San Diego.

He put the van in drive, and started to pull off. He considered going back inside and asking Pat what had him so frightened about these *vory* fuckers, but decided that that wasn't necessary. If he went back in Pat might just decide that it wasn't worth the trouble having ol' Spence back, or he might push him for more information about how he escaped Leavenworth.

You wanna know how I got what I needed from the metal shop boys, Pat? Marty. Alone. In the shower. How could Spencer explain that he had given Marty a sympathetic ear, then used him like currency with five guys from the metal shop who wanted his sweet white ass? How could he describe setting Marty up to meet him in the showers on a certain day at a certain time, and then leaving him to the jackals that tore him to pieces? If Spencer told Pat that, then how long would it be before Pat realized he was also just a tool for ol' Spence, the Loony of Leavenworth?

Some secrets are best left untold. That piece of advice had come from Marty's very own lips late one night in their cell when Spencer had dared to ask him just how many children he had actually raped. "Some secrets are best left untold," he'd whispered so that no hacks could hear their late-night conversation. "If anybody knew everything about everybody, then nobody would ever have any friends." For all his faults, Martin Horowitz had been right about that.

Spencer checked his rearview mirror. A black sedan was coming right down the street from behind. He waited for the sedan to move on ahead. The man in the driver's seat was a boulder. He took his parking spot along the sidewalk, and switched off his lights. Spencer turned on his headlights and pulled away, heading west for Maple Street.

There was a puddle for Leon to step in as soon as he opened his door. Even though there hadn't been much rain, this pothole had retained a great deal. The street was cracked and sloped, all the water running down into this hole like a clogged drain.

He waved to the minivan as it went by, but the streetlights and the water on the windows obfuscated the driver, so Leon didn't know if he or she ever waved back.

He checked his watch. It was 1:09 AM.

Someone hollered up the street. Leon checked on the noise but never broke stride. A simple glance showed him a man fifty yards up the street spilling his shopping cart full of pots, pans, plastic jugs and other assorted scavenged goods from the day. Another man had stepped out from the shadows and kicked the cart away from where he was sleeping in an alley just off the road. This was the area of the Bluff where the homeless began to gather. Public interest in aiding the homeless had waxed and waned like the phases of the moon. Lots of condemned or destroyed buildings from those various projects, and the gentrification of other neighborhoods, had pushed the homeless farther into the Bluff. Some ended up in the homes offered by the local Baptist church; most were anywhere but.

Somebody hollered from up the street. Someone else hollered back. There was joined laughter echoing up and down the vacant alleys.

Pat's shop had a few lights on in the back, and some of it illuminated the front lobby where customers would enter during business hours. He heard the drills going on in the back of the shop, so he went around back and knocked loudly on the big red door that said **EMPLOYEES ONLY**. Someone inside stopped drilling for a moment and said, "Hey, Pat! Somebody knockin' at this door, holmes!"

Then *all* the drilling stopped.

A few seconds, then a piece of metal on the door at eye level slid to one side. The eyes looking at Leon regarded him with a species of mistrust. No words were exchanged but there was final consent in them. The peephole was closed and then the door opened. "God damn," Pat sighed, looking up at the much taller

Leon. "Who tha fuck else gonna come up in this piece tonight? You comin' with a warrant?"

"No, Pat. No warrant. No one else. Just me."

"What'choo doin' here then, nigga?"

"Can you step outside for a minute?"

Pat blanched. "Outside? It's chilly as a muthafucka out."

"Pat, if I see anything inside that makes me, I don't know, *suspicious*? I wouldn't have any sort of plausible deniability."

This changed his tune. Pat perked up and hollered back inside, "Hey yo, I'm steppin' out fo' a minute. Get that shit cleaned up." He stepped and closed the door.

Hands in his coat pockets, Leon walked away from the shop. His brother-in-law followed in behind, and remained silent. Once they got far enough away from Pat's Auto that they could no longer make out the sound of pneumatic drills at work, Leon cleared his throat and said, "You and Melinda still tight?"

"Yeah." Pat put his hands inside his pants pocket and shrugged. "Well, kinda. She mad right now, stayin' with ya moms right now, but, ya know, we still talkin' on the phone. She be back."

"What are you guys fighting about this time?"

There was ample derision in his voice. "You know yo sista," he complained.

Leon nodded. Yes, he knew her. But that wasn't why he came here, so he wasted no more time and got right to business. "Came across a Toyota Tacoma tonight, Pat. Black. Plates from Troup County. Stolen less than a day ago. Hotwired by a pro. What might you know about that?"

"Nothin', man."

"Don't bullshit me, brotha."

"I *ain't* bullshittin', Lee. I don't got no people workin' Troup County, an' if anybody brought me somethin' from that county, or any other county that ain't sure about or where I don't have an in with the local DMV, then I ain't about it. A'ight?"

Leon fixed him with a look and studied him at length. After a moment, he decided that his brother-in-law was telling the truth. He'd never lied to Leon, not once, even though he lied to Leon's sister often. What the hell his sister had ever seen in this man he would never know. He certainly wasn't faithful, and if all she needed was a provider for her two kids from her previous marriage then she could've relied on her little brother, and Melinda knew it. But he suspected she resented the idea of getting support from Leon, if only because he was her *younger* brother. *So she went and married this winner.* He said, "All right, then. Anything else happen recently?"

"Like?" said Pat, with a barely controlled attitude. Leon knew that if he wasn't careful, this could turn into a full-blown family-style argument. Pat was a pugnacious little prick at times, especially these days, since he was so used to getting his way in their relationship. Pat was an informant, but only for Leon, and Leon had settled on turning a blind eye to his operations, rather than handing his sister's husband over to the APD.

"Like any unusual visits. Maybe some new guys from outta town? Maybe some new competitor? Anything out of the ordinary for you. Help me out here, Pat."

"Various folks come, an' various folks go. Can't say anything particular."

"What about a white man? About six feet tall, maybe a little taller? Dark hair, blue eyes. Very pale. Wearing a black hoodie, jeans, and Converse shoes."

Pat said nothing, just looked him up and down.

"That's a yes," Leon said, reaching into the inner pocket of his jacket and pulling out his notepad. "Just give me something and it'll never come back to you. I'll chalk it up to one of my other street-level informants, I'll say they spotted him and your name will never be mentioned. Now, who is he?"

Pat still said nothing. His hand fidgeted inside his pockets as he cocked his head back and looked at the sky from one end to the other.

He looked down at his brother-in-law more judiciously. Leon knew that his height made him more domineering in negotiations, and never hesitated to use it. "Pat, you owe me."

"Yeah?" he said, folding his arms to ward off reason. "For what?"

"You owe me," was all Leon said back. And he did. Big time. In every way conceivable.

For a time it seemed like Pat might just withhold what he knew for all eternity. Then, at last, he said, "His name's Spencer."

"Got a last name?" Leon asked, his pen moving.

"Pelletier. I dunno how the fuck you spell it."

Leon started jotting that down, then stopped. His pen hovered an inch above the paper. "Pelletier…Spencer Pelletier…why does that sound so familiar?"

"He escaped Leavenworth 'bout two years ago. He was famous fo' a minute."

Leon shook his head. "No. No, this was more recent, I think." He shook his head and went ahead writing it all down. "Spencer Pelletier." The name bounced around inside his head in search of something to connect with. "Leavenworth. Two years ago. All right, when did you last see him?"

Pat smiled. "Let's see, I guess it was about, oh, five minutes ago."

"You're shitting me."

"Nope. He left, an' no sooner had I sat back in my office than you knocked at my door, Lee," Pat said, shrugging.

"How long did he stay?"

"I'ow know," Pat said, shrugging. "Thirty minutes? An hour?"

"Which was it? Thirty minutes or an hour?"

"Man, I look like a *God* damn timepiece?" Pat said, shrugging.

"What did he want?"

"A job," Pat said, shrugging.

"That's it?"

"Pretty much," Pat said, shrugging. "That, an' he wanted to sell me this shitty-ass minivan he boosted."

Leon stopped writing and looked up at him. "Wait…wait, he was driving that Ford Aerostar minivan?"

Pat grinned. "Yup-yup. Ya saw him, I guess?"

Leon fumed. "God damn it, yes. I did. Where was the motherfucker going?"

"I'ow know."

"Don't *lie* to me, Pat—"

"I ain't lyin', Lee! This muthafucka didn't tell me—"

"This asshole may be involved in the kidnapping of two children—*two small girls*—earlier tonight!" Leon shouted. He watched Pat's expression change to one of serious doubt and deliberation. "Down by Dodson's Store! Just snatched them right up off the street, Pat! It may be just a bunch o' hoods, but it might also be the *vor*! Now, you gonna help me or not?"

His brother-in-law sighed, licked his lips, and nodded. "How sure are you he took them girls?"

"Not a hundred percent, but I think he *knows* something. He was there, I know that much. Pat, look at me." Pat's eyes had started to wander, not wanting to meet Leon's, but now they locked on unblinkingly. "You know how these cases go. If we haven't found those girls within forty-eight hours they'll already be raped and murdered, and we won't see them again until their bodies turn up in a landfill, if ever. If not that, then they'll be shipped someplace else. God knows where. Now, tell me, where did this asshole go?"

Pat blinked, and made a decision. "I sent him to Basil."

Leon thought for a second.   "The Yeti?   On Maple? Hillside Apartments, right?"

"Yeah.   An' he said somethin' about the *vor* an' this abduction bidness befo' he left. He sounded curious himself. Maybe he just got mixed up with 'em by accident, ya know?"

"Maybe. But we won't know until we ask…" He trailed off. Leon's mind had just leapt to something else. All at once, he had the connection. It came out of nowhere, like an old baseball card collection that suddenly fell out of a dusty drawer when you went to clean the attic. A recent memory, hitherto lost in the attic, rejoined him, and the connection showed promise.   It grew, reshaping Leon's curiosity to something more akin to alarm. After a moment he said, "Wait a minute. Wait just a…*Pelletier*. That's his name? Spencer Pelletier? You're sure about that name, Pat?"

Pat shrugged again. "Yeah, that's his name. Unless he been lyin' to me all these years."

"Spencer Pelletier…*ffffffffffuck*. Fuck me," he said, and took out his cell phone. "Baton Rouge. God damn it. Fuck me sideways."

"Baton R—*hey*! Where the fuck you goin'? This shit ain't comin' back on me an' mine, is it?"

Leon had turned and bolted back to his car.   The text message he sent was to Bernie Gibbons in Missing and Exploited

120

Children.   It was short and sweet: Maple Street.   Hillside Apartments. Maybe caught a break.

He slid inside his sedan and plucked the radio from the cup holder between the seats where he'd left it.   "Dispatch, this is Detective Leon Hulsey. Badge number eight-four-eight-seven. I have a beat on a wanted fugitive who may be at Hillside Apartments on Maple Street. Suspect's name, Spencer Pelletier. Wanted for multiple counts of murder in Baton Rouge. Advise all units to consider armed and extremely dangerous."

"Ten-four, Detective. What's your twenty?"

"Terrell Street."

"Are you heading to Hillside now?"

"Yes I am. Send all available units in the area. Over." He tossed the radio into the passenger seat and instinctively touched the pistol at his side to make sure it was still there before he squealed out. Leon took one last look in his rearview mirror and saw Pat standing there, a lone silhouette on Terrell Street, waving a single hand for his brother-in-law's return.

Or maybe it was a wave goodbye.

Leon looked at the lit-up dashboard. . His clock read 1:17 AM.

City lights streaked past the windows at irregular intervals. Kaley spotted a few cars on the road, and though they were just right there—*right there*—she couldn't reach out to them and let them know her trouble.   Kaley considered drawing the words **HELP ME** on the window with her finger, hoping it would be subtle enough that her captors wouldn't notice, and yet noticeable enough that somebody else driving by would.   Alas, she was squeezed in between two burly men, and could no more reach out to touch the window than she could reach for the moon.

And so they drove on, most of the world asleep, and even those who weren't were oblivious, living their own dreamlike lives.

Once, when she was visiting her Aunt Tabitha, Kaley remembered asking if cities dreamed. Aunt Tabby had asked her where she got that crazy idea. Kaley told her she had read a story at school about a man who got lost inside a city's dream and couldn't find his way out. "If they dream, they have nightmares, don't they?"

Sometime later, Aunt Tabby had followed up on this topic with her. "I thought what you asked was very interesting, girl," she had said. "I actually did some looking into dreams. Everything that has living parts dreams. We might be like blood cells moving through the bloodstream of the city. Like neurons in a brain. If that's so, then we make up a collective thought, don't we? A collective consciousness that is the city's thoughts and dreams."

Aunt Tabitha had seemed quite smitten with this concept, perhaps hopeful that her niece would grow up to take an interest in science like she had. Aunt Tabitha wasn't a genius, but she was the smartest person Kaley knew. She had been a science teacher, and was now mostly retired and occasionally substituted. She had encouraged Kaley to think more deeply about things than the rest of the fools in the Bluff, those who scorned people who made good grades and mocked anyone who showed the least bit of creative talent.

"Misery loves company," Aunt Tabby had said. "They don't want you to escape because *they* haven't escaped. If you escape, then they're all alone with their failures."

Kaley sensed that now from the other little girl sitting in the back next to Shannon. The girl was indeed miserable, and didn't want either Kaley or Shannon to leave, despite the fact that leaving would be a good thing; it would mean being able to get help for her. *She wants us here. If we leave her, then she's alone with her suffering. She sees compatriots in misery. She hopes to bond. She hopes to have friends, like a stray dog edging towards a human, hopin' to be allowed into the home.*

But Kaley's responsibility was to her sister. If she could find a way of getting them all out, she would of course, but priority one was Little Sister. And the Anchor. If Kaley had to make the decision between escaping with Shan and remaining here to make sure the other girls was okay, she would escape with Shan at her first chance and never look back. Well, maybe not never. She would always carry that frightened girl's misery with her, all the way to her grave.

She looked out the windows on either side of her, watched the streetlights standing sentry at regular intervals. Kaley might've recognized the area if it were daytime and she wasn't so confused about how far they'd come already, but at the moment she didn't recognize a single landmark. All storefronts were closed and the windows were dark. A few people walked the streets, and every so often the buildings parted to reveal skyscrapers off to her right, but she still couldn't orient herself.

Whimpering from the back. She turned her head, saw Shannon, as well as the familiar-looking girl lying in a fetal position next to her. And then she heard a grunt from one of the men sitting on either side of her—it was the man with the jaundiced skin—and it seemed to warn her about making eye contact with her sister.

The vertigo-like sensation kicked in again, causing the world to tilt. Kaley knew what was going to happen next, and instead of listening to her charm (as she promised she would from now on) she fought it still, because she didn't want it to be true. For a moment, there was an image crystallized so perfect in her mind, a set of teeth smiling wide, blood leaking from the upper lip, and a background smattering of distant screams. She pushed it away. She was willfully oblivious, looking down at her feet, then out at the streetlights, then back to her feet again.

If cities do dream, she decided, they must have nightmares as well. Tonight, Kaley, Shannon, and the other terrified little girl were caught in one.

6

Though Spencer would never know it, the flaming car that he passed by on Dixon Avenue was just one more cog in the machine of tonight that would bring about so much death. This particular cog happened to buy him the time he would need to escape.

The car-b-que was off to one side of the road, popping like fireworks. Red lights flashed behind him. The fire trucks were already on the scene, as was a HERO truck. Spencer's minivan was one of the last vehicles to get through before the roadblock was set up, and pedestrians from the nearby crack houses and apartments were gathering either beside or in the streets, despite warnings from a man with a bullhorn.

If anybody's in there, sucks to be you, Spencer thought as he coasted past the smoking vehicle and delivered a salute. It was a yellow Eclipse. Fire licked out of each window and smoke plumed from the slightly parted hood. There was no sign of an accident. No other car was nearby. Spencer concluded that either someone was ditching a body or ditching a car they needed to get clean of. *Dangerous night to be out,* he thought. But maybe this was normal for the Bluff.

He turned down two more streets before he finally made it to Maple Street, which was as far as most white folks ever got to Hillside Apartments, and cruised right on over to the complex where a couple of late-night get-togethers were going on. A few young black youths were sitting on a second-storey balcony while their music blasted from a stereo system inside. Another small assembly, this one peppered with a few females, was outside of one of the terraces. Again, music boomed from an open door, and the thrumming bass drowned out all other instrumental nuances.

Spencer found the apartment building labeled **APARTMENTS 0400-0500**, and slid into the only available parking spot. He hopped out of the van. Two older black guys were

124

stepping out of their apartment and Spencer lifted his chin at them by way of greeting. One of them mumbled "S'up," and they kept on towards their car.

He wasted no time at 448. He didn't knock with his knuckles, he pounded with his fist on the door with its peeling white paint and faded number 8. "Yo, Basil! It's Spence! Open up, assfuck!" he shouted. Ten seconds went by. Nothing.

A group of four guys in their early twenties scooted by, hollering and laughing. One of them chucked a bottle into some bushes. Another glanced in Spencer's direction, fixed him with a look, then turned away.

He banged on the door again. "Yo, Basil! Open up!"

Again nothing.

Behind him, a door opened. Spencer turned reflexively to touch the Glock tucked and hidden at his waistband. A Hispanic woman was stepping out of 449 across the hall. She wore stockings and a garter, along with an oversized fake fur coat. As she walked past, Spencer noticed that a price tag still hung from the coat's left sleeve. She lit a cigarette and gave him the briefest of appraisals, gauging his interest, and then discounted him when she saw he had none.

Spencer took in the narrow corridor he was in. He heard shouting from behind closed doors down the hall. A man and woman kind of fight. There was the sound of something hitting the wall. *That's about to get bad*, he thought, and hammered on 448's door again. "Basil! I'm gonna kick this door in, man! You wanna lose your deposit?" Spencer took a step back, and slammed his right Converse hard near the doorframe. "I'm comin' in!"

"Hold on! Fuck me! *Hold on!*" someone called from inside.

Spencer jiggled the doorknob. "You got maybe five seconds, Yeti. *Maybe.*"

"I said *hold on*, man!" There was the sound of a chain rattling on the other side of the door. Spencer touched the Glock again, just in case there was a surprise waiting for him. When the door parted, it did so slowly. A tall, anorexic sasquatch stood on the other side. At least 6 ½ feet tall, the sasquatch had been shaved only around his eyes and some of his forehead. There was gnarled brown hair that descended from his head and merged with a scraggly beard, which created a great mane that captured the occasional crumb. The top of his head had random bald patches. Where you could see skin, it was red, like a dog with the mange. The sasquatch wore a black robe that hung from its skinny body like a long coat would hang from a coat rack; it had no form, wasn't filled out at all. Besides the robe, which he wore open, the sasquatch had only a pair of white briefs. "The fuck, Spence? Man, it's like, after one o'clock an' shit. Almost one-thirty."

"Fuck you," Spencer said, stepping inside uninvited. He paused at the threshold for a second, holding his breath against the smell.

The apartment was a landfill, just like every other place that Spencer had known the Yeti to reside. Styrofoam containers, mostly empty, lay atop balsawood tables that looked ready to buckle. Black curtains clung to one window while bed sheets blocked out the light from others. There were various pillows and blankets on the floor to indicate someone slept there, but it was questionable who and how many. An N64 and a PS2 lay with wires strewn across the floor almost like trip wires. Replica paintings were stacked by the dozens against a wall, but none appeared to adorn the walls themselves. Though it was hard to tell, between the mountains of refuse and a carefully arranged stack of cereal boxes, there was little wall to see. There was a similar stack for *Motor Trend* magazines against another wall. There was a pile of clothes in the shape of a couch at the center of the room, and a variegated assortment of stains across these clothes. Bits of carpet could be seen here and there, but the floor was mostly covered by cardboard boxes, empty water bottles, Sprite cans, old newspapers, Japanese swords (lying on the floor without much care), chewing gum wrappers, four of the seven Harry Potter novels, eight broken lamps, six car stereos, a toolbox (opened and with most of the contents strewn about), a Bowflex with a food tray balanced on it, and perhaps most dubious of all, forty or so empty tampon boxes arranged neatly beside the door. There were medical dictionaries and college study books collected in one corner, along with folders bursting with papers and CD cases of Rosetta Stone's series "How to Speak Mandarin." There was a 20-inch TV sitting atop an old box of a 52-inch TV (presumably broken and now serving as a table), and all around that there was a smattering of keyboards, computer monitors, CDs, printers, copiers, fax machines and scanners. A radio played a familiar Fiona Apple hit from the late 90's.

"God damn, Basil."

"I know, man. Sorry about the mess."

"Mess doesn't begin to…you got my shit or not?" he said, deciding not to get sidetracked.

"Um, yeah. Yeah, let me just…" The Yeti now started frenetically digging around the room seemingly at random.

Once a computer engineer and then an investigator at a bank's fraud department, Basil O'Connor had become what he had become for very simple reasons: he preferred to work from home, and at his own pace. At least, that's what he'd told Spencer almost a decade ago when they first met. Spencer had just been getting his feet wet back then, had happened upon a couple of people who introduced him to some rather influential members of Atlanta's seedier side. Knowing the good contacts from the bullshitters, Spencer had thrown away the useless ones and maintained relationships with those who were worth the time. Basil was one of those worth the time. Basil the Yeti, master forger and counterfeiter, who so far had never been caught, was worth the time. He'd gotten his nickname not just because of his appearance, but because he was so elusive. Constantly moving, constantly changing cell phones, emails and IP addresses, one only knew how to find him if one knew others who knew him that could arrange introductions.

"This is a, uh, surprise visit," said Basil.

"I paid you months ago, Yeti. You said they'd be ready next time I rolled through," Spencer said, shutting the door behind him with his foot. "Well, here I am."

"I know, I know, man," Basil said, his high-pitched voice nowhere near as fearsome as one would suspect from a sasquatch. He scratched at a red bald spot on his scalp, and the muscles around his neck spasmed. He'd been hitting the pipe recently, and like all addicts was trying (fruitlessly) to conceal the fact. "I got 'em all, too. You know me. They're right here."

Spencer snapped his fingers twice and waved his fingers towards him, a sign of gimme.

The Yeti nodded distractedly and moved about with renewed quickness. For all his disgusting habits, the man had a certain organization in his brain that only he understood. He pushed aside a few pizza boxes, two pairs of pants (Spencer had never once seen him wear pants) and six empty Mountain Dew bottles to reveal a small end table. This place reminded Spencer of that incident in Manhattan back in 1947 with those Collyer Brothers, Langley and Homer. Homer, who was blind, had been seen to by Langley, an engineer who designed their house to be filled with tripwires, traps, and a maze of trash, all to keep people from getting into their home and taking his brother away from him. Eventually, Langley had been crushed by his own trash and Homer, unable to help himself, had died of thirst and starvation.

Maybe that'll be the end o' the Yeti, too, Spencer thought. He snapped his fingers impatiently. "C'mon, c'mon, c'mon, I got work to do tonight."

"Yeah? Did you see Pat? He get you some work?"

"Yeah, that's what I'm working on. I gotta get moving."

Basil nodded jerkily. Long ago his central nervous system had lost the war against all the H he was putting in his system. These days it was so bad he could barely stand up straight. "You couldn't wait on these, Spence?" he said, handing over the packet of fake IDs. He bent over against his will, then straightened up against his will. The H was wracking his body. He scratched at his skin and winced. "Like, I dunno, until morning?"

"Naw, I might not be stayin' in the A-T-L too long. Might have to fly fast. Never know. So, I'll be needin' these." He opened it up, checked them out. He glanced up at the Yeti.

"Yo, man, they're all cool. You paid for the best and you got it."

Spencer had no doubt about that, really. Basil wasn't just some moron who threw together a few pieces of paper with a new name on it and laminated the shit at Kinko's. No, he was one of those rare and beautiful types in the criminal underworld, completely indispensible to all of the major players because he didn't just invent IDs, he grew them.

Anybody could go to a cemetery and find the name of a child who'd died soon after birth, then go to the courthouse and look at their records to get the dead infant's social security number and start using it. That was probably the oldest trick in the proverbial book. But the feds were onto that trick, and modern computer systems had made it easier to check and double-check the background of an SSN. So gathering SSNs were only good if a person grew them. This meant that a professional forger like the Yeti had to keep his records regularly updated, and by whatever means. The old cemetery trick was sometimes good, but these days the best thing to do was steal someone's ID from the Internet. A number of confidence scams made it easy to get people to hand that information over, even the information of a dead infant.

Once the Yeti had this info, he grew the ID, used it to open a credit line with a bank, maybe just a hundred bucks, maybe a thousand, and then quickly paid it off. Then he might enroll this fake person in a school system. Doesn't matter that they don't show up, especially if it's an inner city school where the attendance was always shoddy anyway. This all cost money, of course, and the more cultivated you wanted an ID to be, the more you had to pay. For instance, enrolling this fake person in college would be a little more costly, because for Basil, this meant spending his time filling out documents for online courses, maybe even completing a degree in the liberal arts if the client wanted something impenetrable.

Some clients even wanted a picture ID of themselves from their early years placed into various databases to make it appear as though they had carried this identity for all their lives. This might entail taking their childhood school photos and placing them into old newspaper clippings that were now kept online, which required hacking, of course. This way, a person could appear to have been enrolled in, say, a chess club when they were twelve, and then a swim team competition when they were eighteen, and so on. All of this helped fill out an identity so much that it would take a superhuman feat to unravel it and determine it was 100% fake.

Basil kept this information in reams of folders, probably the folders strewn all around the apartment. He stored it for years, gathering new identities while simultaneously cultivating old ones. He waited until they ripened, held onto them for prospective customers, and then finally attached the necessary faces and finalized a few things. It was a full-time job that allowed him to work at home and at his own pace doing something he loved—

hacking and research, both of which provided a creative outlet for his talents.

The computer age and technology had done a lot to inform people, but people like Basil O'Connor were using it to *rewrite* history.

So, with some credit history and an education background, Spencer had two new identities he could choose to disappear into. One of them was Paul Quinton Ramsay, a 32-year-old man from New Jersey with a credit history and an MBA from DeVry University. The other was a little less cultivated, a man named Michael Frederick Voigt, a 31-year-old from Tuckerville, Georgia. Voigt had a little credit history but no education history.

Spencer kept looking at the Yeti, who shrugged and said, "I gave you one great one, and one pretty good one. And, hey, that's a real charity, man. You know? I did it because you paid everything up front. Few people trust me with that."

The Yeti was big on trust, and Spencer had known that. That's how he played him. Still, it had been a gamble. If the Yeti had gotten busted (not likely) or had moved someplace where Spencer couldn't find him (more likely), then he would've been out the fifty g's he'd fronted the tall hairy beast.

"We square, Spence? Everything cool?" he asked, in the hopeful manner of a schoolboy who was offering a gift to a bully he didn't want a beating from anymore.

Unfortunately for the Yeti, this was, to Spencer, another obvious avenue to manipulate him and keep him honest. "Yeah," Spencer sighed, putting the IDs back in the folder. "I guess they'll do." But something else was bugging him. He still couldn't say why, but it was. Maybe it was the way Pat had spoken about those *vor*, maybe it was just that his interest had been piqued. *Maybe I'm still pissed off about Baton Rouge.* "But this is bullshit an' you know it," Spencer added, taking a step towards him.

The Yeti took a step back, almost tripping over a stereo speaker. "Wh-what do you mean?"

"A 'charity,' you called it?" Spencer said. He shook his head. "No, man. That's not how this works. I know how much you charge—"

"Rates go up—"

"Not with me, they don't," Spencer said. "And don't give me inflation or cost o' services fluctuation. I don't give a *shit* about economics. I've been one o' yer oldest customers. I've brought you other work. I gave you the intro to Pat an' the others, remember? I'm the whole reason your operation *exists*."

"Yeah, man. Hey, chill. It's like this, man, I had to—"

"No, it's like *this*. I want a discount. Cash money. Now."

"Man, you know I don't deal with cash," he laughed, shifting his weight. "All my shit's in the Caymans, dig? I put my shit there because it's a tax haven. You dig, man, right?"

Spencer had taken two more slow steps towards him. He'd never hurt the Yeti before and didn't plan to, but the Discovery Channel would be interested to know that the Yeti was a frightened creature when trapped alone in the wild, even when in the company of familiar animals. "Alright," Spencer said. "Alright, fuck your tax haven, then. I need somethin' else done."

"Wh-what, man?" He was fidgeting. The Yeti scratched at his skin, his left eye was twitching and the muscles in his neck started going through spasms again. "N-Name it."

"AXC 371."

"What?"

"A license plate number. I need it looked up." He didn't know why, but something about the way Pat had talked about them, like he was warning Spencer away. Like he was afraid of them himself. He even said he didn't want to do work with Spencer if he was mixed up with the *vory v zakone*. It was like…

Well…

Like they're untouchable. Just like the bullies at Brownfields Elementary School had once felt. Just like Miles Hoover, Jr. had once appeared. Yes, the *vory v zakone* had a certain amount of clout, evidently. And clout and perceived power was something that Spencer Pelletier inherently felt he needed to test. The same thing when Brummel had leaned in and shouted in his ear, "You ain't *ever* getting out of my prison! You understand me, boy!"

The challenge had been issued. It practically begged to be done.

"H-hey, man, it's late," said the Yeti, "a-and I ain't got that kind of hookup no more—"

"That nigger that works down at the DMV still hooks you up," Spencer said, taking a step over to the Yeti's computer array and looking over it. "He gave you that back door into the DMV's system. C'mon, I know that's how you keep up with the updates on driver's license designs and whatnot. Don't bullshit a bullshitter. You still got that back door, don't you?"

"Oh...oh, *that* hookup. Hey, y-yeah, man," he laughed nervously again.

"Look it up. License plate AXC 371."

The Yeti hustled over to his computer desk and pushed a few files to the floor, as well as a copy of *The Making of Citizen Kane*. "Hey, y-you got it, m'man. Coming right up. AXC 371. You got it. Coming riiiiiight up."

"Oh, and a cell phone," Spencer said. "A prepaid one. I know you've got three or four of 'em lying around here somewhere. I want one."

"H-hey, you got it, man. Whatever."

The fire trucks had every lane blocked, and the sidewalk was no good because the burning wreck was on one side and all the rubberneckers were on the other. Hydraulic rescue tools (those Jaws of Life) had been pulled out, and they were all excited to see a dead body pulled from the car-b-cue. The air was filled with the acrid smell of upholstery turned to carbon. Leon fumed and tried to back up, but by now half a dozen cars had stacked up behind him. He put it in reverse and honked his horn numerous times, rolling down his window and yelling for those behind to back up.

When finally he had enough room to get off this street, he had a decision to make. He could take Nickel Ferry Road to get there quicker, but there was no way to Hillside from there and he'd have to leave his car on the sidewalk and run through a short patch of woods to get to the apartment complex. If he wanted to be able to park his car someplace relatively safe and use it to block off the entrance and Pelletier's escape, then he'd need to head down to Johnston Street, take a right onto Perris Way and then another right onto Roundabout Road (suitably named for this night's errand).

Leon had to decide. It took all of three seconds to opt for Nickel Ferry Road. He drove halfway up, parallel with the woods separating Nickel Ferry Road from Hillside Apartments, then pulled up onto the sidewalk. Hopefully, he wouldn't be sorry he left his car in this neighborhood.

Before getting out of the sedan, he made sure to take the radio and his cell with him, of course, so that he could coordinate with the backup which should be on the way.

As he shut his door, Leon's right hand went for his pistol without even thinking. He pulled it out and put it at ready-low position, and dashed through the woods. If he was just questioning a suspect or a witness in a kidnapping, he would never have drawn his weapon. But this was the sick fuck from Baton Rouge, the one who killed six men in a public park, cut the nuts off one and, according to one terrified thirteen-year-old, laughed while he shoved them down the dead man's throat.

In all the excitement, he forgot his flashlight. It wasn't his only mistake. In his hurry, he'd also forgotten to lock his car.

Spencer clapped Basil companionably on the shoulder as he stepped outside. "Thanks, Yeti." He had the printout from the DMV's records in his hand. He folded it and placed it inside his hoodie's pocket. "You're a good guy, I don't care what others say behind your back." Another clap on his arm. "Just kiddin', man. You're the best."

"H-hey, Spence, man. Anytime, you know?

The Yeti smiled big, splitting that beard of his in half. Many in the world thought that the Yeti was elusive because he wanted to be left alone. But Spencer knew the truth. The Yeti was alone only because he didn't know how to make friends. He *wanted* friends. Just like Martin Horowitz had wanted a friend. Everybody wanted a friend, Spencer supposed. Forgers and pedophiles were no different. Spencer was happy to oblige them when they showed a use.

"I appreciate this, Yeti. You do good work. Maybe I'll see ya around?"

"Yeah, hey, definitely," he said. Basil glanced back inside anxiously. His pipe was calling. Human interaction, as much as the Yeti desired it, still agitated him to no end. Though he wanted it, there was one thing he wanted more. "Yo, p-peace, Spence."

"Peace in the Middle East."

Basil laughed. "H-hey, I like that, man. Peace in the Middle East! For sure. And tell Pat I said hey, if you see him."

"Cool, man. Thanks." Spencer offered him his parting smile. The door shut in his face, Spencer turned to walk away, and knew something was wrong almost immediately.

Someone in the joint had once called it street sense. It was the same with another inmate he'd known named Daniel Patterson, who'd shown keen prison instincts because he'd been incarcerated since he was fifteen years old. Patterson called it the "ebb and flow" feel, the ups and downs, action and reaction. A wilderness survival expert Spencer knew years ago called it the "concentric rings of nature"—a squirrel jumps on a tree and scuttles to the other side, so you knew that danger was coming from the opposite side of that tree.

Whatever you wanted to call it, it was there, yelling at him. And it came to him from every direction. The first thing he recognized—without knowing he recognized it—was that the music had been turned down. No more loud bass bumping from the other apartments. That was especially interesting because the party on the second storey had been the loudest. They probably had a bird's-eye view from up there. What had they seen? What put a damper on the party?

The second thing he noticed—again, without knowing he noticed it—was that the Hispanic prostitute was back. She walked by him quickly, and took something out of her purse. She walked casually by a row of bushes and her hand moved. Did she drop something? If so, what for? What was she ditching, and who was she hiding it from?

By the time the third clue came (someone hollering "Five-oh!"), Spencer had already turned away from the parking lot and was walking into a patch of woods on the south side of the apartment complex.

Though he never saw one of the cars, he spotted flashing blue and red lights from around a small hill. The lights quickly switched off. That was the final clue. They were entering without sirens blaring. The lights had gotten traffic out of their way, but they'd switched off the lights at this point in order to serve a clandestine "no-knock" warrant.

Somebody's apartment is about to get hit. Alarms were going off in Spencer's head.

The forest was nearly pitch-black. Spencer heard other footsteps around him. He saw the silhouette of one fellow rushing out of the woods about forty yards up from him, his trench coat flapping behind him. *Big fucker, that one,* he thought. *Has to weigh two-forty, two-fifty.*

The big fellow ran across the parking lot, disappearing behind a few cars. Now came the sound of several car doors opening and slamming. A few men shouting orders to one another, coordinating an attack.

Definitely a raid. But on who?

But Spencer already knew. Somehow, it all just added up, and the glance back only confirmed it. Indeed, they were headed for the building marked **APARTMENTS 0400-0500**.

All right, so they're onto me, he thought calmly. How they'd gotten onto him was anybody's guess, and, as it happened, not very important. Could've been Pat, could've been a witness who saw him hop out of the Tacoma earlier and then boost the Aerostar, it could've been a lot of things. The important thing to do now was to walk away normally, no rush, no haste in his step, just keep moving.

Spencer took out the piece of paper Basil had given him and reviewed it.

VIN: WBLLV82746KT77311   Class: Upscale – Near Luxury

Year: 2007   Engine: 5.4L V-8

Make: Ford   Country of Assembly: USA

Model: Expedition   Vehicle Age: 5 year(s)

Style/Body: SUV   Calculated Owners: 1

Registered To: Brenton Jordan Richards

Mailing Address: 12 Townsley Drive—Atlanta, GA 30314

He memorized the information, then tore the paper up and threw the pieces into a drain at the edge of sidewalk. Part of him was of a mind to run right now. Just boost another car and take off. They'd probably never catch him. But if they pressed Basil—it would be easy with all they would find in his apartment, and the Yeti had proven he was easily pressed—then it wouldn't be hard to get the full story out of him.

But the *vory v zakone* wouldn't let him be. They were with him now, like an irritant, a speck of dirt in his eye.

They think they're untouchable, eh? For some reason, he just couldn't let it go, the same way he couldn't let Miles Hoover, Jr. go. Not that day. Not in the library of Brownfields Elementary School. Not at that particular time. That's how they all found out who Spencer Pelletier really was. That's how his parents found out. That's how his older brothers found out. That's how the school found out.

If he were present, Dr. McCulloch from Leavenworth Federal Penitentiary would remind Spencer that psychopaths typically lacked realistic, long-term goals. They make decisions based on impulse, and though they lack standard emotions, they feel very passionate about carrying through with their spontaneous decisions.

But Dr. McCulloch's advice did no good. Like the Yeti in 448, Spencer had an itch, too, and it needed scratching. He was only human.

Resolute, he started looking for yet another car to boost. As luck would have it, there was a black four-door Nissan sedan parked on the sidewalk almost as soon as he stepped out of that short patch of woods. He went over to test the car door, figuring he'd need to bust the window. But both Fate and Destiny had taken him for a pet tonight, because the door opened right up for him.

Spencer sat in the driver's seat and, just for a moment he thought this car looked familiar. He glanced into the passenger's side seat, saw a comic book called *The Dark Knight Returns*, as well as a folded copy of *The Atlanta-Journal Constitution*. He immediately disregarded this feeling of acquaintance with the car and tore off the ignition cover with the same screwdriver he'd kept in his back pocket for his three-hundred-mile run across the Bible Belt.

The cell that Basil had given him was a smartphone with full bars for Internet access. He found the appropriate maps online and within seconds he was bound for Townsley Drive.

Leon moved slowly, his gun still down at ready-low. Hillside Apartments was a cauldron of various gangs, drug dealers and random hoodlums, and he didn't want to provoke them unnecessarily. He was approaching the door of apartment 448 when he stopped in his tracks. The SWAT van was pulling up. The SWAT officers hopped out the back and filed out quickly. They moved in a direct line and did not stop running until they were in position around the building. The team jogged up to Leon before the lead guy, a man that Leon knew named Hennessey, shouted, "You sure he's in there?"

"God damn, they called *you* guys in?"

"Feds at the station couldn't get here fast enough," Hennessey said, holding up a fist for the rest of his eight-man team. "He in there?"

Feds? Leon wanted to say, but instead addressed the most pertinent dilemma. "Well, yeah, I'm pretty sure our boy's in there."

"Pelletier?"

"That's what my source told me."

That was all Hennessey needed to hear. He waved to his guys and they all filed in behind him wordlessly. Leon now stood to one side, a bit let down that he was going to have to take a back seat for this arrest.

Lieutenant William Hennessey was the man beside the doorknob. Across from him was Sergeant Gil Warwick. Hennessey's men were lined up as they approached the door. The lead man, Rorion Vaulstid, had his MP-5 up and aimed at the door.

The man behind Vaulstid was Joey Heinrich, who had his Glock in his right hand, and had his left hand placed firmly on Vaulstid's shoulder. Behind Heinrich was Lawrence Klein, who had his hands and weapon similar to Heinrich. Down the line, all the men had their handguns drawn in their right hand, while their left hand squeezed the shoulder of the man in front of them. This way, everyone knew the man behind was ready.

Hennessey nodded to Vaulstid, who nodded back, and then three things happened at once. The Benelli combat shotgun disintegrated the doorframe at doorknob level, Lieutenant Hennessey kicked the door in, and Warwick tossed in two flash-bang grenades that he'd already pulled the rings off of, letting the fuses burn just long enough so that when they hit the floor inside they went off almost immediately.

It all happened within the span of two seconds, done exactly as they had rehearsed hundreds of times before.

SWAT moved in. The first two men in the line shouted as they moved in, "Atlanta PD! Search warrant! Search warrant!"

They moved through the doorway in what was termed a button-hook pattern: one man turned a hard left, the next a hard right, the next a not-so-hard left, the next a not-so-hard right, and so on. They spilled into the room, each operator covering his own sector of the room. They could be fairly confident that the tremendous bang and exploded magnesium powder would have deafened and blinded any immediate resistance.

But they hadn't counted on the trash. Rarely had the SWAT team encountered such a packrat. They moved as best they could around stacks of Tupperware filled with books and random knickknacks, as well as a mound that would prove to be a sofa under closer inspection later.

"Atlanta PD! Search warrant!" Warwick called out. He was the last man to enter the apartment.

Vaulstid had been the first through the door. "Clear!" he claimed of the living room, and moved to the side of a hallway entrance. So far, no sign of the tenant.

"I've got deep!" Heinrich called out. He took a position on one side of the hallway, and then proceeded to "slice the pie" as he crept out from the hallway corner and held his Glock out, slightly

138

canted, waiting to see a sign of a bad guy waiting at the other end. "Clear!" he shouted once satisfied.

Lieutenant Hennessey called, "Anyone down there, you better drop to the floor and don't make a move! We're coming in!"

The others moved up. They waited for the lieutenant's signal. He held up all five fingers on his left hand, then squeezed them into a fist.

They filed down the hallway in a bounding overwatch, advancing quickly and clearing a bathroom that had a floor littered with the empty cylinders of toilet paper rolls and grime growing up out of the shower and onto the curtain.

"I've got movement!" shouted Klein. "Runner! Runner! Out the window!"

The Yeti was halfway out the bedroom window, stumbling blind and mostly deaf for the moment. Klein and Vaulstid got hold of him by his robe, yanked him back, and flung him to his cluttered floor. The big, skinny creature twisted and screamed like a banshee caught, not knowing what had hold of him and clawing at their helmeted faces. Klein grabbed an arm and twisted it so that Basil flipped over, and Vaulstid placed a knee on the Yeti's lower back.

"This place fucking stinks," someone called out. "I can smell it through my helmet. How is that possible?"

"Clear!" someone else called. Then others followed.

"Clear!"

"Clear!"

"You have the right to remain silent," Klein was saying as he was putting on the cuffs. "Anything you say can and will be used against you in a court of a law. You have the right to an attorney—"

"Hey-hey, look at us!" Heinrich laughed when he came into the room. "We caught ourselves a Yeti!" Everyone laughed.

Kaley was very tired, but couldn't fall asleep. She was glad to see that Shannon and the other girl could, though. *Or, at least, they're pretending to be.* Kaley actually hoped that was the case, because it meant they were trying to lull their attackers into complacency.

This was actually Kaley's new plan. She wouldn't show any sign of aggression, no kind of trickery. She would appear docile. *Playin' possum*, as Nan would've said, though Kaley still wasn't entirely sure what that saying meant. Living in the Bluff her whole life, she didn't think she'd ever seen a possum. But she had gotten the gist of what it meant. *The guy on the* Discovery Channel *that one time said that if you ever get attacked by a bear, you should play dead.* Same principle as playing possum. Trick the predators. Lull them into a false sense of security. Then, when there was an opening, and the time was right…

But, as much as she was hoping Shannon was pretending, too, she couldn't be sure. Kaley wasn't close enough to truly sense what was going on inside Little Sister's mind or heart. And the other girl, the familiar-looking one holding her locket, she was too petrified to think or feel anything more than dread.

The vehicle slowed down. Kaley looked out the window. They were in another unfamiliar part of town, pulling into a row of buildings she didn't know at all.

Oni, still in the front, said something to the driver in that weird language. The driver laughed and looked in his rearview mirror at Kaley. Kaley looked away. She'd been trying to recall all the landmarks she could in case she needed to run—streetlights, a Waffle House, a liquor store that seemed to be simply called Liquor Here—but most of it was starting to run together. She had remembered the number of turns, and the order they had been in, though: left, right, right, left, right, left, and now right.

Her eyesight was good enough to see the lit-up dashboard up front, too. Kaley had watched the green-lit mileage counter go from 46,819 to 46,828. *Nine miles*, she thought. *Just nine miles.* She hoped all of this information would be useful eventually.

Kaley didn't know it, but she was trying to prevent her premonition from coming true.

7

When the black SUV pulled into Hillside, Leon knew at once that it was a G-man's ride.

They were just finishing putting the cuffs on the Yeti when the SUV pulled to a stop behind the Aerostar minivan, which was parked without anyone inside. So far, all he'd heard on the radio was that the SWAT guys inside had found O'Connor alone. That meant no Pelletier. *Fucker got away.* For a moment, for just a second, Leon wondered if Pat had called ahead to warn Pelletier. But he didn't think Pat was that stupid. He didn't want any more trouble than this Pelletier might've already brought him.

Two black men and one white man hopped out of the SUV. All of them wore street clothes. One of the black men had a beard. These men doubtless performed various undercover tasks, but tonight they were flaunting what they were. Their jackets were the only thing not normal street attire; they had the yellow FBI letters written across the backs and the left breast.

The bearded black man nodded at Leon and said, "You Hulsey?"

"That's me."

"Special Agent Jamal Porter," he said, shaking hands without looking at Leon. The first thing Leon noticed was that Porter's cologne was very strong. He had intense eyes fixed on the doorway of apartment 448. He introduced the others still without looking at the detective. "Agents Mortimer and Stone," he said of the white man and other black man, respectively.

"Guys." He nodded to them, and they nodded back, saying nothing.

"Pelletier inside?" Porter asked.

"Doesn't look like it."

Porter hissed by breathing in through his teeth. "God damn it. Anybody see him?"

"Got some officers canvassing neighbors right now," Leon said, trying to keep his tone from sounding defensive and failing.

"Where'd this lead come from?"

Careful, Leon. Careful. "Street-level informant. One of mine." He knew that he had, on some level, mentioned that last bit as a means to establish that he knew this territory well. It was another automatic defensive gesture.

"What's his name?"

"Deep cover. Can't divulge it." Part of him counted on his large, imposing body to do as it had always done, and shut the other man up.

"You can if he's got information about Spencer Pelletier, Detec—"

"He didn't have information about Spencer Pelletier specifically," Leon lied. He thought, *The things we do for family.* "He gave a description. I thought it sounded familiar. I went to FBI-dot-gov and showed my informant the picture from the guy who did the six guys in Baton Rouge. I thought it was a long shot, but it turns out I was lucky as hell. He IDed Pelletier—and this informant is never wrong—but said he didn't know him by that name, and didn't know him before last night," he lied again. "He said the guy was looking for Basil O'Connor."

Agent Mortimer, the white one, spoke up. "Who is this O'Connor guy?"

"Not entirely sure," Leon said. That part was true, for the most part. He knew O'Connor was somehow connected to Pat's operation, and knew he'd worked in forgeries a few years back but didn't know to what extent. "My informant has worked in a certain capacity with O'Connor before, though, and reported suspicious behavior to me, but nothing serious." That was true, too. Though "report" was a strong word. Pat had pretty much told him some street gossip that occasionally had the name Yeti or Basil attached to it.

"Detective?" someone called out. It was Hennessey, stepping out of 448 with his MP-5 slung at his side and his Glock re-holstered. He was speaking formally of Leon, not using his first name, because the G-men were present. Leon and Hennessey had unconsciously assumed the stations of a unified front against feds

142

taking over their case. "You might wanna see this, Detective Hulsey."

"What's up, Lieutenant?"

"I tell you, it's a God damn mess in there. The place is a fucking wreck. It's…just come look at it."

"Mind if we sneak a peek with you?" Agent Porter asked.

After hearing that, Leon wondered if he'd been too hasty in automatically assuming he would have to fight to keep his clout in this investigation. It seemed as though Agent Porter was trying to show a gesture of peace and cooperation. "Sure," Leon said. "Why not? Let's all go take a look."

The Yeti's home was an utter disaster, with random patches of organization that only made the scene more bizarre. An odor reached out beyond the open door, so pungent that the brain and the olfactory nerves never really learned to ignore it. The big man himself was sitting on his ass on the floor, his robe spread wide open and his balls completely hanging out of his stained white briefs.

Leon said nothing. He'd never seen so much junk in all his life. He glanced over to the G-men. Agent Porter and his two pals were looking about the apartment with mild interest. One of them, Stone, had gone directly over to a pile of computers, printers and stacked manila envelopes. A nest of wires clung all around the nearest wall by a mix of duct and electrical tape.

Sergeant Warwick was bent down to one knee, asking a few basic questions about the Yeti's well-being, just making sure that he was recovering suitably from the effects of the flash-bang grenades. So far, he just gazed with tired, indolent eyes at something on his foot.

"Bunch o' H," someone said beside Leon. He turned, and found Heinrich offering him a tin *My Little Pony* lunchbox that was opened and filled with a bag of eight-balls and hypodermic needles. "Vaulstid said there's more in the back. I'll bet there's a lot more hidden all over this apartment."

"There's a lot over here," said Agent Mortimer, who had joined Stone by the computer array. "Not heroin, but a whole lot of forging going on."

Leon walked over. He pulled his rubber gloves from his back pocket, slipped them on, and started rummaging through the piles of what looked like garbage, but was one man's livelihood. Agent Mortimer had moved aside a 2009 edition of *The Merck Manual of Medical Information*, and was lifting a packet filled with driver's licenses. The pictures were mostly of black men and they came from all over: Houston, Hackerville, Las Vegas, Cumming, Jonesboro, Lafayette, Tutte, Kansas City, Thomasville, Milwaukee, on and on.

"Laminate over here," Agent Stone said, lifting up sheets of plastic, no doubt used to seal a phony license in place. "This kind of laminate is good to use for holograms on a driver's license. Various kinds of ink over there." He pointed. There was an enormous toolbox on the other side of the computer desk, hitherto concealed by a mound of clothes. The toolbox was filled with inks and tools necessary to emboss or add complex designs to a driver's license.

There was Teslin and Artisyn NanoExtreme paper, some butterfly laminate pouches, a thermal pouch laminator, and an encoder to encode the magnetic strip on each pouch. There was a pigmented based inkjet printer, an Epson printer with DuraBrite ink, pretty much the best for making fake IDs. There was also plenty of Pearl-Ex paint and Photo-EZ paper for creating convincing holograms. There were numerous books on how to manipulate images on Adobe Photoshop. There was also sandpaper. Only the best forgers went through the trouble of sanding down holograms to remove the jagged edes on the synthetic paper.

Some of the IDs Leon saw were EDLs, Enhanced Driver's Licenses, made with the specifications of the new Federal Passport Card, which made a document not just good for proving one could drive, but for proving one's citizenship of the U.S.

"Quite the operation for a pig," said Agent Porter, turning away from it all. "Now let's hear him squeal."

"We still haven't confirmed that it was Spencer Pelletier who was here tonight," Leon reminded him. The G-man stopped and looked at him. "Until we confirm that, this is technically still a local matter of nothing more than a possible kidnapping. Missing Persons has authority and jurisdiction on it. I don't mind you guys hanging around, but I'll ask *my* questions, and then we'll see what we'll see."

To his great surprise, Agent Porter showed no chagrin. He smiled humbly and said, "It sounded bad, didn't it? My fault. It's your ball, Detective."

"No harm, no foul."

"I need to ask you, though…" Porter paused, gave some of the cops and his fellow agents a glance that indicated a private conference would be appreciated. They all obliged and moved away. Agent Porter turned back to Leon, who prepared himself for a line of bullshit. "Detective Hulsey, you *are* aware of why we're here." It wasn't a question.

He shrugged his massive shoulders, which were so thick with muscle they barely moved anymore. "I assume you followed the stolen cars faster than we did."

Porter nodded. "It's been tough, but we've been in touch with several insurance companies and police stations across the South, trying to get a beat on every single stolen vehicle reported. The most promising trail led to Mobile. We knew that Pelletier had old contacts in Atlanta, so we hopped on a plane and tried to head him off. We were just getting into contact with the Atlanta Police Chief when the report of the Tacoma came in through the system. We lost track of the stolen vehicles somewhere near Troup County, which was where the Tacoma was taken from, so we knew we were getting close. Me and my guys here," he glanced over his shoulder, "we're all pretty high-strung right now."

"I understand, Agent Porter. I do. I know how pissed off a man gets when his target gets away, and I know it's exciting being on the cusp of catching him—"

"But did you know we've been chasing him for two years, ever since he busted out of Leavenworth?"

Leon shook his head. "All I heard on the wire was that he escaped prison years ago, and was a suspect in that shit over in Baton Rouge. Didn't know from which prison or exactly how long ago until you just said." By "on the wire" Leon meant the transcripts and news updates that LEOs (law enforcement officers) got way before the news programs thanks to a New Age network of communications tools modeled after Interpol's ECHELON system. The FBI had hardly gotten it off the ground yet, and already it was showing promise. Atlanta was one of the cities testing the system to see how fast news would travel through law enforcement, and how long the information could be in their hands before the media got wind of it. It could prove vital in getting to the bad guys before they knew they were being hunted.

"I used to work SIS," Porter said. "You know what they do?"

"Sure. SIS is like an FBI inside the prison system. Investigates prison gangs and plots inside the joint."

"Yes. We were very upset when Spencer Pelletier escaped us. He did so in a very humiliating way for us, I don't mind telling you. But it was the U.S. Marshalls' jobs to track him down once he was gone, not mine. Then I got into the FBI and it was on again. He's stayed quiet for these two years, and now we're closer than ever to reeling him back in. We've found out a lot about him since he left Leavenworth. Detective Hulsey, he's not what he seems. Not just a thief or a bank robber or a con man. He's a monster. A real one, like they keep writing books about fifty years after they're dead. He's a violent, manipulative killer."

Leon nodded. "You think he had something to do with my two missing girls?"

"It wouldn't surprise me. His goals...well, they're amorphous, let's just say that. Constantly changing. One minute he's a small scam artist, then he's a car thief, then a bank robber, then a car thief again, then aiding in a counterfeit money ring, then performing dead drops for drug dealers, then stealing cars again. He shows a, ah, *proclivity* for switching his game. Very unusual. Most criminals and psychopaths are specialists, not jacks of all trades. But at the same time as he's doing all this, almost as an afterthought, he kills people." The FBI man put his hands in his pockets and looked around at the other officers in the room, as if to make sure none were within earshot. "Lots of them."

Leon considered this for a moment, and figured the man for the kind of guy who knew his job well, and didn't seem like the kind of guy who was given to wild exaggeration. And Leon liked to think he had a perfect bullshit detector.

Then, Porter shrugged, showing marginal doubt. "At least, that's the theory me and my team have been working on. We've found bodies over the last couple of years that, once forensics pinned down approximate times of death, started forming a

146

timeline. A timeline that coincided with another timeline we'd made for tracking Pelletier."

"I never asked you, Agent Porter. What department of the FBI are you in?"

"Serial Killer Task Force."

Leon said nothing as a pair of SWAT officers walked in between them, issuing "excuse mes" as they went past them. He sighed. "Well, let me just talk to my captive over here. I'll see what he knows about my missing girls and your Pelletier. You can listen in and, when I'm done, he's your witness and I'll listen in. Fair?"

"Sounds great to me." Porter smiled, showing a row of perfectly aligned white teeth.

They walked over to the Yeti, who was just now blinking and looking around like a man waking up from a terrible dream, hoping against hope that he wouldn't have to go back there. A couple of forensics guys came in with their equipment—luminol, Dictaphones, lifting tape, ultraviolent flashlights, scalpels, scissors, and of the course the increasingly essential cyber forensics kit. They looked at the Yeti, then at the apartment. Their dismayed faces showed they understood they were in for an all-nighter.

"Mr. O'Connor," Leon said, kneeling in front of him and wincing as his knees popped. There were no chairs that could be easily cleaned off to sit on. "How are we this evening?"

"B-b-been better, I guess," O'Connor said.

"Yeah, I get that. Listen, we have some questions for you." Leon waved a hand around, gesturing generally about the apartment. "So listen, we've found a veritable mountain of evidence here that'll send you away for a long, long time. And we've barely even scratched the surface."

"Wh-who squealed on me, man?"

"It's not important—"

"Who *talked*, nigger?" That last word hadn't been said an invective. It was more desperate and pleading than anything, and junkies will say what junkies will say.

"We're looking for a certain individual," Leon went on, trying to keep this from going anywhere near the name or topic of Patrick Mulley. *The things we do for family*. "We came in search of someone very dangerous, and I believe he left here within the hour."

"S-say nothin' else," O'Connor said. "You came for Spencer Pelletier, you got him."

While Leon masked his surprise, Agent Porter was unable to conceal his own excitement. He knelt down beside Leon quickly, but remained respectfully silent. That was good since, technically, this just became a federal investigation. "Spencer Pelletier? He was here, then? That's what you're saying?"

"Yeah, man. I gave him some stuff."

Leon could put two and two together. "New identities."

"Y-yeah, man."

"What else?"

"I dunno. A cell phone and an address. That's it."

"What cell phone? What address?" Leon had his notepad out, his pen poised to jot. If they had the cell phone's number they could trace it, especially if Pelletier made a phone call anytime soon. Pinging was the latest rage amongst law enforcement, and if a call was made by a known number then it was no longer very difficult at all to find the phone's exact location. Warrants were rarely ever needed, either, thanks to bills like the Patriot Act.

There was a stall here, though. The Yeti, half out of his mind from all the H and the flash-bangs that had disoriented him, now seemed to drudge up something vital from the deepest, darkest recesses of his brain. Survival mode kicked in. "I...I need a lawyer first," he said. "I was read my Miranda, and I w-wanna see some follow-through from that p-part where I'm guaranteed an attorney."

Leon tried to hide his frustration. He furrowed his brow and, once more, counted on his great size and deep voice to be imposing. "Mr. O'Connor, I want you to listen to me very carefully. You can of course have your attorney, but what we're dealing with tonight is time-sensitive. You understand? Two small girls were kidnapped earlier—Kaley and Shannon Dupré. We believe Mr. Pelletier knows something about that. The better you can help us tonight, the better it'll reflect on you in court."

Here, O'Connor's cloudy eyes seemed to have a moment of crystal clarity. Something dawned on him, and he said, "Is this about the Rainbow Room?"

"The what?" Leon said, blanching. His pen started writing automatically.

The Yeti looked between all the law enforcement people standing around with uncertainty. A couple of SWAT officers loomed like towers on either side of him. "You said it was little girls," he said. "I h-heard these guys from L Street talking about the Rainbow Room guys. Th-they started off on Craigslist, then moved and made their own website wh-when things got too hot for them there. They move around a lot b-b-because Interpol's after them. I hear they've got helpers in, like, Germany an' Australia, an' some other countries. They abduct kids, y-you know? Rape them. Tape it all. Put it on the Internet. The more you make the kids cry while, you know, fucking them, the higher your status in the Rainbow Room. The higher your status, the more access you get to all their videos."

Leon just stared; around him, the room seemed to grow quiet. The Yeti had spoken about it all so casually. Leon had known human trafficking was on the rise in Atlanta, but hadn't known they had anything like this on their hands. Could it be true? Certainly Interpol had been busting up operations like this all over the planet in the last ten years, but nothing like it had yet come to Atlanta. At least, not to his knowledge. "Mr. O'Connor, you *know* for a *fact* this is going on?"

"No. Like I said, th-the guys on L Street were telling me. I, uh…I sold them some IDs, all right? Okay? A-and they were asking me how's b-business, how's the money flowin', shit like that." The Yeti licked his lips, and his neck muscles went through spasms, causing his lips to press tight against his teeth and stretch. "They s-said these Rainbow Room guys were involved in some big g-g-gangster types from overseas, and that they were looking for locals to help them get to kn-know the city and snatch some kids off the streets. S-s-s-sounded like bullshit to me, but they warned me not to do business with no ch-child rapists, and I s-s-said of course I wouldn't."

"Who were these guys who told you about the Rainbow Room?"

"Couple o' El Salvador guys who've already split the c-country. This was six m-months ago, man. I haven't seen them since they split and I ain't heard anything else about th-the Rainbow Room since then, so maybe it was all bullshit."

Leon started to ask his next question, but here Agent Porter finally could contain himself no longer. "You mentioned a phone and an address that you gave Pelletier," he said. "Give us those numbers."

There might've been a testy exchange between Leon and Porter if that hadn't just so happened to be what Leon wanted to know, as well.

At first, it seemed like the Yeti wouldn't reply, then he said, "You're...you're for real about s-s-s-some girls gettin' kidnapped, man?" It once again amazed Leon just how quickly criminals and cops could become allies, even if for a moment, all because of the nature of the crime. He shouldn't have been so surprised, though, because the most repugnant things in the criminal underworld were child rapists, especially organized ones.

"We are," Porter said. "We are for real about that, Mr. O'Connor."

The Yeti swallowed hard, and his left eye twitched uncontrollably. "The n-number to the cell I gave him is programmed into my other phones. Bring me one an' I can show you. The address...I c-can't remember it, but it was from the DMV. I don't recall the license plate he had me look up. B-b-but it's the last thing my printer printed out so I can recover it if you'll let me at my computer."

Though he didn't know it, Officer David Emerson still had a part to play on this violent night. A very important part.

The call went out to all vehicles in the area, but it came in to car number 1A4 when Emerson and his partner had pulled into a Steak'n Shake on Elm, just outside of the Bluff. They had finished canvassing all of the neighbors around Dodson's Store—a vain exercise if there ever was one—and had just placed their orders when dispatch gave the all-points bulletin.

"All available units in and around Vine City, please converge on 12 Townsley Drive," came the call from dispatch. Beatrice hollered at the guy taking her order over the speaker to hold up one second while they listened. "Repeat, 12 Townsley Drive. Suspect is Spencer Pelletier. He is believed to be at or on his way to that address. Suspected of multiple murders and wanted for questioning in the abduction of two girls. Move in without sirens or lights. Consider armed and extremely dangerous."

"Well, damn," said David, half let down about missing his meal until he glanced at the computer screen situated at the center of the dashboard. The new computers linked directly to a variety of networks, allowing more than just quick license plate checks and the recording of witness statements. Dispatch had sent a picture of Spencer Adam Pelletier, which filled the screen. An exact match of the description he'd gotten only two hours ago from Terry "Mac" Abernathy. Thirty years old, Caucasian, very pale complexion, 6' 1" tall, 182 lbs., black hair and feral blue eyes. *A predator.* Pelletier stared directly at whoever had taken his prison photo with the ghost of a smirk on his face. *A confident predator.* "All right," he said, tugging on his seat belt. "Let's get moving."

Beatrice didn't offer an apology to the drive-through guy for wasting his time. She pulled right out of the parking lot, flashing her lights briefly to get through a stoplight that was immediately off the Steak'n Shake's property, and then kept them on for the time being.

"This is one-Adam-four, responding to that call for Townsley Drive," David said into the radio.

"Copy that, one-Adam-four. What's your twenty?"

"We are on that side of town about three or four minutes away."

"Ten-four. Be advised that others have called in, but they are farther out so you'll probably be first on scene. Do not approach the house until backup has arrived. Detectives and SWAT are on their way."

"Ten-four, dispatch." David's eyes had been grazing over Pelletier's rap sheet. The computer was touchscreen, and he scrolled his finger to get an overview. "Jesus. This guy's been busy over the last decade."

Beatrice checked her rearview quickly, then zipped into the far right lane. "Oh yeah?"

"Yeah. Armed robbery when he was nineteen. Then a bunch of GTAs, a couple of bank robberies, a prison escape—from

Leavenworth, shit—and some drug-slinging days back in the beginning of it all. FBI addendum says he's now suspected of…waaaaaaait…holy shit!"

"What?" Beatrice said. "What is it, partner? Don't leave me in suspense."

"You heard about that shit over in Baton Rouge?"

"Yeah."

"They're saying he's suspect *numero uno* in it all," David said, reaching for his pistol. He glanced up to look at the street signs. They were on Glenwood, a mile and a half from Townsley, which he knew to be an out-of-the-way little hole in the wall around Fenton Park, a failed dog park that had turned into a failed community park a decade ago. There was a small forest all around that area and empty duplexes that were filled with crackheads. APD sometimes had to chase them out like cockroaches when the lights came on. David had helped with that a few times.

The trees hid everything that goes on back there at Townsley. *Like a bandit cove*, David thought. *It always reminded me of a bandit cove.* Two dead bodies and a stash of money found there within the last year helped that fantasy along.

A few specks of rain hit the windshield in a small burst. Beatrice switched the wipers on then off. Townsley Drive was ahead on the left.

The neighborhood wasn't just quiet, it was dead. Spencer killed the lights and pulled to a slow stop as soon as he spotted the two familiar vehicles parked in the front yard of the only house on the right.

He switched the car off and sat there, taking a moment to look around. There were lights on inside the house, but no sign of movement. His window was rolled down but he heard no sounds, either.

There was a body lying facedown in front of the porch. "Huh," he chuckled. "You don't see that every day, either."

Spencer had found two packs of Tic Tacs and a pack of gum in the middle console while driving. He took out a piece of Wrigley's spearmint and popped it in his mouth. A dog barked someplace off in the distance. There was the distant roar of a jet plane somewhere. A fire truck siren blew far, far away. Wind blew lightly, pushing a forgotten page of coupons slowly across the street.

A song of the night, he thought, reminiscing about another neighborhood he'd known like this.

He glanced across the street to a dilapidated home that looked like it hadn't been occupied since the Great Depression. The trees all around both homes ensconced this little zone of the city from everything but a helicopter pilot's view.

This was one of those Forgotten Places. That's what Hoyt Graeber had called them. Hoyt, ever the criminal philosopher and the man that had introduced Spencer to the criminal lifestyle, had spoken of places like these. Wilderness survival experts, some of which Spencer would encounter in his brief, one-year fascination with primitive survival skills, called these areas "dead spaces," and said that some dead spaces were large and some were small. They allowed people to hide in plain sight. A dead space might only be the corner of a room that psychologically most people were *incapable* of looking at when they first entered, or a dead space might be an entire neighborhood or road that people drive by their whole lives and rarely look at, even if they live in the area.

Forgotten Places, he thought. *Dead spaces*. Both were adequate descriptions here.

Spencer savored the spearmint gum a couple seconds longer, then hopped out of the sedan and pulled out his Glock. "Here we go." He approached in a crouch, with his weapon at ready-low position. He moved first behind the El Camino, peeking through the windows and seeing nothing but a sawed-off shotgun in the floorboard. The window was rolled down and he reached inside to lift it. "Yoink," he whispered with juvenile glee after checking to see if it was loaded. He moved on to the Expedition. Nothing of note inside there.

Spencer tucked the Glock back in his waistband and held the shotgun firmly in his hands. He sidled between the Expedition and the porch, made it to the house, and pressed his back against the wall. He looked at the dead body at the foot of steps. It was a black man with cornrows wearing a black leather jacket and sagging jeans. They'd sagged enough upon his death to show the crack of his ass. Spencer smiled. *Wonder if he knew how the sagging pants fad started. Wonder if he ever knew it was for fags advertising themselves for sex in prison.*

Still chewing, he peeked through a screen door into a living room with more dead bodies. The first he saw was another black man lying face-up on the floor near the door, his eyelids slightly parted, his head tilted unnaturally and in a way that allowed Spencer to see that his eyes had rolled back. "Fee-fi-fo-fum, how many motherfuckers tried to run?" he chuckled.

This was probably one of the most exciting moments of his entire life, second only to the suspense he'd felt while walking out of Leavenworth, wondering if the guards would recognize him and send him back inside.

He savored the spearmint a moment longer, then tentatively opened the screen door. Thankfully, the hinges didn't squeak too much. He stepped inside and moved to a nearby TV stand to take cover.

He waited.

After ten seconds, he stood to move. He saw a dead man relaxing in a recliner and a sad-looking crumpled body lying dead on the other side of the TV stand, the man's cornrows drenched in blood. He crept through the house, moving slowly at first, but then faster and with more recklessness. If anyone was here then they probably knew he was here, too. *Better to move quickly and take them by surprise.*

Another dead body was in the kitchen, and another splattered all over the wall in the bedroom.

"God damn," he laughed, lowering his gun. "If I'd known you guys were gonna have *this* much fun tonight, I would'a followed you assholes."

At the very end of the hall, he found a room that was mostly empty except for a space heater and a scattering of small children's toys tossed helter-skelter on the floor. A ceiling fan blew lonely for no one. A Marilyn Manson poster adorned one wall, but the rest of the walls were naked.

Spencer walked back to the bedroom and approached the body of the man lying on the other side of the bed. Beside him was a paper bag. He guessed there was one of three things inside:

booze, drugs, or money. It was the latter. Four grand in hundred-dollar bills.

He shoved the money into his hoodie's belly pocket and knelt by the body to check it, laying the shotgun across his knee. It looked like a twenty-year-old skinny gangsta wannabe. He wore gold chains and a long silver necklace with a dollar sign wreathed in diamonds. A single bullet had entered his chest. He wasn't bleeding that much on the inside, which meant it was a very bad story for his insides. Or was it? Spencer reached out to check for a pulse. Just as he was realizing that he might be feeling a faint beat, the eyelids parted, and Spencer pressed the shotgun to the kid's forehead.

"Help..." the wannabe whimpered. His facial expression never changed. If he didn't have enough energy to move his body or face, then he didn't have long. "Help...help me...I..."

One of the chains on the thug's chest held a cross. *Of course, because what sort o' gangster would he be if he didn't worship the Almighty?* Spencer reached down and lifted the golden cross, held it up to his face so the thug could see. "Any sins to confess, my son?"

The eyes were pleading. Drool fell from his lips, drool that was slightly red. In the faintest of whispers, he said, "Help me...just...please..."

"Nuh-uh. Don't work like that, son. I need me some sins confessed. Now, you're shot pretty bad and you're probably gonna be meeting Tupac pretty soon. You can confess your sins an' meet him with a clear conscience. Or, you can take your chances and end up in hell with only Insane Clown Posse fans to keep ya company. An' *those* are some dumbasses."

"Please," the thug whimpered. His eyes glistened. There was perhaps enough moisture for tears. Perhaps.

"The Bible says we're all bound in error, homey," Spencer said. "You won't be the first fella to confess somethin' he ain't proud of."

"Please...just..."

"What's it gonna be, nigga?"

The eyes closed for good. Yet still, the lips moved. "Rainbow...Rainbow   Room...don't know...talk...Yevgeny...Yevgeny..."

"Yevgeny? I'm hearing Yevgeny?"

"Yeah…yeahhhhh…"

"Yevgeny who?"

"Served time…with Yevgeny…my boy…he's my boy…"

"I'm sure you're good friends," Spencer said hastily. "What's Yevgeny's last name?"

Nothing but a faint hiss came from the man's teeth, but then the lips moved a little. Spencer leaned in, put his ear right next to the dying man's lips. He heard something so low it could scarcely be called a whisper. Something like *Tiddov* or *tits off*. There was a last breath. Then a loud, low groan passed from the thug's nether regions, and the room was filled with an acrid odor.

There were three sharp, violent spasms from the thug's body, and he went silent. Spencer held his nose and stood to leave, but paused to watch the body go through two more sharp spasms. *Somebody taught him how to walk, how to talk, how to read and how to write. They taught him how to add, subtract, multiply and divide. Probably taught him how to apply for a job, too. And now he's here. He gave his last words to me. I breathed in the last breath that he breathed out. An' who the fuck am I?*

It was one of those thoughts that had Dr. McCulloch write down a word in his file that Spencer thought rather interesting: *pensive*. Dr. McCulloch might've been onto something there. At such moments when others would be shocked or sickened, Spencer was dreamy, wistfully thoughtful, and often found humor.

Spencer broke the spell on himself and moved quickly through the rest of the house, checking cupboards for any extra cash or drugs that would be easy to sell later. He was constantly looking out the windows for the headlights he knew would be coming, and listened for the sirens he knew would be blaring. *Or maybe not. Not if they come silently like they did at Hillside.* Even knowing this might happen, he didn't immediately leave.

In the kitchen, Spencer removed a few suspicious-looking metal containers. He found a blue Folgers Coffee can containing five hundred dollars and a bag of what looked like the ol' aurora borealis (PCP), if he was any judge, and he was. He dropped the cans on the floor after he'd gathered their contents and was headed for the back door.

Then, he heard the front screen door open. Someone was stepping inside. "APD!" they shouted. A woman. "If anybody's in here come out with your hands up!" A few seconds passed while Spencer waited beside the refrigerator in the kitchen. He knelt, shotgun at the ready. "Call an ambulance, I've got more bodies inside the house," she called back to someone else, probably her partner.

The distance between Spencer and the back door was maybe five steps when he'd first made out the woman's voice. There was a straight line-of-sight through the living room to the kitchen, where the back door was. If he stood up right then and went for it, there was a better than excellent chance that the officer would see him, especially if she had already dared to step inside.

"Anybody in here?"

" 'Step into my parlor,' said the spider to the fly," Spencer called out. " 'Tis the prettiest little parlor that you ever did spy.' " If they had him surrounded and he was going to die (and he *would* fight to the death to keep his promise of never returning to the pen), then he would at least have some fun with it.

There was silence for a moment. Then Spencer heard the lady officer mutter the word *shit*. Then she mumbled something low, probably into her radio.

"Come out of the house, walk backwards with your hands up where I can—"

"No, no, silly! Why do *you* come *in*?"

No response.

"C'mon, live a little!"

No response.

"You know, they say a coward dies a thousand deaths!"

No response.

David knew they were supposed to wait for backup, but the body in the front yard had changed things. If the man lying facedown was still alive then he obviously needed medical attention very soon. There was no guarantee that he wasn't an innocent.

They approached after calling in the body and requesting an ambulance. David had paused at the sight of black Nissan sedan. He registered it mentally, realized it was Hulsey's, but discounted that little weirdness right away as he took the lead, moving by cover around the Expedition until he and Beatrice came to the body. Beatrice had moved wordlessly up the porch and pressed up to the wall beside the door.

David checked the man in the yard. No breathing, no pulse. David had just stood up when Beatrice had called out, identifying herself as APD. He winced when he heard her do that. He wished she hadn't, but perhaps she had felt it necessary to keep the heads down of anyone who might be inside and thinking of taking a potshot.

"Call an ambulance, I've got more bodies inside the house," Beatrice hollered at him.

David had his radio out and was doing just that when his partner hollered for anyone inside to identify themselves.

That's when he heard the challenge issued. " 'Step into my parlor,' said the spider to the fly." David's blood went cold for a second. He looked up at Beatrice on the porch, and she looked at him with an "oh no" look on her face. A cowboy. They had a God damn cowboy on their hands and he was willing to die. " 'Tis the prettiest little parlor than you ever did spy.' " The voice was sweet and taunting, like a little girl teasing the person who was *it* in a game of hide-and-go-seak.

"Shit," Beatrice hissed.

They waited a moment. David moved up slowly to the other side of the door, his pistol at ready-low. Beatrice called out another order, but halfway through it they received a fresh taunt from the maniac inside. "No, no, silly! Why don't *you* come *in?*" David looked at his partner. Beatrice looked unnerved. They'd seen some shit in their time, but this scene, this taunt, the genuinely humored voice—even David had to admit it was a bit much. "C'mon, live a little!"

With his right hand, David silently signaled for them to stay put. They were dealing with a volatile individual here. Beatrice nodded her agreement.

Where's that God damn backup?

"You know, they say a coward dies a thousand deaths!"

Where is it?

David did exactly what he'd been trained to do at the academy, in all his pistol courses, and in all his stress courses. He breathed in for a count of four, held it for four seconds, and then exhaled for four seconds.

The doorframe exploded a few inches above his head before he ever arrived at a completely calm state of mind. Splinters ripped into his face, causing him to fall back. The size of the explosion and the sound that came from the house left no doubt in David's mind that it was a shotgun. A second shot ripped through the center of the screen door. Steel pellets slammed into the porch and sent more splinters at his face.

David peeked his gun around the corner with one hand and fired blindly, hoping that if the maniac was charging then he'd either hit or stall him. He fired several times, never counting the rounds he let off. When he finished, he touched his face with his left hand, and it came away with blood on it. The pain was like intense wasp stings all over his left cheek, and he worried that bits of his face had been torn off. He wouldn't know until he checked a mirror.

"Beatrice!" he yelled. "You hit?" No response. "Bee?" Specks of wood had gone into his eyes, he couldn't keep them open, and what he could see was blurry. "Bee, talk to me! Are you hit? You with me, Bee? Bee!"

"*Ffffffffffuuuuuuuuuuuuuuck!*" someone shrieked. He knew it had to be Beatrice, but the voice wasn't familiar at all.

David rubbed at his eyes profusely. His heart was hammering in his chest. "Beatrice! You hit?"

"*Shit yes!*"

"Where?"

"My fucking hand! My fingers are gone, Dee!"

In all the craziness, David had forgotten what ought to come next. He touched his radio and shouted into it. "Officers down! Repeat, officers down at 12 Townsley Drive! Send more ambulances!"

David wanted to walk over to Beatrice, but if he crossed the doorway (what many LEOs called the "fatal funnel") then he'd be exposing himself to any gunmen inside. Beatrice was moaning, but said nothing else. He told her to stay calm, to keep taking deep breaths, that it would all be all right soon.

Then, from somewhere in the woods to his right, David caught words on the wind. They came from someone retreating. "Fast as fast can be, you'll never catch me!"

"*Fuuuuuuuck you!*" Beatrice screamed.

When the vehicle stopped, Oni was the first one to get out. No one else moved. Kaley sat perfectly still with only a glance back at her sister, who still hadn't opened her eyes. The last street sign she'd seen read Umway Street.

We're on Umway Street, she thought. Though again, she didn't know of it, and what she would do with this information was quite beyond her.

Directly ahead was a large brick house, one that looked like it had once been impressive but was now as run down as the rest of the neighborhood they had passed through. A number of deciduous trees just starting to lose some of their leaves were lined on each side of the street like sentries, all of them evenly spaced, watching to make sure Kaley and the other two girls did not escape. Probably once, there had been great order in this neighborhood. Those trees had been planted in just such a way. But the neighborhood was now likely leagues away from what it had been. Trash along the gutters told Kaley that it had been quite a while since this area had been on a city street sweeper's regular route.

The house that Oni had just stepped into had cracked windows. There was a second storey, but the windows there were all boarded up. On one side of the house, someone had spray-painted a large penis with testicles in white paint. Someone else had used black paint to send the message **L-Ray runz this shit!!!** but someone *else* had spray-painted a big red X over that.

While they awaited Oni's return (at least, Kaley assumed they were waiting for him), Kaley glanced up the street to the left. She spotted three other houses, only one of them with lights on and that was on the top floor of the farthest house. *If that person in that upstairs room only knew that we were here, and that we needed help, we'd be all right.*

But Kaley checked herself. She didn't know that for sure. Whoever these men were, they obviously had friends. It might be that this whole neighborhood was loyal to them.

She swallowed. Her jaw was beginning to seriously hurt because the gag had been biting into it now for...well, what time was it?

Kaley looked at the glowing clock on the dashboard. 2:13 AM.

She heard snoring behind her. She looked back to see Shannon fast asleep. *Good, let her sleep through it all.* Kaley was still fooling herself into thinking that the vision she'd glimpsed tonight before stepping into Dodson's Store would not come to pass. It's important to hold out hope, and sometimes it's important to lie to oneself. At least, this was wisdom she would stumble upon much later.

The SUV remained dead silent.

Umway Street. Remember Umway Street.

Then, up front, a phone rang in the driver's jacket pocket. He fetched it out and said, *"Allo."* Someone said something on the other line. Somehow, Kaley sensed that it was Oni calling from inside. *"Govori pazhaluista gromche,"* he said. A few words from Oni. The driver glanced in the rearview mirror at Kaley, eyeing her. *"Ya ne znayu,"* he said. *"Net. Net. Olga doma?"* A few seconds went by with Oni talking a lot on the other end. *"Da. Peredayte ey chto zvonil Mikhael."*

In the silence of the car, Kaley could make out the silence on the phone. Oni wasn't speaking anymore. When a voice did return to the phone, she could hear that it was distinctly female. *"Allo."*

The driver said something very rapidly. When he was finished, he said, *"Ya bystro gavaryu?"*

He got an answer. It was short. Then, he started talking fast again. After a few seconds, he hung up and said to the men in the back, *"Baz prablem."*

One of the men, the jaundiced one, said, *"Vsyo v poryadke?"*

"Net. Baz prablem."

Kaley thought that word *prablem* sounded an awful lot like *problem*. She wondered if there was an issue between all the involved parties here that she might exploit. After all, hadn't Oni just killed half a dozen co-conspirators of his? Maybe there was something in this she could use.

The doors opened, and Kaley was hauled out. The jaundiced man kept an iron grip on her elbow and had a pistol out, though so far he hadn't pointed it at her.

Immediately, Kaley's attention was turned to the back of the SUV. Her heart ached as she saw her little sister and the other little girl lying there, both their eyes shut, being grabbed by their arms and pulled out of the rear. Shan barely stirred. Her eyelids barely parted as the bad men lifted her and put her on the ground, where her feet touched so lightly that surely she was still half asleep. Shannon let out a single, somnolent moan. *She's really exhausted to sleep through all this*, Kaley thought. *Exhausted because it's way, way past her bedtime, or else emotionally exhausted by all the—*

That thought was dashed in an instant. Kaley felt what would happen next. She both saw it via the charm and felt it via the Anchor. She was close enough for the Anchor. Something swelled up inside her sister, something tiny that quickly became volcanic. It hit Kaley like a fist to her gut.

It all happened so fast she barely registered it. One minute the driver was yelling something to Oni, who had stepped out of the house for a minute and was calling to him from the front door, and the next minute Shan suddenly punched one of the men in his balls with a viciousness she had never seen in her sister before. It was all so sudden that the man holding her elbow let go and she was off. He would've snatched Shan's pigtails at once if Kaley hadn't acted. Big Sister threw herself bodily onto the large man, who staggered backwards, trying to recover from the attack on his groin and Kaley's dead weight.

RUN! she sent to her sister. *RUN! DON'T LOOK BACK! JUST GO!*

The nameless other girl squealed and dropped stupidly to the ground, looking at Shannon's retreating little body with a mixture of hope and dread.

Kaley wrestled with the big man, who finally grabbed her by the throat, hauled her off the ground and slammed the back of her head on the pavement. The wind was knocked out of her, and she almost swallowed the bundled cloth in her mouth. She twisted her head around so that she could see Shannon get away from—

There was a gunshot. It was deafening. Shannon dropped face first on the pavement, and for a second Kaley screamed through her gag and almost choked on the cloth again. She knew her sister had been shot. She knew it. The little body lay there, motionless. Kaley hadn't felt Little Sister's death as she had Nan's, and didn't feel the still-dying sensation as she had from those thugs back in that house of death, but her mind told her the truth.

Shannon, her gorgeous, most valuable possession, was dead. Kaley's life was over. Without Little Sister, there was no life. Such a simple yet elegant truth, it could never be denied, because Mom was no kind of mom at all. Ricky was gone. These men were going to take her places, make her do things…and without Little Sister—

It's a mercy, she told herself. *Better off dead than with these monsters.*

Then, her eyes showed her something that her charm already knew. Shannon moved. She wasn't dead. Kaley looked over to her right. The jaundiced man was standing there, pistol in hand, aimed at the air. The barrel was smoking. He had fired a warning shot at Shan. "Come back now, little girl!" he cried, and aimed the gun down at Kaley. "Or I kill sister!"

"It doesn't matter!" Kaley tried to scream. "Run, Shannon! Run! Don't worry about me! Just run!" But nothing more than garbled screams came out, and poor Shan probably thought they were screams of fear. Little Sister perceived wrongly. She thought Big Sister was terrified for her *own* life.

Kaley's heart sank when she saw Shannon stand, turn, and take her first step back towards them, almost as bad as it had sank when she thought Little Sister was dead. Oni ran across the yard, looking left and right, probably concerned with who might've heard the shot. He snatched Shannon up by her arms and flung her over his shoulder.

Someone shouted from somewhere behind Kaley. It was a woman. *"Vsyo v poryadke?"*

"Da!" Oni shouted. He pointed to the jaundiced man and the driver, and then pointed to Kaley and the nameless girl. He gave a quick series of commands that Kaley couldn't follow. Shannon was handed off to the woman who came around the side of the SUV. The woman was tall and pale, with long, curly black hair with oily bangs hanging in her eyes. She wore an *American Idol* T-shirt and tattered jeans. For just a moment, seeing Shan handed off to a female gave Kaley hope. But then she saw the supreme look of disgust on this woman's face, and hope faded for the dozenth time this night. *Not a safe female. Not a good one.*

"Prostite chto vas pobespokoil, Olga," said Oni.

Kaley had heard that name said a few times now—at least, she thought it was a name, it was said with a kind emphasis, almost barked—and so she started to think of this woman as Olga. *Who are you, Olga?* Kaley wondered as the jaundiced man jerked her up by the arm. *What are you doing with us? What are you going to do to my sister?*

They started the march inside the house. Kaley walked in between all the men, utterly surrounded. Olga, with Shan in her arms, had taken the lead. At the porch, Shan looked up with tearful eyes. She blinked hopelessly, not knowing what she should do, *if* she should do anything. Kaley tried to send out waves of reassurance, but again, she had to feel it *herself* if she meant for it to feel genuine at all.

Behind her, the other little girl whimpered. Kaley glanced back, and saw that the jaundiced man was walking right in behind her. He had raised up the back of her skirt with one hand and was pinching her butt with his other. Kaley saw the nauseating fear on the girl's face, and for a moment was infected with it herself. The nameless girl wasn't just scared as Kaley was scared, she was near paralyzed.

The screen door creaked open and they stepped inside what would become a true house of horrors that night.

For everyone involved.

The first ambulance to arrive at 12 Townsley Drive had just now sedated Officer Beatrice Fanney. Leon had arrived in a squad car driven by an old beat cop friend of his named Edmond Rosario. He'd radioed dispatch for a lift once he realized his car was stolen. It had pissed him off to no end, but confusion had replaced anger when Edmond had gotten the call from dispatch, saying, "Uh, Officer Rosario, have you Detective Leon Hulsey in the car with you?" When Edmond had confirmed that he did indeed, the dispatch lady had said, "Then you can tell him we found his car. It's at Townsley Drive."

Leon now stood staring at his car. It didn't make any sense at first. None at all. The flashing red-and-blue lights from all the cop cars now present splashed against his Nissan as he went through it all. He found nothing missing. Nothing at all. It wasn't until bodies were being pulled out from the house and the ambulance was speeding Officer Fanney away from the scene that he finally stepped out and said the obvious to himself. "Son of a bitch stole my car."

Special Agent Porter was standing on the porch talking with his fellow agents, who then stepped inside the house. The three of them had arrived way ahead of Leon because he'd been carless. Now Porter walked silently over to him and said, "Seven dead altogether. Fucker who did it was a decent shooter, too. He was firing pretty tight groups. At least he did on the thugs. He fired willy-nilly with a shotgun at the officers."

Leon nodded. He put both hands on the roof of his car and fumed for a moment.

"Find anything missing? Any guns or extra ammo you keep—?"

"No, nothing missing," Leon said. A fire truck honked behind him for one of the patrol cars to get out of its way. "Didn't take my comics or my newspaper. Far as I can tell, nothing's wrong except damage to the ignition cover and the wiring." He took in a deep breath, and fought screaming. Then, he lashed out and kicked the door, denting it significantly. Agent Porter just watched him. "Motherfucker stole my car. *Had* to be a coincidence. But what are the fucking odds?"

"*Maybe* it was coincidence," Porter said, shrugging.

Leon pushed himself away from his car. "But you don't think so."

Again, Porter shrugged.

"Tell me. What's going on here tonight?"

"Nothing out of the ordinary for this individual," Porter said.

"I'm going to have to ask you to try better than that, Agent Porter," Leon said, taking a step towards the other man. Leon knew he was a big man, and had always noticed how people moved out of his way whenever he walked, well, *anywhere*. Hallways, restaurants, sidewalks, anywhere. But Agent Porter had obviously seen a lot in his time, had been intimidated by some of the best, and worst, pieces of shit that the street could regurgitate. He didn't back away even a noticeable millimeter when Leon loomed over him. "Beatrice Fanney is a damn good cop. Always backs up her partners without flinching. All the women *and* men at APD respect her. David Emerson is my friend. A good cop. Cares more than most would about the assholes in the Bluff. So I'm pissed off. But there's also seven bodies to account for, all murdered. Who the fuck is this guy? I'm not gonna ask you again."

"Con man, escape artist, psychopath. That's all I can—"

"Details."

At first, Agent Porter appeared reluctant. He looked over his shoulder, perhaps to make certain that his fellow agents were adequately busy for the moment. He touched Leon's elbow, a gesture that no one had done since his mother when he'd been in trouble, and started to guide him away from the hubbub. Hennessey and his SWAT team were now on the scene and were moving through the nearby woods with search dogs. Townsley Drive, a bleak zone of forgotten prospects before tonight, now had life churning through it again.

"I don't see any reason why I can't shed a little light on some of the details," Agent Porter said. "But there are parts that...well, aren't something we want as public record. I'll tell you which parts those are and why we don't want them known yet."

Leon nodded. This was a start, at least.

"Spencer Adam Pelletier killed his first victim when he was thirteen years old," Porter said. "He attacked and killed a kid named Miles Hoover after he had said something to some other kid named Roberto Castillo. Castillo was new to the country, fresh over from Mexico, and Hoover thought it was funny to mock his thick Spanish accent. Now, there is absolutely no indication that Pelletier and Castillo were ever friends, but one day, in science class, Pelletier told Hoover to lay off Castillo. Hoover was a pretty big kid, but Pelletier had been held back a bit in school even though he'd shown to be very smart in previous grades, so he was as big as Hoover. But Hoover didn't take his threat seriously. He laughed at Pelletier and started calling him a fag and shit like that. Then one day, Pelletier attacked Hoover in the school library.

"Now, Pelletier didn't just *attack* this kid. He moved in a way that showed careful preplanning and finesse. See, once a week, second period classes were required to take the kids to the library to get a new book. To promote reading, right? Well, according to other students, Pelletier had noticed that Hoover always asked to go to the bathroom right as the class was returning from the library. Pelletier had checked out a book a week previously, and neglected to exchange it. We believe it was intentional neglect, because he used it as an excuse to return to the library very quickly, alone, to drop the book back in the return box, sparing him a late fine.

"Pelletier had a plastic zip tie in his pocket when he left the classroom. He timed it so that Hoover would be on his way to the bathroom—Hoover was one o' these kids who always tried to get outta class all the time, for any reason, for any amount of time he could finagle. Always asking to go to the bathroom when he really didn't need to, complaining he was sick, shit like that. Pelletier knew that Hoover would cut through the library on his way back from the bathroom, like most kids did.

"There wasn't anybody in the library at the time. It was closed during those hours, but the door was almost always left unlocked. Again, something Pelletier knew. All the kids knew it. He was *counting* on it. And when Hoover dipped into the dark library, we can imagine Pelletier probably stepped out from behind a bookshelf or a desk, and then put the zip tie around Hoover's neck and squeezed it tight before Hoover could put up much of a fight. Hoover suffocated to death while Pelletier watched.

Pelletier used a pair of scissors from the librarian's desk to cut the zip tie off and then returned to his classroom.

"Miles Hoover's death was determined a murder right away—the ligature marks, right?—and after a few weeks' worth of investigation a detective got it out of a few kids that Hoover and Pelletier had been upset with one another, and Pelletier had been gone at that exact time of death. When asked what he'd done, Pelletier didn't deny it. In fact, he laughed. According to the reports, he laughed until tears came out of his eyes and he couldn't catch his breath."

Leon and Agent Porter had been walking very slowly away from the crime scene, over to the rundown home on the opposite side of the street. The large detective pulled to a stop, nodding thoughtfully. "They try him as an adult?"

"Nope," said Porter, smiling strangely. "See, Pelletier was a psychopath before very many people really understood that psychopaths are *born*, not grown. They can't be changed, can't be made to empathize with anyone—they have absolutely no empathy. And since a person can't just grow a conscience, there was no hope for him. Not ever. But, people didn't know it back then, and even today many counselors and shrinks are reluctant to curse a kid for life by branding him or her a psychopath. They wanna believe all kids can get help.

"Pelletier was able to convince people that it was all innocent, that he was just playing a game with Hoover, that they were even doing 'something gay together' as he put it. Erotic asphyxiation, shit like that. It had just gone too far, that's all. And since he'd been held back in school, he was able to play like he was partially touched in the head. Confused the courts bad enough that he was first placed into a wilderness therapy program in Utah—that's, you know, where they take kids out in the middle o' the woods and try to analyze them while reconnecting them with nature, gets them away from drugs, or their lives as prostitutes, all that shit—and then from there he went to a boarding school.

"Pelletier fucked up in boarding school, too. Stabbed an instructor in the cheek with a pencil. Then he was sent to a youth reformatory in Roarke, Colorado, which he stayed at until he was eighteen. It was his last chance, and he did *incredibly* well there. Of course this was long, long before people fully understood that

168

psychopaths are incredible liars and manipulators—there's evidence that, while at the reformatory, he got a few of the guards upset at one another, convinced one of them that another guard was lying about some money borrowed, or some such. Just like a psychopath to spread discord, pit one friend against another.

"So, he got out of the reformatory a model inmate-patient," Porter went on. "It's not *entirely* clear what happened next—the file on his life at the bureau has been mostly pieced together by me since I took this case—but it seemed he hooked up at some point with an old friend of his from school named Hoyt Graeber. Now, Graeber was just one o' these kids who got involved slinging dope early, a jab here, a jab there, and eventually developed enough skill at it that he got recognized by Rico Nashton. Heard of him?"

Leon squinted, thinking. "Sounds familiar."

"Nashton was one of the guys who—"

"Oh, right! The Gold Club." The Gold Club was a strip joint in Atlanta that received national attention back in 2001 for the indictments of several of the owners, managers and employees. The place had been shut down for a while now, but another place called the Gold Room had opened in its place. "Nashton was caught moving drugs through some of the strippers there, right?"

"That's right," Porter said. "Pelletier and his friend Graeber were involved with Nashton's operation for a number of years, just long enough for Pelletier to pick up a few tricks. First he started driving cars full of heroin across from Mexico into the States, and through these interactions he met the kind of individuals who could teach the fundamentals and advanced techniques of the criminal lifestyle—useful info like robbing a bank on Fridays because that's when they got their money, to using knock-off capecitabine, which is a chemotherapeutic pillthat makes your hands peel and makes it so that you never leave any fingerprints.

"In 2001 Nashton takes a hit, gets sent to the pen for a dime, and the Gold Club shuts down. Graeber overdosed on his own H six months later. That left Pelletier alone. At that point, he disappeared from all public records. He probably had fake IDs— maybe taken from this O'Connor fucker, or somebody like him. We don't know where he went, but when he reemerged on the grid a few years later he was armed with all sorts of new techniques.

We called him Musashi for a while after that. You know who that is?"

Leon thought for a moment. "Japanese swordsman, right? Samurai?"

"Yeah. A *ronin*. A wandering samurai with no master. One of the guys at the bureau, Hector Freedman, was a history buff, did some shinkendo—that's a Japanese sword-fighting style—and read all about Miyamoto Musashi. Apparently Musashi was only a decent swordsman, but then he disappeared into the wilderness for several years, and when he came back he was unstoppable. Nobody knows what happened to Musashi during that time, just like we don't know what happened to Pelletier during his little self-imposed exile. He was into this and into that. One minute it was a counterfeit scheme that netted him a hundred grand, then it was a sizable drug deal that gave him two hundred more.

"Pelletier was all over the map with his scams. He's one mercurial son of a bitch, this guy. Fickle. Changes his game constantly. The bureau first picked up on him doing this scam where he created this website for men living secretly with homosexuality. He sent out fliers and shit. He got a few dozen responses. Pelletier pretended to be a conflicted young man looking for an older gay gentleman to show him the ropes. He would get replies from all over, everything from dirty old men living in log cabins and poring over the Internet for company, to some wealthier, established guys with families. He focused on the wealthy family men because they had more to lose by being exposed. He revealed who he was to them and started blackmailing them, threatening to expose their secret unless they paid X amount. Got away with this for a full year, made some good cash and then split when one of his victims finally got up enough guts to go to the police. FBI figured out who it was by tracking the IP addresses of the websites he created, finding where his base of operations was, which was some apartment building in Biloxi, and then getting a copy of his photo ID from the landlords and running his face through facial-recognition programs.

"Pelletier's face was now in the FBI's National Registry system. His face popped up all over the Bible Belt over the next two years in video surveillance—auto theft, mail-order scams, confidence scams, and some other shit. It wouldn't be until after he escaped Leavenworth that we were able to work out a timeline that matched all of this activity perfectly with a series of murders committed throughout the southern U.S., with a couple up north."

One of the ambulances was leaving with a load of three bodies in body bags. They had just closed up the back of the ambulance and blared their siren just once to tell a few cops to get out of their way. Leon and Agent Porter pressed up against a patrol car to let it pass. "Who were the victims?" he asked.

"Nobodies," Porter said. "Absolute nobodies. *But,* Pelletier's face popped up on a security camera here, a cell phone camera there, and the first few times that it happened to be in the vicinity of a murder that the bureau was investigating was considered a coincidence. But coincidences are only coincidences for so long.

"First one that we *know* of was Kevin Baxter. Forty-two-year-old father of three and devoted husband to a wife dying of stage III-A lung cancer. There's every reason to believe that Pelletier knew this, because he had loaned Baxter some money for unknown reasons—my theory is that Pelletier was trying to break into the loan shark business at that time—but none of Baxter's wife's problems or their children mattered much when, if you believe the forensics guys, he lured Baxter to a meeting in a dark parking lot and beat his brains in with a baseball bat, and then took his body out into the middle of a swamp and dumped it."

"What was the motive?" Leon asked.

Porter didn't answer. Instead, he moved on to the next victim. "Six months later a nurse named Miriam Downey turned up in the Tennessee River outside of Huntsville, Alabama. She was shot twice in the head. She was last seen in the company of a white male by four witnesses who described a person matching Pelletier's description. After forensics came up with an approximate time of death, it matched with the time that Pelletier was confirmed to have been Huntsville, stealing cars for a chop shop that Huntsville PD have since busted up.

"There are four other bodies that we can line up with Pelletier's criminal run through the South. The shit that happened in Baton Rouge was a result of what happened when he was back in CRC, before he was sent to Leavenworth. All signs begin to show that Spencer Pelletier is the most active serial killer in the U.S. A monster that none of us predicted, not even Drew McCulloch, the psychologist at Leavenworth, who we believe was his last victim before Baton Rouge."

Leon's eyes widened. "He killed his prison shrink?"

Here, Porter made a face. "I told you that I would tell you when you were hearing things that haven't been confirmed and shouldn't be repeated. This is one of them. Dr. Drew McCulloch died in excruciating pain a week and a half after Pelletier escaped prison."

"He tracked him down after escaping?" Leon asked incredulously.

Porter shook his head. "No. Poisoned him. At least, a lot of us think so. See, amongst the other two thousand inmates at Leavenworth, Pelletier had kind of *vanished* in a way. He receded into the background, didn't cause any trouble. He was assigned prison work, did it, and didn't complain about it. And sometimes he helped out in the kitchen. The day before his escape, a few prisoners had been caught smuggling in some leaves from rhododendron plants." Leon shook his head, not understanding. Porter explained, "They can be ground into powder, put into a drink or in some food, and they cause excruciating death. You've got them all over Georgia here, especially up north. Indians sometimes used the leaves to commit suicide. Anyways, we *think* Pelletier managed to get some of that into McCulloch's food or drink somehow when he appeared for their last session. Pelletier knew he was getting out, but made sure he took care of McCulloch first."

"Why?"

Porter shrugged.

Leon glanced over at the house, saw the medics still huddled calmly around David Emerson. Leon hadn't spoken with him yet, but the man had looked more pissed off than scared when he first got here. None of David's injuries were serious, he said he just had a lot of stuff in his eyes. The medics were insisting that he go and get checked out for a serious corneal abrasion, but he was still refusing them.

"Jesus," Leon said. "This guy's a fucking maniac."

"Yes," said Agent Porter. The word had the ring of a man who was hearing a theory of his, long held in contempt or at least doubted by his peers and/or upper echelons, finally vindicated. "He passed through the system slick enough in his youth, and obeyed and disappeared frequently enough to become forgotten. But he's a killer. His psych eval in prison and those he underwent in the reformatory point to extreme narcissistic personality disorder, undiagnosed all these years, and coupled with a highly volatile temper. The fights he got into in prison, and the shit that happened with the kid Hoover, were all reportedly over relatively mundane things.

"He tends to build things up in his mind, sees aggression everywhere and in anyone, depending on the weather and the day o' the week, and reacts violently. One of his old pals in Biloxi that we talked to said that Pelletier once said to him, 'I like killing. It makes me feel better about myself.' End quote."

"So what's he doing here?"

"We don't know, really. Running from retribution in Baton Rouge? Maybe he's finally flipped for good? Going on one last final rampage?" Porter shrugged.

"What exactly *happened* in Baton Rouge, Agent Porter?"

"A hit."

"A what?"

"A contract killing. The AB put it out on him for what he did to one of their guys in prison."

"The AB? You mean the Brotherhood?"

Porter nodded.

Leon was about to ask him what exactly their psycho had done to the Aryan Brotherhood when Agents Mortimer and Stone came hustling around the patrol car. "Yo, boss," Mortimer said. "Forensics found a twisted wad of ethnic hair in the back room with the space heater. They said it looks recently pulled out. All of the vics here have short hair. They say its length and the smell of the shampoo used, probably a girl's wad of hair."

"They were here," Leon said. "God damn it, the girls were *here!*" They all absorbed that truth for a moment. Leon looked at the El Camino and the Expedition. "What happened, then? The buyers show up and kill the kidnappers?"

"Hard to say," Porter said, looking around the street. "Seems likely."

Leon turned to him. "What about this...this Rainbow Room, or whatever? You ever heard o' these guys?" They hadn't really had time to discuss it all at the Yeti's place before they each took off for Townsley Drive in their own vehicles, and the fury that Leon had felt his car being stolen (and now discovering that it had been Pelletier who'd taken it) had temporarily pushed the Yeti's words from his mind.

Agent Porter shook his head. "I've never heard of the Rainbow Room before, but I'll be very interested in seeing where this leads. 'Scuse me a sec," he said, reaching into his pocket and pulling out his cell. Someone was sending him a text message, and he sent one straight back. "Well," he sighed. "Fuck me. Just...fuck me. *That's* anticlimactic."

"What is?" Leon asked.

"Spencer Pelletier."

"What about him?"

"I think your boys just shot and killed him five blocks up."

8

The foundation of every society, Spencer had decided long ago, was the same. The Weak had gathered in great numbers in resistance against the Strong. The Strong, formerly in power because of their obvious advantages, were suddenly out in the cold because even a lion can be torn apart by a bunch of mangy dogs. But then, something had happened that had irrevocably changed all societies forever. The Strong-*Minded* had found ways of ruling the Weak, ruling without real physical strength or power or any willingness to get their hands dirty themselves. This left the Strong even more isolated, and gave the Weak a sense that they were truly protected from the Strong for all time.

But the Strong still lived. In pockets and alleyways, at the edge of a city or deep in its heart, hidden away in a chamber where few ever glanced. *Forgotten Places. Dead spaces.* In accordance with the laws of evolution, the Strong had adapted a sense besides the basic five. This sense helped them find these Veins, these lanes and arteries that moved through a city built by the Weak and forgotten.

Even though it had been years since Spencer had really driven the streets of Atlanta, she was still a city. Her curves were the same as all the others. Certain amenities could be found in all the same places. The arteries through which the city's blood (the people) flowed were the same, some were just small and neglected. He found these easily.

Spencer's heart was racing, but only from the run, not from any real adrenal dump. He had dropped the shotgun in the middle of the woods and kept running. He was still tittering to himself.

He paused at the edge of the housing development to allow the patrol car to go past. Only its headlights were on when it passed him, but halfway down the street a spotlight switched on and grazed over the very ditch where he was hiding. The ditch was shallow, but Spencer was confident that as long as he didn't move, he wouldn't be found. The human eye caught movement before it caught color or pattern; that much he remembered from his days studying wilderness survival.

The patrol car slid on by, and once it had turned down another street Spencer hopped up and jogged across to the other sidewalk. He jogged through the back yard of a house that wasn't finished yet and had three squatters sitting in the back over a small fire. Spencer nodded to them amiably, and the three homeless waved back, watching him with incurious eyes. He scaled a chain-link fence and ran through a short patch of trees and sages until he emerged in another Forgotten Place.

There was a park bench to indicate this place had once been inhabited, and an **UNDER DEVELOPMENT** sign to show that it no longer was. Little more than mounds of dirt and flat grassless earth covered this area. There were three large stacks of two-by-fours that looked like they'd been left here since time immemorial. Spencer decided to rest a spell. He pulled up a truncated piece of wood and took a seat in between two of these stacks. He pulled out his cell and pulled up directions on Google Maps.

His stomach groaned. He hadn't eaten since he'd had the burger at Dodson's Store. Cursed with a high metabolism, Spencer was already growing hungry.

Thunder rolled someplace off in the distance, a reminder from a monster in retreat. A few specks of rain fell on him. Spencer checked the time on his cell. 2:32.

Somewhere far off, a gunshot rang out. Then several more in return. He thought, *Somebody else is havin' a bad night.*

The house was a great deal more furnished than the one they'd left. But it had creaking wooden floors with a dark-brown finish that had scrapes and chips that lent more than just character...some of them, at least one long, wavering scrape, looked like a drag mark. Paintings of no particular design, *impressionistic* one might say, hung from the walls, most of them canted to one side or another. A large, widescreen HDTV was on in the living room, through which they passed. A fat, shirtless man was sitting on the ratty couch, acknowledging them only by

176

showing his annoyance when they marched in front of his view of some sci-fi series. It looked like *Battlestar Galactica*. One of Kaley's friends at school, Paula, really liked that series. It was weird watching it now under these circumstances.

There was a tattoo across the fat man's voluminous belly: **Мир ненавидит нас**.

"*Prastite*," Oni muttered to the fat man on the couch. The fat man waved a dismissive hand, and when he did Kaley spotted the same red, roaring bear tattoo on his arm as Oni had.

Down a hallway with black-and-white pictures hanging a bit straighter on the walls, they encountered a younger-looking kid, this one blonde-haired and blue-eyed, maybe seventeen or eighteen years old. He looked at Oni and asked, "*Chto ty delayesh?*" Oni laughed and hollered something at the kid, then reached out and messed up his hair. Kaley wanted to ask the teenager for help, but had the strangest feeling that everyone inside this house was okay with kidnapping children. *It's a family business.*

The teenage boy then regarded her, very briefly, with hungry eyes. It was so brief it could scarcely be said to have happened at all, and then he moved on down the hall, out of sight.

They passed through a kitchen, where yet three more men waited, playing cards and smoking cigars. One of them spotted Oni and said, "*Dmitry! Kak tvaya mama?*"

"*Takzhe*," said Oni.

Dmitry, Kaley thought. *Oni's real name is Dmitry.* What she would do with this information was quite beyond her, but it was something to cling to. She knew something else about her abductors. It gave hope.

Just outside of the kitchen was a door. Olga was moving to open it. Kaley knew what was on the other side without having to see it. She could almost feel the dark shadows creeping up the narrow stairwell. She could almost see them moving under the door.

The men backed off a little and Olga turned to face all three children. She bent over to look the smaller ones in the eye. "*Skolka vam let?*" Olga asked, with cloying sweetness. Then, she laughed. "Sorry, I forget myself. They don't teach Russian in your schools here, do they? A pity. They should." Kaley said nothing. Shannon said nothing. The nameless girl looked down at the ground sucking her thumb and holding the cross about her neck. "I'm Olga. What are your names? Let's start with you." She snapped her fingers, and just like that knives were in the hands of her captors. Kaley was tugged at the back of her head. Then, all at once, the pressure was off her face. Her jaw popped as the tape was ripped from her face and the sock fell from her mouth. "Your name, sweetie."

Olga made it sound like a command, not a polite request. *She's done this before. It's old habit for her.* Kaley still couldn't believe she was here, now, experiencing this with her sister. *How many times? How often do they do this kind of thing?* Then, her eyes drifted to the dark chasm beyond the door. *What's down there?*

Olga moved her head so that she blocked Kaley's view of the stairs. "Now there's nothing to be scared of, my girls," she said. "You're safe now. You're in my home. Now, I've told you my name. What's yours?"

"I wanna go home," Kaley said. It sounded like the most logical request in the world, yet in these circumstances it also sounded like the dumbest. There was no way it could go that way. No way at all.

Olga, predictably, took on a hurtful frown. "Now, why would you want to go home? Your mother isn't very kind to you, now is she? No. She's very neglectful, isn't that right?" Olga turned her frown upside-down. "Here, you'll be *very* prized. Very valued."

Kaley's nostrils flared automatically. "How do you know our mother?"

"We know. We pick little boys and girls up all the time who we see having problems at home. We know, sweetheart. We know your pain. We know you—"

A wad of spit smacked Olga in the face. It took Kaley a moment to realize it had been hers. She'd done it before even planning it. "Fuck you!" she said, just as involuntarily. "You fucking cunt! You've been watching us? How long?"

"*Olga,*" said one of the men beside her.

"How long?!" Kaley demanded, tears welling up.

Olga didn't blink. She had never blinked, not once since Kaley had been watching her. She reached up and pushed the spittle away with her sleeve and said, "Very well, you little bitch. Let's cut this shit. I know your names already. You are Kaley Alexandria Dupré. And this is your sister, Shannon Alexis. The girl on your right is Bonetta LeShanda Harper. You were brought here unharmed out of the kindness of my two brothers' hearts. That's Mikhael and Dmitry there. You will all get to know them very well." She reached out and touched Shannon on her head. *"Ti takaya privlekatelnaya—"*

"Don't touch her!" Kaley shouted and lunged. But Oni, or rather Dmitry, was there to snatch her by her hair, just as he'd done before, and yanked her back. She fell to her knees and he twisted her head back so that he could scream straight down into her face. Kaley didn't understand a word he said, but she took the meaning. Dmitry finished by spitting in her face, then tossing her down onto the white, cracked linoleum.

Olga sighed and whispered something to Mikhael, the driver of the SUV, who nodded and turned to give the jaundiced man an order. Dmitry and the jaundiced man then led the girls downstairs. It was dark. Oily shadows caressed and drew her forward.

They moved slowly with Kaley in front, the men blocking their only exit. They all had their guns out. It was strange, seeing such men afraid of what little girls might do. *Shannon showed them that we might fight. They're prepared now. And they've trapped us all by threatening not to kill the escapee, but the one who remains behind.*

Even before the lights were switched on, Kaley's charm had already informed her. She saw the brightly-colored walls, the purple and pink unicorn cutouts that were taped up, the pink bearskin rug and the colorful teddy bears. She saw it all a full two seconds before the lights came on and showed her exactly all that.

The low-ceilinged basement had many rooms. There were doors all around them, but all of them were closed. There was a sandbox, and an area where a small playground had been erected— a playground designed for children no older than three or four. There was glitter on the ceiling, along with stars and moons and galaxies. But, dominating most of the ceiling was a wide, holographic rainbow. Kaley stared up at it. It was something she would find incredibly pretty if she weren't in this predicament.

From this point forward, rainbows would be objects of dreadful portent.

The lighting in the room was quite spectacular, and came from every direction. Special spotlights covered every little "scene," including a section that was as big as Kaley's room and Shannon's room put together, and it was filled with dollhouses.

If Kaley didn't know instinctively that this was a place where children were raped and murdered, she would've thought it a lovely place to spend her afternoon playing with Little Sister. Knowing it caused every slide, every doll, and every rainbow to assume grotesque depths and dimensions.

Everything smelled fresh. Nothing like upstairs, which had the smell of old men. No, down here everything was sanitized and made perfect. Lysol disinfectant cans sat on a table close by, as did a vacuum cleaner and a broom. There was a mop...slightly tinted red. Beside the table was an array of video cameras, including a Canon Rebel T3i on a tripod (which she recognized because her friend Shala's dad had had one briefly), and a bunch of microphones situated on long, metal poles. There was a rack of children's clothes nearby, everything from schoolgirl uniforms to bunny rabbit costumes, from a pink tutu to a Team Jacob shirt.

"You...fucking freaks," she breathed, turning to look at her captors, who had just finished cutting off Shannon's and Bonetta Harper's gags. "What are you going to do to us? How will you fucking live with yourselves?"

Dmitry didn't acknowledge a word she'd said. He pointed to a door at the far end of the basement and said, "Over there."

"If you wanna kill us, then do it right here. Right now. This...this is fucking..."

"I told you, we don't want to kill you," Dmitry laughed, glancing over at his brother Mikhael. "We want to fuck you." They laughed together.

Kaley felt nauseous. But instead of throwing up, Shannon did. Little Sister collapsed to the floor and started retching all at once. Kaley's nausea had passed from her to Shan via the charm, the Anchor, she was sure of it. *Why can't I do something useful with it, like pass it on to Dmitry and the rest of these monsters?* Then, while kneeling and hugging her sister, she thought, *Why can't I?*

Dmitry had stopped laughing long enough to shout up to Olga in Russian, presumably to tell her to come clean up this mess. Kaley tried to send a wave of her own nausea and fear outward. She closed her eyes and took a deep breath, trying to focus it. For a second, for just one single second, she had it in her hands. It was like trying to hold onto a large balloon filled with water without dropping it and letting it explode. Kaley directed it at Dmitry quickly, and fumblingly flung this…this…*thing* at him.

There was a moment where she felt it strike him. She *felt* it. Dmitry, halfway through screaming at Olga, stopped, lurched, and belched. Mikhael laughed and slapped his brother on the back. Then, perhaps he caught some of it, too, because he staggered back uncertainly, though still laughing.

The two monsters regained themselves. *"Boleesh?"* Mikhael chuckled.

"Net, net," Dmitry said, waving his brother away. But Dmitry's lips looked incredibly pale, his face drained. He waved at the three girls. "Go. Over there. In that room." It had worked. For the briefest of moments, her charm had worked *for* her. She had been able to manage it in such a way as to make it a weapon. But could she do it again? She tried, but it was no good. She couldn't even get a grasp on what she was trying to do. The power, if it could be called such, was gone for the moment.

Kaley looked at her sister and held her hand. "Are you okay?"

Then, her sister asked her the most innocent question. "K-K-Kaley, what do they m-m-mean, *fuck*? Wh-what does it mean? I mean, *really* m-mean."

"We're not gonna die," she whispered fervently. "We're not. You have to hold on to that. 'Kay?"

With the Anchor reforged for the moment, Shannon showed a surprising bit of resilience to the moment. "M'kay," she whimpered and wiped her eyes. Then she said, "I threw up."

"I know."

"You made me."

"I know," Kaley said. "I'm sorry. I didn't mean to." And just like that, they were discussing the charm, as though it had been a secret kept between them all their lives, something that was thoroughly known.

Nearby, the Harper girl sat with her back against the wall, her hands clutching her cross.

"I said, *get up!*" Oni shouted, reaching down and yanking them to their feet by their elbows. "In that room! Now!" Shannon's throw-up spell had left him in a terrible mood, and almost throwing up himself left him…embarrassed? Yes, she sensed that. He and his brother had a lifelong game of I'm Better Than You going, and in Dmitry's mind Mikhael was always in the lead. Vomiting in front of his older brother—older? yes, it seemed that way—had set him back even more in their competition.

They stepped around the various scenes, but had to walk through the sandbox to get to the room. Here, at the door, Kaley paused. There was a smudge on the floor, a dark-red stain that she was not stupid enough to discount as spilled fruit punch, though Shan might have.

Kaley now felt other things. Coldness. Fear. Fear from all around. The walls of this low-ceilinged basement were saturated with it. Fear and pain and degradation. Nan had told her that her charm would allow her to feel the imprint others left on certain things, certain objects, certain rooms. Kaley had never really experienced anything like it until now.

She heard…screaming. She empathized with old fear and humiliation. It saturated *her*.

As Mikhael opened the door, Kaley dropped to her knees. Dmitry put his shoe to her back and shoved her inside. Mikhael turned on the lights. It was a room with two beds, a mirror on one wall, a sink and a shower with no curtain. There was a wooden table with four foldout metal chairs, on top of which was stacked four board games: Monopoly, Candyland, Battleship and Hungry Hungry Hippos. There was a certain inviting quality to the room, one that made her sick again and she tried to redirect it at her nemesis.

"We bring you food later," Oni said, unfazed this time.

The door was shut behind them. There was a sharp clicking sound from the other side. She could hear Dmitry and Mikhael talking to one another as they ascended the steps. Kaley stood slowly, her legs turning to water for a moment before stabilizing. She tested the doorknob, and of course it was locked.

Then, there came a wailing like Kaley had never heard before. Shannon leapt into her sister's arms. But it wasn't Shan who was wailing. It was the Harper girl. She was backing up against a wall, clawing at her face for a second before falling on her ass and crying into her palms. "This isn't happening…this isn't happening…this isn't happening…this isn't happening…"

Fear, old and new, washed over Kaley. She was the bearer of her sister's burden, the bearer of Bonetta Harper's, and the bearer of every single child who had occupied this room before.

"I'm scared, Kaley," Shannon said, shivering in her arms like a freezing puppy fresh out of its bath.

"It's all right, Shan," she said soothingly. "It's all right. We're going to be fine. The police will find us soon."

"You promise?" Shan whimpered.

Kaley nodded. "I promise." She thought, *They'll rape us until we die.*

The dead body of Spencer Adam Pelletier wasn't a satisfying sight for Leon, despite what Agent Porter had told him about the man. He needed the SOB alive to tell him what he knew about Kaley and Shannon Dupré, but it appeared he might just take that secret to his grave—

"It's not him," Agent Porter pronounced before he'd even reached the body. "That's not our Musashi."

Or maybe not. "You sure?"

"This guy's nearly bald, and not nearly pale enough. He's white, though, and wearing a black hoodie. In a black neighborhood like this I can see why your people thought they'd bagged him. Close enough, in other words, but no cigar." He pronounced it *cee-gar.*

The body lying on the sidewalk in front of Leon was that of a heroin addict, that much was certain. The sleeves of his hoodie were pulled up and both his arms had tracks going up and down them. He had a quizzical look on his face, like somebody had just stumped him with the Double Jeopardy question of the day. Blood leaked from his nose and mouth, as well as from the center of his chest, where Officer Grissom had tapped him twice. The .44 he'd drawn had been kicked away from reach of his hand, lest today be the first day of the zombie apocalypse.

Other officers were now on the scene, as was yet another ambulance. *We're running them ragged tonight.* He walked over to Officer Grissom who was halfway through retelling his story to the other officers for the fifth time. "—and the neighbors reported seeing him snoopin' around, too. I, uh, I knew they'd been reporting a Caucasian snoop for weeks now. They filed a complaint, so we added this little alley here to our new patrol for the last couple of weeks. I happened by here, saw this guy, saw that he matched the description of the guy on the APB. I got out, asked him for his papers, that's when he threw down."

"Did you see anybody else with him?" Leon asked, butting in. He shot his hand out. "Hi. Grissom, right?"

"Yeah, Detective Hulsey, right?"

"You got it."

"No, I didn't see anybody else with him. But he's your guy, right?"

"Nope," Leon said. "Not according to Agent Porter over there, anyway." He pointed to the bearded agent, now hunched over the deceased heroin addict's body.

When Leon looked back at Officer Grissom, the man looked crestfallen. "Well, shit," he said. "I thought for sure that he...hey, look, he threw down on me anyway! Must've had somethin' to hide."

"Yeah, must have." But Leon wasn't certain the dead man had thrown down first, and he wasn't going to go there, at least not tonight. He had bigger fish to fry.

He walked over to Agent Porter, who was just standing up and finishing sending off a text. "There's no ID on this guy," he said. "Just an unfortunate white boy moving through a neighborhood on a night when a few dozen pissed off cops were looking for a white boy who nearly killed two of their own. Shitty-ass luck, you ask me."

"Pelletier and our girls are still out here somewhere. White boy can't be too far, he doesn't have a car."

Porter inclined his head. "You sure about that? He hotwired yours fast enough."

Leon had to admit that it had only been wishful thinking. He nodded. "Yeah."

"I didn't get a chance to force this issue back at Hillside Apartments, but I really feel I must do so now," Porter said. Leon looked at him. The next words came as no surprise, he'd known this was coming. "I'm gonna need to know the name and whereabouts of this contact of yours that spotted Pelletier and gave you Basil O'Connor's information."

This wasn't a pleasant prospect. Not at all. Once Agent Porter had Pat Mulley's name, he would naturally want to do a thorough background check on the man. He would find out every place the man had worked in his entire adult life, would check and see how much time he'd served throughout the years, and, of course, would want to know about his friends and family. It wouldn't be long before he knew Patrick Mulley's wife's, Melinda Mulley, wasn't living with him anymore and that her maiden name was Hulsey. How quickly before Agent Porter figured it all out?

Earlier, while speaking about Pelletier, Agent Porter had said, *Coincidences are only coincidences for so long.* Eventually, he would determine that this coincidence was no coincidence, either. And then how long before he figures out Detective Leon Hulsey, an iron horse of the Atlanta PD, had been turning a blind eye to activities he knew to be detrimental to law and order, as well as keeping information vital to countless auto theft investigations, all because some of it involved his sister's husband? What would come next? Suspension without pay? Criminal charges for aiding and abetting? Melinda would lose a brother and a husband, the only two men who could ever take care of her high-maintenance ass.

"His name's Charles Gracen," Leon lied. "I can probably call him, set up a rendezvous. He moves around a lot, though, so no guarantees."

"Fine. Set it up."

"All right," Leon said, taking out his cell phone and walking away from them all. "Give me a few minutes." If Agent Porter detected any kind of deception he didn't show it. He simply nodded and went back to his own cell phone, texting and talking with the other two agents.

Leon walked half a block up. A shirtless, hobbling crackhead crossed the street, and a pair of skanky women were peeking their heads out a window. Three stories above them, a few more heads poked out of windows. All of them were drawn to the flashing police lights and the aftermath of the shooting.

The phone rang once, twice, thrice. "C'mon, you skinny fucking crackhead," Leon whispered. "Answer the God damn phone." Another ring. Then another. Then finally the voicemail picked up. "Hey, yo, you just reached Cee-gray. Leave a message at—" Leon cursed, hung up, and dialed again. Seven rings, then the voicemail again. He hung up, dialed again. Same thing.

He did this six times before finally a groggy, high-pitched voice answered, "Hey, what the fuck, yo? Stop callin' me! It's like three o'clock in the goddamn moanin'—"

"Get your lazy fucking ass out of bed," Leon said. "We've got work to do."

"Whu...?"

"You heard me. And don't talk back to me or I'll make sure the ATF pays a visit *tonight*! You feel me?"

"What the fuck, Hulsey? What's goin' on?"

Leon glanced over his shoulder, making certain no one was within earshot. "I've got feds in town, and they wanna meet one of my informants. You're it. You gave me information earlier tonight—"

"I ain't seen you in a *month*, motherfucker!"

"Yes, you did. You saw me earlier tonight. That's what you're gonna tell them or I guarantee I'll find a reason to send you back to Georgia State Pen! Are you awake? Are you listening to me?"

Charles Gracen, better known as "Cee-gray" to his peeps, sighed heavily. "Yeah, I'm listenin'. So, what did I *tell* you tonight when we had this mysterious meetin' that I'm suddenly recollectin'?"

Leon told him, and after issuing one last threat, he hung up and walked over to the three agents. Porter was sitting in the front passenger seat of the SUV and checking a few things on the dashboard computer. Leon saw that it was a map of Atlanta. "Well?" he said, not looking at Leon.

"It's on. Thirty minutes. About three blocks up in a parking lot behind Grady's Bar."

"Great. Hop in."

Leon had traveled with the agents in their vehicle since his was now evidence and needed to be swabbed for prints. A tow truck would get around to Townsley Drive later to pick it up.

He took a seat in the back with Agent Mortimer, the white man who was sitting quietly to himself behind the driver's seat and looking deeply concerned with something on his iPhone's screen.

"So, I've had people back at the bureau looking into this Rainbow Room," Agent Porter said.

"Oh, yeah?"

"Yeah. Wait'll you hear this."

9

It was perhaps a long shot, but one worth trying. Spencer had his phone out and was thinking about the story he would give to the Parole Commission's office. A brief check on the Internet had given him the number to the Valdosta branch. Now he only needed a plausible excuse to search the name.

The excuse was right at the front of his mind, but it was hiding in shadow. This wasn't like him. It was the third time tonight he'd gotten distracted by a thought that wouldn't leave him alone, and it was terribly frustrating.

The thought that had so constipated his regular fluid thinking was an image of a fat man. It came to him out of nowhere, but stayed like it had import. He'd been drinking earlier, and sometimes when he got a little buzz on he would think about the past. Spencer was susceptible to that kind of thing, being as "pensive" as he was (thank you Dr. McCulloch for that wonderful word). The fat man in his mind was sitting on a throne...or no, a sofa. His face was in a haze, like how a spot disappeared thanks to your blind spot, but the belly was this great, voluminous orb, and on it was a message.

Is it a message for me?

Spencer pushed the thought aside and started dialing the Parole Commission in Valdosta. Then he paused. He couldn't think of the next number. He couldn't think of anything besides the fat man. *What the fuck is this shit? Am I high? Were Pat's cigs laced with somethin'?*

"The only way to deal with your demons is to face them." That was Dr. McCulloch's advice. No, wait...no, that was from that asshole at that wilderness therapy program he'd been put through in the North Georgia Mountains, way, way back when some people in Spencer's life had still been convinced there was a chance to lead him away from the road he was on. *What was that guy's name?* Spencer smiled. *Gary something. Ehrlich? That's*

188

it! Gary Ehrlich. I called him "Gay Lick." Fucker hated me worse than cholera.

The memory was a fond one, and Gay Lick's advice was good advice. "Meet the demons head-on," the councilors had said around their usual circle jerk that Gay Lick called the "Circle of Truth," where everyone shared what was on their mind. None of the counselors had liked this confession period when Spencer spoke, and neither did any of the kids, no matter their disposition.

What the fuck am I seein'? A tattoo of...

Letters. Strange font. The letters and font were both familiar, yet different.

"All right, all right, Spence ol' boy," he said out loud to himself and the piles of lumber all around him. "Face those fuckin' demons head-on." And so he closed his eyes and took deep, steadying breaths just like Gay Lick had advised. Back then, it had worked surprisingly well, though he'd never given Gay Lick the satisfaction of knowing it. And it worked now, too. Spencer saw...well, he wasn't sure what he saw. The letters looked familiar in some way, perhaps he'd seen them in a movie before.

He definitely saw a big letter *M*, but then there was a reverse letter *N*: **и**. Then there was a small *p*. **Mиp** didn't spell anything that he knew of, and neither did **Мир**. *All right, what's the rest? Just get it outta yer head, Spence ol' boy. It's like a bad acid trip. Just ride the shit and get it over with.* There was an *H*, then a lower-case *e*, and then another capital *H*. And then a lower-case *a*. Then a capital *B*, and then a...a...

What the fuck is that? he thought. Some kind of a...an *A*, maybe?

Without really realizing it, Spencer had already opened his eyes and started moving his fingers across the keys on his phone. He felt like that guy in that urban legend who had woken up suddenly in a bathtub filled with ice, only to discover he'd been kidnapped and left there with one of his kidneys removed. The story went that that guy started off quite calmly looking down at himself, half-dazed, unwilling to believe what he was seeing, and then with increasing alarm he'd fumbled through the hotel room piecing together what had happened to him.

A part of Spencer did not wish to acknowledge that maybe, just maybe, he was losing it. *Dr. McCulloch always said it could get this bad if I didn't try to keep it in check.* "A messy mind makes a messy life," he had said. It had been just one in a string of useless platitudes.

His fingers moved across the phone's keypad until he'd pulled up Google Translate. He was able to find a menu that showed all sorts of alphabets. Greek, Chinese, Japanese, Latin. He cycled through them all, looking at samples of them until he landed on Cyrillic, where he saw the weird backwards *N* and the not-quite-*A*-looking letter.

Using his finger on the touchscreen, he typed in the letters he saw in his vision: **Мир ненавидит нас**. He figured he'd get just a bunch of gobbledy-gook. Spencer was surprised when he got the English translation: **The world hates us**.

With rain starting to fall again and smearing his screen, Spencer read the message again and again. *What're the odds that I came up with Cyrillic letters that just so happened to form a complete, coherent message?* Perhaps it had always been there, at the back of his mind, a message someone had given him a long, long time ago, maybe one of the assholes back in the pen. Spencer thought about the fat, grotesque belly he was seeing this tattoo wrapped around. Was it maybe someone from cellhouse A? Somebody he'd half known and his memory of them was just now bubbling to the surface after two beers and a bit of nicotine?

It took a few seconds of pondering to make him suitably bored of the topic. As pensive as he could be, he was also prone to just dropping something whenever an immediate answer didn't present itself. Dr. McCulloch had always told him that psychopaths showed that tendency for quick boredom and a constant need for stimulation, and warned that it would continue to get him into trouble if he didn't attempt to control it.

It took a few seconds to get past the befuddled. Then, Spencer recalled what excuse he wanted to use with the Parole Commission and started dialing again.

Two rings was all it took, but it was an automated machine that picked up, telling him to hold for the first available representative. After a few minutes of listening to the soft but ominous musical stylings of Phil Collins with "In the Air Tonight," someone finally picked up. "U.S. Probation Office, Valdosta," a woman's voice said. "How may I direct your call?"

"Yeah, uh, hi. My name's Wagner. Stewart Wagner," said Spencer. "And I have a complaint to file against a man I believe to be on parole," he said. It was a long shot, but many criminals were either on parole or had once been. And the dying punk back on Townsley mentioned serving time with "my boy" Yevgeny. A long shot, but one worth checking out.

"All right. Maybe I can help you. What's the name?" Spencer could hear long fingernails clicking at keys.

"See, now, that's the thing."

"You don't have a name?" She said it with dismay.

"No. Well, maybe. See, I can't quite pronounce it. I think it's Russian or Ukrainian or some shi…sorry, some *such*."

"Hm. That could actually help narrow it down some, if you could remember even a bit of his name."

Spencer sighed. "It's something like, um, Yevgeny?" he tried. "I'm not sure if that's a first name or a last name. I *think* it *might* be the first, and his last name might be something like Tiddlov, or Tidiv maybe? I dunno."

"Let me try a few different spellings," the woman said.

"Thank you, miss. I really appreciate this." Spencer paused for a moment, taking deep breaths. A sudden nausea had come over him, and he wasn't sure if it was all the excitement, the burger from Dodson's Store, his anger at the man with the bear-claw tattoo, or a combination of all three. Part of him knew that the nausea wasn't his, though. Somebody had sent it to him. Somewhere out there, someone was very, very sick.

"While I'm doing this, Mr. Wagner," the lady said robotically, "would you mind telling me what this individual did?"

"Oh, certainly! You bet your *tukas*!" Spencer chuckled, doing his best impersonation of a concerned citizen suffering righteous indignation. "That son of a you-know-what rear-ended me in the middle of the highway while movin' through Atlanta. He was trucking at—oh, hell, I dunno, eighty, ninety miles an hour?"

"Mm. My goodness."

"Yeah," he laughed bitterly. The nausea was starting to lift from his body, returning from whence it came. "That's what me an' my wife said. Then I saw the piece of crap talkin' on a damn cell phone. He didn't even know he'd rear-ended us. No, I take that back, he *had* to know, he just didn't want to acknowledge it. He kept movin' on, never even slowing down. I sped up—I shouldn't have, I know, but I did—and I waved him over to the side of the road. It took a minute to get his damn mind off the phone, but when he pulled over we had an exchange on the side o' the road. He threw the first punch. My wife got out and he slapped her to the ground!"

"Oh, my."

"It was my own fault, I guess—"

"Well, he was driving dangerously," she said cautiously. "You have every right to file a complaint. Probably should've taken his license plate down and just called the police on him. Not wise to get out of the car and start shouting."

"I know, I know. I was just…I was about to get into my car when he beat me down. My wife got out and he just…well, he took off and I got inside my car and followed him. Shouldn't have done that either, I know, but I did. I followed him to a motel he was staying at in Downtown. I got his name. The clerk seemed to know him, said he'd been staying there a few weeks, just gotten outta prison, might be on parole. I dunno. The motel clerk said he'd kicked a pregnant woman in the elevator at his motel a couple weeks before that, threatened to cut the baby outta her."

"Oh my God." The woman was truly offended.

"Yeah, so, I figured I'd call you guys, file a formal complaint with any parole officer he has, let 'em know that this fucker's crazy. Sorry, ma'am, forgive my language. I'm just…what he did to my wife, and what the clerk said he did to that pregnant woman…" When he first made the call, he'd only had the outline of his story. But the colorful details and the extra surprise at the end about the pregnant lady was all improv. Brian, his oldest brother, had told him he ought to go into acting, do some stuff on stage, improvisational comedy. *You think fast, bro*, he'd said many a time.

"I completely understand," said the woman. More typing from her end. "Yevgeny, you said? Maybe Yevgeny Tidov?"

"Hey, that sounds about right," Spencer said. "You got him in your system?"

"I do."

"White guy, right?" Yevgeny Tidov, whether Russian or Ukrainian, was almost certainly a white man's name. Spencer would let her fill in the rest.

"Uh, yes. Blonde hair, blue eyes, heavyset, has several body tattoos?"

"Sounds like him."

"He lives in Downtown Atlanta, too. You said that's where you encountered him?"

"Yes, ma'am. Is it okay to ask what he went to prison for?" he asked, knowing the answer was yes because these things were a matter of public record for any concerned citizen. If a person was on parole, the average citizen could get them into a lot of trouble. Basically, the parole officer and John and Jane Q. Public owned a parolee's ass.

"Yes," she said. "Double armed robbery six years ago."

"So, I guess he's a U.S. citizen?"

"Yes, not born here, though. Earned his citizenship a year before he got arrested."

"You've been very helpful, ma'am. Um, could you possibly get me contact information?"

"I'm not allowed to give you his address," she said, "but I *can* give you contact information for his parole officer."

"Yeah. Hey, I just need to report this guy. I'd like to call the parole officer personally. Do you have his officer's name and number? Any way to get in touch with him?"

Of course she did. "His parole officer's name is Eugene Evans."

"Eugene Evans?"

"Yes, sir."

"Phone number?" She rattled it off. "Thanks so much. Hey, by any chance, does it say like how often this guy has to visit his parole officer? Or when his last visit was supposed to be? Maybe he missed it. Boy, I'd *love* to get this guy in bigger trouble than he already is."

The woman's voice had a note of humor. "Once a month," she said. "The fifth of every month. Mr. Tidov has made every single one of his meetings with Mr. Evans. Last update has him working a third-shift job, overnight stock at a Target."

"Aw, dang it. Well, I had to try. Thanks so much, ma'am. You've been a great help."

"No problem. Make sure to include everything you've told me in your report to Mr. Evans."

"Oh, I will, ma'am. Trust me on that."

"And try to be more careful next time. You never know whom you're dealing with," she added, blind to the irony.

"Heh, yeah. You bet. Thanks again."

Spencer hung up, and started dialing again at once. Somewhere, a siren was blaring. He was aware of it but did not care. Somehow, he understood that it wasn't meant for him. On some level, he knew that he was meant for the fat orb of a belly, the one that someone had branded in Cyrillic, proclaiming to anyone who cared *The world hates us.* He also knew that the passing nausea he'd felt while making the phone call was from some outside source. As insane as all of these things sounded, he knew them to a certainty.

A dog barked from somewhere up the street, past the squatters on the other side of the chain-link fence. A helicopter *whup-whup-whupped* somewhere close, but not close enough to be a concern to him.

The phone rang six times, and halfway through the seventh someone picked up and the voice of a grizzled old man answered. "Eugene Evans," he said.

"Hello, Mr. Evans? Eugene Evans?"

"That's what I said." A not-so-stifled yawn.

"Hi, my name is Stewart Wagner, I just got into contact with the Parole Commission's office in Valdosta concerning one of your parolees, Yevgeny Tidov."

"Hm. Yevgeny?" he grunted. He then gave a slight, painful moan. "He done something?"

Spencer laughed. "You could say that." He then went through the exact same spiel as he had with the woman at the Parole Commission. It took several minutes of repeating himself because this Evans wasn't a sharp thumbtack. He also seemed to be hard of hearing. An old fellow, but stern-sounding. He demanded to know the details again, and the more he listened, the more he seemed to awaken. Spencer could almost hear him writing all of it down.

Over the line, Evans gave another grunt. "Sorry, I move slowly. Fibromyalgia. It's a bitch." Another grunt. "This isn't like Yevgeny at all. He keeps his nose clean. You're *sure* it was Yevgeny? You might be mistaking him…"

"Blonde hair, blue eyes, heavyset, has a tattoo of a red bear, right?" That last part was improvisation, as well, and Spencer caught himself a second too late before adding that little morsel. But the woman at the Parole Commission's office had said he had a body covered in tattoos and it was a pretty safe bet that the red-bear tattoo would be there because the name certainly sounded Russian and Pat had said these *vory v zakone* were Russians, so—

"That's him," Evans sighed. "Well, I am sorry, Mr. Wagner. I'll have this checked out immediately. I can tell you that this is most unusual for Mr. Tidov but he's about to receive a stern lesson."

Spencer didn't doubt it. Oftentimes the people selected to be parole officers were judicious sons o' bitches who enjoyed keeping an eye out for misbehaviors and indiscretions. "Well, that's good. Is there an address where I can send a formal letter?"

Another grunt of pain. "A what?"

"My father always taught me that if you have a problem with a man, you tell him to his face. An' if face-to-face won't suit, then a finely-crafted letter will suffice." Interesting fact: that was no lie. Spencer's father actually *had* granted him that piece of advice.

"Well, it's certainly not necessary to do that, Mr. Wagner—"

"All I need is a mailing address. P.O. Box will do if that's the case. I don't just want him to hear it from you, I want him to hear a personal account of what he did to me, the fear he placed on my wife, all of it. Do you understand? I want him to *know*."

"Mr. Wagner…" For a moment, Spencer thought he would get nowhere with this stalwart old watchdog and he might have to resort to another tactic, but then Eugene Evans surprised him. "Sir, do I have your word, one man to another, that you are not seeking personal retribution? *Physical* retribution?"

"Mr. Evans, I'm five-foot-five and barely a hundred fifty pounds. I *don't* have a Napoleon complex, I'm a realist. If I tried anything with this guy I'd have my head caved in probably."

Evans chuckled. "I dunno. He's actually not violent. Well, not *usually*. This is the first I'm hearing of anything like this. Anyways, his address is 42 Clayton Road. After I hang up with you, I'll be calling him immediately. This kind of behavior is intolerable. I'm going to check on this."

"Thanks so much, Mr. Evans."

"All right," he grunted again, sounding thankful to be done. "Bye-bye."

"Bye."

Spencer hung up and used his phone to look up directions to Clayton Road. It was just nine miles away. He found a bus route, and the schedule that the local buses stuck to. Spencer then switched off his phone and started to put it back in his pocket. Then he paused and looked at it. He looked up at the sky, then all around him. He looked at the stacks of lumber and the flattened earth all around him. Then he looked at the phone. He had a feeling…

"The phone," he said to no one in particular. An image of the Yeti came to him. Then he thought about how much Basil knew, how much he might've given the cops. He looked at the phone again, put it between his teeth and bit it, thinking. After a few seconds, he took the phone out of his mouth, and tapped it against his forehead. "Yep, the phone." He walked around the pile of lumber and hollered over to the squatters by their fire. "Yo! Who wants a free phone?" All three of them looked up, and all three slowly raised their hands. Spencer reared back and flung it at them. "Draw straws for it, bitches!" he laughed.

Spencer left them to decide who got it. He moved through the construction zone, through the trees at the other end and was enveloped.

"Where are they?!" she demanded. Jovita had walked out of the back room where they had been keeping her and slammed her palms down on the front desk, where an officer was busy assisting a man filing a complaint. "Where—are—*they*?!"

"Ms. Dupré?" a man called.

Jovita ignored him and instead stared bloody daggers at the female officer running the phones on the other side of the desk. "I'm sick o' this shit! You got me waitin' back there for three muthafuckin' hours an' ain't nobody sayin' shit! Where are my babies? Who's got 'em? Huh? Answer me you nappy-headed bitch! Tell me where they at, an' *I'll* go fuckin' get—"

"Ms. Dupré?" someone called again.

The officer lady had been on the phone, and now put the phone against her chest to smother it. Jovita stared at her, and the officer stared stoically right back at her. "You tell me, bitch," she hissed. "You tell me what the fuck's goin' on with my babies—"

"Ms. Dupré?"

Hands seized her. She turned to slap the owner of those hands, but was restrained by another set of hands, officers all. Indignant, Jovita shouted at them all, declaring things about their mothers, about their loyalty to their community, about their lack of respect, and about many other things that she couldn't possibly know about them but somehow believed she was right about it all.

They pulled her over to a chair in the lobby. Other people who had been sitting and waiting patiently to be seen hopped out of their foldout chairs and walked away from her. One of the officers was a black man with a familiar face. "Ms. Dupré? Jovita? It's me. Sam. You remember me? Sam Wentworth?"

She looked at him. The man was tall, brown-skinned, with a military-style crew cut. He had a square jaw, with eyes and lips that looked like an old friend's. "Sam?" she said. It took a moment for her to bring the information out of the fog. Her mind was still addled from lack of sleep and lack of meth. "You...you're Patty Wentworth's son-in-law, ain't'choo?"

"That's me. I've got it from here, Tyler," he told the other officer.

"You sure, Sam?" Tyler said. He was a fat black man with chubby cheeks and fat hands. Iron hands that had seized Jovita and twisted her to her seat.

"Yeah, I got it. Just let me talk to her."

"I'll be right over here." Officer Tyler Whoever-He-Was walked only five paces away and leaned against the front desk. A couple of other officers were coming down a set of stairs and looking about frenetically, obviously responding to the outburst they could hear from upstairs. Officer Tyler waved a hand at them, making a face that said it was nothing, go back to work.

"Sam," Jovita said, tears still streaming. Her teeth were rattling. The roots hurt with each pulse of her heart. She needed a fix, and soon. "Sam, wh-where are m-my babies?" Tears came unbidden.

"Jovita, we're looking into—"

"I don't wanna *hear* that shit, Sam! Th-that's all anybody's been tellin' me all night—"

"That's all we can tell you, Jo," he said, lowering his voice and taking a seat in the foldout chair beside her. "That's all anybody knows right now, okay? Alright? There's nothing more that I can tell you. We've got a line on a few suspects, we're tracking them down now. That's all—"

"Sam, y-y-you can do better than that. Who're th-these people? The s-s-suspects, I mean." Jovita could tell she was about to get more rejection. "Sam, I'm they mama!"

Sam sighed. "Jo, I'm sorry, I really can't tell you that."

Jovita snarled, baring her teeth. "You were raised up the street from me," she said. "I remember you cheatin' off o' Lydia Newton's tests in fifth grade! I was goin' to church back when you got that disease—what was it, uh, uh, uhhhhh, spinal somethin'."

"Spinal meningitis," he said.

"Yeah, that! The church took donations an' my mama was one o' them that got that started so you could get all the medical shit you needed," Jovita said. Lies came easily to her these days, but this one was partially tinged in truth. "Yo mama didn't have the money to help you so *we* did! You wouldn't even be alive if it wasn't fo' us! You hear me, boy? An' I babysat fuh yo black ass when yo mama got sick an' yo daddy ran out—"

"All right, all right, just…God damn it, shut up, will ya?" Sam sighed heavily and looked about the lobby. Officer Tyler gave him a look that, to Jovita, seemed to ask, *Do you want me to escort the crazy lady out of the building?* Sam gave an almost imperceptible look that told Tyler to stay back, that he would handle this. "Look, if I tell you a little bit about these people, will you promise to stay calm for the remainder of the night? Will you go home and sit and wait for us to give you a call when we know something solid?"

Jovita nodded, but wasn't sure she could keep her promise. She reached into her purse and pulled out a tissue, shoved it up her nostrils, and stopped the leaks.

Sam glanced around the lobby once more and then leaned in close, whispering. "There's, uh, there's a chance that the girls might've been taken by a group of Russians called the *vory v zakone*. That's the rumor right now, okay?"

Jovita couldn't even pronounced their name. "Russians?" she said.

"Yeah, I know. It sounds—"

"What...who the fuck are they?"

"Russian organized crime. A weird group of thieves, got started back in old Russia, back in, like, 1917 or something. Back in Stalin's *Gulag*."

"Who the fuck is Stalin?"

Sam made a face. "Joseph Stalin," he said, as if this was some very important person Jovita really ought to know. "Premier of the Soviet Union back in...never mind. The important thing is these guys got started up way back then, and they're still active today. We've never seen them very active in America until the last decade or so. A bit of stuff here and in New York, but that's about it. Nothing like this. And, uh...well, there have been reports of people being snatched up off the streets, uh, young kids mostly, some prostitutes, anyone that the *vor* don't think will be missed."

The indignation in Jovita Dupré threatened to become volcanic. "Wait, what, you don't think I take care o' *my* kids?"

"That's not what I *said*, Jo," he said, holding up his hands in a sign of peace. "But if the girls were out alone in the streets at night, there's a chance that *they* thought the girls were, I dunno, homeless? Orphans? Something like that? They might've targeted Kaley and Shannon because of their perceived neglect." Jovita saw it in his eyes. The man was dancing around with words that masked his own true belief.

He became a cop. He's one o' them now. He thinks like them. Well, I caught him jerkin' off to an Ebony *magazine in my best friend's living room when he was twelve, an' I remember him slinging crack with his brothers when he was fifteen, so I know this*

199

nigga better than he know himself. I remember where he come from, even if he don't.

And there was something else. Jovita's mind might have been mush these days, but she knew when somebody was holding something back. She knew this because she had spent the last twelve years watching her oldest daughter's face. Kaley Alexandria Dupré had been a strange young girl, there was no denying that. Besides her constant debilitating vertigo, which freaked all the kids and most adults out, she had also been a careful manipulator. She knew how to ask Ricky for things in a way that would convince him to convince Jovita, and vise versa. It usually had to do with convincing others to do something for Shannon, who Kaley was intent on spoiling. It might be to get Shan a new pair of pants or some fancy new toy.

Kaley was a careful girl, and she rarely spoke to her mother these days. Jovita had come to think it had to do with her brief but intense (and strange) relationship with her grandmother. They had gotten very close for a time, then after her grandmother's death something had changed inside of Kaley. She wanted to be left alone a lot, with just herself or with Shan. They never got into any real trouble, but the two of them were as thick as thieves, leaving Jovita out of their play, always laughing and getting along until *she* stumbled into the room.

"What else?" she said.

"What do you mean?" Sam asked, lying badly.

"What...*else*?"

He considered her for a moment. Then to her surprise, he was very forthcoming. "Interpol—that's the International Criminal Police Organization—they've been called. Uh, Gary, a friend o' mine in Missing and Exploited Children, said he's been talking with a detective works here name o' Hulsey. He says there's some FBI guys just showed up a few hours ago, and them and Hulsey are asking questions about a group called the Rainbow Room. Jovita, have you ever heard of them? Anything at all?"

"No," she said. "Who are they, Sam?"

"Interpol's been after them for some time. Years, sounds like. They're one of these secretive groups, have people all over the planet, and they have this website where They...they abduct kids and... take the kids, and they...um..."

Jovita leaned in, digging her eyes into his. "An' they *what*, Sam?"

"Jo...listen, you really don't wanna know."

"They're my *babies*, Sam. I wanna know."

The boy she knew returned with his next sigh, and he folded, just as he had folded for Lydia when she said he had to be her boyfriend if he was going to cheat off her test. "The Rainbow Room," he began, "has a website that they change, move to other servers, and keep on the go. None of them have ever been caught. They're hackers and, uh, and...well, *compilers*. They compile pictures of different stuff. They change IP addresses, they move around, very organized. They're not the first. Interpol's busted groups like this for years. That's their big thing these days, human trafficking and child porn..." He trailed off.

"An' what does this Rainbow Room *do*? What do they *compile*?" On some level, she knew exactly what he was saying, because he had basically laid it all out. But Jovita's mind wasn't just foggy, it was the mind of a mother, and no matter how bad of a mother one could be, imagining cruelty like she was being told here didn't quite register. Surely there was something else Sam meant by his words. Surely there had to be.

"They, um, they upload pictures of naked children, and of, um," he swallowed briefly, "of children being raped and—*hey!*" Jovita had gasped despite the fact that she believed she had prepared herself for the worst. Wide-eyed, she fell from the chair to her knees and stared at the tile floor. Sam leaned down and hugged her. "God damn it, I *told* you you didn't wanna know! I shouldn't have told you! Hey, it's okay. Listen, it's okay. We're gonna find them, hear? We're on it. We're gonna find them."

Jovita heard little more than her heart beating in her ears.

"My babies...my babies...my babies..."

There was no corneal abrasion. At least, that's what David kept telling the medics to get them to leave him the hell alone. His eyes hurt, especially his left, which stung and watered every time he blinked. He swore up and down that he could still drive, that it would be no problem. There was only a few cuts to his face, and none that needed stitches. Jeffrey Banks, one of the medics he'd known for years, had plucked the two splinters from his cheeks and swabbed them before putting on tufts of cotton with clear tape.

"How's Bee?" he asked Jeffrey.

"Half her hand is gone," Jeff said. "How do you think she is?"

"I'm good to go, though, right?"

"I'd recommend that you take the rest of the night to—"

"They caught him yet?"

Jeff sighed. "Nope."

"My car still here?"

"Yep."

"Then I'm helping to hunt the bastard." He pushed himself up off the top step, where he'd been sitting ever since backup had arrived. Chalk outlines, some yellow evidence tags and the yellow crime scene tape now decorated a mostly forgotten part of town. Three detectives from Robbery/Homicide had been brought in to start in with the scene, and forensics specialists were still arriving by the truckload. The street of Townsley Drive was fast becoming crowded.

Ahead of him a forensic photographer was taking pics of the scene. David staggered around the photographer and waved back to Jeff. "Thanks, Jeff. You're an eye saver."

"I'm telling you, man, get some rest. They've got everyone out there searching for this guy. They're going to find him sooner or later."

"Another set of eyes can't hurt."

"If you *had* a set," Jeff said. So, he knew that David's left eye had a bad abrasion, but he wasn't going stop the cop from going back on duty. David supposed if cops let firefighters and medics get away with driving drunk, then the medics felt it was their obligation to let the cops get away with a few items of indiscretion from time to time, as well. He also imagined that the AAR, or after action review, would probably be forty-eight hours from now, which was standard. He didn't need to do much more than file a bit of paperwork at the end of his shift. Until then, no one was going to begrudge him for going out after the man who'd shot his partner.

The fire truck was backing out when David hopped inside his patrol car. Less than thirty minutes ago Beatrice had been sitting here, driving the car.

It was my decision, he told himself. *I told her that we needed to go and check it out.* And Bee had said nothing. She hadn't questioned him, hadn't given him a look of disapproval, nothing. *And because of it, we're out another good cop in Zone One.*

Zone One cops were hard to keep. Nobody wanted to stay in the trenches of the Bluff and the areas surrounding it. Cops got out as quickly as they could, took a sergeant's test or an investigator's test and then started trying to move their way on out after a couple years of experience. Beatrice had made a pledge to hang around for the long haul.

Those words on the wind came back to him. "Fast as fast can be, you'll never catch me!"

Why were those words so familiar? Where did they come from? David found a bottle of Advil in the glove compartment, popped two of them for the pain in his eye and gave it some thought. It came to him out of nowhere, a memory from his teenage years. It was from the jackalope on *America's Funniest People*, a TV show hosted by Dave Coulier and Arleen Sorkin. He remembered Coulier had voiced the little rabbit with the antlers— the jackalope—and recalled of all the times he'd thwarted some idiotic lumberjack or an uptight businessman. The jackalope would hit them in their groin, or make them step on a rake that smashed them in the center of their face. Afterwards, the ever-elusive jackalope would dart off to parts unknown, shouting in mordant pleasure, "Fast as fast can be, you'll never catch me!"

Later, as he recalled, the jackalope got renamed "Jack Ching Bada-Bing" in a Name the Jackalope Contest.

"Fuck you, Jack Ching," David Emerson swore. He found the keys were still in the ignition, and turned them. "Yeah. It's jackalope season, motherfucker." He pulled around yet another forensics van that was coming up the street. The ballistics and blood spatter experts had a long night ahead of them.

Leon checked the time on his iPhone: 3:04 AM.

About fifty yards away someone was shouting. He turned and looked out his window. A girl no older than fifteen was walking down the street arguing with a man at least twice her age. The girl's belly was swollen. Knocked up before her sixteenth birthday, and angry at her baby's daddy? Hard to say, but Leon figured his guess was probably close.

The rain had started in again, then stopped, then started again, and then stopped. It seemed that would be the way of the night.

"Yo, dawg!" someone shouted. Leon looked. It was some guy sticking his head out of a window half a block up. He was hollering down to his buddy in the street, who was waving up. They had had a brief conversation, the man in the window reminding him to say something to his sister about something or other. There were laughs, and they went their separate ways.

The parking lot behind Grady's Bar had no painted lines. All around, wild tufts of grass had started pushing their way up through cracks in the pavement. An entire piece of the parking lot on the east end had been washed away and a row of wild sages were growing there. Vines clung desperately to the edge of Grady's. To Leon, places like this always reminded him of images he'd seen of Chernobyl after the big nuclear disaster. Strange to think that if mankind were to die that Nature would just reclaim it all again. The estimates he'd heard had it that it would take 10,000 years—just a thousand decades—for there to be no evidence that mankind had ever lived. At least, not on Earth. Ironically, the longest lasting evidence for mankind's existence would be the flags and rovers left on the moon; silent monuments to all that we were, and ever could be.

He'd let his mind wander a bit. He did this whenever he got nervous. Gracen was late, and even if he showed up Leon wasn't sure the fool could play his part.

"So this Rainbow Room," Leon said. "You say Interpol's got a beat on them in Germany and Australia? That matches up with what the Yeti said."

Agent Porter was still sitting in the front seat, conferring with someone on his smartphone. That, or playing Angry Birds. "Yeah. Berlin, Sydney, Dublin, Hong Kong, Belfast, Moscow, and some middle-of-nowhere place out in Wyoming. They're everywhere. The people in Lyon said they busted into a house in Dublin six months ago, but by the time they got there the apartment had been cleared out, just a computer and a desk was all that was left, and the computer had been completely scrubbed."

"Lyon?"

"France. Interpol headquarters. The agents there are the ones that work as liaisons, I'm sure you know. They try to time hits against international cells all at once, before the media can get a hold of it. That way, if the FBI busts someone in a child porn ring over here, the others in the child porn ring in Germany don't get wind of it and take off. They coordinate, hit all these places at once, take as many down as possible."

"But not the Rainbow Room?"

"Not the Rainbow Room," Porter confirmed. "Least, that's what my friends at the bureau are saying right now. Interpol's damn interested in Atlanta tonight. They'll be watching us. They're saying that they didn't think the Rainbow Room had roots here." He scratched at his beard, and shook his head. "They say the Room's like weeds, they're growing everywhere now."

"How do they work?"

"Far as what they tell me, they put out requests. A website was originally started, nobody knows what it was called now, but it got together the original members," Porter said, lifting his head up from his phone to scan outside the window. "Your boy gonna show?"

"He'll show," Leon said, sounding more confident than he felt.

Porter accepted it. "Anyways, before they shut down they always have a few backup sites to retreat to, confer a bit, and then hop, skip, and jump to another server, IP address, all that. They use proxy servers so no one can track them, and Interpol thinks they communicate through fire-and-forget e-mail accounts. They probably also do recruiting through sites where anyone can put up any homemade porn movies they want. X-vids-dot-com, you know, shit like that?

"In places they've left behind, Interpol has found all sorts o' computer drives that the Rainbow Room uses to hide things in code, pretty much just gibberish unless the person has the right cipher. Sneaky bastards, tech wizards. Phantoms. You know the kind these days." He rolled down his window, breathed the fresh air. "Skip-tracing these kinds of fuckers is almost impossible. You can only join the Rainbow Room by being recommended by one of the highly respected members, and you're put on a one-year probationary membership kind of thing. If you submit enough pictures and donate enough to the community, either money or tips, you can become a full member. Then, the more pics and vids you submit, and the greater the quality, and the higher people rate your pics an' videos, the higher up you go. That means you get more access to child porn."

"People do this?" Leon asked, knowing the answer. He wasn't naïve, one couldn't be if you wanted to be a detective in Atlanta, but his worldview and moral compass demanded he ask the question, almost rhetorically and yet still wanting to verify the absurdity.

"Full-time, my friend," said Agent Stone, speaking for the first time in a while. "They go years without getting caught. Kids getting raped in a basement, it all gets taped, the bodies get dumped, the tapes go online, and the neighbors don't know shit because nobody knows their neighbors anymore. People peek from their windows, but they don't knock on doors and greet the new folks in town. Who the fuck knows who's living next to you these days?"

Leon glanced anxiously out the window. *Where the fuck are you, Cee-gray?* "You ever brought people like that in?"

Porter said, "Like what? The Rainbow Room?" He shook his head. "No. I track serial killers, sometimes chase fugitives on the run. Rainbow Room types get passed on to the guys at Migrant and Domestic Trafficking. I'm just here for Pelletier. *But*, I'll do my part until the MDTs get here, I guess, much as I can. And who knows? Might be Pelletier has a hand in this shit, too. Wouldn't surprise me."

Leon wasn't convinced. He didn't know Pelletier as well as Porter did, but this didn't seem to fit. "How would he have gotten hooked up with people like the Rainbow Room?" he asked.

"Who knows? The man's a recidivist. Maybe heard about it somewhere in the joint? We know he's criminally diverse and has a black hole where his moral compass ought to be, so anything's possible." He pointed out the window. "This your guy?"

Leon looked out his window. A pair of headlights came bouncing towards them. When the vehicle turned, he saw that it was a blue Chevy Nova. "That's him," he said.

They opened their doors and stepped out. The Nova halted, its engine dying gratefully after the end of a long, cruel life, and its fat driver stepped out. Charles "Cee-gray" Gracen commonly wore black jackets with hoods, even though he never wore the hood up, lest it cover up his tightly-woven cornrows.

Leon approached with his hands in his coat pockets. He gave Gracen a look upon his approach, and Gracen betrayed nothing as they bumped fists. "S'up, Leon?"

"A whole lot tonight, Charlie," he said. "You remember the guy you were telling me about earlier?"

"Yeah, white motherfucker." So far, so good.

"That's right." He turned to introduce the agents. "This is Special Agent Porter of the FBI. These are agents Mortimer and Stone. Charlie, they wanna ask you about this white guy."

"A'ight. Shoot."

"Mr. Gracen," said Porter, stepping to him enthusiastically. "Detective Hulsey here tells us that you gave him a lead earlier tonight about a Caucasian male, approximately thirty years old."

"True," Gracen said, inclining his head. He gave a brief glimpse to Leon, and privately Leon was willing him not to do that. So far Special Agent Jamal Porter seemed like a sharp man, and no doubt had had extensive training in advanced interrogation. He would know that glancing up and to the right indicated an insincere response, because it meant the person was accessing the creative centers of the brain. If Leon knew that, then Porter almost certainly did, too. And he'd also notice furtive glances for help sent in Leon's direction. *Just act cool, you fat fuck.*

"Is this the man you saw?" Porter said, holding up his cell phone. It was a mugshot of Adam Pelletier from the Bureau of Prisons.

"Hard t'say," Gracen admitted. "Might've been. Looks like him. White boy, black hair, blue eyes." Once again, he unconsciously glanced over to Leon to see how he was doing. *Don't look at me, you fuck. Look at* him!

"What was the nature of your conversation with Detective Hulsey? Why did you contact him earlier tonight?"

"I give him a heads-up, an' he usually lets me alone, long as I keep myself outta trouble," Gracen said, which was true. "I used to run with a bad crew, an' I still pretend to be they friend, listen in on some o' they plans, who they sellin' jabs to, this'n that, an' I give him a call. I called Leon 'cause I heard about these folk up on L Street startin' back up on a meth lab once they brother get outta the joint next week. I told my boy Leon here that I seen this white boy walkin' that way, thought he looked strange. I'd never seen him befo', an' in my neighborhood when new white folks show up it's sometimes a cause fo' concern. I'm a changed man, a concerned citizen lookin' out fo' the kids in my 'hood. I'm a father now, ya heard me?"

Porter nodded. "Mr. Gracen, have you seen anyone about your 'hood with maybe a tattoo of a red bear?"

"You talkin' about the fucking Russians?" Gracen asked. Porter nodded. "Them motherfuckers be around," he said simply.

"Around…where?"

The fat man shrugged. "All over. They ain't got no territory yet, but everybody know they lookin' fo' it. They work with local boys sometimes. I know these cats from the Crips who worked with them fo' a minute. Said it was just slingin' jabs at first, but then they wanted 'em to start snatchin' kids too, I don't know, send a message to they family? Them Russians be crazy. Startin' to get *real* around here, ya feel me?"

As far as Leon knew, none of this was actually a lie. Gracen must have been sitting on this information for some time. *We'll have to discuss this later*, he vowed to himself.

"Do you know where—" Porter stopped to answer a buzzing at his phone. "Excuse me."

While the agent turned away to answer his phone, Agents Mortimer and Stone remained standing a few feet from Gracen and staring at him. Gracen, for his part, tried to look casual, yet still darted glances in Leon's direction. *Dumbass, don't look at me. Don't you fucking fuck this up, you stupid fat—*

"Detective Hulsey." Porter was waving him over. He walked casually over to where the agent was standing near the

SUV. Porter lowered the phone and covered it with his hand. "We got a trace on the phone," he said.

Leon thought for a second, then figured it out. "What, you mean *the* phone? *O'Connor's* phone that he gave to Pelletier?"

Porter nodded and went back to the phone and said, "Yeah, I'm here, go ahead." The next few minutes were filled with nothing but silence, a bit of murmuring from someone on the other end of the phone, and Porter giving out the occasional "Mm-hm" and "Yeah" and "Uh-huh" and "Got that." Finally, he hung up and said, "They're tracing the signal now. They think they can pinpoint it down within ten yards. Motherfucker called the Parole Commission in Valdosta."

Leon tried to connect that with anything that made sense, and found that it was impossible. "The Parole Commission?" he asked. While he was vexed, he was also glad to have this break in Gracen's interrogation. Though, he now realized that Stone and Mortimer were chatting it up with him. *Keep up the ruse, you fat fuck. So help me god, if you cost my sister a husband, I'll make sure you end up in a cell right next to Pat.* "What the hell did he call the Parole Commission for?"

"They don't know yet, but they're finding that out. It'll take a bit to find out which officer he spoke to and then to find the call records from the office in Valdosta. You up for another drive?"

"Where to?"

"Groomes Street. You know it?"

"Yeah. What's there?"

"Pelletier's phone. C'mon, hop in. They don't have an exact location on that street, but it wouldn't hurt to go ahead and get on our way. Stone! Mortimer! Let's head out!" Mortimer broke quickly from their chat with Gracen and went for the driver's seat, and Stone was right behind him. Agent Porter stepped over to Grace and said, "Really quickly, Mr. Gracen. Do you know where the *vory* might have stations or digs in the city? Any rumors at all?"

Gracen shook his head. "Naw, man. They be around, but not 'zactly all that social, ya feel me?"

Porter nodded and said, "Thanks for your time. Sorry to drag you out here like this for so little."

"S'cool, man. Peace."

Porter turned to the SUV.

Leon gave one last glance to Gracen, who stood there for a moment, looking the question at him. Leon nodded curtly, telling him he'd done well enough, and waved goodbye, then hopped in the back seat and left Cee-gray alone in Chernobyl.

10

He used the money he'd taken from the dead thug to buy the bus ticket. He sat in the very back near the emergency exit, slumped in his seat so that only his eyes were visible above the window.

Two seats in front of him sat a fat black woman in a blue coat, red scarf and red fluffy hat. She had a newspaper in her hand. Three rows up from her and across the aisle, an elderly black man sat asleep in his seat, pitching forward every so often and catching himself an instant before he fell to the floor.

Spencer watched the street signs slide by silently, and knew that his stop was coming up here pretty soon. Out his window, he spied a Waffle House. He was hungry, and those were always open 24/7. The bus was now outside of the official terminator line between the Bluff and places that mattered. The change was gradual. There were still a few stop signs with spray paint on them, but also a few Laundromats that dared to stay open all night, and less homeless crack addicts wandering about aimlessly. A march towards progress and civilization.

For no reason, Pat and his order for a 2013 Dodge Dart popped to the forefront of Spencer's mind. He'd all but forgotten about the job he was meant to do for his old friend, and wondered that if he were to finish the task tonight, would Pat still be friend enough to pay him for it?

When the bus driver hollered out, "Clover Street!" he got up slowly and waved his hand. "That's me," Spencer said, yawning and stretching out. His stomach grumbled. He was thinking about that Waffle House back there.

He moved towards the front of the bus, glancing at the headline of the newspaper the woman was reading (**Disasters Continue to Strain FEMA's Resources**) and nodded affably to the old man. When Spencer got to the door, though, he stopped. Coming up the steps were two black girls…and for a moment he

211

was befuddled, because he swore it was the two nigglets from earlier tonight. "How did you...?" *How did you get away?* was what he was going to say, but then he blinked and the two black girls turned into two *other* black girls, slightly older than the ones he'd seen abducted and neither one of them dressed in the blue Jimmy Hendrix shirt. "How do you do?" he said, recovering and stepping off. The girls looked at him queerly, and said nothing.

The street he was on was quiet, but not quite as empty as those in the Bluff had been. Instead of scuttling crackheads on the prowl, there were a few honest citizens out. Two women walked side-by-side, and though they weren't dressed in the nicest of clothes it was obvious by their gait they weren't layabout whores who were so accustomed to street violence that they wished to linger for too long in any one place. No, they were girls who knew to get their asses home and to trust no one and nobody on the way because it might be someone who had escaped from the Bluff.

Bluff people knew each other too well, got too complacent with all the violence going on. These women moved with purpose. They had hopes and dreams, maybe even went to a community college and held high their aspirations to get even further away from the Bluff than they already were.

A trio of old men were stepping out of a car parked along the sidewalk. The *beep-beep* of the car alarm being switched on wasn't something you would hear in the 'hood, and neither would you hear their friendly, jocular conversation. No, old men in the 'hood spoke quietly, wearily. These men seemed quite comfortable here.

Clayton Road was less than a quarter of a mile up from where he now stood. A swift jog ought to get him there in no time.

Spencer moved out of sight first, lest he be spotted by a random patrol car. He stepped into the shadows between a closed gas station and a closed pawn shop. He hopped a tall wooden fence and hustled across the back yards of a few duplexes and then finally came upon Clayton Road, which went downhill for a piece, then dead-ended at a cul-de-sac. House number 42 was second from the end on the left. It was a white, two-storey home that looked well kept. Pink flamingoes in the front yard indicated someone cared enough about the place. There were still Christmas lights wrapped around wooden pillars at the front door. A pair of wicker rocking chairs and a rustic-looking swing were on the porch. A single car was parked in the driveway, a gray 2003 Buick Rendezvous.

There were no lights on.

Spencer wasted no time at all. He walked directly up the porch without stealth. There was a doorbell, but ringing it didn't seem to produce a sound inside so he knocked. A few seconds went by. Nothing. He knocked again. Still nothing. He started hammering the door with his fist.

A light came on in a window to his right and someone pushed a curtain to one side. Spencer held up the wallet of the unsuspecting well-to-do-looking man in Roswell he'd beaten down on his drive across the South. He held it up in an officious, bored manner, evocative of an officer out responding to something he didn't wish to respond to.

The curtain flapped back, and a second later someone was fumbling with a lock. The door cracked open, but what separated him from Tidov was a pair of chains from the door to the doorframe. An eye of pale ice stared out at him indifferently. That's how Spencer knew this guy could easily become violent. Only predators were so confident that they could be calm when some stranger hammered on their door in the middle of the night. "Evans sent me," he said.

Tidov's icy eye looked at him dubiously. "Evans?" he said, his voice coming from a mouthful of gravel.

"He's been tryin' to call you. What've you been doing?"

"Sleeping. You talking about Eugene?" He spoke in a Russian accent. Spencer's man, no doubt.

"Eugene Evans. Yeah. You know another one?"

Tidov was unmoved, unintimidated. "What's he want?"

"To check up on you."

"Why doesn't he come himself?"

"You know he's got fibromyalgia. It's hard for him to get around. Try an' be a little more understanding, okay, Mr. Tidov?" There passed a few seconds of just two monsters staring across at one another. *Come into my parlor*, he thought. *'Tis the prettiest little parlor that you ever did spy.* Only this time, the spider convinced the fly to invite him into his home.

"What's your name?" Tidov asked suspiciously.

"Blake Madison," he said. "Parole Commission, Valdosta branch."

A moment. Then, Tidov slowly shut the door. A second later he removed the chain, and opened wide for him, standing to one side. "His fibromyalgia, huh? Told his dumb ass to try that tramadol stuff, but he wouldn't listen to me." Spencer stepped inside, as confidently as he would if he'd performed random house inspections like any other parole officer. He was mimicking the same air as the guards in cellhouse A had carried themselves with when they performed their random inspections on his and Martin's bunk. "But Evans is into that holistic shit."

Spencer knew when he was being tested. Even if he wasn't, he wasn't about to walk blindly into a verbal trap. "I wouldn't know," he said. "I barely know the old fuck. I just got assigned to help take over his cases when he had to go to the hospital. He was ranting and raving over the phone, talkin' about how modern medicine still won't consider it a genuine disorder. They think it's all in people's heads." Spencer recalled that much from an article in *Time* magazine that he'd read back in prison. Funny what the brain conjured up when under stress. He'd learned to accept these little details and add them to his vocabulary and discussions; peppering them throughout his everyday speech made many people think he was smarter than he actually was, and afforded him all sorts of unearned respect.

The door shut behind him. Spencer kept his hands in his pockets and turned to face Yevgeny Tidov. He was tall and built. Doubtless he went to the gym. He had a scar like a rope burn across his neck. He wore no shirt, and up and down his body was an array of tattoos, intricately woven together. A sunburst at the center of his chest was the nucleus of it all, and from it rose wild animals charging toward the viewer. Spencer checked his right arm. There it was. The crimson bear. Only this wasn't the same man he'd seen earlier, not the one staring out at him from the Expedition challengingly. *I'll bet he knows where to find him, though.*

"Anybody else home?" Spencer asked.

"My sister and her boyfriend are upstairs," said Tidov.

A lie. Spencer didn't know how he knew these things, but he did. The eyes flitted in certain directions, there was a pause that was just too long before his answer, a skip in the beat of conversation that didn't keep the natural flow. It had been conjured up out of nowhere and fast. But Tidov knew on some level that this was a dance. He knew something wasn't right, he just didn't know what. *We're the same. I've just been at it longer, I'm more aware of what I am. What we are.*

"You want a fucking drink while you look around?" Tidov said, moving past him.

Spencer touched the Glock Pocket 10 in his hoodie pocket, squeezed the grip, and said, "I'm not supposed to drink while on the job."

"Not even coffee?"

"Oh, well, *now* you're talkin'," he chuckled, and followed Tidov into the kitchen. While the Russian pulled out the coffee grinds, Spencer opened a couple of drawers, pretended to look over them. He went to a sliding glass door, which looked out onto a back yard with two hammocks strung up between a few pines. "Mind if I check upstairs?" Spencer said. "Tell me which room your sister and her boyfriend are in, so I can avoid waking them."

Tidov glanced over his shoulder. He opened a few cabinets, looking for the coffee cups. "Well, you probably already woke them," he said, still playing the game. "But it's the first door on the right. Please don't disturb them."

"Not to worry. Just gotta check the usual places. Bathrooms, showers, toilets, under the sink, shit like that."

"Evans never does this." Tidov took out an old filter from his coffeemaker and installed a new one. "I've kept very clean. I didn't go to prison for drugs or for hiding any drug money, so he leaves my house alone."

"Every parole officer is different, you know," he said, shrugging and stepping out of the kitchen. "There are tender-asses and there are hard-asses. Guess which one I am." He smirked and walked upstairs, leaving Tidov to his umbrage and coffeemaker.

At the top of the stairs was a pile of clothes stacked beside a hamper, which was overflowing. He parted two wooden sliding doors and surveyed the washing nook. The washer and dryer were both relatively new. He opened each one, both full, one of whites the other of colors. He passed the first door on the right. As he went by, though, he knocked, and got no answer. He briefly tested the doorknob. Locked.

Farther down the hall was a closet, used for nothing but cardboard box storage. There were old Ajax boxes and Sears boxes. Spencer pulled one out, opened it, and found several unopened rolls of duct table. Another box contained rubber tubing. Another one had pieces to an old Dark Angel paintball gun.

He put the boxes back and walked to the end of the hall, to the bedroom he presumed to be where he'd woken the Russian from his sleep. A small lamp was on, suffusing the walls in a dim orange light. A tangle of sheets was half on the bed, half on the floor; the cocoon he'd shed on his way downstairs.

"You like yours strong, Mr. Madison?" Tidov called from the kitchen.

"I do," he called down, stepping inside the room. Many things leapt out at him at once. There was a taste in the air. It was musty. Like sweat forced out. He looked up at the spackled ceiling, looked across at the walls laid bare. There was a desk with a copy of *Atlas Shrugged* and *A Game of Thrones*, as well as a computer, but there were no pictures of family sitting anywhere. No pictures of any kind, actually. Black curtains covered the two windows. The floor was clean. There was no TV in here, which meant if there was one in the house it was probably in the living room downstairs. This was as workspace.

"Sugar?" Tidov hollered from downstairs.

Spencer smiled and muttered to himself, "Yes, sweetie?"

"What?"

"Yeah," he called back, "I'll take some sugar."

Spencer stepped back into the hall. If the bedroom had been vacant and utilitarian, then the room across the hall was its storage counterpart. He flipped the lights on to get a better look, and tilted his head in curiosity. "You keep dogs?" Spencer hollered at him, stepping inside the room. The cages were too big for dogs, plainly. They were latched cunningly together, one set of solid steel chains connecting them in a row, with a feeding trough that ran through the bars of one and into the neighboring cage. A feeder that looked like what Spencer had seen used in his uncle's chicken houses was sitting there beside the farthest cage, no doubt on an automatic timer.

"What?" Tidov hollered.

"I said, *do you keep dogs?*"

The door had multiple locks added unnecessarily, but from the outside, keeping people on the inside locked in. He pulled the door back and forth. It was heavy. The wooden façade hid a solid steel interior, no doubt. These windows were covered by more black curtains, and the walls…covered in soundproofing foam, like musicians would put in their recording studios, and lots of it. Spencer hadn't seen this much soundproofing foam since a musician pal of his and Hoyt's had spent all his drug money trying to make it big in the rapping business, back in the day when Atlanta had been *the* hotspot for hip hop.

Yes, anyone could see that this room was not meant for dogs. But it was worth asking to hear Tidov's pitiful excuse.

"*Da.* I mean, *yes,*" Tidov called up. His feet were plodding up the stairs. "I sometimes train German Shepherds and Rottweilers. Some pits, too, but not so many these days." Spencer stood at the center of the room, waiting for him. When Tidov got there, he stood for a moment with two cups of coffee in his hand, looking at him. Spencer looked at his tattoos, saw a bald eagle and a bear fighting it out, perhaps a symbol of Tidov's Russian heritage fighting with his American citizenship?

I'm getting all "pensive" again, he thought with some amusement.

Spencer stood there. "Sound doesn't carry well in here," he said.

The Russian nodded, and took a sip of his own coffee. "The dogs bark a lot until I train them good. I didn't want it to keep my sister and her boyfriend up at all hours. It doesn't totally kill the sound, but it helps some."

Spencer nodded. "I'll bet it does. And I'll bet from outside you can't hear a thing."

Tidov took another sip. "No, you can't."

He's one cool customer. Very powerful. Very cocksure that nothing can bring down his house of cards. I really, really hate this motherfucker. "Good coffee?" he asked.

"*Da.*"

"Sure smells good."

The Russian laughed, remembering himself. "I'm so sorry. Here's yours." He stepped into the room and held out the other cup. Spencer regarded the cup with more than a slim degree of humor. And that's how the silly game ended.

" 'Come into my parlor,' said the spider to the fly. ''Tis the prettiest little parlor you ever did spy.' "

"I'm sorry?"

Spencer looked at the offered coffee, then at Tidov. "Is this how you do it?"

The Russian put on the most befuddled face. *Oh, he's very good.* "Do what, Mr. Madison?" Tidov asked.

"What's in it?" He smiled. "C'mon, you can tell me. Lorazopam? You sprinkle some in there? Heard about a pedo priest in Jersey used to do that. Or do you prefer to deliver it in a cellulose capsule?"

"What're you talking about?"

"Three grams puts 'em right out, doesn't it? They don't feel a thing. You can do whatever you want. No squealing, no crying, no pitching a fit about all the blood. No, 'I want my mommy' this, or 'where's my daddy' that. Pretty slick op you got goin' here, friend." The Russian stared at him, the coffee still extended. "But here's your problem. I'm not a parole officer any more than you're a dog trainer or Laurence Fishburne's cock. You've got skeletons in your closet and myself, well," he laughed, "I'm runnin' outta closets."

"I...I don't understand your words," Tidov said, trying to take a step back, but a look from Spencer indicated that wouldn't be wise. He stood there a moment, perhaps realizing his hands were full, and recognizing his precarious situation. The door was three steps behind him. Spencer still had his hands in his pocket. The room was made soundproof. "I, um..." He swallowed. "I just train dogs in here, Mr. Madison. I'm a dog trainer..."

"No, you know what you are?" Spencer took a step closer to him. "You're a careless walker in the woods. That's what they call you people in wilderness survival training. Careless walkers. Traipsing about with no care about where your foot goes, no consideration for what rabbit's warren or gopher's hole you might be fucking up. You chop down trees and hunt the shit outta things until they go extinct. But then you step on a rattler, and the whole world changes. For a moment you stand still, lookin' at this thing as it rattles, hisses, and gets ready to bite. An' you don't know what the fuck to do because everyone's always been afraid o' *you*."

The other wolf lowered his eyes. "I'm going back downstairs—"

"Fuck you, Vladimir Putin," Spencer chuckled. "I've got a gun in my hand an' you're three steps away from the door in a soundproof fuckin' room with both yer hands occupied, bitch. You go where I say you can go. You got that?" A few seconds went by while Tidov considered. "Stop thinking! You have no options. Now, drink my fuckin' coffee for me." Tidov looked at him. "What's in it? Lorazopam? Or something to just make me tired like some valium or some shit? Go on, drink up, motherfucker." Spencer took the Glock Pocket 10 out of his pocket. "I'm waitin'.'"

The other predator's eyes showed that he had time for one more defiant thought.

Spencer raised the gun and said, "If the neighbors couldn't hear all those girls' screams, I'm sure the worst they'll think is that you set off a firecracker over here. Drink."

Only two more seconds went by before the Russian made his decision. He sipped at the coffee, and when Spencer smiled at him and shook his head, he knew he had to empty it. Tidov turned it up, emptying it completely.

"Now, turn around and start downstairs." Tidov did as bidden, slowly, sluggishly, like he was wearing a weighted vest. "I want the keys to that Buick outside. You know what? Fuck it, I'll hotwire the bitch." Then, something occurred to him. "Wait! Ho-*ho*, man! Let's stop inside your sister's and her boyfriend's room. Whattaya say? What's really in there? Inquiring minds wanna know, bitch. Open sesame."

Tidov took on the most dejected look. He blinked a few times, then nodded. They walked slowly down the hall. Spencer wanted to hurry because on some level he knew their time alone here was limited, but he also knew that rushing things tended to make a person sloppy. *And didn't Dr. McCulloch always tell me to stop and think about my actions more?* So he allowed Tidov his heavy-shouldered walk to the room. The Russian reached up, tried to turn the doorknob, couldn't. "You've got the key," Spencer said. It wasn't a question.

Tidov nodded, and Spencer watched the Russian carefully as he set one of the coffee cups down and fumbled in his back pocket. There were numerous keys on that key chain, not all of them of the shape for standard doorknobs (no doubt for the cages) and all of them color-coded. He found the right key after a moment, and inserted it. He turned it slowly and the door opened. As soon as it did, Spencer smelled it. A mélange of formaldehyde and other chemicals. There was also that sweat smell again, and decay.

It was dark until Tidov reached over to flip three light switches. He didn't even wait for Spencer to ask, he knew the score now.

The room was bathed in sickly fluorescent lighting, that unflattering kind that brought out every pimple, boil, scar and sweat molecule on the skin. Other than the sad lighting, though, the room was decorated with various rainbows on the ceiling, a playground at the center with a seesaw, and a twin bed at the far corner with plush pink pillows and big, brown, fuzzy teddy bears sitting happily alongside an old Tickle Me Elmo. One of Elmo's eyes was falling off to one side, giving the creature a deranged look. There was a pair of handcuffs beside Elmo, and they were currently open, which to Spencer meant recently used.

Along the walls were setting lights, no doubt activated as needed for greater picture quality. And of course, there was the soundproofing foam double-layered on all of the walls. There was recording equipment everywhere, including a Sony HVR-Z1U camcorder, which Spencer happened to know went for around $2,000 because he'd stolen a car a couple years back with one of those in the trunk and had pawned it. "Classy set-up," he said. "What's in that room?" He pointed to a door at the far side of the room that he suspected led to what would be a bathroom, and something else, too.

"If you're going to kill me—" Tidov started.

"I haven't decided that yet. I told you, I'm a monster, just like you, and I don't care what you have in that room. I'm not here to rescue the children. I'm here because of that fuckwad who stared daggers at me earlier."

Tidov regarded Spencer for a moment before he stepped over to the bathroom door and opened it. He flipped on the lights again without being asked, and when he did, Spencer found yet another soundproof room. Two large plastic tubs, big enough for bodies, were stacked against one wall. Hanging from the opposite wall was a shelf filled bottles of hydrofluoric acid. The toilet remained, but the bathtub and shower had been removed to make room for a waist-high steel table. On top of the table was a child-sized black bag, with a child-sized object inside it.

"Open that up."

Tidov hesitated, but obeyed. He moved lethargically, stumbling once. Whatever he'd put in the coffee to drug Spencer was now coursing through him. *He tried to play it too cool. Should've come at me guns blazin', but then I guess he still wasn't sure about me. He wasn't listenin' to his instincts.*

The Russian moved sleepily over to the table and unzipped the bag without ceremony. He parted the black plastic covers, and Spencer waved him to back off then peered inside. A young girl, no older than nine, half black, half Hispanic, just lying there, eyes opened and rolled back. Her lips were dried. The aroma coming out of the bag was that of urine and feces.

The room required another look. The hydrofluoric acid was smart, as were the plastic tubs. Hydrofluoric acid would melt through pretty much anything, but not plastic.

"Looks like you bagged another one," Spencer said, laughing. Tidov didn't seem to get it. "That's called a double entendre. It's clever shit, motherfucker, *you* didn't think of it."

Tidov shrugged helplessly. He didn't know what Spencer expected of him.

"You know," Spencer said, "I've done a lotta shit in my life, and I've learned the various ins an' outs of all kinds of work. But I wouldn't have the first idea how to run an operation like this one. Looks like you cats have given this some serious thought." He looked at the Russian. "Can I ask you somethin'? Do their screams ever keep you up at night? I mean, when you think back on them, when you're remembering how they sounded, does it mess with your head or do you still get off on it?" Tidov didn't answer. Spencer smiled. "You get off on it, don't you? You sly dog. C'mon, where do you keep the recordings?"

It didn't take any more convincing. Tidov tilted his head to one side to pop his neck, then led Spencer back into the playing room. Beside the recording equipment were a few mics, and connected to those mics was a soundboard. "Cue one up," Spencer said. "I wanna listen." He thought to himself, *Need to hurry up, Spence ol' boy. The five-oh is gonna be here any minute, you know this.* But he had to hear. He had to.

Tidov sat in the only chair beside the soundboard and fiddled with a few dials. He pulled up one file on the small Hewlett-Packard screen, and after a few seconds the room was filled with screams. They came from a pair of small speakers on either side of the computer monitor. There was the smacking of flesh against flesh, loud grunts from men shouting things in Russian, and screams. The shrieking. Tidov sat there, his eyelids starting to get heavy. Spencer listened to one Russian shout in English, "Cry for your mother! Cry for her!"

The next thing to come through the speakers was a girl's god awful plea for help from her mother. The smacking of flesh on flesh got louder, the grunting more intense, the screams greater and greater.

"Impressive," Spencer said. "You can turn it off now." Tidov seemed only too happy to do this. With the click of a mouse, they were once again alone with one another in silence.

In that silence, something terrible happened. Spencer didn't know where it started—he never knew when these things started—but there was a pulse just behind his eyes. Like the migraines he used to get as a kid that came whenever his vertigo came over him. Brief spells, something that came from intense anger that few people ever felt. No one felt rage like a psychopath, he'd read that somewhere. Whereas love and acceptance was at the forefront of other people's minds, anger and an unnaturally strong need to be dominant was all the psychopath cared for. It could be spurred by many things. In Spencer's case, it was always spurred by the thought that someone else thought *they* had power. It offended him, even when not directed at him. Hell, *especially* when not directly at him. He felt like a master artist looking at some lesser artist's work and saying, "No, you're doing it all wrong."

And like any uppity artist, Spencer felt the need to voice his opinion, then *force* it. "I want to know where the others are."

Tidov might've been a monster, but he did have a degree of loyalty in him. He tried to hide the truth of his accomplices. "What...what others?" His eyes closed, then opened again, then closed, then opened. He was starting to go out.

"Oh, c'mon now. An operation like this doesn't go off without a hitch without some pals." Spencer waved his Glock about the room. "Surely there are customers who help pay for this. And there *must* be some overhead, am I right?"

"Fffffuck...yyyy—"

"All right, all right, fuck me," Spencer said. "Stand up. Let's go for a walk outside. I don't want to have to carry you."

At this suggestion, Tidov's eyes opened a bit wider. *He believes going outside is good for him. He thinks he's safer outside than he is inside.* Indeed, the Russian stood up with a bit more verve and exited the room. On his way out, Spencer saw a bottle of sal volatile (smelling salts) on one of the shelves. No doubt used to wake the kids up after they'd been drugged...or after they'd passed out from the pain. He pocketed the bottle. *Be needin' this later.* He also picked up the pair of handcuffs beside the lazy-eyed Elmo.

Spencer didn't turn off any of the lights, nor did he close any of the doors. Whenever the cops finally showed up here, he wanted this to occupy their time, eat up more of the manpower that should be out there looking for him. *It's a helluva night in the A-T-L*, he thought.

They made it downstairs, but by now Tidov was starting to lose a great deal of his balance. *It won't be long before he passes out for good.* On the way to the front door, he spotted a Motorola Droid phone. "Is this yours?" he said.

Tidov, drowsy and leaning against the front door, turned to look at him. "Yesssss."

He picked it up. "Good. Now, out the door with you, Vladimir."

"My name's...Yevgeny..."

"I know your name, fucker. Now ask me if I give a fuck."

"Do you...give...?"

"*Fuck* no!"

The room was quiet for a time. The Harper girl sat against the far wall, not looking at either of them. Kaley sat on the edge of the bed holding Shan. They remained this way for what seemed like an eternity; the Harper girl, isolated and alone and terrified; Shannon, leaning on her sister and lost and terrified; Kaley, brushing the head and patting the back of her sister and terrified out of her mind.

None of them knew how to move on. None of them knew how to accept their new lives as prisoners. Trapped in that worst of in-between zones, where one is placed into a miserable new set of circumstances and yet still clings to what they once had. It was a delicate time. It was a time when a hard decision needed to be made, when a person had to determine whether they were going to fight or submit, knowing that either one could mean termination. It wouldn't take Kaley twenty years to figure out that truth, she knew it right then.

The first thing to do was to make the decision. *I don't want to be raped and killed. And I don't want Shannon to be raped and killed.* Okay, that was easy. Now, what was she going to do about it?

With tremulous hands, Little Sister reached up to Big Sister's neck. The Anchor was once again established. It pulled Kaley down, down, down…

…down…

There, she felt the Oceans of Sorrow churning. That's what Nan had called them. The Oceans of Sorrow. That's where a person's worst thoughts resided, where their dashed hopes went to die and decay.

Once, Nan had told her about her sister Irene, dead many years before Nan went to join her. Irene had been a talented musician by the time she was seventeen. Violinist, pianist, and cellist. She had shown such promise, but the inferiority of her circumstances (i.e. where she was born) had played negatively on where she ended up in life. She was talented, but not so talented that it guaranteed her a scholarship, so college would still cost her. And as practical a woman as Irene had tried to be, she still felt

224

something for one or two of the men from the 'hood she grew up in. Being knocked up at age eighteen, and then again when she was twenty-one, pretty much dashed her hopes. At first she decided to put off college, but only for a short time. A year, no more. But then came her third child from a third father. Ten years later, Nan said she could no longer go anywhere near Irene. "Her sorrow pulled me down, chil'," Nan told her. "All that Ocean o' Sorrow. It was them dashed hopes of what might've been down there in all o' that black water. If I stayed too long around her, I'd sho'ly drown. It even caused her to secretly hate her own children." She had pronounced the word *chirren*. "Oh chil', no mother wants to admit this, but many of them *do* secretly despise their young'uns, at least one of 'em. They may cry at they funeral or when they graduate, but those are tears shed for what *could* have been, what *should* have been. They don't even know that they feel this way. That's my burden to know. An' yours too now, chil'. Yours too."

Kaley had thought Nan a bit silly, even crazy, but then she had to admit that there were times when she felt bogged down, as well. Being around her mother was like that. Kaley didn't have the heart to tell her mother, for she truly was empathetic and could sense those dashed hopes of hers, but she also didn't want it to rub off on her, or on Shan. Shan didn't know it yet but she had the charm, and as long as she was around their mother the more likely she was to drown in the Ocean of Sorrow.

And it'll bring me down now, if I let it.

The attachment Kaley had now to her sister had her feeling the fear of a child. It mixed with her own. It had her feel every little nook and cranny of her sister's terror. Like a tumor, it swelled and threatened to overtake them both.

"I'm sorry I ran," Shannon whimpered. "I didn't wanna get you hurt, I thought if I got away—"

"Hey, shush!"

"—that I could get help for us both—"

"I said *shush*, girl! Don't you ever apologize to me for tryin' to save yourself. You..." She wanted to say *You should've kept running*, but it was senseless to make Little Sister even more upset than she already was. "You're my sister," she said, hugging her.

"Why're they doing this, Kaley?" she cried. "It's not *fair*! We didn't do anything!"

Shannon's fear seized hold of Kaley's heart, and squeezed. "*Shh.* I know, sweetie. I know. *Shh.*" The fear was like a needle of ice through her heart. Then, the coldness spread, and her whole heart seemed to stop.

Shannon shivered in her arms. It was agony being this close to her. But she loved her little sister too much to leave her now. She couldn't do it. Not even for a second. Shan was frightened worse than the Harper girl, and she needed comfort or she would never get through this.

You have to ward yo heart, chil', she could almost hear Nan saying. *Protect it. That empathy you have, that charm, it's like mine. And, oh, chil'! What heartbreak it can bring. Ward yo heart, chil'. Ya hear?*

And that's when Kaley realized what she had to do. She had to sever the Connection. She had to cut ties to the Anchor. It was the only way to find strength. If she wasn't strong enough alone, she could never be strong enough for the both of them.

"Shannon," she said. "Shan? I need you to let go of me."

"Where are you going?!" Shannon demanded at once, clinging hard to Kaley even as Big Sister moved to stand. She looked up at Kaley with big, round, rheumy eyes.

"Does it look like I can go anywhere else but here?" she said, perhaps a little sternly. "Now...*let go.*" She wouldn't. Kaley pushed her away, and Shan fought it, shaking her head and crying. Shan had the charm, too, and didn't yet know that she was in its thrall, that she was *addicted* to Big Sister. *Like Mom's addiction*, Kaley.

"Don't leave me—"

"Shannon Alexis Dupré," Kaley said, in a voice remarkably like Ricky's. Ricky had been the closest thing either one of them had ever had to a father, and the deep command he had held over them had been something that Kaley had actually been thankful for at the time. He was also the one who pointed out that Shan's initials were SAD, and the thought of that broke Kaley's heart all over again. "You listen to me," she went on, now that she had Little Sister's attention. "I am not going to leave you. I can't leave you, not even if you were on the other side o' the world. You know that, don't you?"

Shannon nodded. "Y-yes."

"We have an Anchor. Do you understand what I'm sayin', girl?"

Shannon nodded. "Uh-huh." She sniffled, and Kaley fought back the urge to reach down and wipe away the snot around her nose and the tears streaming around her eyes. Touching her again might poison them both.

"Now, let me go."

The little hands were as unbreakable as iron clasps. But Kaley had discovered a key, and the locks came off. When they let go, it was the most reluctant feeling Kaley had ever sensed out of any person before. Deep need washed over her, and for a moment she fought to resist grabbing for her sister again.

Kaley pushed herself up off the bed before her resolve broke and walked over to inspect the door. It stood about seven feet tall and was made of wood. She tried to will herself to think about something other than Shan huddled up and alone behind her. The other side, if she recalled correctly, had been smooth, whereas this side was flecked with peeling paint. A spot about head height in front of her was dented inwards, and was suspiciously fist-shaped.

Without knowing why, Kaley reached up to touch it.

Her knees buckled.

It held her.

There was a wash of fear and rage. Boundless rage. A young person's rage. A *boy's* rage. There was temerity there, a great deal of it. And there was pain. He'd had nerve and was awash in shame and bitterness. Whoever he was, he hadn't given up.

It held her.

There was a sinking feeling in her stomach, and then it did flip-flops. For a moment she felt nauseas again. She felt a hand touch her shoulder. Someone was trying to reassure the boy, giving him soft promises that it would be okay, that the pain was over with. Then, there was the white-hot rage again. A silken fury that felt disturbingly satisfying. It was directed inwards. The boy felt angry at himself for having believed them, even as they had

227

handcuffed him to the headboard on the bed. He was angry at himself for falling for it a second time.

It held her.

It held her.

It held her.

Suddenly Nan's voice filled her, *Ward your heart!* it screamed. Kaley jerked her hand away from the door, and realized she was drooling on herself. When she turned around, she looked at Shannon and the Harper girl, both staring at her from where they sat. Kaley wiped her mouth and swallowed.

Wordlessly, she walked over to inspect the sink. It dripped brown water every ten or fifteen seconds. A stain on the floor showed that this remained a constant. She tested the faucet. The water that poured out wasn't so brown, but there was definitely a darker hue to it than should be.

Kaley moved over to the wall where the toilet was. Directly above it was an air vent, no bigger than Shannon was wide.

Two steps from her, the Harper girl sniffled.

"Your name's Bonetta?" Kaley asked. The Harper girl treated her like a ghost, like she wasn't there. "Hand me one of those chairs, would ya?" Bonetta Harper didn't move. She held her locket in her hands, shivering.

"I'll get one," Shannon said.

"No, Shan. You stay right there. Bonetta?" Still, the girl didn't move. Kaley snapped her fingers twice. "Yo, girl! Dry it up! I ain't your babysitter. Now hop up and grab me a chair."

"*I ain't yours to boss around!*" Bonetta suddenly screamed.

All at once, Kaley nearly buckled from the girl's fear and rage. It wasn't quite as powerful as the boy's rage that still haunted this room, but it was close. "All right, then. Will you *please* grab me one o' those chairs?"

"Get it yourself," she said, trembling. "Get it your own damn self. Just leave me alone."

"Givin' up just like that, huh?" The Harper girl looked at her. It had been the right thing to say, as well as the wrong thing to say. "You know they gonna *fuck* you, right? You heard them?" Bonetta looked up at her with eyes wide with indignity. *Sometimes, you gotta give some tough love, chil'*, she remembered

228

Nan saying once when she'd been honest with her feedback of a drawing of MLK that Kaley had done. "You know that, right?" Kaley egged.

"Shut your filthy fuckin'—"

"Or what? What'choo gonna do, girl? Beat my ass? I bet I beat yours."

Shan stopped crying, and looked between the two older girls.

Bonetta Harper rose. In that moment, Kaley remembered where she'd seen this girl. She hadn't looked like much while curled up and cowering in the back of the SUV, but now that she had found some reason to rise to her fullest, she took the persona of the bully Kaley knew her best as. "Don't you talk to me like that," she warned.

Kaley nodded. "You go to English Avenue Middle."

"That's right," she said. "I know you." It was a haughty, threatening statement.

"You're that girl that punched Andrea Kessler in her mouth, took out two o' her teeth."

"That's right, yeah." Again, haughty.

Kaley nodded. "And now you're stuck in here like the rest of us," she said. "And you're scared." She took a step towards her, and Bonetta took a step closer in response. The men outside had, for a time, robbed her of her playground powers, all the authority she held at EAMS, but now that they were gone and it was just them girls Bonetta was back. She might've been slightly younger and slightly smaller than Kaley, but she was a firm, wiry girl and everyone knew she would throw down at the drop of a hat. "I know you're very scared. So are we."

"I ain't scared."

Kaley nodded. "You are. I can...I can feel it."

"What'choo mean, *feel* it?"

"It's something I can do. I feel these things. Fear is real. It's...it's an energy. It spreads fast, like love or hate. It's viral. Ya know what viral means?"

"The fuck is this shit?" Bonetta said derisively.

"It means it's catching. The less control you have over your fear, the less control my sister and I have over ours," Kaley explained, reciting something Nan had told her a year before she

229

died. "And the less my sister and I control *our* fear, the less you can control yours. It's a vicious cycle. We...we have to work together, understand? And that means—"

"My daddy's comin' for me—"

Kaley sighed. "You're daddy's not here—"

"But he's comin'!"

Suddenly, Kaley felt herself feeding off of Bonetta's anger. Her haughtiness, her audacity, it was all just too much. Like the fear, it was infectious. "You keep believing that," Kaley said. "Put that hope in your right hand, then shit in your left. We'll see which one fills up first." Now that was definitely one of Ricky's lines.

"What the fuck is that supposed to mean?" Bonetta took a step again, but this time backward, as though she wanted to keep from catching whatever madness had hold of Kaley.

"It means ain't nobody comin' for us. You heard that bitch Olga. They keep tabs on kids like us. They scout around, see who is an' who ain't watched out for. My mama's a meth head, how's yours?"

"My mama's *dead*—"

"And your dad? He ever around? He ever miss you?" Kaley knew the answer. No, she *felt* the answer. *Nothin' cloys like the heart of a battered woman an' a neglected child*, Nan used to say. Kaley had had to look that word up.

> **cloy** v. , cloyed , cloying , cloys . v.tr. To cause distaste or disgust by supplying with too much of something originally pleasant.

And that's what she was feeling right now from Bonetta Harper, a cloying of love. *Too* much love for her father. It was the kind of unhealthy yearning that a woman gets after years and years of worshipping an unavailable man (something else she would learn in years yet to come). Defenses were built around that kind of love, walls that protected people from seeing the truth. *That she's wasted her life loving an* idea *of a father who's never emotionally available. And defending that idea for no good reason.*

This would not be an easy wall to penetrate. "You don't talk about my daddy, bitch," Bonetta Harper snapped.

230

"Will ya'll stop fightin'?" Shan offered sweetly. So sweetly, in fact, that it threatened to cripple Kaley's heart.

Ward yo heart, chil'!

"I don't need to talk about him," Kaley said, trying to remain stalwart here. "I only need you to lose hope."

"What?" Bonetta said, her upper lip rankling.

"I need you to give up. Quit. Stop hoping. And then, I need you to get mad. *Really* mad. And then I need you to *want* to live," she said. "You found something awful about Andrea Kessler, something that made you wanna hit her, made you laugh when she lost those teeth. I need you to think the same way now."

"Are you *stupid* or somethin'?" Bonetta said, and quickly wiped away the tear that leaked from her eye. "Did you see those guns they got? You can't punch a bullet—"

"But we might be able to get outta here."

"How?"

"See that vent?" Kaley pointed to the vent cover above the toilet.

Bonetta looked, and shook her head. "Can't fuckin' reach it. Too high."

"Maybe if I had a chair?" she suggested. "A *couple* of chairs? And someone to give me a boost?"

For a moment, the two girls stared at one another, each one weakened by the other's fears, and none of their fears was worse than the fear of hoping and then having all hope dashed. They had to simultaneously give up on all the hope they had and yet work towards survival. Decide that they were likely going to die, and then try and do something about it anyway. They would have to do so mindlessly, and forget that fear ever existed.

Kaley felt the change in the other girl's heart. She felt the heart flipping its switch, the mind doing the same. There was resolution. The same audacity that had once made Bonetta so formidable on a playground and had given her the strength to knock out Andrea Kessler's teeth now returned. She was just about to agree. That's when Kaley sensed something else.

"All right," Bonetta said. "Maybe we can—"

The doorknob across the room rattled. A second later it was flung open, and in stepped their nemesis. Oni, Dmitry, stood there with Olga. The wave of intrigue and lust had been what

Kaley had smelled from the other side of the door an instant before it opened. Oni in particular had a pretty cocky air about him, and his lust…it was there. *Don't worry, little girls. We fuck you soon.* That's what he had said.

"No," Kaley breathed. If a needle of ice had punctured her heart before, a spear of ice now split it utterly in half. She knew what this was. She knew. The nausea returned, and a vision of Shannon's future hit her like a fist to the abdomen.

Olga looked at her brother. "Which one?"

Oni didn't hesitate. "That one." He pointed at Shannon.

"No," Kaley said. She stepped forward, and Bonetta stepped back, all her courage gone, shattered, depleted, nonexistent. Oni had the gun in his hand, and Olga held something that looked like a Taser. Out there somewhere, no doubt, was Mikhael. And then the men upstairs, they were probably armed, too. Bonetta was not going to stick her neck out for somebody else. "No," she said again as they stepped into the room. She dashed across and snatched Little Sister up by her sleeve and pulled her to the other side of the table, where the board games were still stacked high. "No. No. No, you can't have her. You can't."

"Move out of the way, little girl," said Oni.

"Kaley," Shan whimpered.

"No," she said. But Kaley had made a mistake. Touching Shan had reestablished the Anchor, and the fear swamped the boat of confidence she'd been floating in moments earlier. "No…no, take *me*! Take me!" she cried.

"We don't want you tonight, little Kaley," Oni said. "We want the little one. Don't worry, she will not feel—"

"Bonetta? *Bonetta, please help us!*"

But Bonetta was no help, not even to herself. She was backing up to the other side of the room. Her own confidence was utterly sapped. Sapped by the same virus that had spread from Shannon, who gripped her sister at the waist and screamed as Oni lunged for her.

The boiling rage of every person that had ever occupied their room surged through Kaley, and it came through in a piercing, a white-hot flash that sent her screaming at the man. She rushed forward, slamming the table into Oni's midsection. She pressed her weight into the table to pin him against the wall. "Run, Bonetta! Get help!" Bonetta didn't budge. Enraged by the girl's impotence, Kaley screamed uselessly. *"Somebody help us!"*

Olga came into the room and flashed the Taser at her. Kaley backed up, and, once again, made the mistake of caring too much. Instead of protecting herself, she protected Little Sister. She pushed Shannon away from the two monsters instead of keeping her weight against the table to keep Oni pinned. Dmitry knocked the table to one side, and Monopoly money spilled out onto the floor. Mikhael stepped into the room. The three of them—Olga, Dmitry and Mikhael—now formed a wall at the doorway. They stepped inside and corralled them into a corner, with Bonetta , who cried into her hands and held her locket.

"Bonetta?" Kaley said, backing up while urine trickled down her leg. "Bonetta, help us. We can get them together. *Bonetta!"*

Kaley looked around the room for something, *anything* to use as a weapon. There was nothing loose in here, it was all bolted sinks and sterile walls. Designed to be that way, no doubt. Her hands still groped along the wall as she pushed Shan behind her. "Don't you—" she started, and then Olga lunged forward with the Taser. Kaley leapt to one side. Olga missed and hit the wall. Momentarily inspired, Kaley lashed out with a balled fist and cracked Olga on the jaw. The bitch staggered a bit, her black hair a shawl about her face.

Now Mikhael and Dmitry rushed in. Kaley kicked out at their shins and, for a brief moment, felt the anger of someone else who had once been in this room. It wasn't the boy this time, no, it was another girl. This girl had bitten. She'd grabbed hold and bitten, so—

Kaley grabbed at the first outstretched hand—it was Mikhael's—and held onto it with both hands and bit as hard as she could on the first bit she could shove into her face. It was his right index finger, and she heard a sharp crunch. There was blood, and screaming, and then the world turned to fire.

The volts from the Taser hit her, controlled her, and owned her. She fell backwards stiff as a board and landed on top of Bonetta, who screamed and shrank away.

Olga was standing over her, snarling down at her, her visage a bog hag from a scary nighttime story. She screamed a string of Russian words and then slapped Oni. Mikhael clutched his ruined hand and fell back against the toilet. He screamed. Olga screamed. Dmitry screamed. Olga shoved Dmitry, who ignored this and reached out to snatch Shannon's right arm. He yanked her off the ground.

Kaley tried to scream, tried to tell Little Sister to run. But nothing came out. She was still paralyzed by the Taser's kiss. And once again, the empathic connection had cursed them. Shan hadn't wanted to sever the Anchor. *Get out of here!* Kaley willed at her. Shan felt Big Sister's command, but too late. She was now in the clutches of something far worse than the White Ninja had ever had to contend with.

As they carried her kicking and screaming from the room, Kaley fumbled impotently with her own fear, as well as Bonetta's, and Shan's, and the slimy ink that was Oni's lust. "Shan...Shannon...?"

"*Kaley!*"

"No," she whispered, trying to will herself to her feet. "No...Bonetta...please..."

Bonetta was off someplace crying to herself. *As useless as a rainstorm in the Mojave Desert*, as Ricky used to say. The thought came out of nowhere, and settled in.

They hauled Shan out the door. Before it closed, Kaley managed to scream, "Take me! *Taaaaaaaaaaaaake meeeeeeeeeeeeeeeeeeee!*"

But the door slammed closed, and *SLAM!*

Click.

After that, there was nothing for a while but the screams. Kaley's body continued to spasm, jump, and tingle as it remembered itself. She rolled onto her side, and started crawling. She vomited from the coalescing fear, and watched the white-brown mixture spread out in front of her. Half out of her mind, she watched as chunks of meat floated in that pool.

She felt the hands of the other children in the room trying to help her to her feet. Or was that imagined? Probably imagined, yes. But there was definitely empathy there. There was...

Bonetta's whimpering. Kaley was so sick with anger that she would probably throttle Bonetta Harper with her bare hands were she able. At the moment, all she was able to do was crawl. The door of cracked and peeling paint was a million miles away, it seemed. From the floor, all she could see was Monopoly money, as well as the shoe pawn and the dog pawn. *Shan always wanted to be the dog, and Ricky was always the race car.* Community Chest cards were mixed in with the balls of Hungry Hungry Hippos. She would never play these games again, and in years to come it would be difficult to explain to others just why she refrained from joining in with them.

She made it to the door, and came to her knees. She pulled weakly at the doorknob, and did not stop trying to turn it no matter how many times it failed to open. "Take me," she said. "Take me. Take me. Take me. Take me. Take me. Take me. Take me."

Several minutes passed. Several eternities.

This was all a dream. She was convinced of it. Nothing so horrible could happen to people so good. This sort of thing happened in places like you heard about on TV, in Darfur or Rwanda, not here, not to people like her or her sister. A bullet perhaps, yes, but not—

She was impaled by the pain and terror long before she heard any screams.

And she sank…

In the Ocean of Sorrow, she sank, deeper and deeper. And like any drowning creature she reached out. Not physically with her hands, but with her beseeching heart. It was so frail and timid that it needed someone, some*thing* to show her the way. Her world was darkness. Though her eyes still worked and she was somewhat cognizant of Bonetta Harper standing over her, shaking her, Kaley was blinded. She could see, but saw nothing.

She reached out for someone, anyone at all, to help her. No, not help for her. For her sister. The pain…

Oh, chil'…you got a lotta hurt comin' yo way.

It swirled in great eddies. Much pain churned beneath the waters. It was the screams of anyone who had touched these walls, this floor, the toilet, the door…

…and Shannon.

Kaley gave up. As she imagined any drowning person must eventually do, she resigned herself to her fate. She would swallow the water and drowned. It must be easier at some point to just accept your lot in life than it was to keep fighting it. The fire she had formerly felt was doused. All light diminished. The pain filled her mouth and nostrils, the terror coursed through the arteries of her heart and choked them off. The passion she had felt when fighting back Olga and Dmitry and Mikhael had ebbed, too small a current against the pain. She was exhausted afterwards. The heat of that passion was dwindling.

And yet, at the very center were coals that were still warm. And perhaps, just perhaps, she saw an ember there? Kaley sighed the sigh of her last breath, and when she did, the air touched at the coals and heated them. "You gotta blow on the coals, give 'em some air," Ricky had once told her on the first, and only, camping trip he'd ever arranged for them. It hadn't been far. Kennesaw Mountain, forty-five minutes north of Atlanta. She remembered that trip. It both seemed like not so long ago and yet a hundred years.

Kaley steadied her breathing. She inhaled slowly, slowly, then exhaled slowly, slowly, and felt a calming heat wash over her. "Blow gently now," Ricky said. "Add some more kindlin', I reckon. Then build it up slowly. Add too much too soon, an' it'll smother it. Put some twigs in, then a few small branches, then the bigger stuff. Let it catch fire slowly. Slowly."

And she did. She started with her memories of Ricky. Those were first. She focused on them, breathed, and focused. She saw him sitting in front of the TV wearing his Atlanta Falcons cap, saw him sitting with a smaller version of Shan in his lap while he watched reruns of *Star Trek* and *Star Trek: The Next Generation*. That gave her something. It gave her hope in a well of hopelessness. Kaley had told Bonetta to forget about hope, but in truth it was about balancing hope and reality. She saw that now. She saw it crystal clear.

Now came Aunt Tabitha, her with her kindly church woman's words. There Aunt Tabby was with Shan, sitting on the back porch eating ice cream after having taken them to church and fed them a big lunch. Their one-Sunday-a-month ritual. Hope flared, but threatened to die out without more kindling and soon.

Next came Nan. Yes, Nan was good kindling. She shared something with Kaley. They were both the firemakers. They brought kindling. They were enkindlers. *That's a nice word*, she thought. *Better than "charm." We are enkindlers, and we carry the kindling.* Yes, Nan had enkindled Kaley and her sister each time she passed around a banana sandwich, each time she touched their heads affectionately, each time she—

The pain! It soared to new heights. Shannon's screams were now audible through the door, her resonance felt even more deeply by Big Sister. It wouldn't have been as bad if it was Bonetta in there, but it was her *sister*. Not only that, but her sister was an enkindler too. The feedback was dousing the flames, putting her back where she had been before, utterly lost in despair.

"You need good kindlin'," Ricky reminded her.

Next, her mother…

No! No, her mother was not good kindling. Her mother would be like cold dirt to the flames, dousing them and ruining the foundation of the fire. Kaley needed kindling, and all her mother provided was a void. Kaley needed *fire*. She needed *anger*. She needed *audacity*.

She searched for the charmed touch left by the other kids who'd occupied this room, and found nothing. Those threads had been little more than echoes, shadows without substance. Her mind, her *heart*, groped for something that was truly fire. It could be anything. Bonetta didn't have enough—there was a flicker of something in her now, but Kaley needed more. She needed something to smother that which she felt resonating from the next room.

"Or maybe fire's not the answer."

Who said that? The words had come from everywhere and from nowhere. Kaley figured they may have come from her own lips. Lost in delirium, swimming in the Ocean of Sorrow and being force-fed her sister's agony, who knows what she might—

Him.

She knew it in an instant. It came to her from…from…

Shan? Shannon? Is that you?

Nothing else. No other response, just the screams from the other side of the door.

Kaley ruminated. Not fire, then. No, not fire. So what, then? What could Shan be—

Not fire. Cold. Cold fury! God help us, Kaley! It's too hot! No more heat! Cold!

"Him," Kaley whispered. Bonetta was over her, her lips were moving, but no words seemed to be coming out. Many things were now becoming obvious to her, her senses more perceptive. The light in the room enhancing. Beads of sweat and grease collecting on Bonetta's forehead. The individual glints of light off of Bonetta's locket, dangling from her deck, inches from Kaley's face. The screams. The sound of the faucet *drip-drip-dripping* away.

"The void," she said. It came back to her; that charmed insight she'd had at Dodson's Store. It came to her in full resonating detail, what she had felt, what she had seen, what had seemed to utterly transfixing about him. At the time, she hadn't known what it was.

I have empathy, she thought. *He doesn't.*

"You," she flung at him. "I need you."

Where was he? He was somewhere out there. Now hyperaware of many things, she felt air molecules cascading down her trachea. She felt the air as she pushed it out, felt the bits of spittle that popped out at each hard consonant. "Where are you?" she asked, puzzled at her own certainty. "I'm talking to you. Do you hear me?"

Outside, the screams continued, and she felt Dmitry's climax.

11

"Who the fuck is Yevgeny Tidov?" Leon asked.

Agent Porter had his own forensics kit in the SUV and had pulled out a pair of rubber gloves with a plastic zip bag to place the cell phone within. The three homeless men stood to one side, getting vigorously questioned by Agents Stone and Mortimer, and all of it was being copied by the two Atlanta city police officers who'd shown up as backup first. Another squad car was present, the two officers fanning out. Three other patrol cars were moving around the area looking for signs of Pelletier, including David Emerson who, against all counsel, was still on the job.

"All I know is that they said he asked the officer at the Parole Commission for information on a guy by that name," Porter said. "The call came from this phone. He was standing right about here less than thirty minutes ago when he made the call."

"And then he called Tidov's *parole officer*?"

"Yep. Got all the info he needed from the Commission office. You up for another ride?"

"Where? To Tidov's?"

"Where else?" The agent walked over to hand the phone to one of the officers taking down the statements of the three bums. "Make sure that forensics gets this when they arrive."

"Yes, sir."

Leon watched Porter give Mortimer and Stone meaningful looks. "What do we got?"

"Not much," Stone said. "They said a guy matching Pelletier's description just tossed it at them. Pretty much hollered, 'Here you go' and then took off."

"Must've known we got to O'Connor's apartment after he left. He knew we'd track it. C'mon, you're driving, Mortimer."

They piled into the SUV and took off before anyone had their seatbelts on. Sitting in the back, Leon was checking in on the call he'd made to dispatch to send units to Tidov's residence. He'd gotten the address from Porter's friends at the bureau, who'd gotten it from a man named Eugene Evans, who, to hear Porter tell it, was incredibly confused about what was going on. "Fuckin' Parole Commission needs to run a tighter ship. I've always said that. They don't have enough real oversight, just helter-skelter."

"Who is this Tidov guy?" Leon asked.

"He sounds like another *vor*—"

He was interrupted by a female dispatch officer over Leon's radio. "Detective Hulsey?"

"Hang on a minute, sorry," he said. He touched the send button on his radio and spoke into it. "Go ahead for Hulsey."

"An update, Detective. Units have already arrived at the Tidov residence. They've knocked and there's no answer. Waiting on a warrant now to enter."

Waiting around holding their dicks, he thought. *Do they need reminding how to walk around the house and find an excuse for probable cause?* "Has anybody called Judge Hodgins yet? That man's pretty liberal with a pen."

"I don't know, Detective. I'll pass that along."

"Ten-four," he sighed. To Porter, he said, "Go ahead. You were saying he's a *vor*?"

"Well, Tidov's certainly got a red bear tattoo on his arm, according to Evans. But he didn't have that going into the joint, apparently."

"Who are these *vory*, exactly? They've been in Atlanta for a couple of years now, but I don't know much about them, and I didn't know they were that organized. We'd heard rumors about them abducting people off the streets, but it was pretty vague. They're not standard Russian Mafia, are they?"

"No," Porter said. He then pointed to the GPS and gestured for Mortimer to hang a right at the next light. "No, the *vory v zakone* are an old group. Started in the old country, in Stalin's *Gulag*. Bunch o' prisoners were getting beat down for a time, and got pretty tired of it. So they banded together, made a tight-knit gang of thieves, sneaking in a little o' this, a little o' that, and generally just meant to buck the guards of the *Gulag* to survive that hellhole. The highest a person could ascend to was the rank of *vor*, a high-ranking thief respected for his skill and commitment to the group.

"*Vory v zakone* translates to 'thieves-in-law.' They live by a strict code." Porter used his fingers to tick off the rules. "No gambling without being able to cover losses. Thieves must be willing to teach the trade to young beginners, and make good on promises, but only those promises given to other thieves. They should also never drink so much alcohol that they lose their reasoning ability. They must take the blame for a theft if it will create confusion and enough time for another thief to make a break for freedom. They must also keep secret all knowledge of hideouts, lairs, dens and safe houses. A thief must never join the military, or take weapons from the hands of authorities. A thief must have good command of *Fenya*, the thieves' jargon or cant language, which is always evolving so that they make wiretaps almost pointless for feds. The cant language they use on the phone sounds like complete gibberish, almost no identifiable Russian in it at all. I forget the other rules."

"A thief must never, under *any* circumstances, work," Agent Mortimer supplied, "no matter how much difficulty this brings; a thief must live *exclusively* off of the profits of his thefts."

Porter paused. "Yeah, I forgot that one. There's also to be no molesting of minors, and sex crimes in general are frowned upon. They're usually pretty strict about all of these rules." He thought for a moment. "If they're involved with the Rainbow Room somehow, then these *vory* we're dealing with are probably outcasts, a few rogues doing the job that the other *vory* would never do."

Leon said, "But you said they're all thieves. Which means, outcasts or not, they've got the theft thing down."

Porter nodded.

"Which means that before they got booted from the *vory v zakone*, they all probably received pretty good instruction in how to steal and kill without getting caught." This held far-reaching implications. How long had these men been "stealing" people right off the streets? How long had they gotten away with it? How efficient had they gotten, exactly? How many missing persons could be attributed to them?

Leon would get his answer in about five minutes, when he showed up at the house of Yevgeny Tidov and had his warrant from Judge Hodgins.

Some might've left the Russian his pants, and therefore his dignity, which might've made him more pliable. Others might've cut his balls off right then and there. Spencer Pelletier had never suffered any such vainglorious rectitude, and wasn't like to start.

The smelling salts worked quickly. He waved the bottle underneath the Russian's nose and he jolted and thrashed for a second before he realized where he was. Or, rather, where he wasn't.

Spencer thought Yevgeny Tidov looked as dumb as a retard stepping off the short bus and having a look around at an aquarium. It must have been very confusing for him. He was in a dark, damp tunnel with scarcely a sliver of moonlight. He sat slumped, his hands cuffed to the rung of a solid steel ladder that was embedded in the stone wall and went up to the manhole above him, through which he'd plummeted when Spencer shoved him through. His head had smacked hard, and he was bleeding from the right side of his face.

Spencer's stomach growled. He was still hungry.

Nearby, a Droid phone splashed white light against Spencer's face like a flashlight on a kid gathered round a campfire to tell a spooky story. "You're in a sewer," Spencer announced. He sat on his haunches in front of the Russian. Tidov looked about, blinking, no doubt recalling the dream he'd had where a man named Blake Madison had duped him. "And you're in trouble."

Tidov did not respond to that. Instead, he looked down at his legs and feet, all bare. In fact he wore nothing now besides a pair of boxer shorts.

You, a thought said. *I need you.*

Those words had been hopping around inside Spencer's head for about five minutes. The first had occurred with Tidov still unconscious. At first, he thought he was hearing things, but they weren't exactly words. It was like a song looping through his mind again and again. He couldn't get the lyrics out of his head. What was so strange was that it was just those four words: *You. I need you.* They were light but emphatic, and they had no

242

familiarity to them whatsoever. He wrote it off as merely a line from a movie he'd seen, perhaps from a Scorsese flick that had a scene just like this one—some Mafioso about to get offed in a sewer. Yeah, those were the good ones.

I'm talking to you. Do you hear me?

Different lyrics this time. Different words.

Spencer shook off the feeling and aimed the gun at Tidov. "I've been goin' through your phone. Got a lotta names here. A lotta numbers, too. You also go to Tripple-X-Bitches-and-Hoes-dot-com a lot. Looks filthy. Also looks like some suspiciously underage girls floatin' around in these vids. This one o' those YouPorn type o' sites, yeah? Where you do all your recruiting?"

"Fuck...off..." Tidov's head lolled. He almost went back to sleep before Spencer put the smelling salts back underneath his nose. Tidov gagged and jerked his head back, hitting it on a ladder rung.

"Shit's strong, ain't it?"

"Fuck you."

Spencer felt his temper flare, the same flare that had gotten him in trouble with the AB back in Leavenworth, the same flare that brought down their wraith in Baton Rouge. "Fuck *me*?" he laughed. "Oh, homeboy. No, no, no, no, no. Fuck *you*. See, right about now cops are swarming all over your humble abode, an' it won't take long for them to find all your secrets. Probably got shit there *I* didn't even have time to find, am I right? Yeah, I'm right."

"Fuck you," the Russian repeated stubbornly. He jerked once to try and free himself, and lunged his face at Spencer. Once he was done with this minor rebellion, he met eyes with Spencer.

"Man, you know what they do to child molesters in prison?" he went on, chuckling. "You know what they do to assholes like you, Vladimir Putin? I was in the pen with one. His name was Martin Horowitz. Bet he could tell ya what happens to your kind there. Heh! Rape and child molesting is bad enough. But the body? *Sheeeeeyyyyyiiiit*, son. That dead body in that black bag? That's life without parole right there, probably lethal injection. The long sleep, ya feel me?"

"Fuck you," Tidov persisted.

On his haunches like this, his legs started to hurt. Spencer shifted his weight to alleviate the pressure on one side. He also had shifted his weight to fidget, because the Russian's resistance was exciting him—

You! I need you!

Spencer looked away from the Russian, glanced up and down the long, dark tunnel. *What the fuck's wrong with me?* he thought.

Then, quite inexplicably, he received an answer. *Where do you want me to start, monster?*

Spencer paused. That time, it hadn't just been like a song looping inside his mind, it was like...like...like hearing the rest of the lyrics to a song that he'd been fighting to find. Or, rather, having someone *give* him the rest of the lyrics.

The previous loop returned. *I need you.*

He turned his attention back to Tidov. "Let's talk about the *vory v zakone*."

"Fuck you."

"Hm. You're far more resilient than you were back in your home. Don't let the fact that you're still alive embolden you. I'm a dog with a chew toy, an' I'm only entertained as long as my toy keeps makin' that funny squeaking sound. You know the sound I mean?" Tidov was apparently smart enough to know a rhetorical, and insane, question when he heard it. "I used to have a Pekingese—you know, the little pug-nosed shits—an' he'd bite the shit outta his chew toy. And the more it didn't make the noise, the harder he'd chew."

"Fuck you," he threw back.

Spencer raised the gun and fired into Tidov's shoulder. The bang of the gun was deafening in the confines of the sewer. Flesh exploded and blood splattered against Spencer's face as much as Tidov's. Fragments of bone and muscle were exposed in that hole, opened right about where the rotator cuff was. Tidov screamed and kicked out. He tried to stand but couldn't.

"That's—not—the—squeaky—sound."

The Russian tried to stand again, then cried out in fury and pain. The language that came out was total gibberish. *"Drivet v horavatt gosha pitmurun alba albabarro!"*

"What is that?" Spencer said. "Is that Russian or is that your secret language? It's called *Fenya*, right? I looked it up on Wikipedia on your phone here while you were out. You guys have like a secret language, right? Was that it? Or was that pure Russian?"

"*FUCK YOU!*" His body went through spasms, and he growled like a wild animal through grinding teeth.

Spencer raised the gun to point directly at his head. Tidov squirmed and kicked pitifully, but could go nowhere. "Is that the sound squeaky toys make in the Motherland?"

Tidov glared at him. He did not answer Spencer's question, but he also knew better now than to say *fuck you*. Spencer sat there for a minute watching the Russian writhe. He did this with the same detached curiosity that he had once done to a moth whose wings he'd removed, and a cat whose paws he'd chopped off. The literature said that many serial killers mutilated animals in their youth. That was how they started. As they grew up, their needs grew, just like how a man enjoyed a good blowjob only for so long, then he wanted *two* girls, one for his cock and one for his balls. Then he wanted three. Then he wanted to be dominated, or to dominate, while roleplaying. The needs grew and grew.

You sick fuck, said the Voice. Again, familiar, yet not familiar. *I still need you.*

For the first time, Spencer entertained this rogue thought. *If you need me, why call me a sick fuck?*

Because you are one! came the swift response.

"We ready to talk yet? Hm, big guy?"

Tidov said nothing. He looked straight up at the manhole cover above his head, no doubt hoping that someone would have heard the gunshot.

Spencer smiled. "Sorry, but it's just you an' me, pal."

Tidov looked at him, and Spencer saw the look in his eyes. *He's about to—*

—shift tactics, came the Voice from the other thinker. *Yes, I feel that, too.*

"Feel what?" he asked aloud. This marked the beginning of his belief that he was actually talking to someone else. It wasn't such a strange thing. Spencer was agnostic, but not because he believed it was truly impossible to know the truth of spirits or demons or gods or angels, but because he honestly didn't give a shit.

So, what if this *was* God? Or some agent of His? What if it was Lucifer? That cocksucker couldn't even keep his mouth shut long enough to stage a decent *coup d'état* before his stupid ass was flung down to earth. So, either an impotent God or an inept Devil was speaking to him. *Or not*, he thought. *Could be I'm insane.*

To him, this was far more likely. Though he thoroughly enjoyed *being* Spencer Adam Pelletier, and the human experience that had come with it, fundamentally he knew that he was fucked in the head. There was no escaping that, really. He'd never run from it before. Why start now?

When he received no answer from the Voice, he turned his attention back to Tidov, who was now hyperventilating. He had also gone still, probably so as not to provoke Spencer anymore, and was staring up at him, no doubt wondering who he had spoken to. "You were just about to shift tactics on me," Spencer said. "So go on. Shift tactics. What's it gonna be? Begging? Bargaining? I have to warn ya, bargaining with me when I've got my mind set on something…well, it just pisses me off."

Tidov swallowed, he opened his mouth to say something.

Ask him about Dmitry, said the Voice.

"Tell me about Dmitry," Spencer said without questioning it.

Tidov stopped, looked up at him, and then shut his mouth.

Spencer smiled. "You think I don't know about Dmitry already, friend? You think I just showed up at yer house with a pistol an' nothin' else?" He snorted and shook his head in amusement. "Yevgeny, you've got a great operation going with the other *vory*, but you don't know shit about how this game is played in its entirety."

Tidov lowered his gaze, and then remembered his shoulder. Or perhaps it remembered him. Whatever the case, he spasmed in pain, and looked at it forlornly before casting his desperate eyes up at the manhole cover again.

He still doesn't quite believe, said the Voice. *He still has hope.*

"He still doesn't quite believe," said Kaley. She stared unblinkingly at Bonetta's face, hovering over her. "He still has hope."

"What?" said the Harper girl.

Outside, the screams had risen to a crescendo and then fell away. The pain was excruciating, the fear more than she could bear. And yet, bear it she did. The same way she had bore the burden of the dying men in the house where Oni had killed so many. The same way she had bore the death of Nan at her last moment, feeling her slipping away into an abyss. The same way she had bore her mother's own Ocean of Sorrow for so many years.

My whole life, Kaley thought. *I've carried this burden my whole life.*

Her legs had gone numb. A tingling sensation was running up her spine. Her skull felt like it was split in half. The numbness retreated from her legs, leaving behind a million billion needles stabbing at her every pore, joint, muscle, bone, tendon, and ligament.

"Ask him about something else," Kaley said. "Ask him about Dmitry's brother, Mikhael. And their sister, Olga. Ask him why they should protect him after he's discovered?"

Ask him about something else, said the Voice. *Ask him about Dmitry's brother, Mikhael. And their sister, Olga. Ask him why they should protect him after he's discovered.*

"What do you think Dmitry's brother will think about your exposure to the police at this stage?" Spencer said. Tidov looked back at him, and Spencer was pleased to see his panic. "Mikhael won't be too happy. Olga, either." He sighed. "They're all pretty tight, huh? Yeah, they're tight. But how tight are they with you? You're here, an' they're someplace else. My guess is, you handle one end o' the business, they handle the other. You cage up extras, dispose of the used ones, and get paid later. Pretty soon your face will be all over TV, an' they say to one another, 'Comrades, let's bounce.' And bounce they will, right on out of Atlanta. You stay here, they go free. Unless, that is, you're willing to bargain."

Tidov looked him up and down. His shoulder spasmed, and he ground his teeth. "Y-you want to c-cut a deal?"

"I'm a reasonable man," he said, and could hear Dr. McCulloch laughing from the grave, saying, "Is that so?"

"Th-their lives for m-*mine*?"

"I'm just talkin' here," Spencer said, relishing the position he was in. He recalled reading Euripides: *There is nothing like the sight of an old enemy down on his luck.* Spencer figured that went for any enemy, old or new. "Words are coming out of my mouth and you're hearing them. What do they mean? What can they mean? Who's speaking to you now, a man or a devil? What does that even mean? What do I mean when I say mean? What's the meaning of mean?"

"What…what're you—"

"Your life for theirs, yes."

Tidov cast his gaze one last time upwards, and then looked back at Spencer. "Okay."

"Okay, what?"

"Y-y-you can have them."

"Where are they?"

The Russian's upper body went stiff. "P-Pennington Street," he said.

He's lying, said the Voice.

I know he's lying, Spencer responded. *You don't have to tell me that.*

"Pennington Street?"

"Y-yes. They're all on—"

Spencer made the strident sound of a buzzer indicating a wrong answer on a game show. "Nope. Sorry. You're lying."

"I'm not—"

"A person's upper body always goes stiff when they're about to tell a lie. You freeze while trying to gather your story. Now, tell me again." He pointed the Glock at Tidov's head again. "You get one more try."

Kaley was lost inside herself. Part of her was in a dream. Another part was dipping into the cold fury of the creature she'd met earlier tonight at Dodson's, and her connection had granted her access to his thoughts. And yet, there was a third part of her that was utterly outside of herself, just walking about the room, smelling, tasting, touching the residue left by those murdered here. The walls breathed.

Despair. Loneliness. Rejection. These all came to her, as did a feeling that she somehow deserved this. That belonged to the others, not to her. *Tell the truth now*, she told herself. *You do blame yourself for this. You didn't listen. You didn't listen to Nan, or to the charm.* It was murky in here. There was no guide. No helpful ranger in this forest to lead the way. There were only phantoms.

Umway Street. The thought was in search of a purpose.

The phantoms needed someone to hold onto. They grabbed at her. Little beseeching hands that feared to be left alone, just as Shan had been afraid when Kaley had pulled away from her. *Don't go*, they said. *Don't leave us here alone.* She did not see their ghosts. Kaley wasn't even sure they were ghosts. *Fingerprints*, she thought. *They've left their fingerprints on this room, on this basement, on this world. They left their pleading hearts. They left their aspirations and dreams.*

Kaley smelled them. In this hyperaware state, their scent filled her. She knew which smells were boys, which smells were girls, and though she knew they all were usually very beautiful smells in here they…they…*cloyed*?

Umway Street, she thought. *Remember Umway Street. Don't forget it.*

She eventually came back to the staring, dumb eyes of Bonetta Harper. "Umway Street," she said. "The last street sign I saw was Umway Street, but we turned down more roads that I didn't see the names of…"

"I'm thinking somewhere maybe around the vicinity of Umway Street?" Spencer said, his voice echoing in the tunnel.

Tidov looked at him with supreme dread. He had seen this look before. He had seen it on the face of Martin Horowitz just seconds before he entered the showers expecting to rendezvous with Spencer; oh, how the man had almost picked up on the ruse, but far too late. It was also the look that one AB assassin had a moment before everything went wrong for him. It was the look of a man who got it, who understood, who fully comprehended the immense machinations that had been at work outside of him.

You're not in control here, Spencer thought, relishing, and grinning ear to ear. *I am.*

It was clear to Spencer then that this deal was sealed. Tidov's lower lip sucked in, and it was now obvious that the man, tough as he'd built himself up to be, had been fighting against his own fears, fighting against turning into a blubbering fool. His ego still had control of him. Spencer identified with this, and was repulsed by it.

"Oh, I see," Spencer said. "You're one o' *those*. You're a monster, but not like me. I was born one, but you were *made* one. You actually have feelings, they just got all twisted around. You feel guilt in the wee hours of the night, but not enough once the sun comes up. You're the reverse of a vampire. In the sun, you can bask and forget what you really are." He tsked. "And now you feel guilt. Guilt for turnin' on your partners, your family, your friends."

"P-please..."

Shine a little light on these fuckers, hold up a mirror, an' they fold like a lawn chair. That was the true essence of their weakness, and why they were not worthy of holding power. Like children who grabbed hold of their daddy's gun while he was away, and then fell to the ground screaming when the sound of the gunshot was more than they could take. "So, you were saying? Somewhere around Umway Street, yeah?"

"Y-yes."

Shine a little light on these fuckers, hold up a mirror, an' they fold like a lawn chair. Kaley had a better sense of the white man's thoughts. They moved like glaciers—seemingly slow, yet ponderous, and just beneath there was more going on than what a sailor might view from the ship's crow's nest. Kaley was adrift in the Ocean of Sorrow, and could spot these glaciers standing tall amidst the rest of the endless, cold, flat seas. It was what was underneath that she feared most. There were things there that were unconscionable.

Above her, Bonetta had stopped talking. She was beginning to cry. She did not understand any of this and was beginning to understand what a coward she was, what a coward she had always been.

Lightning behind her eyes. Shannon's physical injuries coming through. Tearing, bleeding, too much pressure.

Kaley pushed these burdensome thoughts away and tried to manage the white monster's thoughts the way one might manage computer files. She separated them according to category—anger, frustration, curiosity, humor—and pushed them into their relegated zones. They were not ordinary, these emotional files, and they did not jibe well with Kaley's own computer, but she was able to grant them approximations.

Somewhere at the back of her mind, Shan was trying to control her pain. She was now aware of the feedback, and had learned to empathize with Big Sister. Dmitry and Olga were finished with her, but they were not going to bring her back into the room with Kaley and Bonetta just yet.

The conversation between the two monsters was going on. *So, you were saying? Somewhere around Umway Street, yeah?*

She heard/felt the other monster's reply through the first monster. *Y-yes.*

"If he starts getting tricky," Kaley said, still staring up at Bonetta who was beginning to back away from her, "tell him you know how they stalk the children, how they select—

—the children based on how neglected they are, said the Voice.

Spencer tapped the muzzle of the Glock against Tidov's ankle. "*Where* around Umway Street?"

Sweat bullets beaded down from his brow, dripping onto his naked chest. Blood still poured from his shoulder. It might be that Spencer had happened upon an artery. If that was the case, he might not have long. "A-Avery," he whimpered. "Avery Street."

Spencer looked at Tidov's phone and pulled up Google Maps. After a few seconds, he had his answer. Yes, Avery Street was definitely in the vicinity of Umway. Although, there were a number of ways to get there, some of which appeared to dead end, or to go *close* to Avery but not quite. *It's own little Forgotten Place*, he thought.

But was the Russian really telling the whole truth about Avery Street, or was he still stalling, trying to save his friends? "They say that a wolf's territorial reach is about thirty miles from the pack's den," Spencer said. "But they have a hunting range of a couple hundred miles. I've heard similar things about organized criminals. Now, if I had to bet," he said, licking his lips, still relishing, "I'd say you guys control everything, or at least a *lot*, for up to a fifteen-mile radius around Avery Street. Especially for an operation like this one. Am I right?"

The pedophile swallowed the lump in his throat, and his Adam's apple bobbed up and down like a golf ball in a snake's throat.

"But I'll bet your hunting ground is, what, like thirty miles? That would entail the Bluff, Vine City, English Avenue, where all o' this started. Tell me I'm wrong."

Tidov lowered his head, defeated. "Y-you're...you're n-n-not wrong."

"I know I'm not. You know why? Because I'm *never* wrong. I don't ever open my mouth to speak unless I'm sure about something. All other conjecture I keep inside here." He tapped his temple. "Do ya have anything else to say, my friend?" He waited. Tidov shivered, and shook his head. "Oh, I bet you do. Like this territory you control. Avery Street's your wolf's den, yeah? You drive through neighborhoods and stalk children that you perceive as being neglected, but Avery Street's your staging ground, your launch point, an' I'll just bet you have all kinds o' help. So then, how many houses on that street you control? How many relatives an' cohorts live in that area?"

"N-none," he said.

"He's lying. Earlier tonight a shot was fired by one of the Russians, just to scare my sister, and they weren't even afraid that someone might hear it," Kaley said aloud, speaking to air, speaking to the ceiling, speaking to Bonetta, speaking to the children who still occupied this room somehow, and speaking to the monster. "He fired with perfect confidence. He never feared anybody hearing the gunshot."

Spencer focused on the first four words of that last sentence: *He never feared anybody*. That part in particular stung. It hurt. It hurt the way that it hurt to hear a heckler give a stand-up comedian a hard time with total impunity, and to know that that person would never act that way if he didn't have his friends surrounding him, backing him up, cheering him on. And no one in the crowd would do anything about it. No one would ever do anything about the Miles Hoovers of the world because they were too afraid to appear rude themselves.

"Prime Minister Vladimir Putin," Spencer said, "I have reason to believe you are lyin' to me, sir. Ya see, I have spoken with the other members of the United Nations and they all agree, based on the word of informants we have amongst some o' yer people, that you're full of shit. Savvy? Now, I'm gonna hold up fingers, and you're gonna tell me which number seems most appropriate. If I catch the lie, you die. If you tell me true, no harm will come to you." He laughed. "How 'bout that? I'm a poet and I didn't know it."

Spencer held up his right hand, and started ticking off fingers. One? Tidov didn't move. Two? Tidov remained still. Three, then? The Russian looked apprehensive. How about four? The Russian watched the hand carefully. Five? Tidov swallowed. Six? Tidov finally nodded.

"Six? Six houses in that area belong to yer outfit?"

Tidov nodded. "Yes. J-j-just those six."

"All on Avery Street?"

"Yes."

"Family?"

"S-s-some," he shrugged.

"An' what about badges?"

"Wh-what?"

"Police, asshole. How many cops are on your payroll?"

"N-none."

"Thank you." Spencer raised the gun and squeezed the trigger.

Kaley jerked once, and went still. She felt the dying man in the sea with her. She felt the fear, the unease, and the confusion of death. Then, just like that, there was nothing. Nothing but Little Sister's pain and humiliation.

"You killed him," she said.

"I had to," Spencer said, standing up. A brain fragment clung to his left sleeve. He shook it off and said, "What other purpose could he serve except to give me away later?"

We could've used him, said the Voice.

"For what? For leverage?" He waited. There was no response from the Voice. "These people would burn that bridge as soon as I offered him up as a hostage. They'd probably kill you, too, if you are who I think you are. They'd slit your throat an' then bug out, head for Mexico. An operation like this, they all probably have bug-out plans, probably have go-ready bags in the trunks of their cars, an' everybody in the operation knows the code words to cut an' run at the drop of a hat. Naw, I ain't lettin' anybody get away. Not tonight."

Call the police, the Voice insisted. *Tell them where we're at.*

"And let them have Dmitry? I don't think so."

There was another pause from the person at the other end. He felt suspicious thoughts crawl across his brain, tickling and teasing. He rather enjoyed it. Then, finally, *How do you know which one's Dmitry?*

"This connection works two ways, sister." It was true. He wasn't entirely sure what he was experiencing, but he had a genuine curiosity about it all and was starting to explore (quite unconsciously) the limits of it. He didn't really feel all that much, but he saw images, colors, and certain identifying terms leapt out at him as she unwillingly shared the image of the asshole who'd looked at him from the window of the Expedition in front of Dodson's Store. And he knew. *That one's…Oni? Naw, Dmitry?* That seemed right. The owner of the Voice called him Oni, but he was really Dmitry.

You're going to leave us here to die so that you can get what you want?

"I didn't say that," Spencer said. He'd unzipped his pants and was now pissing in the brain hole he'd put in Tidov's head. He felt the person on the other end of his Connection recoiling…and then looking back on in fascination, and vindication. "I'm not stupid. See, any minute now the people on Avery Street are gonna start getting word that Mr. Tidov's house is swarmin' with cops. That ain't good. It'll be the same as if I'd called them and made a useless bargain with his life. Avery Street's almost twenty miles from where I am. Many of 'em will have bailed before I can get there."

You're still leaving us here so that you get what you want!

"He lied."

What?

"Tidov lied. There *are* police helping him out. I saw it in his eyes," Spencer said. "And besides, it makes sense. An operation this big couldn't go unchecked without *someone* in authority gettin' paid to look the other way, to take Avery Street off o' the regular patrols of the Zone One cops, or to at least decrease the amount o' patrols that go through that neighborhood. They may not know that Avery Street is full of rapists and murderers—they probably just think it's more meth labs or drug havens—but they'll look out for Dmitry an' his ilk just the same. If I call the cops, some badge somewhere will tip off the guys at Avery Street."

There are no cops in on this!

"Of course there are."

How can you know all this—

"Because it's what *I* would do if I were settin' up this kind of op." Spencer listened. Silence from the Voice. A thoughtful pause, perhaps? He didn't know, but while he waited for another response he prodded at that tickling feeling at the back of his brain, that part that he had just started becoming aware of. He wanted to see her thoughts, as he suspected she was seeing his.

You...you want Dmitry? The Voice finally said, sounding incredulous.

"I want 'em all. My hungry ass is staring at a buffet, and I'm one o' those that likes to take advantage. Don't know the next time I'll get to eat again," Spencer said, shaking off the last few drops. "But I'm all the way over here an' they're all the way over there." He added, "Where you are."

Another pause. Then, *You want me to stall them?*

"There's a good girl."

But how?

"I've done enough talkin'. Why don't *you* figure it out?"

But...I can't—

"Think, girl. Where are you at?"

A pause. *I'm in a basement.*

Spencer thought about this for a second, and then the answer came to him. But he wondered how obvious it was to her. "Locked in a basement? With amenities provided? A bed, a toilet, all that?"

Yes.

"An' how do you suppose they're keepin' an eye on you?"

From the feeling of consternation that swam over him, he could tell this hadn't yet occurred to her. *Keeping an eye on me?*

"Yeah. How do they monitor you?" More silence from the Voice. He popped the clip out of his Glock and counted how many rounds he had left. Eight. Satisfied, he tapped it back into place. "Think now. Is there a vent? A hole in the wall of any kind?"

There's...there's a vent, yes.

"Pretty small? And outta your reach?"

Yes. How did you...? The Voice trailed off, and there was the feeling of dawning. Hope sprang, hot and uncomfortable for him. *A camera?*

"And boom goes the dynamite."

More consternation. Then, *But, what can I do about that? I can't reach it. And even if I could I can't do anything with a camera.*

256

"But you can control what they see," Spencer said. "Or, at least, what they *think* they see."

I don't understand.

Spencer sighed. "Pretend to start escaping. Pretend—oh, I dunno—pretend like you know how to pick locks, an' then start pickin' the lock."

But I don't know how to pick locks!

"Doesn't matter. They don't know that."

They won't believe it.

"They will."

How can you be so sure?

"Because people are stupid. Even the smart ones."

I...I can't...

"Then give up. Die. Lay there and fucking die, an' see if anybody gives a shit about you or yer sister. You better find some kinda distraction if you wanna live. If not lock-picking you can always dazzle 'em with a magic trick."

"I...don't know any magic tricks," Kaley said, speaking very rationally to the air in front of her lips.

Says the girl speakin' to me via telepathy.

The glaciers ran deep. Kaley explored them with her own brand of curiosity, and, on some subconscious level, she knew that the monster had noticed her. She was like an amateur thief who came through a convenient opening in the screen window, and the monster was watching from the shadows, curious as to what she would do with what she found. Kaley cringed from his sight. *He's searching for me, too.*

She saw something. A flash, lasting only a second, maybe less. In that second she saw the six men in Baton Rouge. For an instant, she was him. She was there in that moment, and she was experiencing *his* brand of curiosity. She saw what *he* was capable of when he got hold of someone he found worth his time.

Kaley closed that vault and looked away, hoping to never again remember it. But she would. Forever. There would even be times when she dreamt of it and woke up at night thinking it had been committed by her. She would tell this to shrinks, all of whom would tell her that it was common for traumatized persons to have reoccurring dreams of violence. She would never be able to adequately explain it. Never.

Now you know, said the monster.

Wet warmth spread from her legs. In her hyperaware state, the urine was so pungent that it made her gag several times, though she hardly noticed, so reflexive was it, and so far removed was she from herself. "Yes," she said to him. "Now I know you."

From a thousand miles away, Bonetta said, "Kaley? Kaley, what's goin' on? Did...did you hit your head? Who're you talkin' to?"

He zipped up his pants and considered his next move. The Glock was replaced at his waistline, and he stood looking down at the piss-covered thing that had formerly been Yevgeny Tidov. Now, it was merely a temple for bacteria and germs. For so long they had been kept in check by red and white blood cells, but now, the day of the bacteria and germs had finally come. The world was their oyster—at least, Tidov was their oyster—and they lapped up the savory juices of him. Any moment now, the bacteria and germs would realize a major tectonic shift had happened in their favor.

Get moving! the Voice commanded.

It shook Spencer from his reverie. Usually, he would've been pissed at someone issuing an order at him, but at the moment he was still so focused on Dmitry (*She called him Oni*, he thought) that little else mattered.

Spencer climbed up the ladder, purposely using Tidov's head for his first step. He slowly pushed the manhole cover aside, and then peeked out. The spot he'd chosen was a block away from where he'd parked Tidov's car. He'd carried the fucker in a fireman's carry behind an alley of a store that was closed but nevertheless had the words **MONEY TO LOAN** flashing in a garish neon pink sign.

There hadn't been anyone in the vicinity when he took his captive to the sewer, and there still wasn't anyone around. He couldn't return to the Russian's car, though, because the cops would be at his house by now, and would probably put out an APB for Tidov's Buick.

He would have to find something else to drive him the nineteen or so miles to Avery Street. Without a vehicle, he'd never make it in time, not on foot, not before the *vory* slit the throats of the only witnesses who knew their faces and bugged out completely.

"Seasons don't fear the Reaper," he sang. For no reason at all, the Blue Öyster Cult was back in his head. "Nor do the wind, the sun or the rain...we can be like they are...come on, baby...don't fear the Reaper..."

"...baby take my hand," she sang. "Don't fear the Reaper...we'll be able to fly...don't fear the Reaper...baby I'm your mannnnnnnn..."

12

At 4:12 AM, on the authority of Judge Roy Talbot Hodgins, the Atlanta Police Department busted down the front door of 42 Clayton Road. They were joined by one sheriff's car outside and a Georgia state patrol car at the end of the neighborhood, blocking the street and checking all cars that moved through.

SWAT moved in first. Judge Hodgins had been so alarmed by what had been told to him over the phone—the bodies on Townsley Drive, an injured APD officer, the probable involvement of a wanted serial killer, the involvement of the *vory v zakone* and the Rainbow Room, and both the FBI and Interpol's interest in all of this—that he'd been granted a no-knock warrant.

The battering ram separated the door from the doorframe, sending splinters inward as the second man stepped forward and gave the door a swift kick to send it swinging wide. They moved inside, screaming, "Atlanta Police Department! Search warrant! Search warrant!"

Leon waited outside on the front lawn. Clouds had gathered overhead, and thunder rolled nearby. He was joined by Agents Porter, Mortimer, and Stone. They'd hung back by their SUV and held a conference between themselves. Flanking the front door on each side were two APD officers, each one with their Glocks drawn and at ready-low. Leon watched the operation with mounting frustration. He wanted to be inside with them, but had to wait for the all-clear.

A squad car pulled up behind him to join the others. It was car 1A4. Leon knew that car. He turned and walked quickly over to David Emerson, who was rubbing at his left eye profusely as he stepped out. "What the hell are you doing?" Leon demanded. "Why didn't those medics send you to the hospital with Beatrice? I swear, I should beat their asses, and *yours*—"

"I'm still good for duty," David cut him off.

"The hell you are."

"I don't have a corneal abrasion, I don't have any serious injuries, I won't need stitches, and no body parts are missing."

"You were involved in a shooting—"

"And my shift's still not over," David returned. "You're still hunting him, so you need every set of eyes you can get."

Leon was about to say something when his radio blared. "Detective Hulsey?" It was Lieutenant Hennessey, and he sounded urgent.

"Go ahead for Hulsey," he said into the radio.

"We're all clear, Detective. You need to come in here and take a look at this. We've got a body and some contraband with some pretty serious implications."

"On my way up." He gave David a level look, and then turned towards the house.

Inside was an average-looking bachelor's home. Not many decorations, but there was a couch that was probably bought used with a few tables and a Sony VPL projector situated on one wall so that it could project against the opposite wall. Wires from surround sound speakers were covered by a cheap rug, and the windows were covered with black curtains.

Leon sniffed. The house smelled…sweaty. Uncleaned. It wasn't particularly filthy, but it definitely had the smell of cramped humans. Years back, Leon had been on a team that opened a U-Haul truck filled illegal immigrants, all bundled up and packed tight like sardines. That truck had smelled something like this.

Footsteps behind. It was the agents, stepping inside, taking a pair of blue rubber gloves from their pockets and squeezing them on.

"Up here, Detective," called Hennessey. He was at the top of the stairs immediately to Leon's right, peeking out from the first door on the right. He hustled up the stairs, slightly resentful of the quick steps of the feds behind him. No matter how much he knew they needed these feds, a part of him would always resent the feeling of being watched over, no matter how illogical it was.

Hennessey had removed his helmet, and he pointed with his MP-5 rifle into the room. "Recording equipment. Sound and audio. A stage of children's toys and clothes set up."

Leon had to brace himself against the smell of ammonia. "Jesus Christ," he said, eyes watering. "Where's the body?"

"Bathroom. Or, what used to *be* a bathroom." Hennessey led him past three other SWAT officers who were inspecting the room further. When they came upon her, the black bag was already opened, and the little one looked like she could be sleeping, except for her eyes, opened and rolled back as they were. "Hydrofluoric acid in the bottles along the wall there," Hennessey informed him, pointing about the room with his black gloved hand. "Bathtubs been removed. Plastic tubs probably used for melting vics down. God damn, Detective, what the fuck's goin' on here tonight? What've we stumbled on?"

Leon was about to answer when suddenly the room came alive with screams. It was the screams of a little girl, and someone shouting at her in another language. The volume was tremendous and shook the walls. The sound stopped as abruptly as it started, and Leon screamed, "Fucking *Christ*, what was that?"

"Sorry," one of the SWAT officers called. "Touched a button."

Leon swept back into the staging room and said, "Hit it again, but this time find the volume knob and turn it the fuck *down* first." The officer did as told, and a few seconds later the seven or so men in the room stood there, transfixed by what they were hearing. In all his years on the force, Detective Leon Hulsey had never heard torment quite so bottled, crystallized, and packaged, to be replayed again and again. Few people knew what it was like to have a job like a policeman. *Somebody* had to watch those tapes created by pedophiles in order for the taps to be submitted as evidence, *somebody* had to chronicle what was in those recordings, so that *somebody* could testify later as to what was on those tapes. It fell on people like Leon Hulsey to go through video evidence of people being raped and murdered in order to ascertain the truth in an investigation.

But this was different. He'd been forced to both see and hear some of the most disgusting things human beings could do to one another, men and women, young and old, black and white, religious and non-religious, but never had it been served up like this. Never had the screams been so well recorded, made so crystal clear.

The girl's dying screams rose to a crescendo, and Leon said, "Turn it off. Now."

The officer did as told, and when he did the room was left in an unbreakable silence. Most of the guys in the room looked pissed off, a couple looked queasy, and none of them would have any humor for the rest of the night. Police officers and firemen saw a lot in their day, and made morbid japes about a lot of it, but not tonight. Tonight, none of these men would be able to sleep. Leon would stake his badge and his life on that. "All right," he said. "Enough's enough. I want this motherfucker pulled in. I want *all* of these cocksuckers pulled off the streets. Tonight. We need to find Tidov. And Pelletier."

Agent Porter said, "I've already called the bureau and they're putting out a description of the Russian to all police agencies in the state. And Pelletier's face is gonna be on every news channel for the next forty-eight hours, I can guarantee that."

Leon nodded, for the moment glad of the feds' involvement. "We've been going around and around with this all night. We've been one step behind him all this time, and we've just barely missed him at each stop. I'm fucking fed up."

Lieutenant Hennessey cleared his throat. "There's more you should see down the hall, Detective."

They stepped out of the room and walked a short ways to the end of the hall, and there they found the cages, as well as the animal feeder and a few empty buckets in the corner that looked good and washed out. Undoubtedly waste buckets for the captives who remained here. "Inch-thick steel," Leon said, gripping one bar and tugging on it several times. It never budged.

"God damn," Sergeant Warwick said. "This is what monsters do. I mean, true to life, no bullshit, *monsters*. Like something out of a God damn Stephen King novel."

"Stephen King never dreamt up something like this," Leon said darkly. He bent to examine the locks, which were heavy-duty ADEL Trinity-788 biometric fingerprint lock. It wouldn't open for anybody without the right fingerprint, and no amount of lock-picking would work on it.

Leon jumped as someone shouted over his radio, *"We've got a live one down here!"*

Lieutenant Hennessey got on the radio, "Say again?"

"A survivor! In the basement! Pulling him out now!"

Leon turned and looked at Porter, and then all at once they fled from the room and raced down the stairs. The house was filled with the thunder of dozens of booted feet clomping their way down. Rorion Vaulstid and Joey Heinrich were standing there in the doorway that led down a set of bare wooden steps. Vaulstid was on the radio, calling for the ambulance. Leon hustled downstairs, Hennessey just ahead of him and the agents behind.

It was a finished basement that was brightly lit with both lamps and overhead fluorescent lighting. A workbench with a wide pegboard dominated most of the room, the pegboard adorned with tools of any sort one might imagine, from commonplace to industrial, from Black & Decker drills to monobolt guns to a jackhammer. There were soldering guns piled high on a tungsten welder, and a smattering of old *Hustler* magazines spread across the floor. There was also a stack of comic books, a *Daredevil* graphic novel and a bundle of *Savage Dragon* issues. Leon recognized these at once, because he'd gone through an Erik Larsen phase of his comic reading.

"Where are you?" Hennessey shouted.

"In here!" another officer cried. They followed the sound of his voice, and came to a darkened room at a corner of the basement. The door had been kicked down, and inside it was nothing but a concrete floor and a trap door. Two SWAT officers were inside, one kneeling at the trap door's edge, the other pushing out a creature in a small bundle. When he got close, Leon saw that it was a boy, African American, his skin ashy and his arms skinny as rails, his eyes wide with terror, his face covered in soot, fingers caked in dirt and clutching at the purple blanket around him. Leon could smell the filth on him. "It's okay, son," the officer said. It was Klein. "It's okay, you're gonna be all right now. Warwick, get that light outta his face!" The boy had winced and shrank from the light. "Clear a way!"

Leon stepped aside, and got a glimpse of the child's terrified face. He looked out from the blanket hood around his head with the eyes of one who didn't know if he was with the good guys or the bad guys. *He may never know the difference again.* How would his life be different? How would he view basements now? How would he view people with Russian accents? How would he view the whole fucking country of Russia? Impossible

264

to say, but a single glimpse told Leon that the boy would never live a normal life again. Nightmares waited for him, awkward conversations with people who joked about man rape in his presence without realizing what he'd been through, and relationship problems that would run deep.

When they stepped back outside, neither Leon nor the agents were speaking, though Porter was certainly doing a great deal of texting. David Emerson approached. He'd hustled over to see the kid into the ambulance, but now looked at Leon staunchly. "What the fuck is in there, Hulsey?" he demanded.

"Find this fucker," he said. "Find him. Find Tidov. They're running right now. They're all going to ground. This is an operation, one they've worked on for years, and gotten *damn* good at it, and at keeping hidden. If we don't get them within the next few hours they'll have closed up shop and left town. They'll just open up somewhere else, and do this all over again. That's what they do. We have to *find them*, David."

Leon had never gotten to know David Emerson well. He didn't know what sort of TV shows or women he liked, he didn't know what high school he'd gone to, he didn't know if he preferred Coors to Budweiser, he didn't even know what David thought of him, but he knew the guy was committed to his job and that he had a bullet waiting for anyone that fucked with his partner. David nodded wordlessly and turned and bolted for his patrol car. He was gone before the ambulance carrying the kid could get out.

For a minute, Leon stood there, looking back at the House, rubbing his cheek with the back of his right hand, considering. Then he turned and looked for Porter, who was standing beside his SUV talking to Mortimer and Stone. He hustled over there and said, "Baton Rouge. What happened there? Anything connected with this?"

Porter halted midway through discussing what they'd seen inside with his fellow agents, and looked at Leon. "No," he said. "I told you. We were just onto Pelletier, I'd never even heard of the Rainbow Room before tonight."

"So what happened in Baton Rouge?"

At first, Leon thought the agent would keep hush, but Porter surprised him. "Pelletier killed six contract killers that the Aryan Brotherhood sent after him. They were still plenty pissed at him for what he did to one o' their boys in CRC. It was their complaint that helped fuck him over, got him transferred to Leavenworth, where the biggest prison population of AB members was at that time. Word travels through the grapevine fast, even in prison. Pelletier probably knew if he hung around in Leavenworth long enough he'd get it in the shower or in the work houses. He got out before they could get their payback."

"Six assassins? They wanted him that badly?"

"That's what the Brotherhood is best at. They account for only one percent of the prison population, but they're responsible for about twenty-five percent of all prison murders. They work in extortion, prostitution and murder-for-hire. They're exceedingly good at it. Before a person can get inducted into their ranks, the person has to show that they're well learned—AB members aren't just dumb rednecks, they're educated inside prison on Nietzsche, Sun Tzu, Socrates, Plato, Buddha, and they're encouraged to learn about the many different religions of the world. You have to show undying loyalty. Blood in, blood out. Only the most committed of men can join, and so it's easy to put out a hit when they want it done."

"How'd Pelletier survive it?"

"He got a heads up of some kind. One of them made a mistake."

"What mistake?"

"We don't know. All we know is that six are dead and one was mutilated pretty badly for several minutes postmortem, maybe as long as an hour. He killed the guy and spent a while working on his corpse. Cut his dick off and shoved it in his ass. A woman was nearby, terrified from all the gunfire that had just gone off, scared to the point that she couldn't move. She covered her eyes, but still peeked. Said she saw Pelletier...eat one of the testicles." Porter shrugged. "Then he cut the belly open, and pulled out the intestines. Played with 'em. She said he...um...ah, hell, *what* did she say he did with them?" he asked of Stone and Mortimer.

Mortimer said, "She said he tossed the intestines around his neck, and looked at her and said, 'Do I look like Greta Garbo?' The woman said she looked away, but said she heard the sound of pants being unzipped and a belt buckle rattling, then some squishy noises. 'Lots and lots of squishy noises.' That's how she put it."

266

"And laughing," Stone put in. "Don't forget that."

"And laughing, yeah."

Leon didn't blink for a moment. And while he imbibed what the agents had said, they went back to their chatter. He finally turned back to the house of horrors, and had the briefest of insights. He was fortunate he had been born relatively sane, to relatively sane parents, and not anywhere near the Bluff.

The rain started in again.

At first, the sky completely dropped on him, drenching him in a torrential downpour to end all downpours. It lasted only a few seconds, though, and petered off to a drizzle. Spencer was already upset about having come across no vehicles that could be easily stolen, and now he would have to walk the rest of the night soaking wet. Not only that, but his quarry was likely to get away. Not only *that*, but he was still hungry.

Then, he spotted lights up ahead through the drizzle. "You still there, partner?" he asked of the wind.

Yeah, came the Voice, from everywhere and nowhere. *I'm still here.*

"Are ya movin' yet?"

Silence.

"That means no. You better *get* to moving, savvy? I think I've found a way to get to you, but you're still gonna need to buy me some time. It won't be long before the police get to Tidov's place and somebody gives Dmitry and the others a heads up. Cops are probably already there now."

I…hurt.

"What's wrong with you?" he said, leaping over a chain-link fence and moving ever towards the light. He saw a parking lot wreathed in the orange glow from various lampposts.

I got hit with a stun gun, and my sister…and Bonetta…I can feel their pain and fear, too. It's…crippling.

"Let me rephrase that: what the *fuck's* wrong with you?" he said, stepping around a few cars which undoubtedly belonged to the late-night workers hitting that third shift grind. Up ahead was a warehouse of some kind, a manufacturing plant. A sign nearby read **Keegan Corporation – Building Better Trucks**. "Ya just gonna lie down and let these fuckers get away with what they've done to you an' yours? Huh?" He peeked at a few of the cars, but saw none that would be easily boosted. Then, he looked fifty yards up at the manufacturing plant itself. Two large bay doors had opened up to let a pair of Penske trucks out. *An assembly line. They build Penskes here.* "After all they've done, you just gonna lay there an' take it? Let 'em fuck you like they fucked yer sister?"

Don't you talk about her! Don't you use that filthy fucking mouth to—

"An' what're you gonna do about it?" he said, laughing and walking through the rain and speaking to air. *"Nothin'!* That's what. Nothin', because you're nothing but a fucking loser who gives up. Fuck you, you little bitch. Lay there and get raped and fuckin' die. Die without even givin' them a fight. See if I give a fuck. See if *anybody* gives a fuck."

Don't tell me I'm nothing—

Spencer wasn't listening to her anymore, at least not for the moment. He saw things inside of her. He saw her own private fears, her shame at her lot in life, an unspoken self-loathing for being the daughter of a woman named...named...Jovita Dupré! Yes, that was her name! And he saw something else, he saw that her teeth were rotted, her eyes sunken and hollow. "Jovita Dupré," he said aloud. "That's yer mother, right? A crack whore and a—"

Shut your mouth! the Voice cried. *Don't you look at my thoughts! They're not yours! They're mine! Stay out of my head!*

Spencer smiled.

The Voice babbled on as he approached a pair of guys who'd stepped outside for a smoke break. They stood underneath a tin overhang, protected from the rain. "Hey guys! Is Terry in?" he said to them.

They looked between one another. "Terry?" one of them said. He was a bearded guy wearing a checkered flannel shirt and work gloves.

"Yeah, ain't he the plant manager here?"

The bearded man took a puff of his cigarette and said, "Naw, man. Plant manager's Nathan Hunter. You might be

268

thinkin' o' *Perry*, not Terry. Perry's second shift manager. Who're you?"

"I was supposed to drop off some new quarter-inch washers," Spencer said, pulling a story right out of his ass. "I guess I should speak to Nathan about that, huh?"

"Probably."

"Where can I find him?"

"Ah, he's probably back in QC right now."

Quality control area. "Great. I appreciate it. You guys pushin' anymore trucks out tonight? I don't wanna keep my truck in the way." Spencer didn't have any automobile, of course, and he certainly didn't have anything parked in their way. But it didn't matter, all he had to do was keep his lips moving, keep asking questions, and unless they were incredibly sharp folks (and they couldn't be because they had found themselves so desperate in life that they worked third shift jobs building trucks on an assembly line), they wouldn't pick up on it.

"Yeah, but the rest'll come outta QC later. Probably out back. You can park yer truck up here, it oughtta be fine, man."

"Thanks, man," Spencer said, and started to step inside before he stopped himself. "Oh, hey! I got another delivery tonight to Avery Street. Either o' you guys know how to get there?" Spencer had looked up the directions to Avery Street on Tidov's Droid phone and had gotten conflicting reports. Some of the streets were probably recently renovated and the maps were updating poorly.

The other smoker scratched his scraggily beard. When he spoke, he revealed blackened teeth that had to be the work of meth or heroin. "Yeah, uh, Avery...yeah, that's...first, you head north on Mansell. That's this road right out here," he said, pointing through the rain. "Go about four stoplights up, then turn left onto Huckleby Ridge Road, go about a mile I wanna say? Then turn right onto Kingsley Street. Stay straight, 'cause that road turns into Umway Street. Go another mile, you'll see a big billboard that's fallin' apart, turn left. That's Avery."

"Thanks, friend," he said, and stepped on inside like he was meant to be there. "Hey, I don't guess I could be a total prick an' bum a cig off o' you, huh?" The man obliged, if only because he appeared to find it too awkward to say no. He also lit the cigarette before Spencer went on his way, smiling his thanks.

They didn't stop you, said the Voice. Spencer felt the other's dull curiosity creeping across his brain. She was in shock, and in such a detached state. Brain dead, like when watching TV.

"Of course not. Why would they?"

You're not supposed to be here...there at the plant.

"They don't know that. Those guys probably see two dozen people a day that they've never met before just come traipsin' into the plant. Regional managers, district managers, plant inspectors, what the fuck do they know about them? Those two knuckleheads work the goddam third shift on an assembly line." Spencer walked past the area labeled **ROOF PIT**, where an aluminum roof was being situated on top of a yellow Penske truck. One of the men looked down from the catwalk at him. Spencer called up, "Hey, man! Nice to see you again!"

The man had a look of confusion, but nodded back and said, "You too!"

Spencer smiled, winked, and gave him a companionable thumbs up.

He doesn't even know you, said the Voice.

"He doesn't know that," Spencer said, taking a puff of his cig. He continued moving through the plant like he belonged there, checking his watch and waving to guys along the assembly line. He gave a wink to one lady with a clipboard, and she smiled back, then looked away, no doubt embarrassed that she didn't remember him.

There were at least fifty men drilling boards and slapping the sides onto the wooden floors of the big boxes at the back of the trucks. One man hollered at Spencer, perhaps asking who he was, but above the din and confusion of all the pneumatic tools going at once he just shouted, "I'm a penguin and this is my dog shit," and kept walking with an air of importance. The other man just looked away, went back to working.

That didn't make any sense.

"Doesn't need to. Just needs to sound authoritative," he said. Their shared Connection went two ways, and Spencer could feel the careful steps the girl was taking through his mind, simultaneously wanting a peek and *not* wanting a peek. "Seventy

270

percent of what people respond to is how a person looks, twenty percent is how they *sound*, an' only ten percent to what they actually *say*. If ya decide to, ya know, actually stand up and fight for yer life tonight, ya might live long enough to read a book on psychology. This shit's easy. Like takin' candy from a baby. Observe."

Ahead of him was a Penske truck, one that looked like it was almost ready to leave out the back bay door. A big red sign over the bay door read **QUALITY CONTROL INSPECTION AREA**, and Spencer moved right past a man with a clipboard standing at the back. He knew the keys would probably be left in the ignition, and when he opened the driver's side door and hopped in the cab he was not disappointed to find that it was so. If they hadn't been, he would've just asked someone, and they probably would've just given him the keys. Spencer started it up and put it in gear.

The man with the clipboard walked up to the cab and shouted, "Hey, where the fuck you goin'?"

"Some o' Nathan's bullshit! Penske reps called an' said they want this truck jackfrost-butt-fucked-a-turtle! I'm as unhappy as you are! Go talk to Nathan!" he shouted, and drove out the front bay door into the rain, leaving the QC inspector standing there shaking his head ruefully. "One thing you can always count on," he told the Voice in his head as he switched on the windshield wipers, "is that no matter where ya go in the world, people hate their bosses. There's always bullshit goin' around that makes no sense. The system's a façade. An illusion. Just do the barest amount o' homework an' then bullshit yer way through the rest of it. You'll come out on top every time."

You're a liar. A thief. And a murderer! You're no different than Dmitry!

"No, Dmitry kills for a reason," he said, inhaling smoke. "I don't. He rapes to fill a hole in his heart, and kills to get rid o' the shame as much as the evidence. I kill because I'm bored an' I take offense easily. An' I get away with it because I'm the greatest guy in the universe. I'm not sayin' that's an excuse, and I'm not *askin'* to be excused. It's important to me that you see the difference."

Why?

"Because I'm comin' to save yer ass, an' I'm the only one who can do it. I need you focused an' I need you to trust me."

Talking about Dmitry was invigorating. He still recalled that look he'd given. So even, so confident, so smug. Well, okay, the smugness was probably just imagined—Dr. McCulloch had pointed out that Spencer was prone to imagining sleights, and was absolutely right, he knew that much—but the guy was still obviously a shit-eater in need of correction. *He thinks he rules the roost. He thinks this whole city's his roost.* Spencer smiled. He could not wait to prove otherwise.

You could still call the police! the Voice pleaded.

Spencer pulled out of the rear parking lot and onto Mansell Road, heading north. "I already told you that Dmitry an' his pals have somebody on the force—"

You can't know *that—*

"Bet me," Spencer chuckled, taking another toke.

What?

"Bet me," he repeated. "I'll tell you what, if you an' me survive this, an' it turns out I was right, then I'm gonna visit you on yer twenty-first birthday, and you'll pay me every nickel you've got in the bank. How's that sound?"

You're playing with my life! With my sister's life!

"And you're *not*, and that's the fucking problem, sister. Now, get up and start stalling those dickheads. Or lay there an' die. Either way, I'm on my way." Spencer made it through the next four stoplights, and, just as the man had said, there was Huckleby Ridge Road on his left. He made the turn and glanced in his rearview mirror. So far, no one was following him; no sirens, and nobody from Keegan Corporation was coming to reclaim their property. "Smooth sailin' from here," he said, and reached to his waistline to make sure the Glock was still tucked snugly away.

Kaley had been speaking to air for several minutes. She was well aware of Bonetta crouched in a corner on the other side of the room, terrified of so many things. The fear now washed over her, fed her, gave her nourishment. Something had changed inside of her. Kaley didn't know what it was, but she was almost certain that it had to do with a chemical imbalance.

Chemical imbalance. That's what the doctors said of her vertigo.

Ricky used to say that he believed what the Chinese believed, that everything in life must have a *yin* and a *yang*, and if anything ever had more *yin* than *yang*, or more *yang* then *yin*, then there was sickness, depression, mental problems, instability. Did the psychopath, her monster, therefore have too much *yang*?

So ya think that's *my problem?* she heard him say from somewhere right beside her. *I don't have enough* yin *in my life? What about you, then? Not enough* yang? Kaley could feel him laughing, and it sickened her.

Something else sickened her, too. It was Little Sister. She was alone out there, shoved into another room and locked up. In pain. In darkness. Shannon was scared of the dark.

Kaley lay there practically catatonic, exactly as Little Sister was. They didn't have the Anchor from this distance, but they shared the charm, and thus a loose Connection. She felt the painful swelling of her sister's lower regions, the burning, the tears, the bleeding. Kaley lay there with the knowledge that her sister had been the victim of something horrible, it had happened just on the other side of the door beside her, and she hadn't been able to do a damn thing about it. Now Little Sister was alone with the shame and the pain. Well, not entirely alone. They both shared the sickening emotions, so slippery and cumbersome, holding them back from fighting back, from doing what must be done.

The monster's words came back to her. "Lay there and get raped and fuckin' die," he had said. "Die without even givin' them a fight. See if I give a fuck. See if *anybody* gives a fuck." And he was right. Nan was gone. So was Ricky. Aunt Tabby might care, and Mom would care, but only so much as it affected her. That was Jovita Dupré's way. And that would always be her way. She thought she loved her two daughters, but really and truly she only loved the idea of them, something that gave her life purpose, two little pets that made her feel loved unconditionally, made her feel like she had accomplished *something* in life. On some level, Kaley had always sensed this. The charm had told her the truth. Love was mostly selfish. While Jovita Dupré would certainly fight for her daughters (if she even knew they were in trouble), she would only be fighting for a part of herself. Jovita Dupré would be sad to

273

see her two loving pets go, the pets she hadn't quite trained to love her back, but she imagined they did. Otherwise, Kaley and Shan would've been out on the street just like any other strays.

Yes, love was selfish. At least, most love was. Some love was truly empathetic, self-sacrificing. Minutes ago when Kaley screamed for Olga and Dmitry and Mikhael to take her, she had meant it. She would've done anything to spare Shannon that pain, and she could sense Shannon's own guilt for bringing the emotional pain on Big Sister. And Kaley felt horrible for making Little Sister fell so horrible. They were thinking of *one another*, a truly empathetic feedback, not any kind of stingy, self-absorbed idea of compassion.

Then, Kaley began to see. She couldn't say exactly where the dawning came from, only that once it came, it cast its light far and wide, pushing away the shadows that ensconced certainty. *You have to ward yo' heart, chil'*, Nan had said. That meant shut it off. Shut it *out*. Shut out all empathy and compassion. Turn away from it. Was that what Nan meant to say?

Then, she heard a voice coming through the walls, a voice that Bonetta Harper never heard. *Listen to the monster, Kaley*, Shannon was saying. *Listen to what he's saying. He knows what he's talking about.* Little Sister sounded incredibly lucid. Whatever had happened to her had transformed her. There was anger there...that was unusual for Little Sister. Little Sister had always been so compassionate.

"But...I can't," she whispered. "I can't shut you out, Shan. I won't...I won't leave you. How can I?" Tears and snot leaked down on either side of her face. How could she? How could she just dump all of her attachments on Little Sister? How could she just be rid of them all at once and focus? There was too much history between them. It was the same predicament a person had on a sinking ship, holding onto a loved one being sucked down into the vortex created as the ship went down. If you let go, you survive, but the other person...

Kaley knew despair now. She knew the despair of those unfortunate souls who became so overly emotional that they took their own lives. Those despondent folks who committed suicide rather than live another day with their Ocean of Sorrow. It was not so easy as one might think to make oneself *not care* anymore about anyone.

If ya can't stand on your own two feet, how are you ever gonna help anybody? Those weren't Shannon's words. Those words had come from another place. A slippery place filled with quicksand and swift traps. It was the monster, of course. So confident, so stubborn, so sure that he had all the answers.

Listen to him, Kaley. Listen to what Nan said. Ward your heart. You…you have to do this for us. I can't. I…I just can't. I'm not strong enough.

"Neither am I," Kaley said.

Then you're both fuckin' dead. The monster. He could hear them? He could hear Shannon, too? *'Course I can fuckin' hear you. You're* both *in my head. It's gettin' awfully fuckin' crowded in here.*

"Get out of my head!" she commanded.

You get outta mine first, he said, laughing alone in his Penske truck. *You saw what I did, an' I've seen some of what your mother has done to you. Neglected you. Neglected everybody. Neglected her sister Tubby—*

"Tabby!"

—and yer dear ol' Nan, he went on, unfettered. *Yeah, sweet Jovita Dupré. So selfish. An' look at her. She's survived how many years with how many different men? That's how she survived, little girl. She whored herself out an' fucked whatever would have her to survive. It's called a survival mechanism, every creature has it, some stronger than others. Now get the fuck up! I'm tired o' hearin' this shit.*

"I can't—"

Jovita Dupré's lived her whole life as a selfish cunt. Ya figured out love yourself just a second ago. It's mostly selfish. So, how come you *don't get to be selfish? Just this once?*

Kaley started to say something in retort, but discovered that she was out of excuses, out of places to run to, out of time, out of everything. It frightened her with just how much sense the monster was making. Then, for just a moment, she let the Connection slip. She lost all sight and feeling with the impressions the other children had left in this room. She lost her Connection with Bonetta, with the monster, and even with Little Sister. Then, the discipline wavered. Just when she felt herself about to give in to the monster's logic and let go, the charm reconnected her to everyone and everything.

Her body and mind were suddenly wracked with guilt, shame, pain, and above all fear. The guilt was then so powerful that she felt hate. She hated herself. It twisted in her gut and soured. She almost vomited. Kaley had never hated herself so much, and was suddenly trapped in a world of self-loathing.

Ya know what Carl Sagan said, the monster said to her playfully.

"If you wish to make an apple pie from scratch, you must first invent the universe," Spencer said, turning the big yellow Penske truck onto Kingsley Street. "Lao Tzu said the journey of a thousand miles starts with a single step. Now that's two people who are smarter than you tellin' you that you gotta start somewhere. Got it?"

No reply. Spencer didn't bother pushing it.

The street ahead was ill-lit, and the houses on either side were somewhere on a scale between brand new and decrepit, utterly unremarkable except for two that had cameras posted on the front porch over the door. Spencer noticed these almost at once. Security, and how to circumvent it, had been something of a hobby of his for the better part of a decade, and so cameras stuck out to him as he was sure a wrongly mixed oil paint would've stuck out to van Gogh.

The thought of Dmitry's cocky face returned to him. It came from out of nowhere, and it made him hard. The rain had stopped, but there was electricity in the air.

"I have a feeling I'm gettin' closer," he told the owner of the Voice. "But there's still a ways to go. I'd recommend creating any confusion that you can. I'm gonna need it when I get there. This truck's hard to miss. When I pull this big bastard up, they're gonna notice me pretty fast if they're all still awake. You there? Ya still with me, partner?"

A moment of silence.

Then, *Yeah. I'm here. And I'm moving.*

Spencer nodded, smiling. So far this night had been the most remarkable of his life. Well, actually that was debatable, but it certainly ranked. As he drove down Kingsley Street, waiting for it to turn into Umway Street as the man at the plant had said through his ruined teeth, Spencer felt as though he were driving deeper into the Twilight Zone. If that were so, then this would be the part where things turned out to not be as they had previously seemed, and there would be some unexpected moral that come from it, a logic that only made sense in the realm that Rod Serling occupied.

His stomach growled. He was still hungry. *I need to eat somethin'.*

The time on the glowing dashboard said 4:37 AM. It had been four hours since he ate that burger at Dodson's, and his entire plan for the night had changed. The job he'd meant to do for Pat was almost totally scrapped, but if he finished with Avery Street quickly enough he might just be able to grab the necessary RFID chip and the Dodge Dart and be out of town with some extra scratch.

Up ahead, he spotted a yellow sign that said Umway Street was just a mile up.

Spencer smiled, and whistled the familiar theme song. "You unlock this door with the key of imagination. Beyond it is another dimension: a dimension of sound, a dimension of sight, a dimension of *mind*. You're moving into a land of both shadow and substance, of things and ideas. That's the signpost up ahead. Your next stop, the Twilight Zone!"

Kaley rolled over onto vomit that she didn't recall vomiting, and pressed her hands against the floor. She'd never been any good at push-ups, yet she managed one. Well, half of one, her knees came up to help her the rest of the way. "I'm moving," she told the monster. She hoped this satisfied him. The more she appeased him, the less he went prodding around inside her mind.

Bonetta Harper said, "You...you okay, girl?"

"Girl," she says. So we're supposed to be friends now?

Kaley made no reply. She stood up on wobbly legs. She felt as though she'd been raped herself, as though she'd been drugged, as though she'd been clubbed over the head repeatedly. A migraine started just behind her eyes and traveled to the back of her brain. She staggered and touched the wall for support. When she did this, a thrill went up her arm, and she felt the torment of others who had imbued the wall with their essence, their fears, their torment. She pulled her hand away quickly, and then warded her heart as best she could. Kaley then tested the wall by touching it again, tentatively at first, with only her fingers. The charm didn't assault her this time, and the migraine started to abate.

"You okay?" Bonetta asked again.

And again, Kaley made no reply. She sighed a quivering sigh, and turned around and around, taking in the room. Her eyes, whether on purpose or by accident she didn't know, finally landed on the vent cover she had been going for only minutes ago. *A camera?* she thought. The monster had suggested as much. It made sense, she supposed. They would have to monitor their captives somehow.

You can control what they see, the monster had said. *Or, at least, what they* think *they see.*

"Bonetta," she said. "Come here."

"Are you okay?"

"I'm okay. Just…just come over here." The charm was still strong enough that she felt the swelling power of Bonetta's trepidation, but eventually the girl overcame it enough to stand up from the corner and approach. She still squeezed her locket hopefully, though. "Come here," Kaley said. Bonetta stopped just short of her, as if afraid to catch a disease from her, and Kaley started whispering. "I want you…to come over here and give me a hand."

"A hand with what?"

"I know how to pick locks," Kaley said. And all at once, she knew that the monster had to be right. Not only did it make sense that there would be cameras watching them, but just think about the *timing*! Olga, Dmitry, and Mikhael had all come in at once, at the exact moment that Kaley had been looking up at the vent, at the *exact* moment that she had been convincing Bonetta to give her a hand getting up to it.

278

Guilt threatened to destroy her. They had come and taken Little Sister away because of her! They had come and taken Shan and...done things to her. *All because I tried to escape. I had to be so damned smart. What'll they do to her if they think I'm trying to escape again?*

Then came the monster's words. *You're doin' it again. Thinkin' of others when ya oughtta be workin' on a way out.*

Kaley felt like arguing, but knew that it was no use. The monster was inexorable. He would continue taunting her from an impossible distance, and she would never be able to touch him or punish him for it. "Not unless I get out of here," she said. Bonetta looked at her strangely.

That's the spirit! he said.

Bonetta looked her up and down. "Who're you talkin' to?"

Kaley swallowed. "Nobody. Now, come over here and stand by the doorknob."

"What? Why?"

"Just do it. I've got a hairpin here," she said, improvising before she realized it. She had pulled it out of her hair. In truth, she had no idea how to pick a lock, but as she approached it, she realized that she did. Kaley bent one of her hairpins to be the torsion wrench, and bent the other one so it could act as a rake. She wondered how she knew how to do this.

Because I know how to do it, my precious, said the monster. *That's somethin' I didn't count on. I meant for you to fake it, but if you can do what I can do, then go for it.*

Kaley wanted to deny it, because it meant that she and the monster were...conjoined. Bonding this empathically with another human being was not a pleasant experience. Emotions were good. They were powerful and fueling, but what emotions the monster had were too intense. The important ones were missing—love, hope, sympathy—and in their place was the most concentrated selfishness. A person must be selfish to some degree in order to take care of oneself, but in this instance...there was too much...it...

Would you say it cloys? asked the monster. A nauseating humor came over her. He saw everything. She was naked before him, and him her. But whereas she had shame, he had none.

Kaley slipped the two hairpins into the lock, and started working on the tumbler. She had never known how a tumbler worked, but for the moment she did. There was more to skills like lock picking than just knowing the names of things and the concepts of a technique—one had to have a certain finesse with the hands, there was muscular control involved, the tiniest of movements from one finger to push this way or correct that way without *over*correcting. Additionally, there was even a pattern of breathing involved in order to help maintain focus, a habit that many skilled people picked up while doing whatever it was they were good at without knowing they were doing it.

What surprised Kaley, and would surprise her for decades to come, was that she didn't just know the concepts of lock picking. For a time, for that window of her life, her muscles, lungs, and focus were that of an expert picker. She *was* the monster. He fed her, whether he knew it or not. The monster knew his thieving craft, no one could ever deny him that. And he had drive. A will.

Out of nowhere, Kaley was reminded of an old *Star Trek* episode. Ricky had been fond of old sci-fi—Isaac Asimov, Robert Heinlein, Douglas Adams—and both Kaley and Shan had been subjected to his interests, and made to watch *Lost in Space*, *Battelstar Galactica* (the old version), and others with cheesy special effects. In one episode of *Star Trek*, she recalled the guy with the pointy ears says to the captain of the starship *Enterprise*, "Jim, madness has no purpose, and no reason." Then, he ominously adds, "But it may have a goal."

You were right about that, Mr. Spock, Kaley thought, her hands working furiously at something that felt utterly natural. *It does have a goal.* She felt the slimy humor of the monster. He had detected her morbid critique, and he relished it. He was closer now. Their Connection felt stronger. Kaley almost reached out for Shannon, to speak with her, to comfort her…and immediately she stopped herself. Or maybe it was the monster stopping her, pulling back on her reins like a rider on a horse. *Don't think that way. That way lies your end.* She wasn't sure if that was her voice, the monster's, Shan's or even Nan's. Either way, it sounded like good advice right now.

Ward yo' heart, chil'. Definitely Nan that time, but was it really her speaking from the ether or was Kaley just losing her mind?

So lost in thought was she that at first she didn't really take note of the sharp *click!* that signaled a finished job. Kaley felt it more than she heard it, and she knew that she had successfully picked all five of the tumbles in the door lock.

Kaley turned the doorknob, and the door parted slightly. She turned and looked at Bonetta, who was wide-eyed and daring to hope. That hope cascaded over Kaley and emboldened her.

Good job, the monster said. She could feel the sinister delight. He was happy that his plan was coming together, not in the saving of her life or anyone else's. *I'm on my way. And, if I'm right about that camera,* they *are too. Prepare yourself for the fight o' yer life.*

"I'm ready," Kaley said, both to him and to Bonetta. She looked at the Harper girl and said, "Are you?"

At first, it did not appear so. Bonetta looked at the door, then back at the room that had been their prison. No doubt she was recalling the weapons and superior strength and numbers of their enemies, and weighing that against the thought of possibly remaining here forever.

"Bonetta," Kaley said, and for the first time found (quite by accident) that she could reach out and *change* others via her charm. Like a child maturing with its newfound gifts of balance and dexterity, Kaley had stumbled upon a way to manipulate Bonetta's emotions. She groped for her attachment to her father, to her anger that day on the playground, and fortified Bonetta with it. "Bonetta, if you stay here, you won't just be a prisoner. You're a future victim, girl. They gonna kill you. You know that, don't you?"

Silence in the room. Any moment now, the Oni's (as Kaley had started thinking of this fucked up family) would be coming down the stairs for them. Finally, the large Harper girl looked back at her and said, "Let's get the fuck outta here."

Together, they stepped out of the prison, and into the Rainbow Room.

"Attention all units," said dispatch. "Five-oh-three reported at the Keegan Corporation on Mansell Road. A stolen yellow Penske truck was taken off the lot. Suspect's description matches that of Spencer Adam Pelletier, wanted in multiple murders and a shooting that wounded a police officer earlier tonight. All units in the vicinity, please respond. Consider armed and extremely dangerous."

Officer David Emerson touched the radio on his lapel. "This is one-Adam-four, responding to that five-oh-three. I am in the vicinity and presently conducting a search for the suspect. En route. ETA, four minutes." He flipped on his siren without listening to dispatch's confirmation, and turned left quickly at the next stoplight. "I got you, Jack Ching. You're mine, motherfucker. Gonna have me a mounted jackalope at the center of my living room. You're fucking *mine*."

"Yo! Porter! We got something!"

That was Agent Stone, sticking his head out from the SUV's driver side. Leon had been standing next to Porter watching the coroners pull out the little girl. A moment of silence had befallen the entire scene, all police officers in the yard and across the street had removed their hats without being told. Most of them had either heard the recording of the girl's screams (if they had, in fact, been hers, and even if they hadn't there was no doubt this girl had suffered tremendously) or had heard the others talking about it.

Porter dashed across the street with Leon jogging directly behind. "What's up?"

"Get in! Mansell Road! He walked into a Penske manufacturing plant and drove right off the fucking lot with one o' their trucks!"

"A *Penske* truck?" Leon asked, diving into the back seat. He'd had the volume on his radio turned low while the girl was being pulled out, and hadn't heard the update.

"Yeah."

"They have a heading?" Porter asked. "A visual on him?"

Stone cranked the SUV just as Mortimer hopped in behind him. "Not yet. Two helicopters in the area are sweeping with searchlights."

Outside, the other officers were getting the same update. Hennessey and his SWAT boys were piling back into their large armored van, ready to be redeployed again elsewhere.

"A big yellow Penske truck?" Leon asked again. "That's getting sloppy of him. He tossed his phone so he wouldn't be found, but those Penskes stick out like sore thumbs. He had to know a stolen truck would be reported. He's either gonna ditch it soon, or..." Or what? Was he leading them someplace? Was he having just that much fun? Leon had flashbacks of seventeen-year-old Colton Harris-Moore, the "Barefoot Bandit," who had evaded police with such mischievous glee and had left notes and pictures in his wake to taunt them. Some men did strange things in defiance of the law.

"Yeah," Porter said. "He must've gotten desperate, and he'll definitely ditch it soon as he can."

Leon nodded wordlessly.

At his phone, Porter received another update. "Well, shit on me, we may have something here."

"What is it?"

"Avery Street. You know it?"

Leon had to think for a second. "Yeah...yeah, I think so. Never worked it, but I know it. It's a really obscure back street, surrounded by some underdeveloped neighborhoods that got foreclosed on. Why?"

"Your boys at Atlanta PD just sent an update, and Interpol's all over it. The bureau just got it that the APD interviewed a few guys from Keegan, and two of them said that Pelletier stopped and asked them for directions to Avery Street." Porter tapped the screen on his phone a few times, then looked down in consternation. "The map o' that place looks screwy."

"Yeah," Leon said. "That area's kind of fucked up. It got zoned weird and divided into different sections, some of which got cut off from other main roads but none of them ever got officially renamed, so there's a few different streets that *look* like different streets but essentially are fragments of old Avery Street. A series of neighborhoods got foreclosed on; it wasn't a priority to rename anything."

"Why not?"

Leon shrugged. "Nothing gets delivered there anymore. No pizzas, no mail. Almost nobody lives there."

"Huh," Porter said, his tongue touching his upper lip thoughtfully.

"What're you thinking?"

"Probably the same as you," he said. "A thousand bucks says we find a whole group of Russians taking up residence in at least one house. Stacked up like Mexicans."

Nobody took that bet.

The rain suddenly started in even harder. It came down in great sheets. Leaning back in his seat, Leon thought about Pat. He thought about Pat's connection to Pelletier, and how that might come back to haunt him. Leon thought about his sister, Melinda, married to Pat. He wondered how this could negatively affect her once all was said and done. He thought about the *vory v zakone* and the Rainbow Room. He thought about the screams he'd heard come from those speakers.

13

The neighborhood along Avery Street was one grand Forgotten Place. That was Spencer's assessment. One of those zones that existed only on a map, but in no one's memory. He could tell by the buildup of leaves in the gutters, the trash along the sidewalks, and the bent, rusted and graffitied stop sign that no one had bothered to fix.

It had been difficult to find, even with the directions the Keegan worker had given him. There were *four different* Avery Streets, or at least it seemed so because of a strange engineering anomaly where Avery Street, most likely an old street, had zigzagged around this area and two other streets—Montpelier and Crowe Street—had been laid along it longwise. Like a slinking, wavy snake that had been cut while curling, there were now many different slivers, all of them called Avery Street.

The road was winding and hilly, with unchecked trees choking off some of the sidewalks. Vines grew amongst the branches, and even reached out at the road, as if ready to snatch up some unwary traveler.

The wind was blowing lightly when Spencer stepped down from the truck's cab and onto the pavement, pocked with potholes. Cracked streets yielded a path for some determined grass. Trees stood sentry on all sides, some firs, one oak, a smattering of beeches. It was clear to Spencer this had once been planned as an upscale neighborhood, but somewhere along the way someone lost it in a bankruptcy, possibly during the big Housing Bubble that ruined everyone. It was new old, or old new; one of the two. Some builder had lost his ass and been forced to stop developing this area, leaving the few planted trees to grow wild and selling the houses for whatever he could get.

Spencer knew the story. He knew it without even having to research it. He knew how the world worked. He understood its ebb and flow, comprehended how its blood flowed through its veins, the way thinking creatures thought, and the way the deck was stacked against almost every single entity trapped in it. The game was the same. Criminals would always take advantage in desperate times. They would squat in houses that sat empty, or else buy them at a steal and turn them into meth labs. *Or rape clinics*, he thought, smirking.

The houses on either side of Avery Street were just short of those large ones that had been such a quick and easy build that they had been the craze in the late 90's and early 00's. Not quite McMansions, but pretty big. *Yep, definitely pre-Housing Bubble.* The American builder had lost his ass in that shit, and then had come a few Russians, ones with the money to answer his prayers since no Americans had the dough to buy *any* house at that time, much less these.

Avery Street had four houses on either side, but at the cul-de-sac, where it ended, there were two others, those being the most well kept in the neighborhood. The yards looked regularly mown, and the waist-high fences, though as jagged and darkened as a crackhead's teeth, looked at least sturdy. Only the big brick one at the end of the cul-de-sac had any lights on. However, Spencer did spot a trio of white goons sitting in a swing and in some wicker chairs on the front porch of the house closest to him.

"You ready, partner?" Spencer said, taking his last toke of his cig and tossing it on the ground.

There was no hesitation this time. *I'm ready.*

The Connection was still felt. Spencer had already gotten used to it. It was refreshing, this new perspective on life. He'd enjoyed tasting the girl's love for her sister, had found her fear intriguing. "I'm on the move."

So are we.

He smiled. "There's a good girl."

How is it out there with you?

Spencer started moving down the street. "Reminds me of that ol' Western, *A Fistful of Dollars*, where Eastwood was in a dying town with two feuding gangs living on each side of a single street. Funny scene. Eastwood walks past the town's only coffin maker and tells him to get three coffins ready. He shoots four dead, and walks back to the coffin maker and apologizes, saying he ought to have said *four* coffins." There was no response from the

286

Voice, but he felt her. He felt her fear, and for a moment he toyed with it. He found it sticky, as sticky as she found his thoughts in general. "Don't worry, I'm not gonna shoot anybody. Least, not yet."

Spencer nodded and gave a polite wave to the three white boys on the porch. The one sitting in the swing stood up and walked inside, alone. The other two remained seated in their wicker chairs, watching him.

Twenty steps later, a light came on in the upstairs window of the house on his left. Another eight steps, and a light came on in both a downstairs window and an upstairs window of the house beside it. Then, just as the first houses on his right and left were behind him, he heard a door shut. Spencer glanced behind. A man and a woman had stepped out of the front door of the first house on the left and switched on a porch light. The man was bare-chested, and had something in his left hand.

Now I'm stepping into their *parlor*, Spencer thought. *And it's the prettiest little parlor I ever did spy.*

Another light switched on. Then another. A man stepped out onto the porch of the last house on the right. Inside each house, calls were being made. Avery Street was its own little nook, a rift in the fabric of the space-time continuum, where only a few knew how to venture in and out of safely. Spencer's sudden appearance was probably a surprise to the inhabitants who probably rarely ever spotted such a bold traveler.

"I don't know which house you're in," he muttered, looking at one of the white fellas who'd wandered out onto his porch and taken a seat. "You there?"

I'm thinking, said the Voice. A few seconds, then, *It's a big brick one, on the front somebody spray-painted L-Ray runs this shit. That's all I—oh…oh God…*

"What is it?" Fear bloomed across his mind, and he liked it. Then, all at once, the Connection was lost. He no longer tasted the fear, the sadness, the shame. Without knowing it, Spencer had started to relish it, much the same way as he'd relished having Tidov dead to rights, but there was a key difference. The sensation that came with the Voice was a little soothing. He felt like a man in a desert who'd been granted a sip of water—the cleanest, purest, coldest glass of water on Earth—and now it was gone. "Partner?" he said. "Partner, you there?"

To his right, one of the men had stepped off of the porch. He was a large man, also wearing no shirt, and his big belly had tattooed letters: **Мир ненавидит нас.**

"The world hates us," Spencer said, half in wonder.

"Hey there!" someone called from behind. He glanced over his shoulder, but never stopped walking towards the big brick house. He spotted it from here, **L-Ray runz this shit!!!**, and never broke stride. "Hey, man! What's a guy like you doin' wandering around here at night? Huh? You a Peeping Tom? Eh? A thief? Maybe you're scouting us out. Is that right?"

Spencer kept walking. He listened to the footsteps behind him and estimated their distance. About twenty feet. The big guy with the round tattooed belly was walking parallel to him on the sidewalk about twelve feet away.

"You gonna talk to me, punk?"

"I'm meetin' a friend o' mine," Spencer said, making it to the fence and stepping right on into the yard.

"Yeah? Who's that?"

"Dmitry. He inside?"

"There's no fucking Dmitry lives around here, asshole. Sounds like you got yourself lost. Time to turn back around—"

Spencer did turn around. Smoothly, and with purpose. His right hand went to his waistline, where he withdrew the Glock. The man walking behind him had a moment for his cocky smile to linger while he processed how the world had turned on him here on his own turf. Another young man was walking behind him, this one with jeans and a Metallica T-shirt, who turned on his heels and ran a second before the bullet ripped through his friend's skull. The sharp bang caused a scream from someplace. He heard a window break, strangely enough, and shots were fired at him. At least, he thought they were.

The big man with the tattooed belly ran for cover behind an old silver Izuzu Rodeo parked at the curb. Spencer turned and fired twice, just to make sure he was down. Someone else fired at him from the window of the house on his right. It was a semiautomatic weapon by the sound of it. Bullets danced on the cracked pavement but nowhere near his feet.

Spencer ducked and ran around the side of the big brick house, bullets slicing at air just behind him, some of them smashing into the picket fence and the earth. He heard someone shout, "*Gde?*" Someone else cried, "*Chto ty delayesh?!*" and someone else screamed, "*Vsyo pad kontrolem!*"

Mere seconds before things erupted on Avery Street, Kaley Dupré felt a familiar, slippery, slimy mind approaching her. She felt the feelings more than the thoughts. She felt the lust, and white-hot anger that accompanied it.

They started across the room, moving slowly at first but then with more purpose. Kaley and Bonetta both paused when they spotted the blood on the floor. It was just beside a small, rounded saddle, and there were stirrups around its legs where her sister had been tied down. Kaley fought back another bout of vomiting—there couldn't be much left in her stomach—and shouted, "Shannon?" Her eyes went rheumy. "Shannon!"

"*Shh!*" Bonetta hissed. "You want 'em to hear us?"

I don't know which house you're in, the monster whispered into her mind and heart. Kaley didn't immediately answer, because she felt the pressure from the Oni's. They were on their way; she knew it even before she knew she knew it.

There was too much going on at once and Kaley didn't know which to act on first.

She knew exactly where Shannon was being held, and suddenly that trumped all. Kaley was terrified to see what physical shape her sister had been left in, but the green door at the other end of the basement had what in years to come Kaley would come to call Resonance. Her little sister resonated from that location. She knew it as well as she knew her arms were attached to her shoulders. She knew it the way that a spider knows it has something in its web, by sensing the vibrations throughout the web itself.

She moved over to the green door, and looked at the lock. She tried to find the knowledge again to pick it, but couldn't. The knowledge was leaving her. The Connection, so strong a moment before, was slowly being severed. Like a fire that burned so bright that it burned up all its fuel and died quickly. *Too* much *kindling this time*, she thought.

You there? the monster said.

"I'm thinking," she said.

Beside her, Bonetta said fervently, "Thinking about what? Let's go!" Now that she was free of the room and had space to move about, and now that Kaley's charm had worked to embolden her, Bonetta had found her courage.

It was all happening so fast. Kaley tried to give the monster an answer. She would still need his help since she couldn't pick this lock. She pictured the big brick house, and the brief look she'd gotten before Shannon had attempted her escape. "It's a big brick one," she told the monster, while Bonetta stood there glowering at her, "on the front somebody spray-painted L-Ray runs this shit. That's all I—oh…oh God…"

She almost vomited.

They had just crossed over the sandbox in the Rainbow Room when she felt the waves of lust and murder preceding the Oni family. Footsteps. Rapid ones coming down the wooden stairs. Bonetta whimpered, "Oh no…" Kaley rattled the door. She banged on it, called out her sister's name, but heard no reply. She hadn't sensed Shan's death, so she was still alive in there. "Oh, God!" Bonetta screamed from behind. Kaley turned, and found Olga and Mikhael standing on the stairs. Olga had her Taser again, and Mikhael stood right behind her, pistol in hand.

"Get back in your room, little girl," Olga said.

Kaley started to say something. Then, all at once, she felt defiance rise inside her. It belonged to Bonetta Harper, and it came from that place where we hide all our secret rebellions, where we send them to be consumed by more logical thinking, and yes, even by our own fears and insecurities. The rebellion was bright and hot and Kaley was overwhelmed by it.

Before they knew it, Olga and Mikhael were assailed by Bonetta, who lifted something from the floor. It was a whip, a prop, laid down beside the saddle and the stirrups. She ran screaming at her captors and was on Olga before she could raise her Taser. Shrieking like a banshee, and tearing at Olga's face and hair, Kaley felt the battle internally more than externally. Red and black swirled in eddies, rage that had germinated from neglect

290

suffered over ten years. And…something else. Something that was here, in this room with Kaley, with all of them. She couldn't feel the monster anymore, but she didn't need to. Something had been shared, however briefly. Just as he'd unconsciously given Kaley his lock picking skills, he'd also dumped in a bit of his humor, his delight at what had happened in Baton Rouge. When someday she had her doctorate in psychology, Dr. Kaley Alexandria Dupré would know that that's how such creatures worked, that it was much like the meth to her mother, how one hit used to be enough, but after a while only a single hit didn't satisfy for nearly as long. So an addict must up the dosage.

The monster had upped his dosage. His need was great, and he'd shared it with Kaley. It was there, inside of her, tugging.

This all happened within the span of a second, while Bonetta struggled, and yet the days and weeks and years seemed to crawl by for Kaley. It started out…slowly…slowly…from the back of her mind forward. It crept across her eyes and there was a splitting sensation. Then, she was spinning around and around. It was like the vertigo she used to suffer through, only now it wasn't nauseating, it was…thought-provoking? Yes…yes, it *did* provoke thoughts. Kaley now found herself in a position of moral flexibility. In one nanosecond she was empathetic to all of the creatures around her—from Bonetta to Shannon to Olga to Mikhael and even to a moth she detected somewhere behind her, feeling so hungry and yet exhilarated by the lights all around it. Then, she wasn't empathetic at all. She actually found herself repulsed by all of these people, even by her sister, who, for just a millisecond, she saw as weak and pathetic.

Something turned over inside of her. There were glaciers of her own that she hadn't yet charted, much like the monster's own glaciers. The landscape of her own heart was opened to her, and it was a tortured, treacherous thing. Kaley did not like seeing the things she saw. At once, she was both pitying and reviling herself.

And there it was. A mentality that she normally would've looked at askance. Olga and Mikhael were wreathed in a viscous fluid. Kaley saw it, even if Bonetta did not. Olga and her brother saw it, too, and acted as if snakes had leapt at them. They crawled away from Bonetta, who Mikhael had wrenched by her hair and flung to the floor at gunpoint. Now, Mikhael looked at his gun hand, and saw the dark-red liquid slowly pouring out from his fingertips and going up, up, up his hand.

Olga's own attack came from her mouth. From her gums came lines of blood, which crawled around her lips and into his nostrils. Next it came from her eyes. She cried tears of dark red blood and fell back onto her ass, looking at her hands, where the flesh had started peeling back. Now Bonetta screamed, for she saw it, too. As it turned out, this might not just all be in Kaley's mind. It appeared this was actually happening.

"*Kak dela?*" someone said. Kaley half realized it was her. She spoke Russian now. "*Ti takaya privlekatelnaya*," she told Olga. Translation: You are so pretty. Olga looked at her. She was trembling, and looked over at her brother, whose own flesh had started to melt. It wasn't boiled, there was no smoke coming off of him. The flesh sagged, and though it was not heated, it took the viscosity of lava, slowly falling, falling, sloughing off of him. He turned and looked at his sister with desperate eyes, one of which hung from the socket. He looked at his own hands and staggered backwards, up the stairs, his flesh dropping off in great clumps behind him.

She had boiled over. Kaley could no longer contain the flow. It came bursting out of her like seas over the New Orleans levies. She stood there letting it pass from her and into the room. It touched all corners of the basement. She felt the plaster on the walls and ceiling, felt the dust mop and the drops of semen, the cracked walls, the stuffed animals and their threading. Bonetta's own mind was assailed, and she lost her mind. Kaley felt it go. She, after all, was the one who destroyed it. Shannon had warded herself, either out of practice or instinct, and was safe. That was good, because Kaley now had no way of protecting her. The waters that burst those levies were taking Kaley for a ride as much as anyone else.

Visions melded with one another, became conjoined, and then dissolved. Curtains of flame appeared, then peeled back to reveal an endless darkness, and beyond that endless darkness was herself, staring back at her from across an impossible gulf. Other things came to her, terrifying and seductive all at once. It inflated her. It was beyond her. *She* was the kindling, and not the enkindler.

This was what she would come to call the Rapture.

The back yard gave little cover against the rounds that burst out at him from the top floor of the brick house. Spencer blindly fired two shots behind him as he made for a parked red sedan near a rear garage. Just as he dived for cover, a man stepped out from the back door with an Uzi with a suppressor. The barrage of gunfire lit the sedan up, shattering glass and flattening the front right tire.

Spencer pressed his back against the rear wheel for maximum cover, even as the neighborhood came alive all around him. The yard was about fifty yards squared, mostly grass except for the two-car garage and a doghouse with no dog.

The windshield of the sedan was spackled with bullets from a silenced weapon. He could no longer tell exactly which direction it was all coming from. Someone started firing from a second storey window in the neighboring house, at least he thought so, and two more pistols were fired from somewhere on either side of the sedan. They would want to hem him in, pin him down, and finish him off quickly before the cops showed up and started asking questions.

But a flash of light and a steady *whup-whup-whup* changed all that in an instant. The helicopter came seemingly out of nowhere. For all the gunfire, Spencer never heard its approach. The searchlight splashed against the yard, but on the opposite side from where Spencer was huddled.

All at once, all gunfire ceased.

The police chopper (for what else could it be?) crested the top of the house, and swept its spotlight across the side of the house. Spencer poked his head over the top of the sedan, spotted a large shadow dashing across the lawn towards the back door of the house. His pulse didn't budge. He stood up, took careful aim, gave a bit of a lead on his target, and squeezed the trigger. It took the bare-chested man in the neck. He did a comical little dance, spinning around and around while trying to keep his feet beneath him, until he finally collided with a porch post.

Spencer darted across the lawn, making for the house. The searchlight would actually grant him cover as long as it wasn't on him—anyone on the other side of the searchlight, which was most of the neighborhood, would not be able to see *through* the light to the darkness beyond. For the moment, he could move freely, and the chopper's own propellers had masked his gunshot.

"This is the Atlanta Police Department!" announced an authoritative voice from Among High. *"Lay down your weapons and put your hands in the air!"* Doubtless, while gunshots wouldn't be easily heard from the chopper's cockpit, the flashes of muzzle flair moments ago would be familiar to the officers inside.

As Spencer made for the back door, he could just see around the side of the house. He spotted at least three sets of flashing lights, one of them belonging to a large van. *No*, he thought. *No, I'm so fucking close!*

At the porch he halted, and knelt briefly over the dying Russian. The dying man had jaundiced skin, and pleading eyes. "Look at me!" he shouted above the din of the chopper and the commands its pilot was still issuing. The man's neck was shooting jets of blood. "Look at me! Look at me! Look at me!" he said over and over, until the Russian finally looked up. He had a crimson bear tattooed on his forehead. "You see me? I did this to you! *I* did!" And he laughed as he scooped up the man's silenced Uzi. The Russian looked up at him stupidly. To Spencer, he seemed to be considering how awful his last moments were, how utterly *wrong* it was to have his killer laughing over him.

Then, gunfire erupted all around him. Left, right, from the windows of the neighboring house, and even from up above. Yes, the helicopter had gone on the offensive.

Spencer went to the back door and stood to one side of it. "All right, boys!" he howled. "I'm a fucking Portia! Know what that is? It's a fucking spider that eats other spiders! I'm comin' into yer parlor, bitch!" He tittered, barely able to contain his excitement as he kicked open the door and moved inside. What he saw next, he would never forget.

David was the first car on the scene, but only by about fifteen seconds. The chopper was already hovering above the big brick house at the far end of Avery Street, on the right side of the cul-de-sac. Its searchlight was on but no longer sweeping, which suggested it had locked on to something, or someone. That was the first thing that struck him. The second thing was the Penske truck, parked at the side of the street without any attempt to hide it behind something of equal size or larger.

Then, the first bullet came through the rear window on the passenger side, ripping through the leather seat in the back. David slammed on his brakes and put the vehicle in park, then ducked out of the door and used it as a shield as he hunkered down and gauged his surroundings. He was about twenty yards into Avery, with the first two houses on either side of him. Lights were on in various windows. Behind him, another squad car was on its way, its coming foretold by the red and blue flashing lights that flickered against the threes around the bend.

Fucking jackalope!

He shouted into his radio, "This is one-Adam-four, Officer David Emerson! I'm at Avery Street and taking fire! Repeat, officer taking fire! I've spotted the yellow Penske ditched at the side of—" He stopped when two more bullets panged off of the hood of his car, and a third cut the air over his head and smacked into a mailbox thirty feet away. "More shots fired! I need more backup!"

The squad car he'd seen coming had now rounded the bend, and was speeding up towards, no doubt having heard his call for help. It screeched to a halt just behind his car, and out came Officers Walt Keitrich and McDevitt. "Grab some cover!" he advised them, just as the first shots bounced off their windshield. David peeked over the open door, saw a few open windows on the house on his right. There were two quick flares from a window on the top floor, and gunshots rang out, both round bouncing off the other squad care. "Top floor, second opening from the left!" David fired the first shot in retaliation.

Keitrich and McDevitt peeked over their own open doors and saw where he was shooting, and fired warning shots of their own. Two more answered them, then David fired another and waited. There was no more return gunfire from that window. He was down on one knee, waiting…

Suddenly, the world came alive with booming guns, panging bullets, and shattering glass. The bullets came from everywhere at once, perhaps even behind him. David dived back into the driver's seat and ducked his head towards the floorboard. He heard hissing and felt the front of the car tilt to one side. That's how he knew the run-flat tires had taken serious damage, since it took a great deal to empty them of air so quickly.

Outside, he heard Keitrich and McDevitt returning fire. He heard screaming from one of them. *"Officer down! Officer down! Officer down on Avery Street!"*

A curtain of flames greeted Spencer at the threshold, though he didn't think the flames were real because he felt no heat. "You open this door with the key of imagination," he said. The flames defied the standard laws of fire, licking down from the ceiling, as well as out from the walls, rather than climbing upwards. An ocean of roiling liquid fire churned on the floor, spreading around his feet, parting for him as he passed, revealing unburned carpet and furniture. On the floor was a bottle of Michelob light, a Styrofoam container holding leftovers from Buffalo's Café, and a Mary Kay catalog unburned, despite flames dancing around it.

Someone screamed.

Inside, he moved with greater care. Somehow, he knew this wasn't meant for him. It was someone else's hell, and he was just getting a glimpse. Yet still, something moved on the floor, something with hooks in its face and desperate eyes. A hand reached up to him, a beseeching hand. It belonged to a younger man. A boy of maybe seventeen years, eighteen tops. He writhed on the ground, the hooks in his skin connected to chains that came out from openings in the walls, which pulled at him, peeling his lips and nose back over his face. His pants were down around his ankles, and there was a hairless, oily four-legged creature pumping on him endlessly, tirelessly. The creature paused to look up at

Spencer, regarded him for a moment, and then went back to his business.

"Sunny days," Spencer sang, for what else could he do? "Everything's *A-okayyyy*! Friendly neighbors there. That's—where—we—*meeeeeet*! Can ya tell me how to get...how to get to Avery Street?"

Spencer stepped over the pleading boy, holding his Glock in one hand and the silenced Uzi in the other. The flames parted at his feet, revealing more of the boy's torment—the flesh on his back had been peeled back to reveal the sinew, the intertransversarii and trapezius muscles, as well as the latissimus dorsi, a triangle of rippling, bloody tissue from the shoulder to the hip. The detail to the illusion—if an illusion it was—was incredible. He looked on with the curiosity of an ornithologist, pausing at a possible new parakeet on his hands, but with many other new discoveries waiting all around, commanding his attention. He moved on.

Flames danced up at him, climbed his legs a bit, children clambering for attention, and he thought he felt the heat now. Someone screamed from someplace deeper in the house. Spencer moved carefully. Though he knew this torment was not meant for him, he knew that he might easily get caught up in it if he allowed himself to be, just the way a bear trap might be meant for a dumber creature didn't mean that a smarter one might not act carelessly enough to get stuck.

More screaming.

The flames shifted. Like grass in the wind, it all blew apart as though a great gust had come through. They moved up the wall, breathing. Yes, the walls were definitely breathing in and out, in and out, in and out. He smelled smoke, and coughed, even though he knew this mustn't be real. It was both real and imagined. Somewhere between shadow and substance, it was as real as it needed to be.

Blood. Blood dripped from a ceiling fan overhead, its flaming blades creating a nightmarish pinwheel. The blood dripped from the center of the fan. This felt real, but he imagined the longer he stayed here, the more all of this would seem logical. Fundamentally, he understood this wasn't all just in his head. It was the girl's doing. *And mine too, somehow.* He understood this, also.

More screaming from somewhere inside the house.

Spencer took a moment to look about the house, get his bearings. The seas of fire parted at times, giving him a glimpse of the furniture, windows, and television—the TV was on the Food Network, and the house was cooking up something that looked *mm, mm good*, glistening sliced ham with pillowy mashed potatoes and gravy with okra glazed with butter. But there was something else in there, too. Just behind the plump, mustached chef with the green apron, there was a woman being flayed alive and pieces of her were being placed out onto the grill, where they sizzled. "Oh, now that smells good already," said the chef. Spencer spotted a piece of the peeled flesh, saw that it had a crimson bear tattoo on it.

It's Olga, said the Voice. It permeated the walls just as the flames did. In fact, the flames breathed when those words were spoken.

Spencer didn't comment on that. "Leave Dmitry to me," he said. "That one's mine. I deserve him."

Why? You could've called the police any time. You could've called them once you had the license plate of the Expedition.

"And you and your sister's throats would've been slit once their cop-on-the-take gave them the heads up—"

You still don't know that—

"Yes, I do, but *you* don't wanna believe," he said, glancing out the windows. What parts of the windows he could see through the flaming curtains were scant images of a charred, tortured landscape. A post-apocalyptic scene that was the antithesis of everything Norman Rockwell ever painted. Someone screamed upstairs. A man. No, several men. "An' ya can't afford to kill me now. Ya still need me."

For what?

"For *this*," Spencer laughed. He approached the steps with the Uzi aimed up the stairs and the Glock aimed down the hall from whence he came. "I hope ya don't think you're doin' this all on your own. No little girl ever thought up shit this fucked up."

The police are here. They'll protect us!

He smiled. "You gonna rely on others to protect ya, little girl? How's that been workin' out for ya so far, eh?"

No reply from her.

"Doesn't matter anyway, sister. They're out there, fighting at least a dozen angry Russians with machine guns. It'll be a while before they clear this entire neighborhood." He started up the steps, aware of the heat climbing up his back. The fire had started catching to him. It had started to become real. "Ya can't keep this goin' forever. You're gonna need me. Now, where the fuck is Oni? He's inside here someplace, isn't he?"

I can feel him, she said finally, desperately. *You have to kill him. But he's…he's…*

"He's what?"

He's like you! He's not as affected by what I'm doing.

"You mean he's immune to hell, or the *idea* of it, anyways," Spencer said, nodding. "Yeah, I smelled that on him. He's ready for hell, always knew he was goin' there, an' had no fuckin' problem with it. My kinda guy. But there's only room for one fuckin' maniac on this planet. Where is he?"

I don't know. He's here. He's everywhere. All around you.

At the top of the stairs, Spencer paused. On the floor were three older men, all of them bare-chested, all of them with tattoos on their arms of red bears, and all of them writhing in exquisite agony. Briars stemmed from their guts, and from their assholes, tearing through the cloth and crawling across the floor, up the flaming walls, and finding purchase in the ceiling. These outstretched vines pulled the three men up from the floor, suspending them in a web of briars and flames and their own blood. These would be the men that Kaley had seen playing cards in the kitchen downstairs when she first came in. Spencer knew this, because she saw his reaction and recalled them for him.

One of the men's pants had torn free thanks to the briars pouring out of him, and his scrotum dangled like a potato bulging from a small leather pouch. And something crawled around inside it, something bubbling, bobbing up and down beneath the skin, poking at the testicles curiously.

Except for the occasional muscle spasm, the only thing moving on the three men were their eyes, which looked out at

Spencer pleadingly. He stepped forward and analyzed them, relishing his position and theirs. This felt good. This felt right. It was as it should be, he standing and smiling, and they twisted and helpless.

Then, all at once, one of them managed to scream. From mouths pushed permanently open by briars that worked their way up through the jaw and up through the roof of their mouths and through their nostrils, this one man screamed. He went into convulsions as more briars suddenly moved, spilling out from his own anus and slowly crawling into his throat.

The flames all around him breathed. Spencer turned and saw something moving. A long, undulating tentacle moved out from a doorway down the hall, its serpentine crawl random, and it piled high on the floor. Its skin was translucent, and its insides appeared to be a gelatinous thing that pulsed with life, even as something inside struggled to get out.

"You see it, too?" Whoever said it had a thick Russian accent.

Spencer looked up. Dmitry stood on the other side of the slithering thing, which had no head and no tail that he could find. The Russian was at the end of the hall, standing inside a small bedroom and bare-chested like all the rest of his comrades, flames licking all over his body and a tiny creature was crawling about his shoulder, the same creature humping the poor lad downstairs. The little imp paused just above the crimson bear tattoo, licked it, and winked at Spencer. "I don't know what you're talkin' about," Spencer told him.

"You see *something*," Dmitry accused, raising a cigarette to his lips. In his other hand, he held a .44 Magnum snub-nose. "I'm just wondering if you see the same thing as me. Or are we both seeing different things? They say heaven is what you make it. I always thought that was strange, you know? If that's so, then everybody's just walking around heaven really confused." He took a toke, blew out smoke, which the imp quickly crawled to the edge of his face and inhaled, lapping up the smoke like sweet juices from a watermelon. "So, is it the same with hell?"

"There is no hell," Spencer said. "Just earth. Good ol' *terra firma* an' a house with a little girl's nightmare occupyin' it." *He's lost it*, Spencer thought. *An' he's accepted it. He's accepted*

the reality around him. The others fight it, that's why they suffer.
As he considered that, he also felt the presence from *her.* She was around him, with him, to the point that, from one second to the next, he wasn't sure where she ended and he began.

"This thing in my hand," Dmitry said. *"It's* not imaginary."

"Neither are these," Spencer said, and raised his weapons. He fired.

Several things happened at once. The slithering thing in the hallway churned, perhaps alarmed by the sudden burst of gunfire. As it did, it absorbed most, if not all, of Spencer's bullets. When this happened, the flames diminished—they didn't vanish, they just lessened in intensity—and Dmitry fired back. He unloaded the snub-nose, but none of the bullets hit Spencer. *Real enough*, he thought, and tossed down his Glock when it was empty. He fired the Uzi in short, controlled bursts until it too was empty. The writhing tentacle slammed against the wall, and where it did, flames bloomed in a way that would've been gorgeous under any other circumstances.

Dmitry flung his Magnum to the ground, and ran out from the bedroom and directly at Spencer, who did the same. The tentacle surged, and amid the cramped hallway, flames, and men choking on the briars pouring from their own bodies, they collided.

David was glad to see the SWAT van pulling up, and the other three patrol cars and the FBI's SUV right behind them, with the three agents hopping out with Leon Hulsey diving for cover behind the rear wheel of David's car as soon as he exited. He moved fast for such a big guy, and joined the firefight before asking any questions. Leon shouted, *"Where?!"*

David pointed up the street, to the open windows from the houses on the left. Leon poked his head out from cover and fired five rapid shots from his Glock, a suppressive fire accompanied by SWAT when they came spewing out the back of the van. They took up cover at the rear of their van, two men peeking around the sides of the open bulletproof doors and firing in controlled bursts at the houses the helicopters (there were two of them now) had highlighted with their searchlights.

The street was alive with echoing gunfire, and very little verbal communication passed between any officers, especially SWAT, who did almost everything with hand signals. Two of them came out the back with Remington 700 sniper rifles and dived for cover behind the other squad cars, and popped up to start setting up their shots.

Shots were rained down from the helicopters, the sharpshooters getting an angle on some of the gunmen in the top floor windows.

This whole thing's a clusterfuck! he thought, and knew that he was partially to blame. Instead of backing out of Avery Street and waiting for backup, he'd stayed and started firing back. He couldn't escape for the hail of gunfire, and this required more officers to put themselves in the line of fire to back him up. This put even more officers in jeopardy, but now their vehicles had formed a wall, and there would be no escaping the cul-de-sac—

One of the SWAT members went down. A bullet had clipped Warwick, who went spinning to the pavement. Within the span of a second, one of his teammates reached down without thought and grabbed the handlebar at the back of his armor, which allowed for easy dragging of a wounded man.

Then, automatic gunfire poured out of two more windows. David spent time enough at the gun range to know the sound of high-powered rifles. Leon and the other agents dropped back behind his car when the glass of the windows exploded all around and the rest of the squad car's tires were finally blown.

"*Officers down!*" he heard over his radio in between salvos from their enemies.

David watched as Hennessey quickly issued orders to his teams. The SWAT team started moving cover-to-cover up the yard of the house on the right. A pair would lay down suppressing fire while four others moved up, and then the two at the front would lay down more suppressing fire, allowing the guys at the rear to catch up. They took cover behind a van parked in the driveway and made their way to the side of the house. The two snipers fired from where they'd set their rifles up on tripods on the hoods of the squad cars. David, the other officers, and the sharpshooters in the choppers also gave SWAT suppressing fire while they moved to the back yard, where they would be in shadows and away from the windows with all the gunmen.

Then, all at once, bullets danced on the pavement on *this* side of David's car.

"Behind us!" Leon shouted.

He turned and saw two men running for cover behind a mailbox, firing not-so-wildly, in a crouch and their weapons held tight to their shoulders. One had a shotgun of some kind, the other something along the lines of an M16. Agents Stone and Mortimer were taking cover behind their SUV, which was the direction the newcomers had come from, and were already gunned down by the time David caught sight of them.

God damn jackalope!

Keitrich was down, and McDevitt had been seeing to him when the gunfire erupted from behind. Keitrich was still conscious, though, and fired his gun one-handed from where he lay half in his partner's lap, bleeding out and possibly dying.

Fucking Jack Ching Bada-Bing! David briefly thought of Beatrice, her marred hand, and how it meant she would work a desk job for the rest of her career, if she was lucky, and she had always despised desk jockeys.

His eye still hurt. And though he would later regret it, that was actually the straw that broke the camel's back.

David stood and ran around his patrol car. He heard Leon shout something at him, but it never fully made it to his ear for all the gunfire. A bullet zipped so close past his head that he felt the wind breaking. He ran for cover behind the same van SWAT had taken cover behind, then darted around and leapt across a short picket fence into the next yard. He took cover around the side of the house, amid shots that tore across the front lawn and drew a line towards him. *You're mine, Jack Ching. Nobody else gets to have you.*

David pressed his back against the wall and peeked around the corner. When he saw that gunfire had been drawn elsewhere, he dipped around to the front porch and crept along in a low crouch.

They were two of a kind, both constructed with the same wrongness at their foundation, yet everything they'd experienced since birth had helped to shape them into different kinds of monsters.

Kaley stood at the center of the basement, standing over Olga, watching as great grasping hands pulled her deeper into the flames, boiling her skin. She'd started to sizzle. She got up to run but was flung against the wall, and then slid along it as though Earth's gravitational pull had decided to go another way. Olga was finally flattened against the ceiling.

Kaley looked around, saw Bonetta lying on the ground, clawing at her own face, bringing blood. Maggots had started pouring from her skin and eye sockets. As much as Kaley wanted to dispel this, she couldn't. Discounting Shan, there were only two other people utterly untouched by what she'd unleashed, but whereas Shan had the charm to protect her, both Oni and the monster had acceptance. They had accepted what they were. *Cut from the same cloth*, Nan would've said. *They be cut from the same cloth, chil'*.

While Olga struggled against hands that stretched out from the ceiling—children's hands, trembling with fear, and rage— Kaley slowly turned back to the door where Shannon was being held. It was wreathed in flame. Inside, there was a dark void, a blind spot to Kaley's telempathy. Shan, the girl who earlier tonight had told Big Sister to watch out for the tiny beetle, had warded herself against the Ocean of Sorrow currently flooding the house.

A hideous creaking noise went throughout the basement. Then, there was a sharp snap. Kaley turned to find the walls breaking apart. One piece came away, and crumbled to the floor. And whereas there ought to have been sheetrock and insulation, there were instead rippling, pulsating slabs of pink, slimy meat that looked like tonsils the size of engine blocks, one piled on top of the other. The walls were filled with them. Green and blue veins climbed up through this meat, and blood coursed through them. The house breathed, and the flames were ventilated in and out through the slight gaps between each tonsil.

A red, viscous liquid poured from the ceiling, and then collected around her feet in great pools. Kaley knew that this was both real and unreal, both shadow and substance.

"What..." It was Olga, up on the ceiling. "What...are...you...doing...to...us?" Then, just as stupidly, "Why? Oh, God, *whyyyyyyyy*?!"

"If you don't know now," Kaley said, "you never will. For what it's worth, I'm sorry. I truly, *truly* am. I...I don't know how to stop it..." But neither one of those things was entirely true. Kaley wasn't *entirely* sorry, nor was she *entirely* ignorant of how to stop it. Part of her—the part shared and enlightened by contact with the monster's heart—relished the Rapture. And, she was ashamed to say, she couldn't stop herself, no more than Olga could stop her loins from going wet at the sight of a new child to torture and film, nor more than Mikhael and Dmitry could stop themselves once they felt their loins filling and going hard at the same thought. It was compulsive, it felt *right*, it felt *good*, and, in many ways, she would hate herself for the rest of her life, much the way the Oni family hated themselves when they went to sleep at night.

All except for Dmitry. He was no one special. He wasn't the patriarch of the family—she now sensed that that dubious honor belonged to the tattooed man upstairs. Dmitry was only unique in that, whereas the rest of the family had a semblance *of* family unity amongst their own, he had none. He was a loner, a divergent creature, one that had learned to operate within a certain set of parameters in order to survive, but was still a man apart.

Just like the monster, she thought. *He doesn't want to admit it, but they're the same, and there can be only one. Just like that movie* Highlander *that Ricky used to like so much. There can be only one.* It was insane to think, but there it was.

"I'm s-s-s-*sorryyyyyyyy*," Olga whimpered from above. The hands had now reached out and grabbed hold of her breasts, had pried them apart to get at her sternum, which they also pried part with slow care, and now reached inside to prod playfully at her innards. "Please...please..."

"I'm sorry, too," Kaley said. "You couldn't stop, and now I can't. I understand you now. I empathize. It just...it just feels *too good*, doesn't it?"

Fire bloomed from their hands as they grabbed hold of one another, their arms crisscrossing and their hands grabbing fistfuls of one another's clothing. The fire swirled beneath their feet, as did the tentacle, or the serpent, or whatever it was. It didn't seem to want to interfere in this, it only swirled and climbed and caught fire randomly. Behind them, the three tortured men had started to move. The briars had started to break free, and just as they were climbing to their feet, more briars shot out of their mouths, choking them and attaching to the ceilings and lifting them into the air by their own tongues.

Spencer saw only part of this. He and Dmitry pushed one another around and around the room of fire until Spencer wound up with his back against a dresser, and Dmitry hammered at his face with his fists. Spencer took them all smiling, the masochistic part of him savoring the pain, his mind diving headlong into the absurdity of everything around him. He caught Dmitry's arm on his fifth punch and then grabbed him about the neck in a clinch. "This is some fucked up shit, ain't it?" Spencer howled.

Dmitry didn't answer, he just jerked at Spencer's hoodie and flung him into another wall. He was stronger than Spencer, and heavier, too. He flung Spencer about not quite like a ragdoll, but close.

When they hit the other wall, the flames spread out, arched around them and formed a hemisphere. Tiny hands reached out from the walls, and they looked so loving, so accepting, so *wanting*.

There was a flash of light, like a bolt of lightning, and the floor beneath them became as lava. The walls behind them peeled back and there was a low tearing sound, like something trying to break through. As the walls crumbled, Spencer saw the throbbing tonsils, and felt them burst and felt the pus run out of them as Dmitry pushed him farther into the wall. The arms still stretched out impossibly, pulling him in, accepting him into their fold.

And he heard them. He heard the familiar voices. Whether real or imagined, they were all there. Dr. McCulloch shouted, "There you are! You sonuvabitch! *There* you are!" And then there was Kevin Baxter, the forty-two-year-old man dying of stage

III-A lung cancer, and who tried to kill Spencer rather than pay back the money he owed him. "You motherfucker! You took me away from my family!" Then there were the screams of Miriam Downey, the nurse he'd killed and dumped in the Tennessee River because she'd tried to blackmail him after selling him the necessary supplies from the hospital to create their startup meth lab. "I got'choo, Pelletier! I got'cho ass now, son!"

It fazed him, though not in the way one might think. He wasn't afraid of these people, if in fact they were even present in the room, but he was *angry* at them. He felt diminished by their taunting, and was outraged at their grabbing hands. After all they'd done to him, after everything *he'd* done to make sure they were wiped from the world, they were still around to belittle him, to disrespect him.

Dmitry slammed a knee into his gut, and shoved Spencer deeper into the wall. "Maybe I let them take you now, eh?" he shouted, smiling that smile that had drawn Spencer from first sight.

And then came a tiny voice. The most taunting voice.

"You snuck on me, Spence ol' boy!" Spencer knew that voice. It could be no one else. Only one kid had ever called him that.

"Hey, Miles!" Spencer laughed, his face pressed deeper and deeper into the pulsing tissue. "How's life?"

"You coming down here with me, Spence ol' boy? Huh? You coming to join me?"

"Probably!" he cackled, watching Dmitry's face go from humored to confused. "Just not today! Lemme introduce ya to a new friend o' mine! Dmitry, Miles! Miles, Dmitry!" The hands groped for both of them now, and Dmitry saw this. He recoiled, and Spencer rejoiced at the sight of fear on the Russian's face. As Dmitry pulled away from the hands, he let go of Spencer and backed up to the center of the room.

Spencer ripped the hands of the damned off of him and pulled himself away from the wall, which had welcomed him like quicksand. Fire still lived on the floor, and was breathed in and out by parts of the walls that had developed flaps of skin like fish mouths and gills.

The flames licked up Dmitry's right leg, and he leapt away, momentarily burned.

"You're startin' to believe it, Dmitry," Spencer said, standing up. "Don't let it get to you. Not before I'm finished with ya. C'mon now, let's imbue this moment."

Dmitry stood there, looking at his right leg in a detached state, like a man standing alone in a dream, wondering if he was going to wake up.

Then, the ceiling swelled like a pimple, and burst just as explosively. Ceiling fans and planks of wood fell on top of them, as well as objects that had been held in the attic—a multicolored tricycle, a few boxes of Christmas decorations, some boxes of old paintings and picture frames—and descending from the sky were meat hooks, at the end of which swung flayed men and women screaming. The barbed hooks clung to their sinew as they tried to wiggle free. The chains holding these people in the air went up for an impossible distance, into a great, enveloping darkness.

The shadows began to tear apart like fabric, great swaths of it separating and cascading into the room as they took shape. A murder of impossibly black crows swarmed about the dangling bodies, some alighting here and others alighting there, pecking and tasting the buffet of dangling flesh. The people on the hooks and chains writhed, but it did no good, the crows did their work unfettered. One batted its wings at Spencer, and dashed to the buffet of hanging corpses all around them.

"*PELLETIERRRRRRR!*" someone roared.

He turned, and spied one particular man dangling from the end of one of the longer hooks. It was Aaron Schmidt, the man of the Aryan Brotherhood who he'd killed and...mutilated postmortem. He swung from side-to-side, trying to get closer to Spencer, who backed up calmly, though not slowly. This was the first time Spencer considered that this might actually *be* hell, that the girl's ability to tap into others empathetically might've somehow enabled her to reach down to the pain and suffering being experienced in other dimensions, other levels of reality.

"*YOU FUCKING DID THIS TO ME! I'LL PUT YOU HERE, AND SEE HOW YOU LIKE IT!*"

Spencer sighed and nodded. "You ready?" he said to his opponent. Dmitry was standing perfectly still at the center of the room like a man who was afraid of tipping over the boat if he moved.   One of the swinging corpses moved near him, an outstretched hand begging for help.

Spencer stared at his opponent. "You ready?" he repeated.

Dmitry looked Spencer up and down, as if seeing him for the first time. "You," he breathed. "You did this. The girl, too?" He was a clever creature, if a punkass, him and his kind would have to be to keep this operation going for any amount of time. Dmitry was piecing it together, a man taking his first steps out of an acid trip. "I'll kill her," he decided. His thoughtful voice made him sound like a man deciding on what he'd have for dinner. Then, his face twisted into rage. "I'll kill her! I'll kill her!" He ran towards the flaming dresser and pushed it over. "I'll kill her!" He kicked over a small table, picked up a flaming chair and tossed it at a glass window, shattering it. "I'll kill her!" he screamed, continuing his fit as he lifted a lamp and stabbed it into the throbbing wall. A murder of crows fluttered away from one of the holes and disappeared into the darkness above. *"I'LL KILL HER!"*

Spencer smiled. "You can kick an' scream an' holler, but I betcha five dollars ya don't touch her again."

"Out of my way. I have to kill her. She's doing this to me. To us. *We* have to kill her."

"I don't think you understand. I'm a Portia, bitch. I came here to eat you."

Dmitry screamed and ran at him.   Just then, the floor buckled beneath their feet and an abyss as endless as the one above them revealed itself. Spencer leapt for one of the dangling bodies, and dug his fingers into the muscle and sinew. Dmitry did the same, only his momentum swung him towards the door, which was now an isolated floating hole of light in this dark corridor of nothingness and chains and screaming people.

Spencer hung there, clinging to the flayed, screaming body of Aaron Schmidt. His flesh that had once donned the mantle of the AB and various swastikas was now completely gone.   His fleshless arms batted at Spencer, pulling bits of muscle and tendons free as he climbed up to the barbed chain and started swinging them both back and forth. "FUCK YOU, PELLETIER! I'LL FUCKING FUCK YER GUTS OUT—"

"Oh, shut up, Aaron!" he shouted. "You did this to yourself!" Spencer swung to the next dangling body, which was the one that Dmitry had swung to freedom with. It was the body of Ramsay Friedkin, recognizable only by his missing right leg and half of a missing right arm, both lost to landmines in Vietnam.

The old fucker had entered into an agreement with Spencer just before he went into prison, and while he was away at Leavenworth Friedkin had taken all his money and ran. Only not far enough, as Spencer tracked him down outside of Baton Rouge once he got out. Spencer was a hunter by nature, though a hunter of a different sort, and this vast black arena was a monument to that work, an assortment of trophies that still talked.

"Spencer?" said Friedkin, taking on a different tone than the others. "Spencer...help me. I'm so sorry for what I done. Please, help me! This can't be real! This can't be! I wanna wake up! Find my mother! Please, *MOTHERRRRRRR!*"

"Shut up, Friedkin. Take it like a man."

Flames shot down the barbed chains from somewhere far, far above, and then bathed every single one of the bodies in its baptizing heat. All his victims screamed louder, if that could be believed, and as he swung to the doorway and hopped off and back to the relative safety of the hallway, Spencer was fascinated to hear the screams almost harmonize. It seemed that when the ultimate summit of torture was reached, all human beings hit the same note. Funny.

The hallway squished beneath his feet. When he stood up, his hands and knees were covered in a translucent green mucus. It smelled of someone's unwashed mouth. The three men from before were now being absorbed into the meaty walls while fire licked around them.

Spencer became convinced that they were, in fact, inside the throat of a beast, at least that's what Kaley's mind and his were constructing, or summoning, or both.

You have to kill him, said the Voice. It was calm, still, supremely certain.

"I'm workin' on it!"

He's coming to kill us.

"No shit!"

He knows we're doing this. Instinctively he knows. He's coming to stop me—

"No *fucking* shit!"

Dmitry had already run down the stairs, on his way to kill the girl, no doubt. Spencer bolted for the stairs and looked down, and for a moment he got vertigo. These were not the same steps he'd ascended moments ago. Now, there was scarcely a step every few feet, and the walls and the ceiling had become lined with ribs pressing out from the meaty walls. The fire still licked up and down these walls, traveling like wind through a grassy field while the creature continued to breathe.

Dmitry was at the bottom of the stairs, slipping and sliding down the mucus-covered floor before ultimately flopping on the floor at the bottom. Spencer took two steps down the creature's gullet, but once he slipped the first time he just went with it and flopped belly first on the floor and slid down to catch up to his prey. Dmitry was just getting to his feet as Spencer slammed against his legs, taking them out from under him. And there they grappled, the flames blooming out from wherever their arms met.

The two gunmen who'd come up behind them had been taken out, one by a SWAT sniper and the other by Agent Porter with a well-aimed and well-timed shot. Leon spotted Agent Porter trying to move cover-to-cover to get to his two downed agents.

Avery Street had become a war zone. The firefight had expanded, and it appeared that they were gaining more enemies, not less. The shots were pouring out from windows and back yards. Leon now realized something that he would revisit sometime later, if he survived. They were in the dominion of the *vory*, of the Rainbow Roomers. They had found the cave where these creatures had kept their secret, had held council, and had carved out a place for themselves while the city slept.

Another officer was hit, a bullet to the shoulder put him down. Leon turned and spotted a second SWAT vehicle on its way towards them. It was followed by three other squad cars with sirens blaring, but barely audible for the din of gunfire. Another chopper had joined the fight, sharpshooters raining down bullets on the house at the right, which was dishing out the most punishment. The two houses on the left had desperate men and even women running out of the house, firing wildly as they crossed the lawn and tried to get to their cars. One woman was gunned down by someone, and a half naked man was clipped in his leg as he dived for cover behind his Chevy.

All of the houses supported one another, all except for the last house on the right at the far end of the cul-de-sac. That one was strangely dark and silent. At least so far.

When the second SWAT van arrived the driver bravely drove it directly in front of the other police vehicles, creating a new barrier with its solid steel body. The driver hopped out and joined the rest of the team assembling at the back. Two snipers took up position at the front and the rear, firing around the sides. A third sniper crawled *underneath* the SWAT van and fired out the other side from cover.

This went on for about three minutes, and finally the exchange of gunfire started to diminish, at least from the enemy's side. Leon hopped up and ran around the side of the bullet-riddled squad car belonging to David Emerson. He almost stopped himself from going after David, and was sure that if he didn't stop himself someone else would. But no one tried. In fact, when he glanced behind him he only found Agent Porter hard on his tail.

No words were spoken. Leon and the agent leapt over the picket fence and ran around the dead body of one *vor*, then made it to the side of the first house. He glanced behind him and gave a nod to Agent Porter, who took the lead, doing a slicing of the pie maneuver to clear the corner.

There were fewer and fewer shots being exchanged, the most were still coming from up the street, in an exchange between Hennessey's team and the remaining enemy combatants.

"I'm gonna fuckin' eat you!" he cried. Spencer head-butted his enemy, then kneed him in the groin before tackling him, sending them both back to the ground. They rolled around in the creature's stomach, and as they did Spencer felt his skin burning, watched his hoodie begin to smoke whenever it made contact with the piss-colored ooze on the floor. It smelled horrible, like bile and shit and another odor Spencer couldn't quite pin down.

He knew it was the gastric acids of the creature, or at least it was what passed for gastric acids in this universe they now occupied. It was corrosive, but it was only so because he allowed it to be.

He laughed. "Did ya hear what I *said*?! I'll fuckin' eat you!"

Spencer rolled on top of his nemesis, clawing at his face and raining down hammer fists repeatedly until finally Dmitry brought his heels close to his butt and thrust his hips into the air, sending Spencer over his head and sliding across the toxic fluids. Dmitry got to his feet, and so did Spencer. The fires had mostly gone out, but a few still lingered, being breathed in and out of nostril-like flaps of meat along the walls. Strangely though, the furniture was still here. Dmitry's back was to the kitchen and he made for it. Spencer knew where he was going, because it had been what he'd been thinking, too.

They both leapt over the flayed kid who now had more imps fucking his flesh and dining on his tongue. First Dmitry hopped over him, then Spencer close behind. Dmitry made it to a rack of Ginsu knives and pulled out the longest, skinniest one and slashed out at Spencer. The blade cut across his brow and he started bleeding at once, and he liked it. Spencer grabbed Dmitry's wrist on the second swing and twisted it down, then slammed it into the kitchen countertop. *The only kitchen in hell*, he mused. *Hell's Kitchen!* He rammed his shoulder into Dmitry and drove him against the wall. Suddenly one of the cabinets burst open and more hands came out, reaching, beseeching, yearning, thirsting.

This worked in Spencer's favor. Dmitry had been snarling at him, a ravenous creature equally hungry as he, but as soon as he saw the outstretched hands his confidence faltered and he was more concerned with getting away from them. His grip on the Ginsu knife lightened for just a moment, enough so that Spencer could wrench it free.

But then Dmitry fought back, head-butted Spencer and kneed him in the sternum. He grabbed hold of Spencer's right hand, now holding the Ginsu, and forced it back at his face. The knife stabbed deeply into his face, entering through Spencer's cheek and going between his teeth. He bit down on it. Dmitry jerked at his hand, ripping the knife back out, opening Spencer's mouth in a ghastly Glasgow smile. Blood poured out from his split mouth, down his neck. Inside his mouth, the blood quickly pooled and went down his throat. Spencer choked for a moment before he had a very simple, and effective, idea.

Spencer gathered the blood in his mouth in one great assault, and spat a jet of it into Dmitry's face, blinding him and causing him to reel back. Here, the hands reached out and grabbed hold of his bare skin, tugging and pulling and even ripping. Dmitry's grip waned for just a moment, and Spencer yanked his hand free and started doing what was termed "sewing machine" in the penitentiary. He stabbed repeatedly at the stomach, one thrust right after another. Some of them got through, but others were deflected by Dmitry's flailing arms. The Russian finally tore free from the wall, losing some of his flesh to the groping hands as he fell to the floor and rolled away from Spencer.

The acids, though, they ate at Dmitry's back and he screamed and stood up at once, backpedaling as Spencer came at him until he slammed into the kitchen table. Spencer screamed as he leapt atop the Russian, pinning him to the table and stabbing downwards. The thrusts only went an inch or two deep, but one of them finally hit a key spot. Right in the eye socket.

Dmitry screamed. To Spencer, it was the most exquisite scream he'd ever heard. This was why he lived and breathed. This was *his* Rapture.

And it only got better. Dmitry's hands went to his ruined face as he spun away from Spencer and fell to the floor. He backed away to the wall. But he'd forgotten about the hands, ever lustful, ever wanting, ever needing. The hands reached out and snagged him, and this time they did it with such sharpness that even Spencer leapt back. They meant business this time.

Dmitry reached out and clawed at the burning ground. The hands peeled and pulled him closer, closer, inexorably closer to the wall. "*Net! Net!* Help me! Help meeeeeeeeeee!*"

Spencer knelt to one knee, and waved bye-bye with the hand holding the Ginsu. "Look at me!" he said with an intensity he had never felt, and feared he'd never feel again. "I did this to you! Got that? *I* did! Don't you *ever* look at me cross-eyed again, motherfucker!"

"*Hellllllllllllllllppppp!*"

"How do you say *fuck you* in Russian?" he laughed.

"*HELP ME!*" Dmitry's legs were now sucked into that churning meat. From inside, there came crunching sounds, like bone snapping and then being ground. "*PLEASE! I HAVE DAUGHTERS! I HAVE FAMILY!*"

"What're their names?" he asked calmly. "Where do they live?"

"*HELP!*" His hips were now consumed. His ruined eye leaked blood and a yellow ooze as one of the hands had slipped its finger inside. Dmitry's other eye was wide, and looked out at him with genuine need.

"Where—do—they—live?"

"*DERBENT! THEY LIVE IN DERBENT!*" he shrieked desperately.

Spencer winked at him. "Good to know."

"*PLEASE! HEL—*" A hand now reached out to his mouth and pressed against his lips. His head was jerked back and licking serpents squeezed his throat. His arms were reaching for Spencer, quivering and beseeching as the gastric acids burned them. Spencer tilted his head to one side, spit out the pool of blood that had been spilling out from his mouth. The blood landed on Dmitry's head, just before he was finally and utterly swallowed. The last Spencer saw of Dmitry, his hand was still reaching, still hoping that Spencer would have a change of heart and grab him and pull him back. The Russian died in vain hope, the same as most other people, Spencer figured.

It's done, the Voice said to him.

"Yep," he said. It felt anticlimactic. Just like the tiredness a man feels after orgasm, Spencer felt quite like a nap.

I need you.

"But I don't need you," he said. "Not anymore."

You do if you ever want to get outta this hell. It'll eventually consume you, too.

"My own little corner o' hell? Sounds like fun. You know what they say? Better to reign in hell than serve in heaven." But those were just words, and he knew it. Spencer no more wanted to stay here than he wanted a lobotomy. Still, it was a fascinating place. He sat there a moment, feeling the blood trickle down his neck and throat, swallowing some of it and listening to the screams of others he'd killed coming up and down the halls. A small part of him figured that he might as well stay here in this land of both shadow and substance. God knows there wasn't any other place for him in the realm of Earth.

But you want to stay alive to see the next part, don't you? the Voice coaxed.

And she was right. There was no denying it. Spencer Adam Pelletier wasn't necessarily fearless, he just experienced emotions differently than most other humans, and that experience had him caring very little about anything besides experiencing more. He wanted to see and do more things, he wanted to challenge and be challenged. It was what got him out of bed in the morning, whether he was in a prison cell or in a luxury suite or in a ditch.

"I'll be right down, sweetheart," he said. "Just don't be afraid when you see me. I ain't too pretty anymore."

He felt a hint of her powerful empathy. *How bad is it?*

"Oh, don't worry about me. I'm a monster. Monsters don't feel anything, remember?" He made for the hallway, and then into the kitchen, searching for the door that would lead to the basement steps. He sang, "Come on, baby...don't fear the Reaper...baby take my hand...don't fear the Reaper...we'll be able to fly...don't fear the Reaper...baby I'm your mannnnnnnn..."

The rain suddenly came in great sheets, but the strange thing was that it did not come down, it came *sideways*. David paused at the front of the house. Gunfire had almost completely ceased on Avery Street, and he'd made it to the house at the far end. He had a moment of strange calm as he watched the rainfall phenomenon, and noted that there was no wind to make it act as such.

David was transfixed for only a moment, and then continued on his way. The front door was a few steps away. He peeked in through the nearest window, but couldn't see much for the black curtains. *Just like Tidov's house.* He thought he caught a glimpse of a flickering flame, but that was about it. With his back pressed against the wall, he thought he felt a deep thrumming, one at regular intervals like a heartbeat. Then, the ground below him quaked. It was definitely a minor earthquake, no denying that. What a strange time for that to occur, but not so freakish because Georgia did have its own fault line that occasionally brought on tremors and quakes.

Now the sideways rain *arched*. It arched inwards, towards the front door and some of the windows. Something was breathing it in. In fact, David felt the oxygen all around him become somehow…unavailable. Like the air was being sucked out of a room. It became hard to breathe.

But he was so close. He was almost at the front door.

Another spat of gunfire erupted at the house on the other side of the cul-de-sac. David hunkered down and made for the door. Something was drawing him there. Cop instincts? Perhaps. Or maybe it was just that this was the only house that had no lights on.

Whatever the case, he made it to the door and touched the knob. It was scalding hot. His hand jerked away from it, and then he willed himself try again.

David opened the door partway but then it flew inwards and he heard something that sounded like someone taking a luxurious intake of breath, like someone coming up for air after nearly drowning. And he was sucked in with it.

Kaley waited at the foot of the stairs, terrified and yet hopeful. When the door at the top of the stairs opened, she wanted to run to the man up there. If she hadn't had her charm, and if she hadn't seen what this creature was, she would have. She wouldn't have hesitated to run to anyone come to rescue her and her sister.

He ambled slowly down the stairs, a creature as disgustingly confident as Dmitry had been, although this one…was somehow different. Cut from the same cloth, perhaps, yes, just as Nan had said, but those pieces of cloth had been woven in with other, different fabrics.

The monster was covered in blood leaking down the right side of his face. He stopped at the bottom of the steps, looking about curiously, and Kaley saw his bloody half grin, saw his teeth through the gaping hole in his cheek, and winced. He shifted his weight to one foot and crossed his arms. "Well, well, well, if it isn't the Tiny Terror."

Whimpering. Kaley and the monster both looked over at Bonetta, lying down in a fetal position in the corner. She'd fought admirably, but she'd also seen something that she could never unsee, and it was still up on the ceiling. Olga dangled by her entrails, flayed and splayed open, yet somehow still alive. Her eyes looked around, begging the world for both sanity and a release from her pain. To her continuing surprise, the monster had words for Olga. He walked out to the middle of the basement, stood directly under her where her blood could drip on his face, and said, "You're gonna know a lot of pain now. Savvy? A whole, whole, whole, whole, whole, whole, whole, whole, whole, whole *lotta* pain. It's gonna be with ya so much from now on, it'll define you. You won't know who ya are without it." He smiled. "Sucks to be you, sister!" Then, as if remembering the Tiny Terror, he turned and faced Kaley. "Where's yer sister? We need to blow this popsicle stand, an' *fast*."

All at once, Bonetta stood to her feet, and ran screaming up the steps. The monster just watched her go, a slightly bemused look on his face.

Kaley swallowed. She felt like she'd been standing there for a century, her knees stiff and her spine made of stone. She turned back to the door behind her and pointed. "I...I can't open it."

"Do ya still have the hairpins ya used before?"

"The...?" She did. They were on the floor, in an area that hadn't been transformed into the veiny throat of a monster.

The monster knelt and picked them up, and made short work out of picking the lock. He opened the door, and stood to one side. All at once, Kaley broke from her trance and dashed in through the doorway, and went to her sister. "She needs a doctor."

"No shit."

"Help me with her!"

"Listen, if the police aren't here yet, they gotta be close. You can wait here for—"

318

"You and I both know that this...*thing*, whatever it is all around us, it's not just *our* making. It'll swallow us all if we stay here. Now, move your *fucking ass*!" Kaley's voice dropped an octave or two, or else she'd been speaking with someone else's voice. *His* voice, perhaps?

Whatever the case, it got his attention. He smiled and nodded. "All right, Carrie White. Let's do it. Teamwork, right? Heh! Go, go, Team Psycho!" He moved into the room and grabbed up the girl, who was unconscious. She had her pants on, but there was blood all around the crotch and legs. Shan stirred, and Kaley held one of her hands while the monster carried her from the room. The Connection was made, the Anchor, and this time they *both* recoiled from one another. It would mark the first of many intimacy changes for them throughout their lives.

Then Shannon's eyes rolled over to look at the monster carrying her.

"Don't worry, Sleeping Beauty," he said. "Your prince has come." And Kaley thought she saw something on his face, and, more importantly, in his heart. Warmth. Hope. Care. It was there for the briefest of moments, and then gone as quickly as rain from a desert floor.

They made for the stairs. Kaley took one last glance behind her, saw Olga there, her eyes turned hopefully towards them. Kaley turned away, leaving the woman to whatever hell they had all created together.

They made it into the hall, and here Kaley saw the many-chambered throats of the beast that she, Shannon, the Russians and the Monster had all helped open. "Step carefully," said the Monster. "An' don't go near the walls. They have hands."

Burning saliva dripped down from the ceiling, and Kaley jumped back from it. There was a deep, deep thrumming coming from the walls. Kaley realized it was the creature's heartbeat, and she imagined this was what it sounded like in the mouth of a blue whale. Only, there was light here, and it came from plumes of flame that jetted out of random flaps of flesh like exhaust ports.

Somewhere, somebody screamed. Lots of somebodies.

They made it through the kitchen where the three men had been playing their game of cards earlier. Down the hallway and towards the back of the house, now at the back door. All at once, something fell from the ceiling. It was a large, pus-filled orb that suddenly shot out like a ruptured hemorrhoid and started bleeding. It split, and blood fell from its wet sack. Inside the deflated sack, there was a body, twisted and turning and writhing in pain. It gagged on a dozen barbed chains forcing their way into its mouth as four little slithering fat imps moved up and down the body, checking and rechecking the chains, as if ensuring their stability. *Like maintenance men*, she thought dumbly, following the Monster, who barely took a glance at the grotesquery.

They made it to the door, and the Monster's hand was on the doorknob when they heard someone say, "*Shhtop.*"

Kaley turned quickly, saw the man first, and screamed. The monster, he turned slowly, still holding Shannon in his arms. "Let's see," the Monster said. "I handed Dmitry over to the demons hands, and Olga's downstairs gettin' buttfucked by briars on the ceiling, so that must mean that you're...Mikhael?"

Mikhael, the last survivor of the Oni family, stood with flesh still sloughing off his body, but he was still capable of standing, and with a sawed-off shotgun in his hands. Parts of his clothes were still on him, though they had charred and melted and merged with his peeling skin, which dangled from his glistening meat and bones like strips of beef on a coat hanger. "Eeeshh theshh you?" he asked. His lips had almost completely melted away, and Kaley thought he meant to ask *Is this you?* He wanted to know if all of this around them was her doing.

"No," said her pet Monster. "This isn't her. This is you an' me, Mikhael. All o' this you see around you, it's just what happens to a mind like hers when people like you an' me come into her life. We fuck up everything we touch." Then, Kaley caught a glimpse of the monster's eyes. They flitted to the side, as if he'd caught sight of something, and for a moment she saw that he was humored again, though he hid it well. "You can be at peace with that, like I am, an' as far as I can figure you'll be left mostly untouched. Or you can fight it, an' well..." He smiled, as if to say *You know the rest.* And Mikhael did know the rest. He was living the rest.

"Churn it offff," he said.

"She can't," said the Monster. "She can't turn it off anymore than you can turn off all o' *yer* fucked up thoughts. This is *us*, man. This is who we are. Welcome to the human race." Once more, the Monster's eyes flitted, and he tilted his head to one side. "I'm sure ya think killin' me an' these girls would end this."

Mikhael raised his shotgun, pointing it at the Monster, and Shannon in his arms.

"No!" Kaley screamed.

"Don't worry, little girl," said her pet Monster, grinning so broad that his garish new smile split even more and poured new blood down his face. "It ain't my day to die, an' neither is it yers or yer sister's."

No sooner had he winked at Mikhael than Mikhael's head exploded. He pitched forward and fell into the oozing earth. Tenebrous hands reached up from the floor and pulled him. Mikhael came apart in pieces, and the hands fought over those bits until he was consumed.

Kaley now stood in front of the Monster. Without knowing it, she had flung herself in front of Little Sister. After watching Mikhael's grisly end, she looked up, and found the police officer standing at the other end of the room. His uniform was a bit charred and smoking. He'd come down the hallway, she supposed, and now stood staring in wide-eyed terror at everything that was happening around him. His pistol was still locked in his hands, and he was still aiming at the spot where Mikhael had been standing.

Then, all at once, hands shot out from the wall and grabbed hold of the officer, who screamed and fought to tear himself away.

The monster had turned towards the door and opened it. Outside, a torrential downpour was drowning the world, and he was dashing out into it. "Wait!" Kaley shouted. "We have to help him! He saved us!"

"When're you gonna stop worryin' about everybody else an' save yer own fuckin' skin?" the Monster called over his shoulder as he ran into the night with Shannon clutched tight to his chest.

Kaley turned to see the officer being pulled into the wall. She was torn in many different directions. Hands licked up from the floor around her, touching and groping at her ankles. She made a decision, and turned and bolted from the house, into the purifying rain. Behind her, she heard the bloodcurdling screams of the officer, but they were lost in the rain and gunfire and helicopters swarming all around Avery Street.

The world didn't make sense. David had been sucked into a universe that made no sense, that defied all reason and logic. The flames billowing out from the meaty, breathing walls licked at him, and his pants leg caught fire almost instantly. He did the classic stop-drop-and-roll, and during this time his right sleeve also caught fire from another plume of flame. He hacked and coughed against the smell and smoke.

When he finally stood up, he'd staggered back towards the door. But he couldn't find it now. Where the door had been there was now a wall of trembling muscle, or fat, or…something. An impression in the rough shape of a door was the only sign that there had ever been a way in.

Screams.

David had turned to find a young man, probably under twenty years old, writhing on the floor and being dragged by chains looped through his flesh. Four or five…creatures had hold of those chains. David aimed his pistol and shouted, "S-stop!" It sounded so feeble and so stupid, probably because it was, and was altogether absurd in this world.

Flames covered the young man, and he disappeared around the corner of a hallway, his hands reaching out as soon as he spotted David.

Smoke filled much of the air. He gagged. Through the smoke, shadowy figures shambled this way and that, some of them lined in the orange of flames, others not so clear. More screams. Something nipped at his ear, and then at his mind.

I died, he thought. *I died and went to hell.*

The feeling came and went within a second, and then Officer David Emerson's logical mind came back to him, and he rationalized it all. The meat on the walls…it was just that, *meat*. It didn't make any sense why someone would wish to line the inside of their house with meat, but fuck it, he had to save his sanity and move on somehow. As for the flames…bad air conditioning. An electrical fire somewhere in the walls. Whatever. Just go with it.

And what about the little creatures pulling the young man? he thought. Yes, what about that young man?

He was halfway down the hallway when he spotted the aberration. The man with his skin sloughing off of him, all of his flesh slowly pooling around his ankles like the slow crawl of lava down a mountainside. He had a shotgun in his hands, and he was aiming it at…

The jackalope. *Pelletier!* And there was a girl in his arms, and another one standing in front of him. The aberration losing its flesh raised its shotgun. Without thinking, he'd adopted a Weaver stance just like he was trained at the academy, and raised his Glock. He took a breath, let it out slowly as he squeezed the trigger, and all at once the aberration's head popped and the body pitched forward. He stood there for a moment, just staring at the Spencer Pelletier and the two girls. For a second, David was caught between commanding Pelletier to freeze and asking the girls if they were okay. And that's when the hands seized him.

"David!" one of them hissed at him. He thought he knew that voice. *Dad?* The thought was too brief to sit with, as the hands yanked at his head, snapping it back against the meaty wall. "David! C'mere to me, boy!" He struggled in vain. He knew it was in vain because his father was there. There was no other way around it.

The hands burned and dug into him. He felt something crawl up his spine, and then burrowed *into* his spine. He fought against screaming, he wanted to accept his death like a man. Just like his father had always told him to. "Be a man, David! Be a *man!*"

Then, something changed inside of him. David suddenly fought against the hands, tearing and scrambling. He then recalled that he still had his Glock in his hand. He fired backwards into the wall. On the floor in front of him, he spotted the young man crawling. The little creatures were pulling him around and around the house, it seemed, taking him on a parade that never ended.

David had no time to really think on this. He twisted around and faced the hands pulling at him. He fired three more shots, and to his surprise one of the hands actually released him. But two more popped out in its place, snatching at his clothing, ripping it free and digging into his flesh. He fired five more shots, then one of the hands seized his gun and wrenched it free. Then the wall opened up. A gaping maw awaited him. Inside he saw the faces that he imagined were shown to all of the damned before they were absorbed, the faces of the ones you'd judged, the faces of the ones you'd turned your back on when you could've helped.

Now, those pitiless faces stood judgment on him as he was swallowed into the great, enveloping maw. He now accepted that this was hell, or at least as close as was ever constructed.

"But…I saved her! I didn't do anything wrong! I did what was *right*!"

Hell didn't care. It had him in its clutches and it intended to enjoy every savory morsel. After all, how often did they get to dine on the genuinely good? After eons of eating only the wicked, he must've been a tender treat.

David screamed.

"Pelletier!" Leon screamed. "Freeze!"

The rain was coming down so hard it was difficult to see much, but the brief sweep of a chopper's searchlight showed him the pale skin and the black hoodie. It was him all right. And he carried a black bundle, while another, shorter shadow followed him into the small patch of trees butting up against the property.

Leon took aim, but dared not shoot for fear of hitting the two girls.

"You saw him?" Porter asked, coming up behind him.

"Yeah. There. He went into those trees." He pointed, and the agent just nodded and waved for Leon to take the lead.

Behind them, all gunfire had ceased. The two SWAT teams had secured Avery Street, and ambulances and fire trucks were now permitted to come down to start collecting the wounded and dead. Their sirens were visible even through the rain, and the fire truck's horn was extremely loud.

A scream. This one from the back door where Leon had first spied Pelletier vacating. Leon wouldn't go in there alone, not before the SWAT team had fully swept and secured it.

He and Porter dashed across the back yard, their feet splashing through puddles now gathering in the dips in the earth...and, strangely, forming small rivers. Leon was only partially aware of this as he moved away from the neighborhood and gave chase, but the rain was coming *towards* him, not from above. It poured towards the house, and what water was on the ground did the same.

A gunshot rang out, and Porter screamed behind him, landing on the sodden earth and sliding. Leon dropped to one knee and fired in the direction the shot had come from. The shooter taking cover behind a black sedan. Holding the gun in one hand and canting it slightly sideways in order to absorb the recoil, Leon dashed over to Agent Porter and offered him a hand. The agent took it and pulled himself up, holding his side. Leon fired two more shots at the sedan just to keep the gunman's head down.

They moved back around the corner of the house, from whence they came. Agent Porter dropped to the ground, moaning "Fuck!" again and again while clutching his side. Blood pooled in his hands.

Leon peeked around the corner, just in time for the enemy to pop his head up and fire a shot over the top of the sedan. The bullet smacked the side of the house, and when it did, Leon was almost certain he heard a grumbling. And his imagination must have been in overdrive for all the adrenaline, because he could've swore he felt the house shutter.

He fired two more shots at the sedan, and then turned back to Agent Porter. "How bad?"

"Bad," he said at once, pulling his hand away to look at the blood. "Stomach."

"Shit!" Leon shouted. He couldn't just leave the man there to die. If the stomach had been penetrated, then it was only adrenaline that was keeping Porter from writhing in agony. Very soon, though, his gut would be burning with a fire few human beings ever had the misfortune to feel. He peeked around the corner once more. The neighborhood had now gone eerily quiet. He imagined his enemy behind the sedan had made a run for it into the trees.

Leon was torn as to what to do. On the one hand the two girls were in the hands of a monster, and Agent Porter, a brother in the law enforcement field, was on his ass, dying and—

"What're you waiting for?" Porter growled. "Go fucking get those fuckers!"

He looked at the agent, who nodded his understanding. Perhaps he'd seen the struggle written on Leon's face, or perhaps he was just that committed to getting Pelletier. Whatever the case, he did not blink, and obviously meant every word. "You got rounds left?"

"Yeah," Porter growled through clenched teeth. "Now...*go!*"

Leon wasted no more time. He took one more peek around the corner and came around with his gun aimed and ready.

At first it seemed like the trees would never end. Indeed, Spencer even sensed they were being followed by them. As they moved through the wood, the trees seemed to bend and creak and *lean* in their direction. The girl knew it too. The girl running at his side, that is. The girl in his arms was still mostly unconscious, though her eyes did open and shut intermittently. "It's raining, Kaley," she muttered once, and went back to sleep.

Then, a bullet whispered through the trees, and smacked against one of them. All at once, he dropped the girl from his arms and leapt for the cover of the nearest tree. The taller girl screamed, "Wait! You can't leave her!" Spencer paid her no mind. When the second bullet rang out he shot to the ground and started crawling. "Wait! Don't leave us!" Spencer crawled around to the side of a fallen tree, his fingers feeling through the sodden earth for any sort of weapon. A rock, a sharp stick, a discarded bottle, anything.

Another shot rang out. Then another. Then another. Spencer then realized what he was hearing. It wasn't just one gun firing, it was *two*. A gunfight had kicked off out here.

Kaley ran to her sister and tried to lift her. It was a bit difficult, they were both so weak, and Shannon was heavier than she looked. She managed to half carry, half drag her sister over to a collection of bushes. That's when the next gunshots rang out, and the rain intensified, if that was possible. This allowed her to move as loudly as she wanted, because no movement could be discerned in this din.

Thunder rolled overhead, but without lightning it was only a dark promise from an unseen beast.

More gunshots. At least that much was audible above the rain. There was a scream. And in an instant, Kaley felt the same, sinking, grotesque feeling that she'd felt at the house where Dmitry had killed his cohorts. It was the feeling of someone not dead, but dying. It swirled around her, a cold blanket that she did not want.

Kaley grabbed Shannon's hand to feel the Anchor one last time.

Leon slowed down as he came into the thick of the trees. It was surprising how dense the trees were considering this was the middle of Atlanta. An old, muddy sign he passed read **FUTURE SIGHT OF ADELL PARK**. He faintly recalled the plans for Adell Park, and how quickly they had been cancelled. Along with the rest of Avery Street, this area of the city had grown wild, and was destined to become exactly like Townsley Drive: forgotten, but never quite gone.

The first gunshot caught his attention. As the first of the thunder rolled he ran ahead. It was nearly pitch black, only some distant streetlights and the occasional sweep of a chopper's searchlight granted him any visibility.

The rain became thick. It continued coming in towards him, directly into his face, into his eyes and mouth, and even the drops that hit him seemed to crawl around his body, as if looking for a way around, and dripped *horizontally* away into the darkness behind him.

The searchlights caused the shadow of every tree to grow and elongate and move. For a moment, he caught snatches of movement—perhaps wind in the rushes, perhaps an arm, perhaps nothing more than a trick of light. Leon kept his gun up and scanned slowly. The water was like needles in his eyes, necessitating far more blinking than usual. The shadows elongated again and again as the choppers moved overhead.

A loud pop, and then a brief incandescent muzzle flash. Something bit his right arm. Leon's massive body absorbed the shock and he turned, firing at the space in the darkness where he'd seen the flash. Three more shots came right at him, one of them hitting him in the left leg. He screamed and went to one knee, still firing at where he'd last seen the flashes. He fired until he was out, and then scrambled to the nearest tree.

The helicopters overhead swooped around, still searching, still finding nothing for the tree canopy. He heard something crash behind him, the crunching of twigs and branches. Leon knew he was about to die. The searchlight from above briefly illuminated the long silhouette from the other side of the tree. He braced himself, and turned to meet the man.

Leon collided with a man equal to him in size, but with considerably more fat. They smacked into one another and fell to one side, two ogres wallowing in mud. A searchlight flashed over the man's body. He was bald and pale white, and his swollen belly had a tattoo written in another language: **Мир ненавидит нас.**

Leon's enemy screamed something in Russian, and battered him with punches and elbows, one of which slammed into his face and shattered his nose. Blood filled Leon's nose and mouth and he tasted copper and silver. The fat man raised something in one meaty hand, a stone or something, and an instant before the blow came down a dark panther leapt out and tackled Leon's murderer to the forest floor.

"Remember me, fucker?" Spencer screamed. Of course he didn't. He didn't remember Spencer any more than he remembered the Spanish Inquisition, because the fat man hadn't been there. He hadn't been there to abduct the two girls, and he hadn't been the one looking out at him from the Expedition. But it didn't matter. For the moment, Spencer needed the fat fuck to be Dmitry again. He hadn't been sated. Probably never would be sated. Every sleight lived inside of him for the rest of his life. He still despised the very thought of Miles Hoover, Jr., and yet savored every morsel of that hatred.

The fat man felt the brunt of that savoring as Spencer mounted him and pinned his arms against his chest. *"Remember me?!"* he screamed, and then grabbed the fat man's ears and used them as handles to slam his head repeatedly against the forest floor. *"Remember me?!"* His voice was now like a woman's shriek. Tears fell from his eyes as he quivered and came. He eventually wrenched the rock clean of the fat man's hands and started bashing his skull.

Spencer drove the rock against his skull until he heard the first crunch. Invigorated by the sound, he went further, hammering again and again until the top of the skull started to split. He then wedged the end of the rock between the gap in the fat man's skull and pried it open, left and then right, then left again, until the brain was laid open in front of him.

He reached inside to get a handful of the brain. It had the consistency of fresh tofu, and when he squeezed it between his hands, he knew he was squeezing the very *thing* that had been his enemy. This was the man's hopes and fears in his hands. This was his knowledge of vocabulary, soccer, TV shows, space, electronics, food, animals, paint, China, sex, as well as all his theories of who he was, what he was meant to do, and why he was here. Spencer crushed all of that. The brain gushed out each end of his fist, and he stared at it. "I did this to you," he told it. If only he'd been able to get Dmitry like this. If only…

"Spencer!" It was the first time she'd ever used his name. He turned and looked at her. For a moment, the searchlights touched her and she was wreathed in that light that came from backlighting falling rain. And she was beautiful, the most radiant thing he'd ever seen despite her disheveled state. "It's over!" she cried. "I need your help now! Just one more time! *Please!"*

The rain no longer poured against him, but directly down as it should.

There was thunder. Spencer heard moaning. He glanced behind him, at the big black man in the trench coat, who was no doubt a police officer. He wiped his mouth. A bit of brains fell from his lips. Had he taken a bite out of it? When had that happened?

He looked around, his eyes finally resting on the girl, and he said, "Kaley, right?"

She looked a little leery of answering, but finally nodded.

"Nice to meet ya. Heh!" He stood, feeling sapped, tired. "There's gotta be a street up ahead," he said, walking over to her. Her little sister was still unconscious on the ground. He knelt to lift her. "There oughtta be a car around. I'm drivin'. Called it. Heh!"

The three of them hustled on into the night, disappearing from the woods, leaving it quiet and sullen. The searchlights swept the area ceaselessly. The rain covered their tracks, and soon it was as though they never were.

Leon stared up at the needles of rain falling on his face. The light of the choppers shone directly on him once, blinding him, then moved on.

His leg throbbed. So did his arm. So did his broken nose and his head.

Raised voices. Shouts. Calls for anyone. Leon tried to roll over. He tried to respond in some way. Nothing worked.

He closed his eyes because that felt best.

Lieutenant William Hennessey's men had found Agent Mortimer and had secured the area enough to bring in the medics. The house he was lying against was empty. Flash-bangs were tossed in just to be sure, but as they swept inside the house and cleared it, all they found was a smoking ruin that looked weeks burned and smelled of barbecued hair. The basement, where it appeared most of the Rainbow Room's filthy acts were conducted and recorded, was mostly left intact. There were a few scorch marks here and there, but nothing else. Nothing besides the fresh blood beside the horse saddle.

The utter lack of bodies was perhaps the most unsettling thing to Hennessey and his team. Something serious had happened here, something more than just accelerant tossed onto a stove fire.

And then there was the thing in the basement. "What...the...fuck?" Lawrence Klein breathed. The flashlight at the end of his assault rifle was aimed at a mound of still-sizzling meat left at the center of the basement, the beam from the flashlight catching wisps of smoke dancing off of it.

Screams suddenly filled the basement. A recording device had been left on, its blinking light showing that its battery was low. The lens cap was still on, but it appeared Heinrich had wanted to listen to what audio it might've recorded. They were screams, but not of any child. They were a woman's. They begged something in Russian.

14

CNN picked it up first, of course, because its headquarters was in Atlanta and it had a powerful presence in the streets of the city. At first, the story didn't appear that surprising. Another gunfight in or around the Bluff, no biggie. However, some were interested to hear that it was not only the work of the *vory v zakone*, but that it involved a child sex ring the likes of which no one had ever seen before. The gunfight on Avery Street was just the icing on the cake, a final showdown between the good guys and people who were obviously the scum of the earth.

Seven law enforcement officers shot, three killed, including two FBI agents, Nicholas Mortimer and Derek Stone. And one of them, Officer David Emerson, was strangely missing. All in all, twenty-two *vory*, including three women, were injured, while twelve of those died of their wounds.

Witnesses and officers willing to make statements had been rounded up for the early morning news. Once seven o'clock was upon the state, all Georgians would come to hear the details, but that was still an hour and a half away.

After the gunfight had ended, six officers were tasked with the duty of organizing the incoming fire trucks and ambulances. Fire marshals and inspectors were rushed to the house at the end of the cul-de-sac to determine whether or not the house was in danger of catching flame again. Strangely enough, the inspectors couldn't even determine whether a fire actually *had* occurred at all. While it certainly *looked* like a flashover, key clues would be found missing in the weeks ahead, most notably that the charred marks did not indicate that the fire had moved towards ventilation, which was a typical post-flashover pattern.

The lumps of melted flesh found sizzling in the basement would never be identified with any one person. Footage would be found that would show the heinous torture and rape of thirty-seven children. Their bodies would never be found, though scant DNA evidence would find hair, blood and skin samples in the two rooms in the basement.

Bonetta Harper was found two weeks later, soaking wet and filthy, living in a culvert several miles away from Avery Street. She would need serious psychological care. Once her story was known, several celebrities donated secretly to her care.

The surviving members of the Rainbow Room would be put to the question in a media frenzy that would haunt viewers and terrify parents for a full year. Six weeks before the first *vor* was convicted, he would cut a deal with the prosecution and name all other cells and collaborators that he knew of. There was a baker who lived in Downtown, a tech guy who lived in Savannah, and even a few partners in Tallahassee, Birmingham, Frankfort, Houston, and Montpelier, and that was only in the U.S. Interpol managed to take information from computers and routers in all six houses on Avery Street and follow links, keystrokes, and e-mails to supporters in other countries. Customers of the Avery Room included two teachers in Ukraine, a mailman in Germany, a police officer in Australia, three nobodies living on the Dingle Peninsula, one of the most remote places in the world, and even a minor politician in China.

But the biggest surprise to many in the U.S. was something that wouldn't come to light until a full year had passed. Vincent Pastone and Jerry Baker, a ten-year veteran of the Atlanta Police Department and a sergeant for Zone One respectively, were indicted on charges of conspiracy and collaboration with members of the *vory v zakone*, including the Ankundinov family: Boris, the father, and his children, Olga, Mikhael, and Dmitry. Though they would later claim they had no knowledge of what was really happening on Avery Street, they did confess to accepting money from dead drops to give heads up to any police activity involving their neighborhood, and Sergeant Baker was able to control frequency of patrols to that area, and rather easily since the place had long been forgotten.

Basements identical to those set up in the burned home were found in all but one of the other homes on Avery Street. Some had video equipment, others didn't. They found large, steel cages in most. Confessions from survivors said that duties for handling captives were rotated, children were moved from one house to another to keep one group in one house from having to listen to all the wailing or handled feeding and cleaning the children.

Facebook pictures of some of the Ankundinov family would be on the news for months, and their faces would go on the FBI's Most Wanted List for quite some time, since they had all disappeared without a trace and none of the Avery Street survivors claimed to know where they'd gone.

Two Rainbow Room members would hang themselves in their prison cell before the next year was out. Also, the Chinese politician would be poisoned, and one of the teachers in Ukraine found a razor to slit his wrists with.

The fallout would last for half a decade, one confession leading to another outlet of the Rainbow Room, which eventually would change its name to Angel's Haven, then to Everyone's Playpen, then to the Little Dollhouse, before it then fell, finally, into extinction.

Two years after the events on Avery Street, Patrick Mulley would get busted and his chop shop shut down, and it would come out that Detective Leon Hulsey was his brother-in-law and many suspicions would be raised over this. He wouldn't be fired, but enough questions would be asked about how much he knew and when that he would eventually feel compelled to resign.

This was all yet to come. For Kaley Dupré and her sister Shannon, the night still wasn't over.

Spencer drove them ten blocks away from the epicenter of all that activity. He found a bridge and pulled under it, remained there until a police helicopter passed over, then pulled on out. It was a green '96 Pontiac Grand Prix, with leather interior. "Ya know," he said, jumping back onto the road. "This year o' Grand Prix was the last for the fifth generation. A sport package with five-spoke alloy wheels an' dual exhaust. Somebody took care o' this thing, she still hums but doesn't rattle like the rest of 'em always did."

In the back seat, the eldest girl said nothing. She glanced up and looked at Spencer's eyes in the rearview mirror, then went back to rubbing her sister's hand and sniffling.

He drove them south, where they crossed over two sets of train tracks and bounced up and down in silence. Spencer took them through an area with plants shut down on each side, which eventually gave way to dilapidated homes that looked long unoccupied.

Blood pooled inside Spencer's mouth, and he spat it out the window. He'd found a rag in the glove compartment and had torn parts of a child's shirt that he'd found on the floorboard, and tied the makeshift bandage around his grievous wound.

He checked his bloodied hand. Bits of brain still clung to it. *Wonder which thoughts that part held?* he mused. *The capital o' Kentucky? The date o' the Emancipation Proclamation? Nah, probably somethin' Russian, like Boris Yeltsin's birthday.* He let the piece hang there. Dr. McCulloch had told him that psychopaths rarely cared all that much about how they looked, but some few had intense grooming rituals. He figured he was more the former than the latter. "You listen to music?" he said, switching on the radio.

"Are you gonna take us to a hospital?"

"Hospital?" he chortled. "That's a joke, right?"

"No, it's not. You're…you're hurt. Your mouth is all slashed up. And my sister's…she's bleeding from her private parts."

"You will too," he told her. "Someday. Someday some lucky guy'll do the same thing to—"

"She's hurt! She's bleeding! She could die!"

"Nobody ever died from gettin' fucked. Besides, I take you to a hospital, an' then there I am, a wanted man. Even if nobody recognizes me, how long before you an' yer sister there start talkin' about the white man who brought ya?"

"We won't—"

"—tell anybody, got it. Yeah, heard that one before," he chuckled, turning the radio dial. He had forgotten all the local stations, and so surfed through Stone Temple Pilots territory, Bonnie Tyler, Janis Joplin and Metallica before finally landing on Jefferson Airplane's "Somebody To Love." He turned it up, and was just about to start singing along when he felt a fist slam hard into the back of his head. "Ow! What the f—"

"*Stop this car, now!*" Kaley shrieked, slapping him several times more.

Spencer slammed on the brakes, screeching to a halt and sending Kaley between the seats. Her little sister almost fell to the floor. He reached down and grabbed her by the throat. "It'd be a mighty tragedy if you were to survive all ya did tonight an' then just die right here, wouldn't it? *Wouldn't* it!" Her mouth opened, but no words came out. She was choking to death. Spencer finally let her go, and then watched her gag and cough as she went back to seeing about her sister.

Once all was settled in the car, he put on the gas again. Behind him, a car honked at him to go faster. He held up his bird finger, and the car must've seen this via its headlights through the rear windshield because it flashed its lights. Spencer put the brakes on again and said, "Please get outta yer car. Oh, dear god, please let this motherfucker get out..." But the driver didn't. Instead, he waited, and Spencer drove purposely slow and held him up even longer to let him know who was boss.

They drove another mile, slowly and obeying all the traffic laws. Spencer checked the glove compartment thoroughly while driving. "God damn it, not a single fuckin' cigarette or stick o' gum or *nothin'*. What do they do while they drive?"

His stomach growled. He still hadn't eaten, and he was still losing blood. Not good.

"Please let us out," said a tiny voice from the back, only this time it was the little sister. Shannon was her name, if he recalled correctly from what he'd...experienced while sharing their unique Connection, which was now long gone and only like a faint echo between his ears.

Spencer glanced back at them in the rearview mirror. Kaley sat with Shannon's head in her lap. They both stared at him with expectant, frightened faces. "Izzat all you two are gonna do now? Say 'please' and 'thank you' and 'would you be so kind,' shit like that? Izzat how it's gonna be?"

"How else are we supposed to act?" asked the older girl, Kaley, a bit defiant. "What way would suit *you*?"

"Well, there's no way to 'suit' me, per se," he said. "But if there's one thing that pisses me off more than the Miles Hoovers of the world, it's the Roberto Castillos of the world."

"The who?"

"Not the bullies, but the bullied. Nobody wants to fight back anymore. Everyone's afraid o' hurtin' somebody else's feelings. Instead o' trustin' their instincts an' tellin' some creep to fuck off, people just duck their heads in the earth like ostriches, hope that it'll all be all right an' that the bad men will pass them by, find someone else to fuck with." He looked in the rearview mirror again. "That's what happened to you, I'll bet. Am I right?" Kaley said nothing. Spencer smiled. "Yeah, I'm right. But hey, ya fought back. Hell, ya just tried to smack the shit outta me. Guess that's somethin'."

"Take us to a hospital or let us go," Kaley said.

"Please," her sister added.

Spencer checked his driver's side mirror, flipped on his left blinker, and merged left. "If I took you anywhere an' left you there, you'd just tattle on me. Sooner or later, you'd tattle."

"I give you my word," Kaley said. "We *won't*."

"Only people in fairy tales keep their word, an' even they spill their beans to the reader," Spencer said. He glanced at them in the rearview. "Do you believe we're in a story right now? Do you believe somebody's puttin' these words in my mouth right now? Or in yers?"

Neither one of them seemed to know how to answer that. "No," Kaley finally said.

Spencer nodded, and swerved around a Mazda to merge right. He checked the skies for any sign of choppers, saw none. "Lotta times, rape victims blame themselves. You two gonna do that?" The big sister shook her head, the little sister made no reply. He nodded. " 'Course ya will. It's only a matter o' time. Lemme save ya years o' therapy. You are *not* what they say you are. Savvy?" This time, there was no reply from either sister. "See, they're gonna tell ya that there's something wrong with ya, that certain traumatic experiences are what changed ya, messed ya up, made it so that ya can't trust anybody. Then they're gonna lie to ya, tell ya that it's all just perspective, probably recommend a few trust exercises an' shit, an' without a doubt there'll be some expensive prescription drugs. An' it's all just to cover up one very simple fact." He tapped the side of his head. "You're fucked in the head."

The girls said nothing.

Spencer laughed, and merged left. "It's all right. Nothin' to be afraid of. I'm there with ya. Only, I had the fortune o' being born this way. I'm okay with it all. Never really had to struggle with it myself. You two?" He chuckled. "You only knew the world one way. Trust an' neighborly love were the daily order. But it was a curtain, an' now the curtain's been pulled back. You're about to see the world with new eyes. You're gonna see how falsely they move, how hard they struggle not to let others see through the façade." He added, "That means a false or superficial face."

Kaley said, "Does all this mean you're gonna let us go?"

Spencer pulled to a complete stop at a stop sign, waved another car to go on, and then turned right. "What all this means," he sighed, "is that you're in for a world o' hurt. So much hurt, you can't even *believe* it right now. You thought what you went through in that basement was tough? *Sheeeeeyyyyyyiiiiit*," he laughed. "Being imprisoned, tortured an' raped is easy. It's like gettin' married an' havin' kids, anybody can do it, it's no great accomplishment. It's what ya do after the kids leave. Can ya survive empty nest syndrome? Hm? Is there anything left after all the anguish o' rasing kids an' being raped? If not, if you're only reason for livin' was just to *be done with it*, then that's pretty fuckin' sad, don't you think?"

"I don't know," Kaley said. "I just wanna go home."

Spencer scoffed. "To where? To Jovita Dupré? Eh? That sounds like loads o' fun."

"You don't know anything about us!"

"I know everything about you," he said, losing all humor and looking into her eyes through the rearview. "I know all about you because I know all about me. Savvy? I sized you an' yer sister up at that store. I sized up Dmitry the minute I saw his sorry ass. I knew what he was. I knew what the Bluff was. I knew the police were after me this whole night."

"You didn't know *shit* about *shit* until I contacted—"

"I been two steps ahead this whole fuckin' night. I knew what was waitin' for me inside that house before I knew what was waitin' on me inside that house. Savvy? I won this fight before I woke up this mornin'." Spencer held her gaze for a few seconds more, then finally looked back at the road. He'd drifted onto the shoulder, and now corrected. Spencer listened to Jefferson Airplane wrap up their song, then chuckled. "You're right about one thing, though. Ya did help me out with Tidov. That's quite a gift ya got there. Ya didn't know ya even had it until tonight?"

Kaley didn't answer.

But Shannon did. "Neither of us knew. It just…happened."

"Hush, Shan."

"That's somethin' else," Spencer said. "One in a trillion. Some real awesome shit."

Shannon asked, "Was that…hell?"

"I said *hush*, Shannon," her big sister said. "Don't talk. Especially not to him."

"Listen to yer big sister. Ya really shouldn't talk to strange men. An' nobody's stranger than me. Ha!" He glanced in the rearview, saw that this got a smile from her, and part of him warmed, if only for a second. Spencer dismissed it. It was probably echoes of their Connection, that's all. "I tell ya what, though. I've seen a lotta shit in my time, but that one took the cake. I dunno if it was hell, but if it wasn't, then it was hell's red-headed stepchild."

Kaley swallowed. "It couldn't be hell," she said. "It…it came after that police officer that saved us. Probably killed him."

Spencer smiled. "Still sore about leavin' him behind, huh?" He snorted. "Well, just because it took a good guy down with it doesn't mean it wasn't hell."

"God wouldn't let that happen—"

"Yeah, probably right. Probably wouldn't let little girls get kidnapped an' raped, either. What the hell was I thinkin'?" Neither one of them said anything for a while. "Either one o' you ever heard o' Epicurus? He was a Greek philosopher. He said that if God is unable to prevent evil, then he's not all-powerful. If he's not *willing* to prevent evil, then he's not good. If he's both willing *and* able, then where does evil come from? And, if he's both

339

*un*willing and *un*able, then why call him God at all?" Spencer laughed. "Fucker's an absentee landlord. You'll see. You've got lifetime o' prayers that I'm sure you're gonna send his way. That Aunt Tabby o' yers, she'll tell ya one of two things: if yer prayers are answered, then it'll be 'God be praised.' If yer prayers aren't answered, it'll be, 'It's God's will, we can't question it, Thy will be done.' It'll beg the question, 'Then why do we pray in the first fuckin' place?' The truth will elude you till yer dyin' day, an' the hard reality is that we just saw hell, an' it doesn't care if you've been naughty or nice. If it gets its teeth in you, you're ass is grass. If God's an absentee landlord, then hell's his pitbull that he left pent up in the apartment with nothin' to eat. It's got no master anymore, an' boy is it *hungry*!" He cackled, and turned right.

"Maybe he's not absentee," said a small voice from the back. Shannon had lifted her head. "Maybe he sent you. Maybe *you're* the pitbull. You're...you're the Portia. The spider that eats other spiders."

Kaley looked at her sister.

Spencer smirked, and spat out another mouthful of blood. His stomach growled again. "I like people who wear their thinkin' caps. So then, you think I'm like Genghis Khan?"

"Who?"

"Genghis Khan. A warlord. He said, 'I am the punishment of God. If you had not created great sins, God would not have sent punishment like me upon you.' If Genghis Khan was right about himself, then he surely killed lots o' folks who didn't deserve it on his way to the folks that did. An' that police officer tonight...well, I guess that just goes to show that yer God believes that ya can't make an omelet without breakin' a few eggs. My kinda son of a bitch!" he laughed, and finally pulled onto the interstate.

I-75 was a major north-south interstate that would take him all the way to the Great Lakes of Michigan if stayed on it long enough. He checked the fuel gauge. He had plenty of gas to last him. But eventually he would need medical care, there was no way around that. And so would the wee girl if infection was to be prevented.

Spencer toyed with the idea of taking them to the hospital the way that a tongue will toy with the empty socket of a missing tooth; for no other reason than to toy with it. "Ya think Jovita's really gonna be missing you two?" he asked. He spotted a chopper with its searchlight, and pulled off the next exit and turned left onto a familiar road. "Ya think she's worried herself sick over you guys?" No answer from either one of the girls. "I'll take that as an 'I'm not sure.' Makes ya wonder, doesn't it? If Mommy don't care, then who will?"

"What do you mean?" said Kaley. Her tone suggested she was quite through with this game, and her eyes were smoldering.

But Spencer wasn't. "Well, you're both damaged goods now. That's for sure an' for certain. O' course, you both were damaged goods long before ya met Dmitry an' his family."

"Why?"

"Because you were born in the Bluff," he said. "Ass end o' Nowhere Important. You've lived there yer whole lives. You were just a pair o' niggers from the Bluff. Now, one o' you's a *raped* nigger. But they'll always say that. People that ya meet at school or at future places of employment. If they ever find out about yer past, where you're from, the fact that you were kidnapped an' raped," he laughed mirthlessly, "they'll cast judgment. Part of 'em will always think ya had it comin', that you're genetically predisposed to be victims. They'll pigeonhole ya, see ya as weak, not worth granting promotions or respect to."

"You don't know anything," Kaley said.

"I know the world's filled with people, an' that ya can't trust one single one of 'em. I thought you would've learned that by now, too." He glanced at her in the rearview, saw the enmity in her unblinking eyes, and smiled inwardly. *That's it. That's what I like to see.* "Nobody's gonna care about your sob story," he went on, turning right to get farther away from the police chopper. "You're both alone now. Even with that gift o' yers, it's nothin' but lonely nights from now on. Ya can't trust any man, we can know that almost to a certainty. Even the ones that help you, you'll fear them, too. Just like ya fear me."

"We're not afraid of you," Kaley said.

"I am," her sister put in.

"The little sister is smarter than the big sister," Spencer mused.

Kaley gripped Shannon's hand tight. She looked out her window, saw the liquor stores of Houston Street. This was familiar territory. It wasn't all too far from Beltway Street, their home. She held out a secret hope that they would survive this night, after all.

Back in that patch of woods, Kaley had panicked. She was too weak to carry Shan herself, and she didn't want to go back to the house where it seemed hell had taken up residence. She just wanted to get away, far away with her sister, and Spencer had been her only means for that. But it had been a snap decision, and she realized now it might've been smarter to wait for the police.

She looked at the driver's seat, at the back of the monster's head. "My sister needs a hospital."

"So you've said," Spencer remarked.

"Kaley?" Shannon squeezed her hand. "Kaley, is he gonna kill us?"

"No, Shan."

"An' how do *you* know that?" the monster posed.

She looked at his eyes reflected in the rearview mirror. "Because, even though you're a fucked up piece of shit—"

"K*aley*," warned Shannon.

"—you don't have a thing for kids. You have a thing for…something else."

His eyes smiled. Kaley could still feel a slight Connection, a ghost of what was there before, and she felt the glaciers moving again. Cold happiness spilled over her, as well as moist intrigue. There was sour greed, and bitter humiliation. There were slippery slopes of morals, and burning rope bridges that crossed a chasm of logic. These things only made sense with the charm, and Kaley knew that she would forever have a vocabulary about emotions that no others would comprehend. No one, that is, outside of Shannon, once she became old enough to articulate. And even then, words wouldn't do justice.

"You're right," Spencer said. "Ya nailed it. But what about you? What're you into?"

"I'm not into anything," Kaley said, feeling Shannon squeeze harder.

"Damn right you're not. Not anymore. It all stops. Right now, it all stops. Every dream ya ever had about bein' a mother or a writer or a teacher or an astronaut, that's all gone. Ya don't even know it yet, but you've already given up. Jovita, Ricky, an' the rest o' the world doesn't know it yet, either, but *they've* given up on ya too."

"You like to hear yourself talk," she said. It wasn't a question.

And he didn't deny it. "I do. Talkin' helps me think." He tapped his temple with two fingers, then snapped his fingers. "Keeps me sharp. But let's get back to you guys an' what you're gonna do after all o' this is over."

"No," Kaley said, raising her voice. "No! I'm sick of this! I'm sick of your...your...your *gloating*! My sister needs to get to a hospital, and...and...we've fucking endured *enough* for one night! We know you don't care about anybody but yourself, and that you're so fucking smart and that you did all this and still didn't get caught! You must be so fucking proud! We're happy for you! Now," she screamed, tears letting loose, "*LET US OUT!*"

The car fell silent. Shannon squeezed Big Sister's hand harder, if that was possible.

In the driver's seat, the Monster was unmoved. Spencer checked his driver's side mirror, switched on his blinker, and merged left. He drove them another block, checking the blood leaking out the side of his face. He spat out the window. Then, finally, he said, "We're all in this together, ya know?" He sounded different now. Kaley couldn't quite say how, but he was a little less...cocky? "Monsters, saints, innocents, psychopaths and telempaths. This is the dance we do. The dance macabre."

Kaley felt a lurching inside her gut. She felt nauseous, exactly like she had in the basement, exactly as she had when she used to get vertigo. Then, she realized it was only because they were slowing down.

Kaley looked out the windows all around her. The car had stopped in the middle of an empty street. There were no cars parked on the sidewalks, no people walking, no stores opened. The street was somewhat familiar. She believed it was Vernon Street, but she couldn't be sure. "What're we doing here?" she said.

"What does it look like?" he asked. "And remember our bet. If it turns out a police officer was involved with the Rainbow Room, then I'll be back in a few years to collect my money."

"What if I don't have that much money?" she asked, stalling and she didn't know why.

"I'm sure you'll find a way to raise it."

"What if you end up in jail? They'll catch you sooner or later, you know."

Spencer shrugged, as if to say *maybe*. "It'll be kinda hard. I won't be in this country much longer. I've got a date with the rest o' Dmitry's family."

The hairs stood up on the back of Kaley's neck. "What do you mean?"

He smiled. "Genghis Khan said somethin' else. 'The greatest happiness is to scatter yer enemy, to drive him before you, to see those who loved him shrouded in tears, an' to gather into your bosom his wives and daughters.' Dmitry said he had daughters."

"You're...you're going after *them*?"

Again, he shrugged a maybe.

She looked out the windows again. "And you're just going to let us go now?"

Spencer said nothing.

Kaley had felt hope rise and fall tonight, had been denied it, and now believed that if she moved, the monster might turn and kill her and her sister. *It could be a trick*, she thought. *He can't trust us not to talk.* The fire that she had felt just seconds before left her. She felt depleted again.

And the Monster knew why. "It's called learned helplessness," he said. "A puppy gets held inside its cage for a year. It sees other puppies running freely, playin' an' havin' fun. Then one day you open that cage an' let the puppy out, but when it takes a couple o' steps you give it a shock with a stun gun or a shock collar. Next time ya open that cage, that puppy won't come out. For the rest of its life, it'll stay in that cage. It learned that it's hopeless, that to even *try* to escape will bring pain." He looked at her in the rearview. "You scared, puppy?" Kaley said nothing. She felt her knees shaking. Spencer smiled. "Yeah," he laughed. "Yeah, you're scared."

Then, Kaley thought of Olga…and Mikhael…and Dmitry. She had kindling then, and burned them in her heart. *"Fuck you!"* she growled, and tore open the door and dragged her sister out onto the silent street. The Grand Prix squealed off before her sister's feet had even hit the ground, and she heard the mad laughter until the car disappeared around the corner.

And she would hear it every night for the rest of her life.

Kaley helped Shan to her feet. Shan was sniffling and quivering, but as soon as she stood up she wrapped her arms around Big Sister and squeezed. Kaley could barely breathe, and didn't care. They both fell to their knees, crying. The Anchor rooted them to that spot. Relief swelled in their veins, baptized them and, for a moment in time, they had each other and nothing else. No pain. No past or future conflicts. And, most importantly, no fear.

Kaley was the first to pry them apart. "C'mon," she said, wiping Shannon's eyes and nose while Shannon wiped hers.

They got to their feet and staggered down one street after the next. Signs seemed to pass *them*. Jerry's Car Titles & Loans. Ray's Auto. Fancy Eats. Cynthia's Furniture Store. Kaley stopped at each of these, slamming her hand on the windows to see if anyone was working there. The sun wasn't up yet, but the sky had gone from pure-black to navy-blue. The clouds were parted, and tearing off in different directions.

Kaley rattled the cage doors of each store, and cupped her hands to look in through the windows. She grabbed Shannon's hand and pulled her on. Her little sister's pants were soaked with blood, and Kaley had almost asked the question before Shan said, "I'm okay, Kaley." These words sounded more mature somehow, not quite so tiny. Kaley didn't know it yet, but those exact words would be repeated back to her by Little Sister for the rest of her life, through many discussions. "I'm okay, Kaley," she would say whenever Big Sister gave her a call in the middle of the night for no reason. "Really, I'm okay. Are *you* okay?"

And that was the question, wasn't it? Despite being so young—or perhaps because of it?—Shannon seemed to be taking what had happened to her better than Kaley was. What had scared Shan the most was the house, and everything about it. She'd been mostly unconscious throughout the entire ordeal, yet still she had experienced it somehow. Tectonic plates had shifted, ruptured even, causing a serious realignment of Shannon's person. Kaley would eventually theorize that she hadn't just empathized with her sister throughout the ordeal, but that she had actually *absorbed* some of her sister's pain, like a sponge. *I am my sister's keeper*, she would come to think, and often. *I bore the burden to lighten her load.*

The house.

The memory came back to her, rattling her. It...it wasn't so much what she'd *seen* as what it all implied. If the Monster was correct, then hell and punishment had no aim, no direction, and there was no "prime directive" of heaven. Some powerful being had made the universe, perhaps as an afterthought, an offshoot of some other experiment, and then had walked away from it without giving it a second thought.

What if he's not even aware that we're here? Kaley pondered, even as she pulled her sister farther down the street. *What if it's, like...like when you make some clay jar for your mother in second-grade art class. It sits on the shelf a year or two, maybe you're proud of it, but eventually...*

"Eventually everyone forgets about it," she said to herself. The clay jar is not just misplaced, it's *forgotten*. It's as though the clay jar never was. If it falls in a garbage dump and gets shattered, who knows that it needs fixing? What's worse, who *cares*? The universe was a happenstance, a side alley to other things, a—what had the monster called it?—a Forgotten Place. Like Avery Street, a place left unchecked, and now occupied by whoever took advantage first.

Aunt Tabby, you were both right and wrong. There is a God, but he doesn't even know about us. He's moved on.

"And so should we," she whispered. Beside her, Shan looked at her. She squeezed Big Sister's hand, this time to give reassurance, not to get it.

All at once, Kaley knew where this thinking was coming from. It was her brief but intense shared link with the Monster. Some of him had spilled over. She hadn't kept all his skills at lock picking, but she had retained something. Something in his character was imprinted onto her, absorbed, just as she'd absorbed some of Shan. Something...pensive.

346

"Kaley?" Shannon said. "I think I hear a car coming."

Headlights coming around the corner up ahead. The motor was getting louder. Kaley and Shan stood alone on the sidewalk. She grabbed her sister's hand and pulled her close to a lamppost and a pair of newspaper stands. They huddled there, watched it drive past. After it was gone, Kaley realized that the Monster had been right. She would never trust another car again. Not another night. Not another stranger. Not another person who looked even remotely like the Oni family.

They plodded on, through the streets, through their lives, searching for someone who cared, for someone who could be trusted, for someone they could love.

The icepack was laid across his face, and Leon accepted it gratefully. He lay on his stretcher, looking across to the body of Agent Porter, who was DOA when the medics got there. A white blanket was laid over his upper torso and head, his hands at his side, and one of the officers saying a prayer over him.

The oxygen mask was placed over his face, and he began to breathe. "Detective?" someone was saying. "Detective, can you hear me? Give me a thumbs up if you can—good. Very good. All right, let's load him up."

Someone grabbed one of his hands. "Yo, Leon!" It was McDevitt. His partner Keitrich had been taken away, but whether he was alive or dead or simply dying, Leon didn't know. "Yo, man, you're gonna be all right. Hear me? You're—"

"David," he said. "David went...to the house..."

"We'll find him, man. Don't you worry about that, all right? You just focus on you right now."

"Find him...find David..."

His stomach growled.

The time on the dashboard read 6:02 AM when he rolled onto Blankenship Avenue, then down Donald L. Hollowell Parkway from the north. This one took him to another street that looked familiar. There was a closed car wash, two small grocery stores, and a car title pawn shop called Strike Gold. *Whattaya know? Beltway Street, my ol' friend, we meet again.*

Not a mile down the road, there was the flashing sign, missing its letters: **D ds n's St e.**

Spencer didn't know where else to go at the moment. He cut a few more pieces of cloth to absorb the blood, which was still pushing out but with less intensity than before. The strips of cloth he'd used earlier had soaked completely through. He'd read somewhere that you should never remove the old blood-soaked bandages, rather you should add new ones to the top of the old ones, to keep damming the flow.

Spencer had been considering Dmitry's last words. He already didn't really trust his eyes with all he'd seen, and wondered where Derbent was on a map. He didn't think he'd ever heard of it. He supposed he could get a smartphone from Hector in Memphis and look it up on the Internet.

He pulled the Grand Prix to a stop right in front of Dodson's Store, and hopped out. The sky was lightening. Morning was come. The street was completely empty. *Not a creature was stirring*, Spencer thought, *not even a mouse.* He smiled, and that was a mistake. It hurt, and more blood flowed out of his face. He checked himself in the mirror. He was turning pale. If he didn't find some blood clot soon and someone to stitch him, he could be in serious trouble. Luckily, he knew a guy outside of Atlanta, and Hector up in Memphis. The two of them ought to be able to hide him for a time. It meant leaving behind Pat and the job he'd been given, but things were too hot for him to stay here now.

His stomach growled. *But first, a fucker's gotta eat*, he thought, stepping out of the car. He spat a gob of blood onto the pavement. When he stepped inside Dodson's, the chime over the door jingled. The music now playing wasn't Akon's, but Nicki Minaj, telling the world that if she got a certain look from a man then her panties were coming off. He tapped his feet to the beat for a minute.

"What...the...?"

Spencer glanced over to the counter. "S'up, Mac?" he said. The big man was standing behind the counter, his little TV showing *Star Wars*. By the look of it, it was that first disaster, *The Phantom Menace*. Mac was still wearing his Falcons jersey, and still as fat Spencer remembered.

"What the fuck happened to you, bra?" He had started to walk around the counter but stopped, either because he couldn't fit or because he wasn't certain what he was going to do with a man bleeding to death in his store.

"Ya got any bandages? Alcohol an' some swabs? Any kinda medical aid section?"

Mac just pointed a fat finger.

Spencer tipped a cowboy hat he wasn't wearing. "Much obliged." He went into the back, and was pleasantly surprised to find that Dodson, whoever the fuck he was, had stocked just two small containers of QuikClot. "Niiiiiice," he said, lifting them off the shelf. There were nine boxes of bandages, and Spencer took all of them, as well. At the counter, he said, "Another burger if you would, please."

"Fuck, brotha, you look like you in *mad* need of a hospital."

"I'm fiendin' for a burger right now, Mac. I need it. I need it like you need to take that jersey off an' throw it in the dumpster."

"I ain't got no more burgers, dawg."

"Somethin' quick then. Like a, uh, I dunno, a fuckin' reheated hot dog or some shit. Nachos to go. Ya got anything like that? An' a Coke...*no*, bottle water?" Mac studied him a heartbeat longer, then nodded and went to get it. When he came back, he tossed a bottle of water and a reheated hot dog onto the countertop and stared at him a minute. Spencer's eyes had gone to the TV. "You ever seen Plinkett's review o' those *Star Wars* prequels?"

Mac shook his head.

"Funny shit, man. Funny, funny shit. He points out all kinds o' bullshit in those movies. Like in the second one how Anakin Skywalker kills the sandpeople's children, and his girlfriend Padmé is okay with it. But then in the third one Obi-Wan Kenobi goes an' tells her that he's seen security footage of Anakin killin' children at the Jedi Temple, an' Padmé's all like, 'No, I won't believe that, I can't!' Strange, stupid, an' just plain *bad* writin' in those movies, man. Total fuckin' disgrace. How much is that gonna be?"

"Seventeen eighty-five," Mac said. While Spencer went fishing for his wallet, he cleared his throat and said, "You ever get with the police about what happened earlier?"

"What happened earlier?"

Mac made a face. "C'mon, man, don't bullshit me. Them two girls got taken earlier tonight."

"Oh, them?" Spencer handed him his last twenty-dollar bill. "They're dead, my friend. Believe that."

Mac reached out to take the money. "How you know that?"

He touched his temple with one finger. "Intuition. They both died tonight."

The big man opened the register and got out his change, handed it back. "You saw what happened tonight, man. You coulda done somethin'."

"There's nothin' you or I could've done that those two couldn't have done themselves. Can I get a bag for all o' this?" Mac watched him another heartbeat, then moved to get the paper bag. He dumped all of Spencer's goods into the bag carelessly, and then pushed it across the counter to him. "Thanks so much." He pointed to the TV. "Enjoy those shitty movies." He turned and started to leave. As he approached the door, Mac called back to him.

"Do me a favor, man," the fat man said. "Don't ever come back in here. I don't wanna see you ever again. Ya feel me?" Mac's gaze was even.

Spencer smiled at him. "You'll still be the only man I ever loved, Mac. But don't worry, ya won't see me ever again. It's better to burn out than to fade away." He winked, and walked out.

The streets were still empty. Spencer felt a little lightheaded. He staggered the last few steps to the car. He took out the bottle of water and flung the paper bag and the rest of its contents into the back seat. He cranked it up, and sat there for a moment. He was slightly aware of the police car that had pulled up behind him. He was also somewhat cognizant of the two police officers that hopped out of the car and were moving quickly into Dodson's Store. Maybe Mac had made a quick call, or maybe he'd pressed the button behind the counter as soon as Spencer stepped inside. But Spencer didn't think so, because they walked in and started chatting, and didn't have their hands resting on their guns as one might expect of officers ready for action.

Probably comin' back for some routine questioning. Mac'll probably rat on me, tell 'em I was just here. I'll need to switch cars again soon. It was time to move.

"Seasons don't fear the Reaper," he sang, and spat out another gob of blood onto the seat beside him. "Nor do the wind, the sun or the rain." He put the car in drive, checked his rearview once and let a truck go by before he pulled out onto Beltway. He did an illegal U-turn in the middle of the street, despite the cops in the store. "We can be like they are. Come on, baby...don't fear the Reaper..."

Only two cars went past him, as did a crack zombie out looking for another fix, as did a woman carrying a baby in one arm and guiding another pantsless child by the hand, as did a police chopper overhead.

Soon, a swift sunrise was ahead of him.

He still had the fake IDs that the Sasquatch had given him, and if he was lucky he just might be able to get the medical help he needed and then get out of the country before the IDs became completely useless.

"Come on, baby...we'll be able to fly...come on, baby...don't fear the Reaper...baby I'm your mannnnnnnn..."

AUTHOR'S NOTE

While much of the Bluff's description and the information on its crime and statistics mentioned here are true, much of it was obviously (and necessarily) changed to create the story. To any lifelong Atlantans who say, "Hey, Terrell Street isn't a real street," you may rest easy knowing you are absolutely correct.

To those of you who found parts here endlessly disturbing, I have news for you that you may find even more disturbing. The Rainbow Room is actually based off of a real group of child pornographers that, thankfully, the good people at Interpol and various police agencies around the globe brought down back in 2011 through careful investigation, cyber-tracking, and coordination. Kaley and her sister Shannon are not based on anyone in particular, but hopefully they served as monuments to those that suffer these horrific ordeals and die alone in some monster's basement, or else live and struggle to find some way to carry on in life.

Spencer Adam Pelletier, I'm a little frightened to say, is a creation of my own. Birthed out of reading countless accounts of psychopaths and how they think, this personality eventually emerged. Spencer was a playpen for this writer to hop into, allowing one to do and say and think some of the most despicable things that would never cross the mind of your typical protagonist.

If there were parts you had difficulty reading, just remember that I wasn't too pleased to have to write them. Spencer's world and philosophy are harsh, and I'm not sure I agree with any of his lessons, but if you have any grievances, please, take them up with him.

Chad Huskins
February 26, 2012

1

Chelyabinsk Oblast, Russia

Zakhar knew that he was being followed. What he didn't know was whether it was just another hunter trying to poach game on his family's land, or some lost homeless squatter. The signs were all around him. A bent sapling here, a pile of crushed leaves where someone had been lying there. He circled the area several times as a matter of habit—this had long been his family's land, he'd hunted it with his father, and his father had hunted it with his father, and so on for generations. He knew the land well, and he knew when a stranger was on it.

Having set out that morning to hunt, Zakhar was upset that some squatter might be inadvertently running off his game. *Nothing worse than having a perfectly good hunt ruined*, he thought.

Presently, Zakhar remained well within the tree line, where the thick pine canopy had protected the forest floor from much of the snow, but not nearly all of it. The snow-dappled ground was frozen solid, even the stubborn Siberian grass crackled beneath his feet as he walked, and it crackled again under his knees when he knelt to inspect the sign a bear had left, perhaps a day prior. The droppings were frozen solid.

Whoever the man was, poacher or squatter, he likely hadn't killed this bear. *I would've heard the gunshot.* Sound carried out here, though few were around to hear it.

He looked up, pulled his balaclava up around his nose so that he could scratch an itch. Zakhar's breath came out in a great fog, like that of a dragon. He had ascended to a hilltop that put him just above some of that aforementioned forest canopy. He looked westward for a moment of peace, out over the Ural Mountains away in the distance, and then pulled the wool mask back down over his face and descended the hill, searching for other signs.

The forest got thicker through here. There were great, climbing vines that threatened to strangle every tree in sight—a stubborn, defiant species, like everything else that lived in the Russian territories—and a host of angry briars and brambles. He paused occasionally to inspect the snow for depressions—footprints that might have been filled in by the quiet and constant falling snow. *They're still out here*, he thought. *Maybe more than one?* If that were so, they were probably poachers, and it would be the first instance of poaching in almost four years, ever since he'd ran the last bunch off and then helped to pass stricter laws against trespassing and poaching, along with his friends at the Slaviansky Trophy Hunting Society.

He checked his watched. It was almost four o'clock.

Zakhar knelt to study the latest sign. It was a sweet gum bur, extremely rare in this part of the world due to climate change, but there were still a precious few left in the Siberian wilderness.

The prickly burs were about half the size of a golf ball, and fell from the trees whenever the harsh winters arrived. Zakhar had first learned of the importance of sweet gum burs in tracking from reading the works of the great Russian hunter Leonid Pavlovich Sabaneyev. The burs remained on forest floors and did not naturally pierce any other leaves. But when Zakhar lifted this bur, he found several leaves stuck to it. Someone, or something, had passed through here. However, he saw no other visible sign of the bear, nor did he see sign of boar or deer. *They've all run off.* Had they sensed him? Or, had they sensed the others that might be out here? He put a hand on a knee and pushed himself to his feet. He took a moment to scan the tree line. "*Otkuda vy?*" he hollered: *Where are you from?*

His words echoed through the lonely forest. But there was no answer, only the stillness and silence of the forest and snow. The forest kept its secrets.

Overhead, a covey of dark-brown gannets suddenly took flight from the trees. A few heartbeats later, there was total silence again. Zakhar started walking, and then his eyes caught sight of a squirrel about ten meters ahead of him dashing across the snow-dappled earth, lunging for a tree, clinging to it, and climbing to the other side. Here was another sign straight out of Leonid Sabaneyev's hunting chronicles: a squirrel that leaps onto a tree and immediately moves to the other side is hiding from a predator.

The birds, the squirrel, these were all signs of what hunters and trackers called the "concentric rings of Nature." One thing alerted one group of animals, and their scattering alerted another group, and so on. A savvy hunter knew to pay attention to these signs.

Zakhar looked in the direction whence the squirrel came. He removed his balaclava this time, and the cold cut to the marrow of his bones. *"Vy mestnyy?"* he shouted, a bit sarcastically: *Are you from around here?* Of course the poacher wasn't from around here. How could he be, when Zakhar Ogorodnikov and his family had owned the hundred square miles all around for hundreds of years?

Zakhar hollered again, this time informing the would-be hunter that he was poaching on private property, and that, because of the new laws passed four years ago, the penalty for that could be as much as a million rubles.

No answer.

After listening to his words finish echoing through the trees and across the white fields beyond, Zakhar pulled his balaclava back on, then lifted the strap of the Tigr-308 over his head to remove it, and checked it. The rifle was self-loading, built to withstand all conditions, and he hadn't even fired a shot today, but it never hurt to check and make sure everything was set and ready to go at a moment's notice. He'd seen violence while in the military, but in all his years living on this land, he'd never even heard of an incident happening between his family and poachers.

And who else besides poachers had any reason to come this far out into the Siberian wilderness? There was no one and nothing else out here to see, not after leaving the main road, which took one far beyond the Ural Mountains.

Could be Tatars, Zakhar thought. He recalled reading about Tatars moving farther this way, squatting on private property. Though he had never seen any of those roving, gypsy-like groups around his land, Zakhar knew that they had recently become a problem in and around the Ural region, large clans of them pulling up stake and driving their busted up cars and pushing their load-bearing mules onto others' private property. The cities had all gotten fed up with their transient ways, complaining of the littering and escalating violent clan disputes, and as a result the Tatar nomads were moving deeper and deeper into outlying forested lands, hoping to become lost again in the great Siberian wastelands.

Hope to God that's not it, he thought. *I'll take anything over a gypsy.*

Zakhar didn't shoulder his rifle. Rather, he kept it in a loose, low-ready position, exactly as he'd done in the military, and started forward. About a hundred meters later, the forest abruptly ended, and he was back in the great expansive fields of his childhood.

He noticed no footprints on the way back to his house by the frozen lake, and heard no other sounds besides the lonely Siberian winds whickering through the forest behind him. Halfway back, the snow suddenly began falling with greater intensity.

Atlanta, Georgia

Her alarm clock went off at exactly 7:00 AM, playing the song "Tainted Love" by Soft Cell, a favorite of one of her mother's many boyfriends. Reflexively, her left arm shot out from the covers and snatched at the clock, her palm smashing against its top and sending it to the floor. Only, that's not how Kaley Dupré saw it happen. Indeed, a great deal went on before she sent that clock smashing to the floor.

The dream had been a deep, ponderous one. She was lost amid a city—a city that was wholly unfamiliar to her. Everywhere, there was water. Not a flood or a rushing river moving through the streets, just standing water that everyone around her was walking through as calmly as you please. Kaley herself stood in the water, and, after having learned her lesson many times before, she did not move.

The water foamed up around the people and objects that moved around her. Wherever the people moved, wherever there was a stop sign or parking meter, it bubbled and licked around the object's edges, almost as if the water was acid, and corroded everything it touched. But nothing appeared to be in decay—nothing except for the buildings.

It was an otherwise normal city street, like Atlanta, only different in all the unpronounceable and textured ways of dreams, yet from the tallest peaks of each building there came clumps of stone and masonry work, all of it plopping into the water and disappearing amid a swell of foam before that foam, too, fizzled and ceased to exist.

"This city is collapsing," she said to the man beside her, quite calmly. It was a man in a gray business suit...or maybe it was black. Hard to say. She knew it was a dream. And so, it seemed, did everyone else around her. In fact, they all moved about like they were mostly bored. Sometimes they looked to her expectantly, as if waiting for her to do something about the city.

Kaley hadn't moved. She had learned it wasn't smart to move when the world was flooded like this. The scenery was sometimes different—sometimes a desert, sometimes a forest, sometimes frozen tundra—but it was *usually* a city, and *usually* it was smart not to move. It was as if the water sensed her, grew irritated with her. Everyone else walking about could move freely and do as they pleased, but the second Kaley moved—

And then it happened. The loud, screeching noise. She knew at once what it was. *The alarm clock.* Knowing it made it no less offensive to her ears, and startled her no less. "Sometimes I feel I've got to—*bump-bump!*—run away!" sang the majestic Soft Cell. "I've got to—*bump-bump!*—get away from the pain you drive into the heart of me!" She jumped, and when she did, the water all around her ankles felt it. A swirling eddy that began around her. *Oh god, not again...*

Now everyone on the street backed away from her. The whirlpool gained power quickly, and the water churned and frothed all around her. Everyone on the street now paused, a look of mild curiosity on their faces, and no one moved to help her, though she screamed and pleaded.

Then, from the foam came long, tenebrous arms. They were the same as before. Black, burnt things, missing flesh and bits of muscle, with sinew dangling from their length. They came up through that churning well and groped at her. One snatched at her ankle, another at her hair. *"Go away! Leave me alone!"*

The alarm was still going off somewhere. "The love we shared—*bump-bump!*—seems to go nowhere!"

Meanwhile, the hands all around her became hungrier. *It's only a dream*, she thought. *It's just a dream.* She had an intuition what they were searching for, like the way you know something in a dream, but don't know it when you're awake. *And that's all it is. Just a dream.*

And that's what frightened her. The first time she'd seen them had been in a dream, too, something she'd conjured up out of necessity, out of a need to survive one terrible night. That was it, just a coping mechanism. Or so she'd thought. But an officer was dead, as were Dmitry and all the others, and at the hands of the terrible things she'd brought into this world. A door had been opened, and she had opened it.

Now they want me, she thought, struggling with the indecision. Should she stand still and hope they finally lost "sight" of her, or try to run and risk attracting even more of them?

"Once I ran to you," sang Soft Cell. "Now I'll run from you...This tainted love you've given...I give you all a boy could give you!"

The whirlpool gained in speed and intensity. Now, even the people in her head were running in fear, but now the power of the whirlpool and its angry foam pulled them in, as well. The hands climbed higher on her, groping, searching for her lips, her eyes, her ears, her everything. The hands were slimy, bloody from the missing flesh and dangly meat. *"It's her,"* whispered one of the familiar voices. It was familiar only in her dreams, and whenever she woke up, she usually forgot about it again. *"It's her, it's her, it's her, we need her. Get her! Get her! She can bring us back! Get herrrrrrrrrr!"*

"Oh God," she wept. "Oh God, no! No, no, no, please God, noooooo! Noooooooooo!"

Kaley finally began to thrash, and when she did, she felt something swelling inside of her. It was like a tight knot, something that yearned to get out. Like vomit, or diarrhea, it would not be stopped. But, also like those bodily projectiles, their direction and intensity could not be controlled. A portion of it went up and down her spine, into her bowels, then up into her head and rested behind her eyes, threatening to split her head before it traveled to her hands, her knees, her heart, her lungs, bouncing all around.

A sickness was rising, one she hadn't felt since…

A trembling. Something from all around. The walls of the cityscape began to crumble even more now. Enormous chunks of stone and contorted gargoyles plummeted down into the water, smashing into parked cars and sending them into the foaming fury. The ground bucked, cracked, then rose, stone riven from stone. Kaley felt herself take in one quick, panicked breath, and then, the thing that was inside her that was waiting to be vomited, was vomited.

There was a tear, something forcing its way out of her…

All at once, she was somewhere else. Kaley had merely blinked, and felt propelled by the same force that was churning inside of her. It was like the feeling you get on a rollercoaster, a tingling up the spine, your stomach rising high into your chest, a sense of being lurched. It was over in an instant, the hands were all gone and she stood in her living room. She could still hear her alarm clock going off, but farther down the hall in her bedroom. "Take my tears and that's not nearly alllllllll! Tainted love…ooohhh, tainted love!"

Was this a dream, too? Or was she sleepwalking? The living room seemed perfectly fine. Unpacked boxes still hugged same walls as before, and the outdated Xbox was sitting in front of an equally outdated Sony big-screen, amid a rat nest-like tangle of wires and surge protectors. There were shelves set up for books or homey ornaments, but so far left bare. The single mounted picture of Jesus was beside one black-curtained window. *Mom thinks it's a talisman, a ward against more evil.* Kaley shook her head. *She has no idea.*

Kaley sighed…but it was strange, because there was no air to breathe. *S'funny.*

Then, she heard something. Whimpering, and close by. She turned, and for a moment she didn't know what she was looking at. Huddled in the corner, garbed in nothing but her Powerpuff Girls shirt and underwear, a tiny girl had retreated, arms over her head as though she were trying to drown out noise and all the terrors of the world. "Shan?"

"Kaley," Shannon whimpered. "Get back. Get back inside before the monsters find you."

"Inside where, Shan?" She took a step towards her sister...and noticed that the carpet felt...slippery? Kaley looked down. It was all perfectly normal, the same puke-brown carpet of their new apartment. Kaley had told her mother how very depressing that carpet was, but Jovita Dupré had said nothing. Unless it was a rebuke, her mother didn't say much of anything these days. "Shannon, what are you talking—"

"Kaley," Shannon whispered. "Hurry back inside. They're coming."

"What do you—" Then, she remembered. *Oh no, it's happening again.* The dream was always the first stage, and then came the next stage, what she called the "false awakening," when she thought she was up and moving but she wasn't. The slippery carpet, the lack of oxygen all around her. She tried to take a breath, but there was none to be had.

"*Get her! That's it! That's it! Don't let her go!*" The hands. Suddenly she felt them pawing at her, wrapping around her legs and ankles, arms and wrists, now her neck and hair, now her waist—

"*Get her! That's it! Almost got her! Almost!*" The same voice as before, the same hungry, desperate voice that always commanded the others.

"Let me go!" she screamed. "Let me go!"

"Don't touuuuuch me, *please!*" shouted the alarm clock. "I cannot stand the way you teeeeeeease! I love ya, though ya hurt me so! Now I'm gonna pack my things and go! Tainted love!"

The trembling returned, this time far more sickening, and vastly more painful. It gnawed at her insides, tore her intestines to shreds, swam through her guts and dove into her bladder.

Whatever it was, it came out from her fingertips, her eyes, her nostrils and lips, her toes and toenails, her privates and her ears. Out of everything. It was an immense expulsion of something grotesque that was rotting her insides, and when it happened, the hands tore away from her, almost painfully…

All at once, she was sitting straight up in her bed and her hand went flying towards the alarm clock. And it went flying from her nightstand, smashing against the floor and skipping over to her small bookshelf, knocking off a low-lying copy of *The Lightning Thief*. Soft Cell finally went silent.

Kaley sat upright, panting, the sweaty sheets falling from her chest as tears fell from her face. She was sobbing uncontrollably. She felt…warmth. A warmth on her bottom and between her legs, like something slithering…

"Oh God!" she screamed, and reached down to rip the sheets off of her. But this time it wasn't bloody hands reaching up from an abyss. It was urine. She had peed herself, and was still peeing.

Kaley let the urine flow. She let it flow and flow, and never tried to stop it. It felt too good. Like a person that had suffered through a night of food poisoning and survived, she didn't care what else her body did, as long as the pain was gone, as long as she was safe and secure and there was no more pain.

With trembling hands, she reached up to wipe her face. Kaley then looked around her room to survey it. All was right, except…*The nightstand*. Something about it was wrong. It took Kaley a moment to realize what it was. *It's so far away*. In her nocturnal thrashing, Kaley had somehow wriggled away from her side of the bed and was now on Shannon's side. The nightstand was on *her* side, out of arm's reach. Then, she looked at the alarm clock on the floor. *How did I reach that?*

A mental fog had grown all around her. All sorts of blockages, brought on by fear and disorientation, muddled her thinking. And like tumbles in a lock, one by one, those mental blockages were lifted and another door of realization was opened. Kaley realized that if she was on Shannon's side…

"Shannon?" she hollered at once, trying to hop out of the bed and nearly falling on her face. The sheets got tangled around her ankle, and for a terrifying moment her mind made it the hands from her dream. But it hadn't been a dream, had it? At least, not all of it.

Kaley was up and searching for the light—at seven o'clock in the morning it was still dim inside their little apartment, especially with the black curtains that Shan insisted they needed. "To keep the monsters from seeing inside," she had said again and again.

Kaley never found the light, and instead stumbled out of her room and down the hall. She made it into the living room, feeling that atrocious, old, flattened brown carpet beneath her feet. The same as always, no longer slippery as slime. The living room was exactly as she'd found it moments ago, the unpacked boxes stacked not quite neatly against the walls, the picture of Jesus beside the black-curtained window, the denuded shelves, the tangle of Xbox and TV wires on the floor. And Shannon, squatting in the corner exactly as Kaley had seen her moments ago. "Shan?" she said, on the verge of tears. Urine was still streaking down her leg. She'd clean it up in a minute, after she checked on her sister. "Shan, can you hear me? You all right?"

"Kaley?" she said, sniffling. Timidly, Shannon glanced over her shoulder, almost too afraid to find the truth. "Is it…is it you? Did you make it back?"

Now with sleep in full retreat, Kaley had her wits about her again and knew what Shannon had meant. "Yeah, baby. Yeah, I made it back." Shannon stood at once and rushed into her arms. They clung to one another like they were sinking, and each of them was the last piece of driftwood that would help them stay afloat.

"They gonna keep comin'," Shannon lamented, sniffling. "The Others are gonna comin' in your sleep, ain't they?"

"I don't know, girl. And that's the truth."

"I don't want you to go! I don't want them to take you!"

"Shhh, I ain't goin' anywhere."

"What do they want with you?"

Kaley kissed the top of her head. "I don't know, baby." But that wasn't true. Kaley had a suspicion, one that she didn't want to voice, lest she give power to the notion.

"I wish they would go away," Shannon cried.

"Me too, girl. Me too."

For several weeks now, it had been like this. First came the dream of some unknown place, the things and the people inside of them were obviously conjured up by her own imagination. This seemed to be the way the Others found their way in (she and Shan had resorted to calling them the Others, for what else would you call them?). With her mind relaxed and at play, they poked and prodded ever so gently, and when they were right upon her, she felt the explosion of...of...some *force* that took her away. In those moments, she wasn't exactly her. She was both in her bed and yet somewhere else, too, in a kind of state where she could be seen, yet she couldn't interact with the world around her. When Kaley was in that state, everything was slippery.

Sometimes at night, Kaley found herself adrift in the halls of their new apartment, trying to touch the walls and yet watching her fingers slide right off. There was no air, and none necessary. Actually...that was wrong, wasn't it? There *was* air, she even felt it on her face sometimes, like when the air-conditioning cut on, it was just that she had no lungs.

"A spirit ain't got no use for breathin'," her Nan had told her once. Kaley had asked some question about angels, asked how they could die. She had asked about chopping off their heads or drowning them. That's when Nan had told her. "Spirits ain't got no use for breathin', chil'. You find that out one day, too." Kaley had assumed Nan had meant someday when she died, when she too became a spirit ascending to heaven. But had Nan meant something else entirely? Did she have first-hand experience? Or had she known how far the charm could carry Kaley?

There had been a few times when Kaley found herself walking through the house alone, touching things experimentally, feeling the slick, soft surface of things. It was almost as if she could pass through them if she wanted. One night, while asleep and fleeing the arms of the Others, Kaley had suddenly appeared in the kitchen—it was a reflex, it seemed, a way of escaping the Others. Her mother had been up getting a late-night snack, her back to the dinner table, hunched over the sink, weeping.

When Kaley had softly said, "Mom?" Jovita Dupré had nearly leapt out of her skin. "What the hell are you doin' there? Ain't you s'pposed to be in bed? Get'cho black ass in there—" She'd cut herself off when she saw Kaley staring at the thing in her hand. "Don't'choo judge me, now," she said. "I'm livin' under pressure you don't understand! I'm tryin' to survive! Keepin' this family together ain't easy! Gawn now, get in the damn bed." But Jovita had stormed off, leaving her daughter's spirit standing dumbfounded where she had found her.

"The laughing man brought them, didn't he?" said Shan presently.

Kaley looked down at her sister. Pity poured to and from Shannon in an endless cycle, one sister assuaging the other. *The laughing man,* she thought. *She still can't even say his name. She'll call him anything else. The monster. The mean man. The laughing man. Anything but his name, even though she knows it full-well by now. She's seen all the news stories about him that came after, and she still won't say his name. As if it somehow gives him power, like saying Bloody Mary in front of a mirror.*

In fact, that's exactly what it was for Shannon, and Kaley knew it, because she could feel the emotions and surface thoughts of others, sometimes their whole mind, and none more so than her sister's.

Kaley pulled away from her sister and touched her face, wiping the warm tears away from her cheeks with her thumbs. "Listen, this is something you and I have to deal with on our own. We can't tell Mom, 'kay? She won't believe us. Nobody will. Just like they didn't believe us when we told them about…about all that other stuff."

"He ain't comin' back, is he?" Shannon said fearfully. Her face contorted, her eyes shut automatically and her lips curled into great rolls as tears began to pour again.

"Shhhh-sh-sh-sh," she said, pulling her sister's face to her chest again. "Nobody's gonna hurt you. Not anymore. And the laughing man's gone, you hear? He's gone and he's not ever coming back. Ya hear me, chil'? He ain't never comin' back." It would be a little while later that Kaley realized she had sounded exactly like her Nan. "What were you doing up in the first place?"

"I was itching again," she said. Shannon had an infection, something the doctors called vaginitis. An inflammation of her private parts, with terrible itching and the occasional discharge. Shannon was the victim of rape, and she wasn't just dealing with the emotional stresses of it—as a matter of fact, she had buried much of that pain, likely thanks to the "charm" she and

Kaley shared—she was also dealing with the infection her rapist had given her.

They had given her another sickness, too, one that removed her innocence, took away that playful youth, that sanguine outlook she'd long had on life. They had amputated a part of her, opened up another door in her mind, one that let all the pain and hurt of the world flood in, left her in fear of what total strangers might do to her. For Shannon, the world was no longer wide open and full of wonder, it was cold and deceitful and evil and crowded with terrors. She wanted nothing more than to keep it out. Hence, all the black curtains.

"I woke up itchin' all over," Shannon said, "and saw you jumping and jerking in your sleep again. I shook you, tried to wake you, but you told me to run."

"I did?"

Shannon nodded meekly. "You said, 'Run away, Shan. They gonna get you too. Run!' I stayed and kept shaking you, but then I felt the hands…or…or I felt the hands around *you*." This was due to the empathic connection of their charm. Almost always, when either of them was under terrible stress, the other one detected it, just like they always seemed to detect the surface emotions and occasional thoughts of others, like a spider detecting movement in its web. The web stretched out from them, and as far as Kaley could tell, the web had no limit. But the closer someone was, the stronger she felt about it.

Or, in some cases, the more powerful the pain, the more it seemed to ripple through the web, along various avenues and arms, and finally resting inside her head and guts. *Inside my everything.*

"I knew you was about to jump out again, that you would be safe enough for a second," said Shannon. By *jump out*, she meant exit her body. Kaley didn't like to think of it like this. It made her feel like her soul was actually leaving her body, and that meant death. And if she died while those things were pulling her down, down, down…

Shannon started weeping again. An alarm bleated obnoxiously somewhere in the apartment for a full two seconds before it stopped. A light suddenly switched on down the hallway. *Mom's up.* Jovita Dupré would be around and about in a moment, and then there would be inevitable arguments, possibly even shouting matches if Kaley elected to retort.

"Hush now, we're okay. Hush it, I said," she told her sister sweetly, quietly. "Now come on, help your big sister clean up this mess," she said, pointing to the wet spots she'd left on the floor, droplets of urine that made a trail all the way to her room. "And let's put those sheets in the washing machine. Before Mom gets up and has a fit."

The hunting lodge that his family once rented out twice a year to members of the Slaviansky Trophy Hunting Society was now empty. The lodge was forty meters away from the main house, it was two stories and fully powered by gas year-round, with air-conditioning and water that was kept from freezing by its own independent gas tank and generator. There was a snow-capped shed with a Subaru Forester parked inside, flanked by two ATVs, all with chains for their tires, and plenty of petrol cans and spare tires.

Zakhar kicked the snow off his boots on the doorstep, pulled his right glove off with his teeth and fished in his pocket for the key—even after all these years of living alone in the middle of nowhere, he still locked it behind him whenever he left. And why not? He had other reasons for keeping people out, and not just poachers.

When he stepped inside, Zakhar closed the door behind him at once in order to preserve the precious warm air. Then he paused, looked around, and listened. The lodge was dark and appeared exactly as it always had: quaint, old, well kept and with lots of character. Two large bearskins were dangling from the rafters, a third one splayed on the wall, and a forth one, the largest one, growling angrily in front of the fireplace. Over that fireplace was an oak mantelpiece, and above that hung a large rectangular mirror, which made the living room appear more spacious than it actually was. A moose was mounted on the far wall and looked straight ahead dutifully, never eyeing him. The place still smelled freshly of the pinewood it was made of. A gun rack over the door was still full, nothing missing there. The wicker couches and chairs still had their plush pillows and cushions, all soft and new from his latest additions.

After a few moments of checking the other doors and giving the windows a jiggle, Zakhar decided the poachers hadn't been this brave. He unshouldered his Tigr-308 and replaced it in its own gun cabinet, which he then locked. He kept the pistol strapped to his side, though. When spending long holidays out here alone, he never went anywhere without it. He even slept with the Colt Woodsman .22 on the nightstand, within arm's reach. Home invasion was highly unlikely out here, which was why he sold his property in the city years ago and moved back home. *But there's was a first time for everything*, he supposed.

The rest of his family in Derbent had found that out the hard way. They lived in the boring part of a boring town, and yet look what happened to them. Some nobody, a drifter some said, had come out of nowhere and shown them how the outside world could intrude on such tranquility.

The lodge was warm, despite there being no fire in the fireplace. He never liked to leave a fire going while he was away from the cabin, but he liked for it to be heated when he returned. *Let's turn that heat off, get a fire started.* He made a brief stop in the kitchen to flip on the tiny radio, and turned it to the weather station so that he could start monitoring this storm.

The logs were outside, chopped during the spring when the Siberian territories were only cold, rather than frozen. Zakhar poured some water into a kettle, put it on an eye of the stove and got it going, then stepped outside. The snow was coming down even harder, so hard that he could no longer see the forests of Siberian Pine where he'd conducted his day's hunt. The cold ignored his gloves and penetrated his bones, and the wind forced those snowflakes into his face, like little needles of ice.

He gathered up the logs covered in hoarfrost, counting out six good ones, then stepped back onto the front porch and paused at the front door. The footprints he'd left coming back from the woods were already getting filled in, and he was struck by their shape. Some of them looked wider, and a little longer than the others. The wind must have had some effect on that, he figured.

Balancing the chopped logs between his chest and left arm, Zakhar used his right hand to open the door, and halfway through, he paused again. He bent to drop the logs on the rug inside, then turned back to the footprints leading up to his doorstep. Zakhar stood there for a moment, examining, his breath coming out in great clouds, his eyes attempting to penetrate the white curtain that nature had covered the world in. He looked east, towards the frozen lake and its single, dilapidated dock. It was also mostly ensconced by the curtain of falling snow.

When he stepped back inside, he shut the door and locked it. He waited, listening to the house, the lonesome creaks and groans. The wind pushing against the windows, causing them to make little snapping sounds. He reached for the Colt at his side, checked it again to reassure himself, then he went about searching the house.

When Jovita stepped out of her bedroom, folding the front of her robe around her waist, she was already shivering. *Cold as a witch's titty*, she thought briefly, but her mind was already working on what she had to get done today. She had to restock the house with some groceries—they were almost sittin' on empty—and she had to talk with her sister Tabitha about that job down at the church she'd been talking about. Jovita's only concern was that it was another ambush, a trap set up to *look* like a job interview, but once she got there they would tell her that she needed to stay clean and go through regular drug tests in order to get her measly paycheck. Tabitha had done this to her once before with another church, an arrangement that was more intervention than interview, and that had turned out…

"What'cha'll doin'?" Jovita asked, stopping short in the living room. Her two girls were bent over on the floor beside the couch, working the carpet back and forth assiduously with a pair of towels.

Shannon looked up sharply, looking guilty and caught, and, as always, she looked to her Big Sister, her Eternal Protector, who said, "I got up early to get somethin' to drink, and I spilled it."

"What'choo drinkin' this early fo'? I ain't even made you any breakfast. You tryin' to take that away from me now, too?" The words were out of her mouth before she could check them. She hadn't meant to say anything like it, but there it was, hanging in the air. For months now she had become frustrated with their little conspiracy of two. Late at night, they walked around in their room after the lights were out, whispering their secrets to one another. Jovita had heard them, and often barged in on them a few times and demanded that they go to bed. It gave her a degree of dark maternal pleasure to interfere with their secrets.

They were up to something, she just knew it. They were still their little conspiracy of two, just like they had been before all that evil had happened to them. Jovita had tried in those first two months, she had really, *really* tried. But the cravings had started, and it hadn't helped that Jerome Denney, one of her old dealers, had moved out this way three years ago and had been calling her up, asking to catch up on old times. Kaley already suspected, already *knew*. And Shannon, well...*She won't even look at me.*

Shan had been through a lot, and Jovita felt for her, went to hug her repeatedly, cried with her and tried to tell her everything was going to be all right. But always Shannon would go limp in her arms, like she was dead. When she was in her sister's arms, though, some ember of life was kindled, and she would grip and hug, even laugh on occasion.

And now they hate me again. It was mostly Kaley's doing. *God damn her, she knows what was done to me. She knows I suffered the same as them!* When a mother's daughter was raped, the mother felt violated herself. Powerless and crippled by her shame, Jovita had retreated further and further into her soft, safe world with Jerome Denney.

Jovita hated herself for not being there for her girls when they had needed her most. Rather, some other lunatic had had some say in their rescuing. *And here I was, laid up an' high as a kite.* And she knew that, come later tonight, she was likely to be in the same state. The same demons as before were calling to her; with each passing year, their song grew more sonorous, and the events in Atlanta had put Jovita in a state where she was willing to listen even more.

No, uh-uh, she told herself. *No, you are not doing that again, Jovita Dupré!*

But Jovita knew better. She was strong right now, right in this instant, but eventually...

Presently, her girls weren't answering her. She jerked her head towards the hallway. "Get in there an' get dressed. You both were late for the bus the last time, I ain't explainin' that again. That Principal Manning already look at me like he know somethin' 'bout me, a secret he ain't tellin'. I ain't got time fuh *his* ass today, so don't you get him on *my* case again." She did another jerk with her head, and the two girls walked by her in silent procession.

As Kaley went by, though, her eyes raked across her mother, assessing her in a moment. Jovita almost said something. *Oh, you think* you *know somethin' about me, too?* But she swallowed the challenge before it could ignite a war. After all, Kaley did know something about her, didn't she? She knew Jovita Dupré hadn't changed much in the last five months. New clothes, a new apartment, and a new school hadn't had any real effect on her, or any of them for that matter. Family and friends in their old neighborhood had heard about what happened, had donated food and clothing, and offered so many tears and support. For a time, Jovita had believed she could change, and perhaps Kaley and Shannon had allowed themselves to believe it for a time, too. But now...

I know you, those eyes said to Jovita as they slipped on by. *What do you know?* she wanted to reply right back. But it wasn't just the eyes. It was the...the...watchacallit? The "*aura*" as her mother used to say. It was an outpouring of something that went further than just a penetrating gaze.

Mama said it skips a generation. Jovita's mother had had that same knowing look, like she could tell when somebody was lying. And not just her children, *anyone*.

But Kaley didn't need to have any kind of intuition to know her mother. A month ago, she'd walked in the kitchen a month ago while Jovita was hunched over the sink, lighting up another crumbled bit of white rock in her spoon. Jovita had been nearly scared to death, nearly dropped the spoon, lighter and all.

But maybe I only hallucinated a little of that, she thought. After she had stormed out of the kitchen that night, Jovita had gone to the room her two daughters shared, to check on Shannon...only to find *both* of her daughters in bed. When she'd gone back to check the kitchen, Kaley was gone. The crack rock, the meth…the horrors that her daughters had faced…her guilt over having done nothing about it…*I'm losin' it.*

"*The girl,*" someone whispered. Jovita jumped, turned, looked all about her. "*Her?*" asked someone else. At once, her hands started shaking. Then, there came a reply. "*No, the other one. This one's the mother, she is no use.*"

"Okay, who the *fuck* is that?" she hissed. No answer. Nothing at all. Jovita moved around the living room, listening for the slightest noise. *Losin' it. Yeah. Fuh sho'. Oh…God…*

The attic was clear, as was the entire upstairs. Zakhar double-checked the downstairs, every bedroom, bathroom, and closet, flicking lights off as he left each room. He checked behind every curtain and under every table, around every corner and inside every shower and tub. The only thing left to check was the basement.

Part of him felt silly, and a bit annoyed with himself for being so on edge. This was supposed to be a place of respite, a retreat from the rest of the world, where he could be alone to do what he needed to do. No poachers had ever been so bold as to…

But Ivan and the others, he thought. *Maybe they thought the same thing.* Considering what had happened to the rest of his family, anyone would forgive him his paranoia.

Zakhar went to check the basement door in the hall. The three locks on it were untouched, as was the small wedge of wood he never forgot to jam between the middle hinge and the doorframe; a telltale sign someone had disturbed it, if it had fallen. He went to his bedroom, opened the middle drawer, rummaged around until he found the key ring tucked behind his thickest winter bedclothes, and returned to the hall to go through the locks, one by one.

When he opened it, the usual darkness awaited him, as did the usual odors. Cleaning solutions, and pine-scented air fresheners. Zakhar flipped the switch beside the door, and fluorescent lights flickered on, casting a pallid, funereal glow about the staircase. He kept the gun in a loose, low-ready position, and started down. The wooden steps creaked in protest beneath his weight. At the foot of the steps, Zakhar flipped another switch, this time casting the room with a brighter, more familial glow. To his left was the food pantry for his guest. To his right was the guest room, also triple-locked. Three different keys opened the locks.

Before he stepped inside, Zakhar knocked twice, then once, then twice again. This would signal his young guest to go to the far side of the room, as he'd been trained. Gun at the ready, he stepped through.

The room was exactly as he'd left it, and his young guest had kept it clean, as he'd been trained to do. Hard, smooth concrete floors, with two couches covered in plastic sheeting and a television mounted on the wall, high enough so that it was out of reach, and behind Plexiglas. The TV happened to be on, and was playing a *SpongeBob SquarePants* DVD that Zakhar permitted him. There was a single coffee table, oak, spotless, and with a glimmering top. The room smelled of Pine-Sol. That was good. The boy had cleaned recently.

Zakhar took three steps inside, and paused. His guest was huddled on the far couch, sitting there obediently in his underwear, thumb in his mouth. Zakhar looked at the TV, then at his young guest. "Are you all right?" he said. The boy spoke English. Zakhar had had to brush up on his own. The boy looked at him, doe-eyed, nodded slowly, and looked back at the television. Zakhar also looked at the TV. Squidward was wroth with SpongeBob, it seemed. "Have you heard anything? Any knocking? Anyone moving upstairs?" The boy continued sucking his thumb. "I'm talking to you!" The boy jolted, and shook his head, trembling. "You heard nothing? Heard no one?" The boy shook his head. Zakhar nodded. "Dinner will be ready in a little while. Make sure you bathe. I'll also bring down your shots." He backed away towards the door. "And don't watch so much TV. It will rot your mind."

Back out the door, locking all three locks, then back up the stairs, switching off the lights in the stairs as he went. He shut the door in the hall, locked every lock, and replaced the keys in his drawer. Zakhar was about to return to the fireplace, but paused halfway through the living room and thought for a moment. Something told him to check one last time. Perhaps it was paranoia left over from his days in the service.

The radio was still going in the kitchen, but the weather report was finished for the nonce. It had gone to commercials now for some kind of aftershave. The water in the kettle still hadn't warmed enough to start squealing yet.

Zakhar swept the attic one more time, the upstairs, then the downstairs again. The wind blew harder outside, pressed against the windows.

Satisfied, he holstered the Colt, and finally returned to the logs. He stacked them neatly in the fireplace and then set up some twigs and kindling. He still liked doing things the old way, using bow-drill kits the way the old wilderness survivalists taught. Zakhar had taken numerous courses on primitive survival skills—living way out here, one never knew when the gas tanks might suddenly shut off, without warning, in the dead of winter. No man could survive the blunt force of a Siberian winter. No man.

It took a while for the punk to ignite, but once he had a workable ember, Zakhar set the nest of burning kindling lovingly into the pile of smaller sticks of wood, where it quickly caught flame and began to spread. He stood up, and saw his stalker in the mirror over the mantelpiece a second too late. Zakhar spun, his hand going reflexively for his pistol, but he saw what his stalker had in his hands, and froze.

"Arrogance before the gods," his enemy said, seated comfortably on the couch, directly below the two hanging bearskin rugs.

Zakhar's heart jumped a beat, but he steeled himself, sighed. "What?"

"I said, get'cho *black behind* out that do', befo' you miss the damn bus! What's the matter? You got wax in yo ears, girl?"

Kaley helped Shannon with her coat. It was a hand-me-down from Kaley, but Shan was small, even for her age, and it was just too big. It was almost comical. *She looks like a turtle uncomfortable with her shell*, Kaley thought, grinning. But she swallowed her smile quickly when she felt the animosity pouring off her mother. Mixed with guilt and fear of the future, it was a disgusting mélange on Kaley's tongue and on her mind.

It was a difficult time for all of them. Kaley and Shannon were victims of something horrid, Shan especially, and their mother felt the burden of guilt of not having protected them. In fact, it had been her that sent them out that night, all alone, for groceries she herself ought to have gotten the day before. Now Jovita Dupré emanated such self hate that Kaley couldn't help but absorb it, and the more she absorbed it, the more she showed her hatred for the insufferable woman. And, the more Jovita Dupré saw the hatred in her daughter's eyes, the more she hated herself.

It's a vicious cycle, she thought. *And it's never going to end. Never.*

The door was hanging open. A new winter's breeze came sweeping in, and it seemed to penetrate their clothes, finding the tiniest of gaps, slipping up around them like icy tendrils. For a moment, Kaley felt swept away. She smelled…pine? And Pine-Sol? *Mom doesn't use Pine-Sol* was the last thing she thought before stepping over the threshold. She shouldered her book bag and handed Shannon hers. "Here," she said, and they stepped outside.

And for a moment, Kaley saw something else. Trees. And snow. But it hadn't snowed during the night and she knew it. She blinked. It was gone, and all that was left was Bentley Drive, in Cartersville, Georgia. Bentley Drive was a short stretch of forgettable road that was a forgettable offshoot of Tennessee Street, and covered by dying oaks and forlorn willows. Of the nine houses on Bentley, there were only two that were actually owned by real homeowners, the rest of the houses were all rented out by the same landlord as the one Kaley's mother had found through one of the officers at the Atlanta Police Department. The nice detective, Leon Hulsey, the big man who never stopped looking for them that night, had suggested it to them before he was swallowed by controversy—apparently, he'd been turning a blind eye to his brother-in-law's chop shop.

The trees blew in a sourceless wind, a wind that felt colder by the second. It blew in hard and fast, pushing against both Kaley and her sister. It had another strange odor to it. It didn't…well, as strange as it seemed, it didn't *smell* like the wind was from around here. *More of that pine smell*, she thought. There were no pines around Bentley Drive.

"Hurry on, now!" said Jovita Dupré, safely in the doorway, hugging her robe more tightly to herself. "Gawn, I got a job interview to get to! Don't be late to the bus!" She waved them away, almost like pests, and shut the door.

Kaley reached for her sister's hand, gripped it, and gave it a reassuring squeeze. They walked fifty feet to the bus stop, where two other kids were waiting for the bus, as well. They were older kids, though, a couple of ninth graders, white boys who never did more than glance at Kaley and her sister with an exquisite blend of pity and disgust.

"Did you get the sheets in the washin' machine before Mama saw?" asked Shan.

Always looking out for me. "Yeah, I got it," Kaley said. At least, that's what she meant to say. Only when her lips moved, the words that came out were. "Arrogance before the gods."

"Huh?" Shannon said.

The man on the sofa lounged for a moment, then stood. In his hand was a Glock. His grip showed it was nothing casual; he knew how to use it. He wore black jeans and a black jacket, unzipped, and the shirt underneath had a message written in English: YEAH, I'M INTO THAT SHIT. The man's complexion was pale, his hair black and wild like overgrowth in the forest, his face…there was an illusion on his face. A shadow, brought on by the dark stubble. But something else was wrong. The hairs weren't growing right. There was some sort of distortion, like a scar that—

"Hubris," said the man. "That's arrogance before the gods. And there's a spirit of vengeance, set against those who succumb to hubris. That's what the Greeks believed, anyway. Guess they're good for somethin' besides makin' a mean eggplant." He smiled, and Zakhar noted that the smile was slightly off, too. "Do you know what they called this spirit of vengeance?" The man stepped around the coffee table, his boots were wet and his jeans were soaked almost to the knees. He took a seat at the edge of the table. "*Nemesis.* That's where the word comes from."

Zakhar started to speak, felt something catch in his throat, and swallowed. After he cleared his throat, he said, "What do you want? I have money—"

"You know, I never much believed in god or gods, still not sure that I do, but it's interesting how they supply a kind of, uh...what's the word...underpinning?" The gunman nodded. "Yeah. Yeah, an *underpinning* for how we describe what takes place around us. A basis, a foundation for the things we don't understand."

"If you want money—"

"If I wanted money, Vladimir Putin, why the fuck would I come way out here to planet Earth's frozen asshole?" Zakhar didn't know the language well enough to place the regional accent.

"You can have anything in the house that you want," he told the man.

"Oh, I've got all I want. Right here, right now."

"I'm...not sure I understand you."

The man smiled, and his smile...didn't quite *happen* the right way. The left side, it twitched a little, and turned down at the edges as the rest of the face smiled. Something had happened there, something terrible. Zakhar reminded himself of the Colt Woodsman .22 at his side, ready to be drawn, ready to be fired. And his eyes constantly flitted to the Glock in the intruder's hand.

The gunman suddenly changed topics. "There's this, uh, this bigass crater in America. Maybe you've heard of it? It's called the Barringer Crater." The gunman raised his eyebrows. "It's outside o' Flagstaff, in Arizona. It's a meteor impact crater. You guys have one like it here in Siberia. I think ya call it Popi-guy? Poppy-*gay*, somethin'?" He waved his gun hand dismissively. "In any case, the Barringer Crater, it's like four thousand feet wide, and like six hundred feet deep. You could fit about five aircraft carriers inside. You could also fill that crater with how much shit I know that you *don't* know. So when you say, 'I don't understand,' believe me when I say, *I know*. Only in this instance, I think you *do* know."

"Know what? What the hell are you talking about?"

The gunman tittered. It was a disturbing little titter, almost girlish, and it made Zakhar think of the boy downstairs. "You're really gonna make me say this, aren't you?" He shook his head in wonderment, and stood up. "You fuckers, you don't even have the guts to own up to what you've done. An' they call me the freak."

Zakhar raised his left hand slowly. "Tell me what you want," he said reasonably, "and then maybe we can work out an arrangement of some kind."

"An arrangement. Like what you've got here?" He looked around at the living room, giving an appraising look at the moose on the wall, the considerable fireplace, and mantelpiece. "Quite the *arrangement*." He took a step closer to Zakhar, and Zakhar took a step back, bumped against the mantelpiece and then walked slowly to his left, to the far side of the fireplace. "I'm no vengeful spirit, but I *am* here because of your little *arrangement* here. Fascinating how you stayed off the grid with your work. A smart plan. Much smarter than the rest of your ilk, the ones in Germany, and Ukraine." He smiled knowingly. "And Derbent? Mm?"

For a fraction of a second, Zakhar's eyes widened, but he controlled his surprise and remained calm. "You?"

"Good brandy in Derbent. Good scenery, too. Nice, sleepy little city. Lots of ancient structures. A mixed and cultured people. Peaceful. Not the kind o' town you would associate with people who have your kind of *arrangement*." The gunman let that sit in the air between them. He glanced at the windows. The wind was getting even harsher, and great chunks of snow were smacking up against the side of the lodge. "I saw you got chains on the front tires o' that SUV outside. Do ya have any more chains for the rear tires?"

Zakhar nodded slowly, calmly. "Yes, of course. I could show you where—"

"Don't you fuckin' move," said the gunman evenly. Zakhar froze. He had just started to turn for the door, aiming the right side of his body away from the gunman, so that he couldn't see his hand moving to the holster. Now, the gunman sighed, looked him up and down appraisingly. "Just tell me where they are."

The logs were being consumed by flame in the fireplace, and the fire was now crackling at his side. Zakhar was close to the flames, and felt his palms growing sweaty, though not just because of the heat. All at once, he was becoming increasingly aware of his isolation. The isolation that had once brought such sweet solitude and respite was now a trap. Even on a clear day, without wind or rain, a man could fire a gun outside and not be heard by anyone for many kilometers around. "The chains?" he said. "You…you want to know about the—"

"Yeah, Vladimir, I want the goddamn chains. I parked my rental car a good ways away from here, hiked in on foot. How d'ya think I got way out here without leaving any tire tracks in the snow?" He snorted out a laugh. "I don't wanna chance hiking back to it, not in this weather."

A sudden inkling of hope sprung with Zakhar. *Maybe he's just on the run. A desperate man, just needs a vehicle to get clear of here.* But hadn't he just said he had been to Derbent? And he obviously knew things. Things about the others. "The chains are behind a pegboard in the shed. I can show you."

"Just tell me. An' the gas, too."

He swallowed, eyes darting towards the Glock, back at his intruder's eyes. "The pegboard is in a hidden closet in the shed. Where…" He swallowed again. "Where the poster with the big bear is hanging. The petrol is in there, too."

"Petrol?" he said.

"*Da.* Er, yes. *Fuel.*"

"Oh, right," said the gunman, glancing out one of the windows. "We say *gasoline* back in the States." He looked back at Zakhar. "That's where I'm from, ya know? The States. You ever been to Georgia?" Zakhar shook his head. "No? Ya know anybody from Atlanta?" Zakhar shook his head. The gunman gave a teasing smile. "Awwww, c'mon now, Zakhar. Don't lie to me. You can do this. You're a big boy."

"I don't follow y—"

"Oh, for Christ's sakes, man! You really can't say it, can you? Huh? Can you?" He chuckled, glanced out the window, and Zakhar's fingers touched the sandalwood grip of his Colt just as the gunman looked back at him. "Ya sit out here in the middle o' nowhere, you've got a basement door with three locks on it, and you've gotta believe I haven't missed those locks, and you're still tight-lipped. I've told you that I've been to Derbent an' that I came from Atlanta, but you're still not letting yourself put the pieces together, are ya?"

Zakhar said nothing, took a slow, deep breath, and let it out quietly, calming his nerves. Thought about the Colt, going for it, watching the Glock trained on him, decided against it.

The intruder was still smiling that not-right smile of his. "What've ya got down there, Zakhar?" *Zakhar, he says. He knows my name.* "Or, maybe I should ask, *who* have ya got down there. Lemme guess, a sweet little piece o' action? Small girl, blonde-haired and blue-eyed? Your people in Derbent were partial to those types. Izzat what you got, Zakhar? Hm? Izzat what you got on the last shipment?"

Trembling with barely controlled rage—rage at the insolence, the indignity, and his impotence in the moment—Zakhar said nothing, tried to remain still. His fingertips were still just touching the Colt's grip.

The intruder laughed again. There was no mirth in it though, only malice, and promises. Zakhar's blood was boiling. He was getting tired of being mocked in his own house by a trespasser, and someone who knew his secret. "Cut this, Jack," said the intruder. "I know all about you. I know what you like doin'. I know you're a part of somethin' bigger, a family of sorts that started out this gig, but now you're more like a customer. You help a little here an' there with the shipping and the details, you still have a little bit o' stock in your family's old shipping business. Northeast Siberian Shippin', right?"

Steady now. Steady. "I'm still not sure I follow you, my friend."

That smile never wavered. "Well, let's see if you can follow me around the world," he said. "Seven months ago I'm in Atlanta, ran into a little bit o' trouble with some Russians. A group of *vory* that fractioned off of the main group of *vory v zakone*, right here in the Motherland, and who started workin' for a few groups of human traffickers. One of their clients was a group of child pornographers called The Rainbow Room. The *vory* were at first only interested in the usual stuff—forced prostitution, maybe moving the girls across borders, through shipping containers. But they still used some old business ties over here in the Motherland; financing, moving some money into some trustworthy family members over here, family members who were holding on to it, like a retirement plan for the whole fucked up family.

"I got into a tussle with some of your pals—that's how I got so pretty," he added, turning his face over and stepping a bit more into the firelight. Zakhar could see the grotesque scar running the length of his face, like a canyon that someone had tried to fill in, and failed. "I dipped outta the A-T-L with the sirens still screamin' for me. I found a doctor who did passable work on sewing me up, an' then I got to looking. The guy that did this to me, his name was Dmitry. I believe ya know 'im?"

Zakhar tensed. He shook his head. "I'm afraid not."

The gunman tilted his head to one side curiously, in a kind of look that said, *How long are we going to do this?* He continued with his story. "Before he died—if you can call it dying—Dmitry told me that he had family in Derbent. Now, I promised this son of a bitch that I'd kill his entire family. It was the *least* I could do after all he put me through. An' I like to keep my promises. Call me old-fashioned." He snorted a laugh. "I read all the follow-ups in the news concerning the story—you probably remember it? A bunch o' human traffickers an' child pornographers operating in and around Atlanta? They finally pinned a last name on ol' Dmitry. Him, his brother Mikhael and their sister Olga were part of the Ankundinov family. Well now, as you can imagine I was happier'n a pig in shit when I found this out, because this narrowed my search down *considerably*.

"But first, I had to get outta the country. This wasn't easy, ya know? I mean, every cop and his dog knew that I was in Atlanta, and they for some reason associated *me* with The Rainbow Room, and so I became a prime suspect. I'm still on Interpol's list, last I checked their website. I never became very famous, because I was just one of a dozen others that eluded police agencies around the world durin' this operation." *Bragging,* Zakhar thought. *He's actually taking the time to brag.* As much as it angered him, it might also be his salvation. *Keep talking. Just keep talking.* "Feds cracked down on anybody who knew me. Lotta colleagues o' mine ain't too happy with me." He sighed. "In any case, after I got sewed up, I hopped from one ride to the next until I got into Canada. Found an old pal that owed me a favor, got a couple fake IDs, and finally, I made it here, to the Motherland.

"In a way, it was like…comin' home, almost. I'm no Russian, but I have a certain, ah, aptitude, an ability to integrate easily into various socio-economic classes. I'm also good at pickin' up on the *vibe* of a city. Ya know, I tend to read the people well. I also take an interest in the customs an' behaviors of my host city—it's important in my line o' work—so I bought a few language CDs, learned how to say 'where's the shitter' and 'fuck you' in Russian—you know, the important stuff—an' then started to check the listings on the Internet. Such a handy tool, the Internet.

"Long story short—I know, I know, too late, right?—I found a few more members of the Ankundinov family, followed a few for the first couple o' months, figured out which ones hung out in the skeevy part o' Derbent, and then offered my services. I'm a thief, specializing in boosting cars, and people always need cars, especially *vory*, am I right? Am I right, Zakhar?" Zakhar didn't know what else to do but nod, so he did. "So, I engendered myself to a few of them, learned a bit about jackin' local cars—you fuckin' Europeans and your reversed ignition switches," he chuckled. "And then I made myself the go-to guy for disposable cars."

Zakhar's eyes wandered about the room, searching for some way out, *any* way. The front door was five steps away, but it was locked. He'd locked it as soon as he returned from gathering the wood. There wouldn't be enough room or time to lay down a few suppressing shots and dive for the door.

"That's where I found out about the Ankundinov family's connections to the Northeast Siberian Shipping Company. Lots o' boats moving in and out of port, and all year round. The company was initially founded and run by an Anatoly Ogorodnikov—your grandfather. More an' more shares have been sold down through the decades, leaving you with very little stake in it, but stake in it you still have, at least enough so that you get a few benefits."

Zakhar shook his head. "I have nothing more to do with Northeast Siberian Shipping. Nothing besides a little bookkeeping."

The smile never wavered, and neither did his knowing look. "Ya know, it's an interesting fact: every year about nine million shippin' containers enter U.S. ports, and about as many leave. Only about five percent of those are inspected before they are unloaded, even after 9/11 and all the fears of smuggled uranium started up. But it's easier to detect enriched uranium hidden inside a container—a good Geiger counter can do that—but finding small children stuffed inside them..." He let the sentence drop.

"I've never hurt any children—"

"Liar liar," he teased. "Pants on fire."

"I swear to you, I've never—"

The gunman put a finger to his lips. "*Shhhh.* I'm not here for the child, Comrade Ogorodnikov." A moment of indulged relief, which helped to calm him, gave him hope. His fingertips were still on the gun's grip. "I don't care about any o' the people you've hurt, or the children you choose to diddle. Honestly, that's none o' my beeswax." He sniffed. "But I made a promise to Dmitry Ankundinov. I told him I'd kill his daughters. Only, they weren't in Derbent like he said. They've moved somewhere else, with some other family. I learned this after a very considerable, and, uh...*bloody* interrogation."

"It was you?" Zakhar still couldn't believe it. He had received warnings, from his people in Moscow and his relatives in Chelyabinsk. They'd told him about a revenge killing, something they believed was associated with "bad blood" between their families and some other foreign families. *It's not, though. It's just him.* "You burned them?"

The gunman elected not to answer this directly. "It seems the Ankundinovs in Derbent heard about Dmitry's downfall in the States, and they had a hunch to hide much of his close family—mainly from Interpol and other agencies, not from me. Still, the results are the same. They're gone. All I wanna know is, where did the *vory* move his family?"

"You...want to kill his daughters?" he said, astonished.

"Don't sound so appalled. What the fuck do you care? You've got someone's son or daughter locked up in your goddamn basement. Now, I can kill you where you stand, an' this'll be the last time you ever visit this lodge. Or, you could give me Dmitry's daughters, an' you get to stay here with whomever you've got locked up down below." He shrugged. "Whattaya say, *comrade*? A child for a child?"

Was it really that simple? Just give over Dmitry Ankundinov's family and that would be the end of it? Zakhar wasn't truly conflicted on the decision—after all, he didn't know Dmitry at all, and had only ever met the Ankundinovs during a few shareholder meetings here and there throughout the years—but would giving the family up really save him now? "What if I told you that I don't know where they are—"

"Then I'd say you're about as useless as an asshole on my face," he said, raising the gun.

Zakhar held up his left hand, still keeping his right hand close to his Colt, inching more over the grip. *Has he noticed yet?* He wondered. "Wait, hold on! Please! *Prastite!* I'm...I'm sorry. I'm sorry, but I don't know where they are, but I *can* tell you about the others!"

"What others?" There was a trick of the light in that moment. Something from the fire, deepening shadows that carved hard lines in the gunman's face.

"Th-the others..." he said, beginning to stutter. "They m-might know where to find the rest of Ankundinov's family. They're the ones...the ones that the *vory* worked with first, when the *vory* first came to my family with the business proposition. That's how my father always told it—"

"All right, shut up. I'm going to ask again, and slowly. Who—are—the—others? Names. I function on names."

"*N-ni znaju*...that is, I don't know their names—"

"Then how does this help me—"

"—b-because I kn-know their faction! Eh, how you say, their affiliation?"

"What, like a club or group name? A gang?"

"*Da, da,*" he said hurriedly. "A gang."

"What's the name?"

Zakhar swallowed once more. "At-ta Biral."

The gunman reached into his left pocket, but never took his gun or his eyes off of Zakhar. He produced an iPhone, one that looked familiar to Zakhar. It took a second for him to realize it was his. "What's your code for gettin' into this thing?"

"Eh...eh...one-four-four-two."

The gunman punched it in, then tapped a few keys on the touch-screen. "What was that word? Atta...?"

"At-ta Biral."

"Spell it." And so Zakhar did. The gunman punched in those letters. Zakhar's right hand was now just about fully wrapped around the grip. He was ready to pull the Colt when the intruder looked up at him. "Eight cats? It says here *at-ta biral* translates in one o' the Bangladeshi dialects as 'eight cats'. You pullin' my leg, Zak?" He gave Zakhar an austere look, glanced down at his gun, clearly saw his hand on the gun, but said nothing.

Unable to admit to raping children, it seemed Zakhar also could not acknowledge going for his gun, even when he was caught red-handed. "N-no. They are, eh, they are the At-ta Biral, the 'Eight Cats' of Bangladesh."

"Bangladesh, huh?" He looked back at the iPhone's screen, then lowered it and tossed it onto the couch. "You don't wanna go for that gun, big fella." Zakhar froze, becoming the very quintessence of a mannequin. "Tell me about these Bangladeshi boys. The Eight Cats, ya say? What are they, human traffickers like yourselves? Heroin? Prostitution? A bit o' all three, be my guess. That's how it works, right? Steal them, get them doped up, turn them out on the streets, and keep shuffling them around, place to place, an' before long they don't even know where they are, where they came from, or what their names are?" He jerked his head towards the hallway. "Is that where ya got your new stock? That how the Eight Cats keep ya satisfied? They send you a new toy every so often to appease you? You know what, don't answer that, just take your goddamn hand off that gun. Slowly, like molasses in a Siberian Christmas."

For a moment, Zakhar didn't believe he had the strength to just remove it. The gun seemed clamped to his hand, and his hand to it. It was his lifeline, his last chance out of this. He couldn't...he wouldn't...

But he did. Slowly, and like molasses in a Siberian Christmas.

"Turn around," the gunman said. Zakhar obeyed as though in a dream. And could it be a dream? Could it? He'd always assumed that if he was found out, it would be police and sirens and the media snapping pictures of him. Not this. Never this. What *was* this? "Kneel." Zakhar obeyed, as a robot might do, the commands registering with a programming deeply embedded while everything else—the firewalls keeping others out, the stubborn administrator guarding all the entrances—was rebooted. "Put your hands behind your head." Zakhar obeyed. "Cross your feet." Zakhar obeyed.

For a few moments, the lodge was engulfed in silence. It seemed the wind had even died down a bit. The radio played only soft static. Zakhar listened as, behind him, the gunman just hummed to himself. He caught a few words being sung. "This tainted love you've given...I've given all a boy could give you..." He hummed a few more bars and moved around behind Zakhar. Perhaps checking windows? "Song's been stuck in my fucking head all day. Like it's on a loop. Don't you hate that, getting a song stuck in your head?"

Zakhar said nothing. What was the right answer? Was there a right answer? So much was racing through his mind in that moment. The signs he'd ignored. His own elongated footprints in the snow leading up to his cabin—*He followed in my footsteps.* But when had the man come inside? How long had he been stalking Zakhar? Had he waited for him to put down the rifle? How much had been calculated?

He heard the gunman approaching from behind, slowly, slowly. Then, all at once, the Colt was snatched from Zakhar's holster and the gunman took a step back. "Stand up." Zakhar obeyed. At least, he tried. His legs had turned to water.

He started weeping.

"Oh, fuck, you're gonna cry now?" The gunman sighed. "Look, I gotta be outta here in like ten minutes. So could you just not...?"

"P-p-please...please, I have money! Lots of it! You see what I can afford! I can pay you! I can pay you enough to...to...to fix your face!" he rushed to say. "T-to run away from these people at Interpol! Enough m-m-money to find these men from Bangladesh! I can gi—"

"*Money* to find them," said the gunmen. "Meaning you don't actually have anymore info about *where* they are, and you don't know *how* to find them?"

"I-I-I didn't mean—"

"I'm just tryin' to be specific here. Do you know where these men are, right now, right this very instant, or not?"

"N-not right this—"

"So you're tryin' to buy yourself some time."

"N-n-n-no—"

"No? You're not trying to buy time? You don't wanna live?"

"I-I mean *da! Da! Yes!* I mean…I can help you. I can…I can help you." *Remember your training,* Zakhar told himself. *Breathe. Just breathe, and stay calm. Remember your training. You were a soldier.* Zakhar's tears stopped at once, he dammed them up and bit his tongue to reinstate control. He listened to the gunman take a few footsteps around to his right side, then around to his left. "Th-there's money. Thousands of rubles in my drawer, as well as other currencies. U.S. dollars, too!"

"Which drawer? Where?"

"My armoire," he said, breathing a sigh of relief. *I have him thinking rationally.* "Top drawer. It's in a large steel suitcase."

"In case you ever had to hit the road fast, huh?"

"Yes…yes, it's true. Everything you've said. It's all true. But you said you don't care about the merchandise, so you can take the money. It's all yours." No more stuttering now. Zakhar was back in control, and he believed the gunman was on track, too. His tone sounded more equitable now.

"Steel suitcase. Top drawer."

"*Da.*"

More pacing from behind. Then, the gunman started speaking again. "Ya know, in Derbent, I got a hold of this one fucker named Andrei. Andrei Ankundinov," he laughed. "He wasn't a brother to Dmitry or anything, not even blood, but he was family through marriage some kinda way. Anyhow, Andrei was into boostin' cars, like me. He's the one I approached first when I started to peg which Ankundinovs were which—they're not quite like Johnsons or Joneses over there in Derbent, but the last name is popular enough. I hooked up with Andrei, found out he was an alcoholic, an' I know the quickest way to an alcoholic's heart is to buy the rounds, drive him home an' don't tell the rest of his family.

"So I did just that, an' enough times that he introduced me to some o' his pals. In less than two months, I'd already met everyone involved in Northeast Siberian Shipping, even if I hadn't shaken their hands. Got invited to a poker game—that was the first time I heard your name bein' tossed around, and I took note, kept playin' my cards. Later that night, though, Andrei was all set to head to a neighborhood outside o' town, to do a dead-drop and a pickup for some cats owed him and his family money. That night, as he was hopping in his Jag, Andrei said, 'You come with me, Yank.' That's what they called me for the three months I was in Derbent: The *Yank.*

"I rode with him outside o' town, and this is when I made my move. See, it's not always about rushing the moment, or trying to force a moment to happen. Nah, see, sometimes it's about *waiting* for that right moment. This was that night. This was that moment. Andrei was shitfaced drunk, I mean just fuckin' hammered, and so I took the wheel for most o' the drive. I pulled over under the pretense that I needed to take a piss, an' I knew he wouldn't argue." Behind Zakhar, the gunman continued to pace. "So we get out, we both take a piss, and then I smash the back of his head with the butt of my Beretta. He was so drunk he went down like a daisy.

"An hour later, Andrei wakes up upside-down, tied up by his ankles by some cords in his trunk, hanging from a tree. He was confused as well, o' course, and I just kept beating him with my pistol. Like a fuckin' piñata, get it? I'm just hammering away. I took a few shots at him from ten feet away, an' I intentionally missed. An' he's screamin' an' screamin'," said the gunman, laughing. "He pissed himself! You ever see a man hanging upside-down and pissin' down on his own face? Comical don't begin to describe it!"

More pacing, more silence, a touch of wind from outside. The gunman chuckled, cleared his throat, continued. "I wanted to know about Dmitry's people. His family, where they'd gone, all that. I was getting a little, ah, *impatient* with not finding Dmitry's daughters. I shot at Andrei a few more times, he blubbered and prayed to God, all o' that. He dropped a few names, most of them were nobodies, people I knew from Derbent, ones that had no connection to Dmitry Ankundinov or his brother

Mikhael or sister Olga. He was coverin' for somebody. But then he mentioned your name again, and so I was intrigued.

"It seems that you, Zakhar Ogorodnikov, are a bit of a connoisseur. You never order the same piece of merchandise twice. That really, really frustrated Andrei and his peeps, because it meant they needed to keep a variety of merch in stock—blondes, brunettes, red-heads. And younger and younger, too, eh? 'Insatiable.' That's a good word to describe you, innit?"

Zakhar swallowed, still trembling, still shivering like he was naked in the cold. And how he did feel exposed. "I've already confessed to you."

"Shit, Zak, I ain't your goddamn priest. I'm not lookin' for a confession. I just wanted to let you know that after all of Andrei's begging and pleading, his bargaining and more begging, I cut him down and told him to start running. I told him he was free to go, that he only needed to promise not to tell anybody. I let him get about twenty feet before I took aim and blew his goddamn brains out."

"I-I don't...I don't understand..."

"I'm sure some o' this just sounds like I'm lording all of this over you. Or just rambling. Some people play chess to win. Others play chess to instruct. I play chess to instruct."

"Chess? I-I don't under—"

"Like a said, Zak," he said, and pressed the cold steel against the back of Zakhar's head. "There's a hole in Arizona that I could fill with shit I know that you don't." Zakhar finally started to react, his old military instincts kicking in at last. Here came his defiance, his rage at the insolence of the intruder, the indignity of it all, but just as he started to turn the bullet snapped through his skull and pitched him forward. His head hit the side of a stand that served no other purpose but to hold up pictures. A tiny family portrait fell beside him, in the pool of blood that began spreading outward from his cranium.

Paralyzed, dying, and blind. Yet by some anomaly, he was still able to hear words floating all around him, floating down from the gunman. It was a song, nice and even lovely. "The love we share...seems to go nowhere...and I've lost my light...for I toss an' turn, I can't sleep at night..."

He also heard the kettle on the stove starting to squeal. *Tea's ready*, was Zakhar Ogorodnikov's very last thought on this earth.